The Bear at Midnight
Orkneyinga Murders IV

Lexie Conyngham

'

ACKNOWLEDGMENTS

Thanks once more to Nanisa, Kath and Jill for keeping me in check!.

Cast of characters:

At Buckquoy:
Einar Einarson, chief at Buckquoy
Rannveig, his diminished wife
Rannveig's daughter Thordis
Einar's son Bjorn
Varin and Sigvat Olafson, Einar's nephews
Atli and Egil, Bjorn's men

Oddr, Einar's councillor
His son Foldar
His daughter Frogunn
Afi the boatbuilder

Hrolf, one of Einar's men, and his wife Helga

Sigrid, a woolworker
Gnup, a farmhand

On the Brough of Birsay (usually):
Thorfinn Sigurdarson, a much put-upon Earl
Ingibjorg, his wife
Bolla and Groa, maids

Ketil Gunnarson, Thorfinn's man

Ketil's men, Skorri, Geirod and Alf
Geirod's dog

Sundry gate guards and a pigman on Birsay

Ljotr Hrutson, a merchant in Kirkuvagr, and his wife Hrefna

Grettir, a traveller from the (north) East

Ozzur and Thorthr and a sow from Westray

I

'Sigrid! Sigrid!'

For a moment Sigrid paid no attention. Her bare feet were numb in the cold water and her fingers were almost useless as she pulled and poked at the stems she was trying to haul out of the stream.

'Sigrid!' Gnup, her farmhand, slid down the last few paces of the crumbly amber cliff and landed with his own feet in the stream. 'Do those not sting?'

Sigrid grabbed the last of the nettles and dragged them on to the sack she had brought, as flat as she could make it on the bank.

'No, not when they've been soaking for a while. Anyway I can't feel anything.'

She stumbled out of the water, bracing herself against the sharp pain as feeling returned to her toes. She twisted the sacking around the heap of soggy stems, and with a flick of the arm had them up and on her shoulder. At once the cold water trickled down into her clothing: her sleeve was soaked.

'Can I get the other ones?' asked Gnup. She shook her head.

'They're not ready yet. Did you come down here to help with that?' she asked, mildly surprised. Gnup preferred working with the animals, though he was a willing enough boy with all the farm work. And he was busy now with their small harvest.

'Oh! No.' Gnup took the bundle from her. He was growing strong. 'No, I came to tell you the news. Einar's dead.'

Well, it had been coming.

Sigrid, her cold feet decently booted, and in a clean shift, overdress and headcloth, sat with the other women of Buckquoy in the great hall that had been Einar's domain. They had prepared the body and now guarded it, just as they ought.

Einar Einarsson made a long, thin corpse, Sigrid thought, so little of him left sideways you could nearly lay him in one of the new drains up on the headland at Birsay. It was an irreverent thought, and she silently apologised to Einar's shade and to that of her late husband, Thorstein, who had been Einar's man. Thorstein had died of water on the chest, several years ago. Einar had died of … he had just faded away, really. He had been quite a warrior once, long ago – not that long ago. Then he had come home and learned to read – Latin, not runes – and surrounded himself with his books and his bored hird. Well, some of the men were bored, missing the summer raiding, and others – and she could name names – were simply too lazy to bother. And then his wife had betrayed him: Rannveig, handsome and clever and Einar's constant companion and counsellor, and she had betrayed him. It had left Einar shattered. You could as well say he had died then, a couple of years ago. If he had lived at all, it was to keep Rannveig where he could see her, under his thumb, with none of her old freedoms to do and to speak. Her betrayal had broken both of them, though the other man was now dead.

'Who will take over, though?'

Her friend Helga, beside her, broke quietly into her thoughts. Sigrid shifted her cold feet. Outside the hall, the endless autumn winds lashed rain against the high wooden door. She wished she could have brought her nettles to work on: her fingers itched when they were idle.

'Whoever Thorfinn appoints, I suppose.' If her husband Thorstein had been Einar's man, Einar had been Thorfinn's.

'Well, yes, but who?'

Sigrid glanced round. Helga's eyes were bright. Could she possibly think her own husband Hrolf would be in the running?

Next to her was Frogunn, daughter of another of Einar's less impressive followers.

'Oh, my father's already in deep discussions over it!' She

was a hearty, bright girl and struggled to keep her voice respectfully low. 'No doubt it will all be sorted out soon.'

It would be an important gift, this hall of Buckquoy. It guarded the landbridge to Thorfinn's settlement on the headland of Birsay, and overlooked the precious harbour down below. Thorfinn Sigurdarson, Earl of Orkney and more besides, might have stepped back from raiding but he knew how to defend his extensive lands. He would not give the place to someone he did not trust, and did not think capable. Hrolf might be trustworthy, but was he capable? Sigrid was not at all sure.

Helga, though, would manage the domestic side of a hall very well.

'It's a shame Einar had no sons,' said Sigrid, dodging the question of Hrolf.

'No sons with Rannveig, no,' said Helga, with a little lift of her eyebrows.

'He wasn't married before,' said Sigrid, knowing that was hardly relevant – if Einar had fathered a boy and acknowledged him, the boy could as easily inherit. 'She was, though. Hasn't she a daughter?'

'Thordis, yes,' said Helga, who knew everything. This, Sigrid supposed, came from her habit of hanging about the harbour, waiting for traders to offer her their goods and sometimes other favours they might have available. 'Thordis has been staying with Rannveig's family in Kirkuvagr, but I think they've sent for her.'

'Is she married?'

'Not yet, no,' Helga said without emphasis. Sigrid wondered why not: Rannveig and Einar had been married quite a while, so this Thordis, from a previous marriage, must be of wedding age. 'Anyway, she's not going to get the hall. I'd say the men are already wondering which of them it will be.'

'Oddr and Ulf are too old.' Sigrid began the inevitable list, quietly, as the women near them were all wives or daughters of these men, too. Frogunn was Oddr's daughter. 'Wouldn't you say, Frogunn?'

'Oh, far too old!' Frogunn laughed again.

'Ulf, yes,' Helga agreed. 'Oddr might think he has a chance. Hrolf of course,' she named her own husband quickly as if warding off any objection Sigrid might make. 'Afi, maybe.'

'Or Thorfinn might bring in someone from outside Buckquoy,' said Sigrid, already disheartened at the possibilities within Einar's hird.

'Didn't Einar have a brother?' Helga ventured, not entirely sure. 'What was his name? And I think he had boys.'

'If he had I've never seen them,' said Sigrid. 'Would Thorfinn even know them?'

'Well, then, someone in his own circle? Ketil?' Helga's voice took on a low, suggestive tone that annoyed Sigrid much more than it should.

'I don't think Ketil is really the man for the job,' she muttered. 'He's barely here.'

'But when he is … I think Ketil would make a very fine leader,' said Helga, now quite caught up with the idea.

'Look at Rannveig,' said Sigrid, desperate to change the subject. 'Did you ever see a woman so – so collapsed in on herself?'

Rannveig, Einar's widow, had been an extremely handsome woman, capable and intelligent. Sigrid had half-admired, half-envied her for years as she ran her husband's hall and longhouse, brewed and baked, oversaw dairy and salting, and even, it was said, was her husband's chief advisor on matters both political and military. She also had excellent taste in her clothing, which Sigrid particularly appreciated as she herself had made much of that clothing in exchange for the fine produce of Rannveig's domestic business. But Rannveig had not ordered so much as a length of braid nor a nailbinding hat for a few years now, and what clothes she wore – appropriate enough for a widow only that she had been wearing them for some time – were shabby and old and showed signs of the daily manual work she still did or oversaw meticulously. But you could feel when a longhouse was not loved, when a hall lacked a heart, and that was the case at Einar's.

The question that tickled the back of Sigrid's mind, though, was what Rannveig might do now? She looked broken and faded, but would Einar's death give her the freedom to come back to life?

A young woman appeared from the doorway at the back of the hall, and for a moment Sigrid took her to be one of the servants. Then she realised she had never seen the woman before, and as for being a servant, it seemed unlikely when the woman went and touched Rannveig on the shoulder. Rannveig straightened a little, and looked up at her. They spoke quietly together.

'Who's that?' Sigrid asked, just as quietly. Helga glanced over, eyebrows raised.

'Oh! Thordis has arrived, then! Well, anyway, who else could it be?'

Rannveig's daughter, brought back from Kirkuvagr. Sigrid gave her a more detailed assessment.

'She's very handsome – after her mother, presumably.'

'Oh, yes, she's her mother's daughter in that respect.'

'Who was her father?'

'No one I ever met. Svein someone, I think.'

Frogunn laughed.

'I thought you two knew everything! I'm disappointed.'

'I'm surprised she's not married.'

'I know,' Helga agreed. 'She's clever, too, like Rannveig, and she has all the right skills. She's supposed to be a wonderful tablet-weaver and wool-worker.'

'Is she?' said Sigrid, instantly defensive. There were too few customers to go round, and she badly needed all of them. But then no doubt Thordis would go back to Kirkuvagr after the funeral, and they would hear no more about her.

'Maybe she'll take Rannveig away to Kirkuvagr too, after the funeral,' she said, finishing her thought out loud. 'It might do Rannveig good to get away from Buckquoy.'

Helga, though, had dismissed the diminished Rannveig, always much more interested in what the men were up to.

'I think I'd watch the nephews,' she murmured. 'They'll think they'll get the hall, anyway: Thorfinn might well give it to one of them.'

'Where are the nephews, though? Where is Einar's brother?'

'Oh, I think the brother's dead. As for the nephews … now, what did I hear?' She began to tap a foot on the stone floor, as if it might jog her memory into action. Sigrid laid a hand on her knee to stop her before she drew attention to herself in the quiet hall. 'Thorfinn's men, of course, though the brother was much less close to Thorfinn than Einar was. Are they in the islands? Hm … I'm sure Rannveig has summoned them.'

Rannveig of old would have had it all worked out: who was to inherit, what position she would hold, unofficially, what influence she would have. Sigrid sighed. It seemed like a lot of work, when one could be weaving.

'Young men, though, presumably?'

'Oh, I should think so. Our age. A match for you, Frogunn?'

Frogunn blushed and grinned.

'You never know!'

Helga, contentedly married, smiled and moved on.

'You might get yourself a new husband, too, Sigrid!'

'Hm,' said Sigrid, unimpressed. She had had one of those: she was not racing to find herself another. It was all very well for Helga: Hrolf was so useless Helga ran everything as if Hrolf were away on a perpetual raid. And that was a thought. 'What will the men do if the new leader wants to go on raids again? They're not used to it at all now.' She tried to sound sympathetic, though in fact the Buckquoy men were a useless lot, in her opinion.

'I think they're over on the east mainland. Deerness, somewhere about there. Not far, anyway.'

'Then Thorfinn will know all about them.' Thorfinn knew most things.

'I still think he might appoint from among his own hird. Someone who deserves a bit of a reward. And you have to admit, Thorfinn's being very generous to Ketil recently: I think he's in with a chance.'

Ketil in charge of Buckquoy. Sigrid had known Ketil since they were children in Heithabyr, on and off, and therefore had a healthy lack of respect for his abilities. If he were in command here, he would need an eye kept on him, that was clear. And who would run his household? It would be chaos.

'Where is Ketil, anyway?' Helga asked, in that creamy tone she always slipped into when she talked about Ketil. Sigrid was fairly sure that Ketil had never actually fallen into Helga's clutches, but there was always that niggling doubt.

'Westray, I believe,' she said, pleased for once to know something Helga did not.

'I suppose someone will have sent word there, too,' said Helga after a moment. 'Westray's not so far away.'

'Well, no. You can see it on a good day,' said Sigrid, and then wished she had not.

Ketil Gunnarson, standing outside a hall on a broad green hill on Westray, was not looking towards Birsay, but then he was not having a good day.

It did not help that Thorfinn, his lord, had clearly thought this was some kind of privileged promotion for Ketil. Not that he was bestowing this gift in the magnanimous hope of some return. Thorfinn was feeling guilty, and since he had become a Christian, Thorfinn felt guilty about quite a number of things that had probably never bothered his head under the old beliefs. Watching Thorfinn trying to make amends was sometimes touching, and sometimes appalling.

In this case it was simply, cringingly, awkward.

'So,' he said, ignoring the soft rain that was trickling down the collar of his new shirt (a gift from Thorfinn's wife: her own way of assuaging guilt). 'So, tell me again, what exactly happened?'

Leaning against the wall, just at the edge of his vision, he could see his three men, ostensibly there to support him but, as he could clearly sense, trying not to laugh. Well, Skorri and Alf were trying. He was not sure he had ever seen Geirod laugh. Geirod's yellow dog, which followed him everywhere, was seated, yawning, by his side. On the other side of Skorri, tethered by a strong rope, was a small black pig.

'I – I –' One of the Westray men before him struggled with the words. He was small, by Westray standards: most of the Westray men Ketil had met had been large, powerful, quick with their fists and with a keen sense of justice. This one was slightly shorter than Ketil, who was himself well above the middle height. As for his sense of justice, well, that was what had brought Ketil here. Or why Thorfinn had sent him.

Westray was a large island, to the north of the Orcadian mainland, north of Rousay, too. The land was rich and fertile even if, in Ketil's opinion, it was dangerously flat for an island. There were several large longhouses, with prosperous farms about them – the one here at Langskaill was perhaps the best he had seen, and commanded a fine view down to the sea, over the skerries to Rousay and with a glimpse of the west mainland, and the Brough of Birsay, beyond. Even on a foggy day, which seemed, to Ketil, to be about six days of seven here, you could sense Thorfinn's eye on you from his settlement on the Brough. In fact, he wondered that there was a dispute to be settled here at all. But even with the rain, he had a niggling feeling that the stuttering man had tears in his eyes.

The small black pig watched the men with interest. After all, she had started all this.

Ketil waited. Was that what Thorfinn would do? No, what Thorfinn would do would be to delegate the various matters that required his adjudication on this island to Ketil, calling it promotion, while he stayed at home and did more important things.

No, that was unfair. Thorfinn did settle disputes within his lands, and rarely delegated. He really did think that this was an honour for Ketil. Ketil, too, had probably thought it was something like that, while the other cases were being sorted out: an insult apologised for there, a fine paid for an injury in another place. It had all been going very smoothly. Well, until he had met the pig.

The bigger of the two men before him, who was propped against the longhouse wall with his arms folded (each one of them the width of one of Skorri's legs, which were not, themselves, small), gave a grunt of disgust.

'He took my pig,' he said. He pointed to the small black pig, as if the identity of the pig was in any doubt.

Ketil nodded. He was glad they had the right pig, anyway. He turned to the smaller man.

'Did you steal his pig?'

'No!'

'He did!'

'I did not!'

'Right,' said Ketil, 'stop. If you didn't steal his pig, Thorthr, why does he think you did?'

Thorthr drew a deep breath, steadying himself visibly.

'I didn't steal his pig. I rescued his pig.'

Ketil blinked.

'You rescued his pig?'

Thorthr nodded.

'From what?'

'From him!' Thorthr pointed at the big man, Ozzur, who pushed himself away from the longhouse wall.

'But it's my pig!' he bellowed.

'But you were going to kill her!' Even the pig jumped. The yellow dog heaved up a heartfelt howl, till Geirod laid a hand on its head.

'But it's my pig! That's what you do with pigs!'

'Not with her!'

Bravely Ketil broke in.

'A man has the right to kill his own beasts,' he said firmly.

'Well, yes,' agreed the small man. On the whole Ketil liked him better of the two, even if he seemed to be making no sense.

'See?' said Ozzur. From his tone you would have thought he was some lad at his mother's knee, squabbling with his sister. But now he pulled out his knife. 'Give her here,' he said to Skorri, 'and I'll kill her now.'

The pig, with a keen sense of self-preservation, hid behind Skorri's broad legs. Alf and Geirod tensed very slightly. Skorri frowned, though, and raised a hand. Ketil nodded permission.

'Why would you want to kill a young sow?' Skorri asked. Unlike Ketil, he had been brought up on a farm. There had been pigs in Heithabyr, disposers of waste and providers of dubious meat, but Ketil had had little to do with them. 'Has she even had a litter yet?'

Thorthr shook his head, sad eyes on the pig.

'I have another one,' said the big man with a mighty shrug. 'I can't afford to keep the two.'

'You could have sold her. She's a fine pig,' said Skorri. 'You'd have got a good deal for her.'

'I offered for her!' snapped Thorthr. 'But he wouldn't sell her. He wouldn't sell her to me, see. So I rescued her. Look at her – a fine pig, you say. A lovely pig. Think of the piglets she'd have! How could you kill a pig like that? What a waste!'

Praise Heaven, Ketil thought: he'd begun to think that the man was in love with the pig.

'I'd rather kill her than sell her to you,' said Ozzur, and spat with admirable accuracy just short of Thorthr's feet.

'So you would sell her to someone else?' Ketil asked.

'Nobody else wanted her. Big litters this year – everyone's got pigs.'

'Except me,' Thorthr put in. 'I'd buy her.'

'I'm not selling to you,' Ozzur repeated.

Ketil sighed.

'Why won't you sell the pig to Thorthr?' he asked

'Because he wouldn't let me marry his sister!'

'That was ten years ago!' Thorthr retorted.

'Who's this?' asked Alf, who had been keeping his eyes open. He nodded his thin head towards a busy-looking man, hurrying along the path from the harbour.

'You have a visitor,' Ketil said loudly to Ozzur, hoping to break up the argument, but Ozzur and Thorthr paid him no attention.

'You've been married to Thora for seven years,' Thorthr was objecting. 'How many years will it take before you'll talk civilly to me again?'

'Never!' cried Ozzur. 'You know your sister wanted to marry me!'

'She has no interest in you, never had!'

The stranger, arriving damply at the longhouse door, looked anxiously from Ozzur to Thorthr and back.

'I'm here to find, um, Ketil? Ketil Gunnarson?'

'That's me,' said Ketil, wondering what further complication was going to arise.

'A message from Thorfinn Sigurdarson – well, you'd know if I just said Thorfinn, wouldn't you?' asked the man reasonably. He was a local: he must have picked up the message at the harbour and offered to bring it up here. He had an air of unaccustomed importance. 'It's bad news, I'm afraid.'

Ketil tensed, eyes on the man, but said nothing. Bad news for him personally? Or more generally bad?

'Go on, then, man,' said Skorri, moving closer with the pig on its rope.

'I was told to tell you that Einar Einarson is dead, and Thorfinn wants you back on the mainland. As soon as you can manage, they say he said.'

II

Father Tosti, the priest at Thorfinn's new chapel, arrived at Einar's Buckquoy hall to pray over the corpse. The rain had eased a little, though the clouds were still low, and the women took it in turns to step outside for fresh air and to stretch their weary backs.

'I want to meet Thordis, don't you?' asked Helga, making sure her beads were sitting prettily across the front of her dress. She always seemed to have one string more than anyone else, and there was usually some fine bead Sigrid had never seen before. Today it was a rounded piece of amber, glinting like gold even in the dull daylight. 'I'm sure you two will have lots to discuss about – well, wool and things.'

Sigrid did her best not to scowl. And to be fair, she was curious about Thordis, and why she had not been living with her mother Rannveig, and why she was not married when she was so irritatingly handsome and competent.

'Yes, of course,' she said, gritting her teeth. 'Let's go and say hello, now that she's not with her mother.'

It was automatic now, this avoidance of Rannveig, since her betrayal. No one ever really spoke to her. It had possibly been the worst part of her punishment, even if it had not been a deliberate one – no one had said 'Let's not talk to Rannveig'. Sigrid wondered whether even Einar had been able to bring himself to have a conversation with his wife in private.

But Thordis looked quite approachable, and there was no

sense in blaming her for anything her mother had done. She was standing at the wall of Einar's practice yard, where the men staged mock fights and competitions to keep in shape when they were not raiding. She seemed to be staring out towards the Brough, but since it was barely visible through the mist Sigrid dismissed this as unlikely: Thordis was just taking the fresh air like the rest of them. Sigrid and Helga trotted over to join her. To add insult to injury, Thordis' graceful form rose half a head taller than Helga or Sigrid. Sigrid felt like a troll.

'Thordis Svein's daughter?' asked Helga, and Sigrid thought that even Helga looked a little unsure of herself.

'Yes? Yes, that's me,' said Thordis with a smile.

'Helga Asmund's daughter and this is Sigrid Harald's daughter. We're neighbours,' said Helga, nodding in the general direction of both their longhouses. 'It's very sad about Einar.'

'Oh, oh, yes,' said Thordis. 'Indeed: he was a great warrior in his day. My mother was devoted to him: they married when I was very small, you know.'

'You've come all the way from Kirkuvagr, haven't you?'

'Well, it's less than a day's walk, not so very far,' said Thordis. She seemed amiable, certainly. As long, Sigrid thought, as long as Helga doesn't mention wool working, this conversation might be tolerable.

'And yet I don't remember seeing you here before?' said Helga, though she softened it with a smile of her own. Helga could be very charming.

'Oh, well, my aunt and uncle have a very busy household!' Thordis laughed pleasantly. 'My mother has been to visit us a few times over the years, of course. And now …'

Now? thought Sigrid. Oh, surely she doesn't intend to stay here.

'Now my mother needs me, and I shall probably come to stay here in Buckquoy.'

Sigrid swore, silently.

'Then no doubt we shall be friends!' said Helga. Sigrid wanted to slap her. 'I hear you are a wonderfully skilled wool worker?'

'Yes, indeed,' said Thordis. 'My customers around Kirkuvagr will be very sorry to lose me. I may have to travel back frequently to deal with their orders.'

'What –' Sigrid found her mouth was dry, and swallowed. 'What in particular do you do? Weaving fine cloth, perhaps? Some kind of stitching work?'

'I do tablet-weaving,' said Thordis. 'My braids are very popular – I design all my own work, of course, and often make my own dyes, too.'

Sigrid's thoughts went at once to her few little dyepots in the corner of her longhouse, that delicate green she had worked so hard to achieve and had used only a few special times. That deep red that sold well – Helga had a cloak with a deep red braid, and even Thorfinn wore the colour on a braided kirtle he believed his wife had woven for him herself.

'Really?' said Helga. Sigrid could see her eyes light up. Helga's longhouse was full, but she could not resist new and pretty things – and Sigrid did all her wool work in exchange for samples of Helga's excellent baking. If the supply dried up, Sigrid and Gnup the farmhand would have to subsist on her own efforts. They might starve to death in a month. 'I'm sure you'll be able to keep your Kirkuvagr customers, then,' Helga went on. 'They won't mind if the work is done here instead of there.'

'And I'm sure there are people in Buckquoy who would appreciate a higher standard of braid,' said Thordis with satisfaction. 'I shall keep busy, no doubt!'

'No doubt!' said Helga brightly. Sigrid thought her friend was avoiding her eye. But before she could find anything useful to say, Thordis, who had kept half her attention on the misty path up to the Brough, stiffened, and an odd, twisty smile caught on her fine face. Sigrid and Helga turned to look.

Along the path came a stocky, dark figure they both knew at once was Thorfinn, their earl. Hardly the style to set a maiden's heart running, Sigrid thought, as she looked more closely at the two men with him. She was fairly sure she had never seen them before: two bright blond men, upright and moving with the confidence of young and successful warriors. Now either of them, she thought, would do very nicely for Helga. She did not have to look round to see her friend Helga quickly check her beads and tug a loop or two of her red hair tantalisingly from her headcloth. She only wondered which of the young men Helga would choose – or at least in which order she would choose them.

Ah, but wait: usually Helga had her choice of any available men, for she was undoubtedly the prettiest and most charming woman in Buckquoy. But Sigrid turned to look at Thordis, with her odd little smile and her determined expression. It looked very much as if Thordis had her eye on one of these men, and with her grace and her beauty – and perhaps a head start with them, for she seemed to know them – Helga might not have her way quite so easily this time. Sigrid gave a slight smile, fond though she was of her friend. What would happen if Helga had to fight for a man?

But already Helga had been left behind. Thordis was leaning over the wall and waving to the two young men, and they both raised hands in reply. In a moment the three of them were at the gate, and Thordis was with them.

'Could this be the nephews?' Sigrid wondered, but Helga was hanging back now, not looking at them. Sigrid watched more closely. Thorfinn paid little attention to Thordis, and strode past towards the door of the hall, the two young men following a little sheepishly behind him. Thorfinn did not look wholly happy. 'Come on,' Sigrid snatched at Helga's sleeve. 'Let's see what's happening.'

They were close behind Thorfinn and the men as they entered Einar's hall. Thorfinn had not before been to pay his respects to the body of his old fellow warrior, and he stopped abruptly at the sight of the long, thin body under its sheet. Tosti the priest, hearing Thorfinn behind him, made to rise from his knees, but Thorfinn waved him back and dropped beside him for his own prayers. After a moment one of the young men followed, and after another moment so did the second, lowering himself awkwardly on to the stone floor. Hm, thought Sigrid, that would not impress Thorfinn. Thorfinn's father, Sigurd, had been forced to convert to the new religion and probably never took it very seriously, but Thorfinn was quite the opposite, and much preferred to have men about him who felt the same way.

While Thorfinn prayed, Sigrid took the chance to slip along the side of the hall almost to where Rannveig sat, staring into space. Sigrid pressed herself back into the shadows as Thordis, with a busy air, hurried past her and took a seat beside her mother. She bowed her head, her shining dark hair glinting in the lamplight, bare of a married woman's headcloth. Sigrid wondered how good her braiding really was, and whether or not she was really going to stay at Buckquoy.

Thorfinn rose to his feet. One of the young men instantly stood, too, while the other at least managed to look as if he were just finishing a phrase of prayer before he also stood up thoughtfully, head still lowered. Thorfinn, with a look of distaste on his face, came over to where Rannveig was sitting.

'My lady,' he said. 'You no doubt know these two. They seem to have thought that they would be better advised to come and make themselves known to me on the Brough before paying their respects to their late uncle and you.'

'Varin,' said Rannveig quietly, 'greetings. And Sigvat, welcome to you, too.'

Sigvat, who had paused before leaving his apparent prayers, bowed his head, taking Thorfinn's rebuke. Varin seemed unaware of it. Sigrid tried to find something to make her remember which brother was which from their appearance: Sigvat's hair was longer over his brow, but that would not help if he cut it. Both were clean-shaven and blue-eyed. Varin was broader, but not by much, and his jaw and shoulders spoke of an easy power. Sigvat was lighter. Each man wore some kind of folded lead amulet on a leather thong around his neck. Sigrid wondered if they were charms or affectations.

'Aunt,' said Varin, bowing, and Sigvat followed. He was presumably the younger, so it was more likely that Thorfinn would give Varin the hall. Not that Thorfinn seemed much impressed by either of them just at the moment.

The men of Einar's hird who were present now took the opportunity to approach, sizing up the opposition. Sigrid thought they would be wiser to assume that one of the nephews would be given the hall and work out what their new leader would be like.

'Travelled far?' asked Hrolf, Helga's husband. As always he was well turned-out, with a new blue shirt and a fine braid on his cloak that had cost Helga quite a few meals paid to Sigrid. Sigrid glanced at Thordis, and was pleased to see her noting the braid.

'We're from Deerness,' said Varin, with a glance at Thorfinn. 'But we've been in Kirkuvagr for a while.'

'Haven't seen either of you round here for a while,' remarked Oddr, a stolid, self-important man who had appointed himself as Einar's chief adviser in the last year or so. He seemed to be anticipating having his nose put out of joint. 'Just turned up for the funeral, have you?'

Sigrid caught a flash of anger in Varin's blue eyes, but Sigvat, his handsome face bland, said smoothly,

'To pay our respects, yes. We have not indeed seen so much of our uncle since he became less active.'

'Aye, well, it's good to see you, lads,' said Ulf, probably the oldest man in the hird, scarred from plenty of battles. 'And I'm sorry it's on a sad occasion.'

Thordis rose gracefully and departed, and in a moment returned with three cups of wine.

'Please forgive my mother,' she said sweetly to Thorfinn. 'She is so upset by Einar's death.' Her smile swept on to encompass Varin and Sigvat. Sigrid, watching closely, was still not quite sure which of the brothers Thordis favoured.

'You're ... what is it, Thordis?' asked Earl Thorfinn, taking the wine. 'Rannveig's daughter?'

'Yes, my lord,' said Thordis, with a smooth bow and that smile. 'I have come to be with my mother at this sorry time.'

Thorfinn gave her a long look, expressionless. He was not much of a man for being charmed by a pretty woman: for reasons completely beyond Sigrid's comprehension he was devoted to his awful wife, Ingibjorg. Thordis, elegant and undeterred, went on to fetch cups for some of the other men of the hird, easily slipping into her mother's place of hostess. Earl Thorfinn took a seat near enough to speak to Rannveig, but still at a marked distance. He, too, no longer trusted Rannveig.

'I've sent for Bjorn,' he said.

Rannveig, who had seemed to be in a dream, looked up suddenly and met his eye.

'For Bjorn? In Norway?'

'He's Einar's son. His only son, as far as I know,' said Thorfinn. He looked down into his wine cup, but did not taste the stuff. Rannveig nodded.

'He knew of no other.' She paused, and Sigrid could almost see her urging her unaccustomed mind into action. 'Are you thinking of giving the hall to him?'

Thorfinn leaned back on the table behind him and looked up at Varin and Sigvat. They, and the hird, were suddenly very intent on the conversation.

'It's a possibility,' said Thorfinn. 'I hear good things of him. But my mind is not yet made up. When he arrives, we shall see.'

He nodded in satisfaction. But Rannveig, her gaze flickering between Varin, Sigvat and her own daughter, looked much, much less pleased with the idea.

'People have sailed to Greenland with fewer animals,' Skorri remarked. They were heading down to the beach where Ketil's boat was pulled up. The pig was coming too.

'I thought it was a good idea,' said Alf. 'Very appropriate. If they can't sort themselves out over a wedding that didn't happen, seven years ago, then they can't have the pig.'

'You realised how ridiculous that sounds if you weren't there?' asked Skorri, though he seemed happy enough to be leading the pig. The pig, too, followed along contentedly. Perhaps she had always wanted to see the world.

'What'll happen now Einar's dead?' asked Alf. 'Why does Thorfinn want us back?'

'He might want us there to help with any disputes over Einar's hall.'

'Who's in the running for it?' asked Skorri.

Ketil shrugged.

'No one very convincing, that I can think of. His hird are mostly old or out of condition: as far as I know, no one has been hovering and waiting for him to die.'

'Has he no sons?'

'I never heard of any.'

'Daughters to marry to someone from outside?' Skorri knew how things worked.

'No, I never heard of any daughters, either. There are nephews, I believe: I met his brother once, long ago. He had two boys, if they still live – I think they're somewhere over to the west of the mainland. But Thorfinn will need to trust them, or he will never allow them to take power somewhere as important as Buckquoy.'

Assuming, that was, that no one took this as an opportunity to challenge Thorfinn himself. He was not getting any younger, and Buckquoy would be an ideal place from which to control what happened on the Brough and in the harbour below. No, whoever took over Buckquoy had to be Thorfinn's man, through and through.

The wind was already picking up by the time they loaded the pig, who seemed to be enjoying herself, into Ketil's boat. The dog followed.

'He needs a name,' said Alf. 'You can't just go on calling him the dog.'

'It's worked so far,' said Geirod.

'You could call him …' Alf looked about for inspiration, absently shouldering the boat down to the water as he did so. Alf was much stronger than he looked. 'You could call him Fjall. He's as calm as a mountain.'

'No,' said Geirod.

'Rock,' Alf tried.

'No.'

'Egg,' suggested Skorri. 'He's yellow enough.'

Geirod did not even dignify that with an answer.

Ketil checked to see that they had left nothing on the shore, and swung himself into the boat, pushing off with his oar. The tide was nearly at the full, and they worked to clear the coastline before raising the sail.

'Won't take long today,' said Skorri comfortably. 'Look at that one go!'

He pointed over to a warship skimming past, a safe distance from the islands, heading south. The sail was plain red, with the outline of an animal on it – a bear, perhaps? Ketil sat up.

'I wonder who that is?' said Alf.

'At least it's just the one, by the look of it,' said Skorri. 'Have you seen it before, sir?'

Ketil shook his head.

'No, but it looks new. It doesn't belong up in Hjaltland, anyway – it must have come further than that.' Was it alone? Were there other ships in the mist? He ran over a list in his head of who might be thinking of attacking Thorfinn in his stronghold. It occurred to him to wonder for a moment if the message about Einar was genuine, or if they might be heading into some kind of trap.

'We'd best be ready when we land,' said Skorri, unnecessarily. They all gazed after the ship for a long breath, fascinated.

Which was why they hit the skerry.

The pig lurched, unhappy. The dog sighed. Geirod, who was steering, cursed, but mostly at himself. Ketil leaned over the side, feeling for damage, as a trickle of water seeped quietly down into the bows. Geirod swallowed hard.

'Sorry, sir,' he muttered.

'We'll get there, unless anything worse happens,' said Ketil grimly. 'Alf, pass a bit of that cloth.' He blocked the crack as best he could without making it worse, and prayed for an easy passage. By the time they were organised again, the mysterious warship had vanished into the mist.

Ketil's slim boat, rowed by the four of them as they approached the harbour, slipped into place on the shore and Alf leapt out to begin pulling it up on the gritty beach. The dog and the pig, very much the passengers in this exercise, remained serenely in their places until Skorri lifted the little sow down on to the sand and Geirod called to the dog with a kind of grunt.

'Odin,' said Alf, nodding at the dog.

'No,' said Geirod. The dog came and sat at his feet.

Ketil glanced up at the Brough above them and the narrow path up to the bridge from mainland to headland. All seemed peaceful, but then, he told himself, it was unlikely that the death of an elderly, frail warrior like Einar would lead to much in the way of violence or uprisings. In his youth Einar would have been surprised if anyone had told him he would die in his bed.

Ketil looked on around the curving beach, to see if Afi the boat builder was about and could take a look at his dented prow before the leak became serious. Afi was an enormous man, easy to spot from some distance: there was no one larger on the Brough or in Buckquoy.

A smart warship was pulled up at the far end of the bay, and you could see from the gouges in the sand that it had not been there for long. It looked from here very much like the one that had passed them as they dealt with the skerry.

The ship almost seemed placed to look as unthreatening as possible, which was wise: an unannounced warship arriving just under Thorfinn's hall might not have a happy welcome. The crew were about it, one or two still on board, throwing things down to the men on the shore. And there was Afi – he must know the men.

Wait, no: that was not Afi. Afi was walking towards them. And the man at the warship dwarfed Afi, like a warship dwarfing a rowing boat.

Ketil felt his jaw drop, and his men all turned to see, and gape, at the same sight. The man's brown hair and beard, which stuck out sharply in all directions, seemed to blend with the fur of his cloak at the shoulders. He wore black leather gloves and boots, and even from here, as he looked about him, they could see bright dark eyes shining with interest and humour.

'Who in the name of Thor is that?' asked Skorri, in an awed whisper. 'Or is it Thor himself?'

'I know who that is,' said Ketil, finding his voice at last. 'Did you not see him in Trondheim? This will be interesting. That is the Bear, Skorri. That is Bjorn Einarson.'

III

A look of relief settled on Afi's stolid face when he saw Ketil approaching.

'Here's one of Thorfinn's men,' Ketil heard him explain quickly to Bjorn. 'He'll be able to, um …' And Afi faded quietly into the background, in a way that was surprisingly efficient for a large man. Afi was never much of a one for standing out.

Bjorn, however, turned broad-shouldered as if he fully expected to be the centre of attention. He bowed, a hand to his chest. Ketil returned the bow and cast a quick look over the ship. Small, but well-equipped, he noted. The crew, however, did not seem to be anticipating a fight – they were tidying ropes and unloading baggage as if they had arrived in their home harbour. Ketil turned his attention back to Bjorn, who was himself giving Ketil an assessing glance. Then he squinted more closely at his face.

'Do I know you?' he asked. 'Have we met before?'

'Long ago, and briefly,' said Ketil, 'at Trondheim. I'm Ketil Gunnarson, Thorfinn's man. And you're Bjorn Einarson, aren't you?'

'That's right!' Bjorn beamed. 'That's me! I don't know that I could have put a name to you,' he added apologetically.

'I was only there for a short time,' said Ketil, pleased that he had escaped general attention. But Bjorn was already looking about him, not much interested in Ketil.

'This is a good little place, isn't it?' he said. 'I was only here once, when I was a boy. I see Thorfinn's been building. I daresay my father's hall is a bit grander than I remember it, too! Can you turn me in the right direction?' He was eager to be off, full of enthusiasm for his visit.

'Did Thorfinn send for you?' Ketil asked, suddenly wary.

'Thorfinn? No. Why should he?'

'Because …' Ketil, who rarely smiled anyway, struggled to

make his face more solemn for the news. 'Because Einar is dead.'

Bjorn stopped, like a mountain troll struck by the dawn light. 'Then I am too late?'

Ketil hesitated, wondering what Bjorn might have wanted. To Ketil's knowledge he could barely have seen Einar since he was a lad. Had he wanted to meet him as an adult? Or was there something more specific?

'He is not yet buried,' he said eventually, 'or so I believe. I have just arrived myself at Thorfinn's summons.'

'Thorfinn summoned you?' Bjorn frowned, giving Ketil a slightly more interested look. 'Why's that?'

'I have no idea: I haven't seen him yet,' said Ketil, not wanting to articulate his own ideas. Probably best not to let Bjorn know that Thorfinn might be anticipating trouble. 'Perhaps we could go together to Einar's hall? My lord Thorfinn might well be there.' He gestured to the path that led up the hill. Bjorn, in silence, nodded, and walked beside him. Ketil's men gathered the bulk of the boat crew, including a few better-dressed men who were probably Bjorn's own men, and brought them along behind them with the baggage, leaving Afi in peace on the beach to do his boat repairs with only a few of Bjorn's crew left behind to guard his ship. Skorri led the pig on its rope, and Geirod's dog followed on at the back.

It was not long before Bjorn's initial shock wore off and he began looking about him, remarking on things he remembered from his previous visit. There were not many: the wind was one, and the green of the land, though now they were coming into autumn that was beginning to fade.

'It's good land, though, isn't it?' said Bjorn with a contented smile. 'My father's land. I knew it was right to come here.' Ketil blinked. Was Bjorn here to claim an inheritance? Ketil was not sure how Thorfinn might feel about that – and the presence of a small warship in his own harbour, the idea that his hand might be being forced, however gently – that would not go down well with Thorfinn at all.

He had little time to think about it, however, for the path to Einar's hall was a short one and in very few minutes they were at the great door. Bjorn stopped and could be seen noting that the door was in fact not that great and needed sealing, that the roof could have benefitted from repair, that the hens wandered freely about the training yard. He was suddenly less sure of himself, and waved to Ketil to go first. Ketil suddenly remembered the first time he himself had entered by that door, hurrying behind a woman who would turn out to be a childhood friend, long lost. He shook his head, and went in.

Sigrid, once again seated with the women in Einar's hall with Einar's corpse, tried to look on the bright side. At least while she was here she was being well fed. The quantity and quality of the victuals at Einar's hall had not diminished even when Rannveig had fallen into disgrace. Einar's hird liked their food.

But she was itching to get back to her wool, and her nettles. It was a long time since she had had the opportunity, and the time at the right time of year, to rett the nettles properly and draw out the fine, silken fibre from their stems. In Norway, where she had learned the skill, they would wrap their hands and arms in linen, seize great bundles of the tough stems in the late summer, when they were tallest (and when the soup you could make from their tips was not as sweet as in the spring), cut them and strip off the leaves and weigh the stems down with flat stones in the fjord. Here she had to make do with a shallow stream, and she was not convinced that running water worked so well. But as long as the stems softened and began to rot it should work. The next challenge, though, would be to dry them out properly so that the hard outer bark could be broken away. Here in Orkney that was going to take a while, or the investment of precious fuel to keep her fire going brighter than she might have managed otherwise. She glanced around thoughtfully. Could she perhaps negotiate for a corner of the hall here? It was always dry and warm. Einar wouldn't mind – ah, but Einar was no longer in charge. How would the new man feel about a rack of decaying nettle stems in his property?

And who would the new man be? Could it be Varin or Sigvat, or someone else?

It could make a huge difference to their lives here. The new man might have a wife that loved fine cloth – but would she employ Sigrid or Thordis, or someone else again? If she employed Thordis, she certainly would not want Sigrid's nettles in the corner. The new man might distance them from Thorfinn, force the men to go raiding again (then there would be more work in sail weaving, an endless, soulless job she threatened herself with when times were bad, lengths and lengths of hard warp and soft weft for every ship), raise taxes – Sigrid's constant nightmare. Who would Thorfinn choose?

As if in answer to her question, the door of the hall swung silently open, and a figure stood against the wet light of the autumn day.

'Ah, here's Ketil at last,' said Helga, pleased. Frogunn looked across, a bit puzzled at Helga's interest in Ketil.

'But who's that with him?' asked Sigrid.

For even that dull light was suddenly extinguished, as a massive man stepped in behind Ketil.

Frogunn's strong jaw dropped. The subdued chatter of the women ceased. Tosti, sensing the silence, turned on his knees, then scrambled to his feet. Thorfinn, at ease on Einar's high seat, straightened, eyebrows high on his dark brow.

'Oh, my,' Helga breathed.

'My lord Thorfinn,' said Ketil, moving swiftly up the hall to pause, respectfully, at Einar's body. He bowed his head for a moment in prayer, then continued to approach the high seat. 'My lord, here, just arrived, is Bjorn Einarson.'

Bjorn Einarson – this Einar's son? Sigrid watched as the enormous man came forward, surprisingly quietly. He looked to neither side, though Sigrid was sure he was fully aware of them watching him. When he drew level with Einar's – his father's – bier, he flung back his great fur cloak, and knelt at the foot, head low. Even kneeling, Sigrid was sure he was as tall as she. It was hard to resist comparing the great heavy man, the sheer presence of him, with the thin strip of cloth that seemed to be all that was left of Einar. Einar had been tall, but in Sigrid's memory he had never been anywhere near as – well, wide – as Bjorn. His mother, whoever she was, must have been a giantess.

Warily she glanced back towards the doorway, where a number of strangers had gathered, solemn and a little awkward. Two of Ketil's men, Alf and Geirod, were with them, which Sigrid took as a sign that the strangers were at least trusted for the moment. She hoped that Ketil had not mislaid Skorri, his other man, somewhere on Westray, but even as she thought about it Skorri appeared and joined the others, nodding to the strangers, then turning his attention to what was happening further up the hall.

Bjorn's great slumped shoulders straightened as he stood, head bowed, and went to greet Thorfinn.

'My lord,' he said, respectfully. 'I bring greetings from Harald of Norway, who gave me permission to come here to visit my father.'

'I am sorry that you find you are too late,' said Thorfinn, with a brief nod at the name of the King. Sigrid smiled to herself. In the view of Harald Hardrada of Norway, Orkney was his and Thorfinn held it, and Hjaltland, and other territories, as Harald's man. This was not quite the way the situation was viewed here at Birsay.

'I too, my lord,' said Bjorn. Sigrid could not see his face, but he sounded sincerely dejected. But if he had really come straight from Norway, the news of Einar's death could not possibly have reached him before he left. He must really have expected to see Einar alive. A strange coincidence, that he should arrive just now.

'Did the King send any word?' Thorfinn asked. 'Does he want someone sent in your place?'

In his place? Sigrid wondered what Thorfinn meant. It surprised her that this man, of whom she knew almost nothing and of whom she had never heard until the last day or so, should be someone so connected with her home here, and someone to whom Thorfinn spoke so familiarly, as though they already had some connexion. But then Thorfinn had travelled – he had been all around the islands and Scotland and over to the western islands, and he had travelled to Norway and to Saxony, and then all the way to Rome. His acquaintance was probably vast. All she had done was to go from Heithabyr as a child to Norway, then from Norway as a bride to Buckquoy, with a bit in Caithness in between. Hardly far. She had never been back to Heithabyr: she had no one left there, but she knew that Ketil's older brother still lived there, married and with children to carry on the family business of cupmaking.

Her mind was wandering again: it was the result of sitting here so long, doing nothing but gossip and eat in the subdued atmosphere of a dead room. Had she left her nettles well enough spread out? Would they be mouldy? She could try to send a message to Gnup to check on them. But who would go? It was as if Einar's body, Einar's death, was some kind of lodestone, constantly drawing people towards it, not setting them free until he was buried. People came, and talked, and prayed, and ate, but they did not leave.

She pinched the back of her hand to rouse herself. Up by the high seat, Thorfinn was summoning Rannveig to stand closer to him: even if she had not heard Rannveig's name, Sigrid could have guessed who he had called by the look of distaste on Thorfinn's face.

'Einar's wife,' he said to Bjorn, and seemed unsure whether to elaborate. Einar's wife who betrayed him, he could have continued. Einar's wife whom Einar kept, in disgrace. Bjorn seemed to be unaware of the story, and perhaps put Rannveig's subdued look down to her grief at Einar's death.

'It is good to meet you, Rannveig, though at a sad time,' said Bjorn, and though the words were formal he could not seem to help a smile. Rannveig's glance flickered to Thorfinn and back to Bjorn, all her old assurance gone.

'Bjorn, welcome. I am sorry you were not here to say your farewells, but happy that you are able to attend his burial.' Her headcloth hung loose about her shoulders, and hid much of her handsome face as she bent her head. For a moment she seemed to tremble, and Thordis, attentive to her mother's needs, stepped quickly forward to take her arm. She, too, bowed her head to her … step-brother, Sigrid thought. How would Thordis like to have one of those?

Her gaze flickered past Thordis and Bjorn to where Einar's two nephews stood a little behind Thorfinn's high seat. Whether or not Thordis minded Bjorn's arrival, it was clear that Varin and Sigvat were horrified.

'I think those brothers must have thought the hall was theirs,' muttered Helga beside her with a grin, as they trotted out to fetch more food for the new visitors.

'It still might be,' said Sigrid. 'Thorfinn will have to decide.'

'Poor things,' said Frogunn briskly. She hefted a large cooking pot up against her hip and waited for them both to gather bread and cheese. The cooking pot was full of raw vegetables, but she seemed to feel no strain.

'Well, it could be interesting, over the next few weeks,' said Sigrid. 'I'm not sure yet which one I'd want, are you?'

'Varin and Sigvat are both very handsome,' said Helga at once, 'but that Bjorn – my, what a man!'

Frogunn laughed, but Sigrid said,

'I was thinking of judging on something more than just looks! Helga, promise me you'll leave them all alone, at least until everything is settled. You'll only add to the confusion.'

'I only want to make sure they all feel welcome!' Helga protested, at which Frogunn almost doubled over laughing, broth splatting out from her cooking pot. Sigrid and Helga started too, a relief from the solemn hours of sitting in the hall with Einar's corpse. When Ketil appeared round the corner of the hall, heading who knew where, he found them sagging against the sharp flat stones of the hall's wall, gasping in the thick, misty air.

'Ketil!' cried Helga, pulling herself quickly upright. 'It is good to see you back safely. How was Westray?'

Ketil nodded to each of them, not singling Helga out.

'We came back early at the news. No doubt we'll have to go back later, when all this is settled.'

'Did Bjorn land on Westray, then?' asked Sigrid. 'How did you come upon him?'

'He had just come into the harbour when we arrived back,' said Ketil. 'Afi was the only man there, and he was working, so I offered to bring him up here.'

'Do you know him?' Helga demanded. 'Have you met him before?'

'I saw him in Trondheim,' said Ketil, 'that is all.'

No doubt, thought Sigrid, Bjorn would have been in a circle closer to the King than Ketil would have been. You only had to look at them: Bjorn, built like a mountain, would have been noticed anywhere, whereas Ketil, lightly built ... But it was more than size. Sigrid felt that even if Bjorn had been quite small, people would notice him. And Ketil seemed deliberately to fade into the background. That was no way to succeed, she was sure, in a royal court. She realised she was staring at Ketil, and quickly looked away.

'... doing there, if he was Einar's son?' Helga was ploughing on with her interrogation. 'Who is his mother?'

'That I don't know,' said Ketil. 'But everyone knew he was the son of Einar Einarson, so Einar must have acknowledged him.'

'He'll inherit, then,' said Frogunn, a little sadly. Ketil glanced at her, and Sigrid knew he had no idea who she was. Frogunn must have realised, too. 'I'm Frogunn, Oddr's daughter,' she added, with a little bow – still holding the cooking pot steady – 'you know, Einar's man with the whiskers.'

Several of Einar's men had whiskers, of course, but Oddr's moustache was notable. Ketil nodded.

'Good day to you, Frogunn, Oddr's daughter,' he said. 'Yes, I think it likely that Bjorn will inherit Einar's goods, but that doesn't mean that Thorfinn will allow him to take over here. He has to be sure he has the right man for that.'

'Of course,' said Sigrid with feeling. 'But what was Bjorn doing at King Harald's court?'

'He was a hostage,' said Ketil.

That explained it. Thorfinn had been anxious that King Harald would expect a hostage sent in Bjorn's place, a token of Thorfinn's own allegiance and good behaviour. Such hostages usually came from prominent families, otherwise they might be thought expendable. And being from prominent families they tended to be treated very well in the court at which they lived. That would be the reason for Bjorn's rich clothing and easy manner.

'But it might also account for Thorfinn's caution,' Sigrid continued her thought out loud, though in a low voice. 'Assuming it needs accounting for.'

'Indeed,' said Ketil. 'Thorfinn has not successfully held all his lands for so long without a fair allowance of caution.'

'But a well-treated hostage, brought up in a prosperous court, might feel his own loyalties wavering,' said Sigrid. 'After all, King Harald's household must be almost all Bjorn has known, so why would he not consider himself Harald's man?'

'But isn't Thorfinn Harald's man?' asked Frogunn, reminding Sigrid how young she was.

'Oh, yes,' said Ketil, 'of course Thorfinn is Harald's man.'

'At a distance,' added Sigrid. 'Requiring very little in the way of direct leadership.'

'Which might look,' said Ketil, blandly, 'like independence, but of course is not.'

'No …' Frogunn agreed, taking it in. 'No, I can see that.' A slow smile spread across her face. 'That makes sense.'

'Can I help you with that pot?' asked Ketil politely, but Frogunn took a step away from him.

'No! I can manage – it's nothing,' she said, and edged

towards the door of the hall, gesturing to Sigrid and Helga. 'Are you coming? I don't want to be late with the food on my own!'

Sigrid wanted to follow her, but she had to ask Ketil one more question.

'What's he like, then, this Bjorn? Do you think he would make a good leader?'

Ketil shrugged.

'He's popular,' he said. 'It might depend what other men Thorfinn might have in mind. Einar's own hird …' He met Sigrid's eye briefly. Helga was still within hearing distance, holding the door open for Frogunn and waiting for Sigrid. 'Who are the two fair-haired men? Where have they come from?'

Of course Ketil had noticed them.

'Sigvat and Varin,' said Sigrid. 'Don't know which is which yet.'

'Einar's nephews?' Ketil's pale eyebrows rose. 'Where have they appeared from?'

'From Kirkuvagr, apparently,' said Sigrid. 'Though they're from Deerness.' She noted that Ketil did not exactly seem delighted at the news.

'Well, well,' he said, then, annoyingly, turned away. 'I can see you're busy. I won't keep you.'

'Where are you off to in such a hurry?' she demanded, irritably.

'I have to see a pig,' he said, and disappeared around the corner of Einar's longhouse.

'A pig,' muttered Sigrid, joining Helga again. 'Does Thorfinn have him farming now?'

'He can come and dig over my infield any day,' said Helga, with a sigh, then turned to go back into the hall and admire the newcomers instead.

IV

Noise and chatter had returned to what had been Einar's hall. The old man – and as he had left his hall for the last time, left his hird and his books and his treacherous wife, Sigrid had even shed a tear, partly of pity for him and partly of worry for herself – the old man was buried at the chapel up on the Brough, the first of his line interred in holy ground. And now where was his line going?

While the burial party, led by Father Tosti, bore the long bier over the landspit to the Brough, the women left behind in the hall had tended to the fire, set fresh pots over it filled with broth, and jugs beside it with wine to warm, sending out teasing swirls of herbs and spice into the air bright with newly refilled lamps. The tables were rearranged, the high seat dusted off and covered with a clean fur for Thorfinn's return, the benches set up, pitchers and plates set ready with ale and cheese and cold meat. Sigrid had helped at several funerals, of course, and usually this was a time of busy relief, the long, quiet period of deep mourning over, and however much the dead person would be missed at least there was hope that life would go on. But as the women hurried around, making sure all was ready in time for the men's return (and, with luck, in time for them to put their own feet up for a little before they had to serve the men again), Sigrid thought there was more to their mood than the usual feelings. Excitement, anticipation, anxiety – it was all there in her own heart, anyway. Bjorn, Varin, Sigvat … or who else? Could Thorfinn have some other candidate up his sleeve? Might one of Einar's hird stand up and make a claim?

She took a pair of jugs from a dull-eyed Rannveig and went to set them by the fire as directed.

'Things would have been very different if Rannveig was her old self,' she said quietly to Helga. 'She would have had the whole thing organised and then made sure Thorfinn came to the same conclusion.'

'Do you think?' asked Helga. 'Rannveig certainly told Einar what to do, but I'm not sure she had the same influence over Thorfinn, did she?'

'Well, she certainly doesn't now, anyway,' said Sigrid. 'Every time he has to speak to her he looks as if he's been eating raw onions.'

'If she cooked it, I'd eat it,' said Helga. 'Smell that whaup stew on the left there. How does she get that flavour? She'll never tell me.' She sniffed at the pot herself. 'Dried plums?'

Rannveig could stand over Sigrid while she was making it and the whaup would still feel it had died in vain. Sigrid relied more on Helga's fine cooking to survive.

'I hope the bier reached the burial ground safely,' she said, changing the subject. 'You could see Thorfinn's dilemma.'

'Oh, yes!' said Helga. 'No one to match Bjorn in height, but he couldn't be left out if Einar's nephews were each taking a hand. It's a good thing Afi came up from the harbour in time. Not that he's quite the size of Bjorn either, but it was a better match.'

'As long as poor Einar didn't slide off backwards,' said Sigrid.

'I don't think those nephews are much impressed by Bjorn, do you?'

Sigrid gave a short laugh.

'I think all they thought they had to do was decide on the hall between them. It's interesting, if nothing else.'

'What do you think of them?'

'I don't know,' said Sigrid. 'We've hardly had them here two days. Thordis is clearly keen on one of them, but I'm not sure which. I've only seen them look contrite at Thorfinn's reprimand, and appalled when Bjorn arrived. I'm not even completely clear which is Varin and which is Sigvat. Do you think either one of them looks like a good leader?'

'Well …' Helga gave the whaup stew a final stir with a sigh. 'Well, no, not really. They look a bit young. What have they done up to now? Played at axe-throwing in Kirkuvagr? You would have thought that a young man with ambition would have been here at the Brough, trying to impress Thorfinn.' She stood and looked about the hall. 'We must be nearly ready for them coming back. I'm not saying,' she added, 'that they are not very fine-looking young men, and I'm looking forward to serving them some ale this evening and getting to know them better, but you're right: they don't look like leaders, either of them.'

'Here they come,' said Sigrid.

Thorfinn led the men into the hall, followed a little too closely by Einar's nephews as if the two men had done their best to beat Bjorn to the best seats. Rannveig stepped forward as hostess but Sigrid noted that instead of presenting Thorfinn with the first cup of spiced wine, as honoured guest, she allowed him to choose from several cups ready on the table. The men following took cups, too, and after some shedding of damp cloaks and gathering of friends they took their seats at the long tables, Thorfinn at the top of the hall in Einar's high seat. A silence fell, and for a moment Sigrid thought that Thorfinn was about to make an announcement there and then. Her breath caught in her throat.

'Welcome to all guests from elsewhere,' said Thorfinn, raising his wine cup. 'A sorry cause for a meeting, but an opportunity to remember all that Einar was – a great warrior, a fine leader, and a good and Godly man. May he be long remembered.' He drank, and sat, gesturing for the food to be served.

If Varin and Sigvat had been quicker, they might have sat one each side of Thorfinn and blocked Bjorn completely, but they could not seem to organise themselves and Thorfinn waved Bjorn to his right hand, leaving the brothers to find space on his left. Sigrid noted that Thorfinn also glanced about the hall until he had found Ketil. Ketil was near the back, as was his habit, not seated with his own men but conversing with, on this occasion, a couple of Bjorn's men. He had a cup in his hand, but Sigrid was sure he would drink little. Thorfinn gave a nod and turned to Varin and Sigvat, apparently relaxed. Sigrid wondered what he thought might happen, and what he expected Ketil to do about it.

Ketil, too, wondered if Thorfinn was up to something. It was a rare day when he was not. It could be challenging to be Thorfinn's man, expected to keep up with him.

'We had no idea Einar was dead,' one of Bjorn's men said chattily, already on his second cup of wine. The wine was very good, as always. The other man was quieter and more abstemious, but tucked into a goose leg with relish. Ketil wondered how long they had been at sea. 'It was a terrible shock for the Bear. He was that keen to see his father again.'

'When did he see him last?' Ketil asked.

'Oh, it's been a while. Years. But here –' the chatty man leaned closer and gave Ketil a nudge with his elbow, 'your man Einar *wrote* to him!'

'He wrote? In Latin, do you mean?' It was true that in the last few years Einar had developed an unhealthy interest in reading and writing. No one could quite comprehend it, except perhaps Tosti the priest, who had helped him to learn. Ketil wondered what would happen now to Einar's collection of books – there were probably three or four, more than anywhere else in the islands. Einar had rarely been seen without one by his side recently.

'Aye, that's right!' The man gave a kind of laugh, intended to indicate, Ketil thought, admiration and appreciation of such a level of eccentricity. 'I mean, the Bear says he did it himself, and all. He didn't give it to a clerk.'

'He didn't have a clerk,' Ketil agreed. 'He had learned to write a little, I believe.'

'I mean, runes, you can understand runes,' said the other man, wiping his mouth with the back of his hand luxuriantly. His beard was currently a little catalogue of what he had been eating since he arrived. He nodded solemnly, emphasising the gravity of his statement. 'Anybody can understand runes, if they put their mind to it. And write them and all.'

'Indeed,' Ketil agreed gravely. 'And did the Bear – Bjorn – did he write back to his father?'

'Aye, but he was able to use one of the clerks to do that,' said the first man. 'The usual thing, you know?'

'So what made him set off just now to see his father?' Ketil asked. He was not keen on coincidences, particularly not where deaths were concerned. Even when the death was a natural and expected one.

'Oh, someone else at court,' said the chatty one.

Ketil raised his eyebrows. It was enough to make the man continue.

'A man at court had been here, and he said he didn't think Einar Einarson was well. It had been a while since the Bear had got word, so in a way he wasn't surprised. He asked King Harald if we could come down here and pay a visit, and he said yes.'

'Unusual to let a hostage go so easily,' Ketil remarked.

'Oh, the King likes the Bear,' said the chatty man, happily allowing a girl to refill his cup. He thanked her politely. 'Yes, the King likes the Bear. Everyone likes the Bear. And we all go off on raids with Harald – the Bear likes a bit of a scrap, as do we all!' He waved his cup, and the other man grunted his agreement. He had started on some roast pork. Ketil wondered how the Westray pig was.

'Where is Harald raiding these days?'

'Oh, it's nothing serious. But you know he fell out with Sweyn of the Danes – that was a few years ago, after they'd been pals for ages!' He shook his head in despair. 'So really, he's just off annoying Sweyn.'

'Harrying Danish lands?' Ketil asked, trying not to let a sudden wariness creep into his voice.

'Aye, that's right. The Danes like a bit of a scrap, too. As do we all!' he repeated, and raised his cup again, finding it was already empty.

The Danes were indeed not averse to a bit of a scrap, Ketil thought. He just hoped it would not affect Heithabyr, and his brother and family, the biggest trading town in the Danes' territories.

There was a busy while for Sigrid and Helga and the others, as they made sure the men's plates were filled, the bread dishes replenished, cups brimming, and then retreated to the sides of the hall for a moment to snatch some food of their own. The whaup stew was indeed a marvel, even after all the good food of the last few days. They ate, for now, with an eye to the men in case they needed anything. As the evening wore on, and more drink was taken, they would be less dutiful, no doubt.

'I'm sure Thorfinn doesn't want Rannveig attending to him,' said Helga thoughtfully. 'Perhaps I'd better take the wine jug over and see to him and his guests.'

'How will you decide which of them to start with?' asked Sigrid,

Helga assumed an innocent expression.

'I shall just have to see which of them is nicest to me!' she said, settled the jug on her hip and slipped round the tables towards Thorfinn. Sigrid looked about the hall until she found Hrolf, Helga's husband. Sigrid knew that Hrolf could be jealous, but he also seemed utterly unobservant: as far as she knew, Hrolf was only aware of one of Helga's many dalliances. Hrolf was seated a little way from Thorfinn and the visitors, engaged in serious conversation with Afi, the big boat builder, Oddr, Frogunn's father (about half Frogunn's height, but oh, those whiskers!), Oddr's son, and a few others of Einar's more senior hird. They had always taken themselves very seriously. Sigrid wondered if it would even occur to them that Thorfinn might appoint them a new leader from outside, not from amongst them.

Her thoughts were interrupted by a squeal from the top of the hall, and a burst of male laughter. Varin, the older of Einar's two nephews, was evidently pleased by something. Thorfinn was frowning, however, and Sigvat, the younger nephew, was holding out both hands to Helga, an anxious smile on his face. Whatever he was saying, it seemed to be directed at Thorfinn, too, and in a moment Thorfinn's expression grew less angry, and Helga, quite pink, hurried back to where Sigrid was standing.

'Well!' she said, and for a moment could apparently say nothing more. Sigrid was happy to wait: she had rarely seen Helga speechless. In fact, she had filled the cups of two of Bjorn's men at the table in front of her before Helga had found words. 'I'm not interested in that Varin, anyway. I prefer a man to wait until he's offered.' She met Sigrid's eye significantly. There had not been much time for anything to happen, so Sigrid assumed that Varin had seized some part of Helga that he should not have seized. He had not looked particularly contrite.

'Sigvat, though: he has nice manners,' Helga went on, undaunted. 'That's what you want. Handy with an axe, or a sword, and then a bit of consideration with you. That's what you need to look out for. Like Ketil.'

'At least that's one of them eliminated, then,' said Sigrid, ignoring the mention of Ketil. She was quite happy as she was: Helga had always seemed fascinated by Ketil. 'If Varin doesn't come up to standard, then you can focus your attention on the other two.'

'I don't even want to look at him,' said Helga, unusually

sour. 'I can see Varin's still laughing.'

'Oh, I'm sure you've had worse,' said Sigrid. 'When the ale flows, the hands wander!'

'Ah, that's different,' said Helga, then stopped, as if she had surprised herself. 'Why is that different? You're right, it can get tricky in here sometimes late in the evening.' Sigrid knew that Helga probably had it worse than she did, but she nodded.

'Is it because he doesn't know you?' she asked. 'He should have spotted that you're a married woman.'

'Maybe,' said Helga. She fetched a basket of bread and refilled two of the plates near them. Frogunn and the maids were still filling bowls with the stew, working tirelessly around the fire: she and Sigrid were lucky to be further back here where it was cooler. 'When our men do it, it's like a joke, isn't it? Or as if they've been dared by their friends. A bit of fun. It wasn't like that with that man. He thought he was just taking what he was entitled to.' She shuddered. Sigrid raised her eyebrows. She had never known Helga react that way to a man before, let alone a young and handsome one.

'Well, then: let's hope Thorfinn doesn't choose him,' she murmured.

'Sigvat, though,' said Helga, 'he seems better. He apologised! He could see I was – well, taken aback, and he said sorry, that his brother was upset at Einar's death and that was not typical. He could see Thorfinn was cross, too: you know what he's like, certainly early in the evening, and certainly with the married women.'

'I didn't think either Varin or Sigvat was particularly upset at Einar's death,' said Sigrid drily. 'They can't have missed him much: I don't remember either of them coming here to see him, do you?'

'No, not for years. No, it was just an excuse, the best he could come up with on the spur of the moment,' said Helga with a sigh. 'I took it more for the good intention than for the truth of it.'

Sigrid nodded, hoping that Thorfinn would not choose either brother. It was all very well for a son, a hostage in King Harald's court, to find it difficult to slip away and visit his father, but at least Bjorn had finally arrived, without receiving word that his father had died. Varin and Sigvat could have sailed here from Kirkuvagr and been back the same day, with good wind and tide. Why had they never visited? Never taken an interest – never mind in their uncle Einar, but in the land, the hird, the people? No, it looked very much as if they had only turned up when they thought there was something to be gained from it, and that did not bode well for experienced, sensible leaders. And were they experienced, anyway? The Buckquoy folk knew very little about them. Was either of them married? Had they campaigned? Did they help their father with his own lands? She hoped that Thorfinn would be sensible enough to find out all these things before he made any rash decisions.

'Any more cheese there?' asked one of Bjorn's crewmen. 'This is fine stuff! I thought your islands would have nothing!'

'Aye, we don't do too badly,' she answered, not wanting to sound too enthusiastic. Thorfinn would not want King Harald taking a greater interest in the islands than necessary – if he thought Thorfinn presided over a few useless rocks then he might leave them to it. 'I'll see if there's more cheese.'

There was none left in the hall, and she could see no sign of Rannveig to ask her. Shrugging, she headed into the dimly lit rear of the hall to see if more was available in the preparation room beyond. She was almost at the doorway when she stopped, catching the sound of an angry voice from within.

'You've taken little enough interest over the years!' A light voice, but full of defiance. 'I know him better than I know you!'

'Just because I wasn't around doesn't mean that I don't want what's best for you.' That voice had an authority Sigrid remembered. 'Why do you think you're not already married off with a place of your own?'

She broke off, and for a moment the younger woman said nothing, either. It was as if neither of them really wanted to hear the answer to that question. Then Rannveig – it was Rannveig, of course – cleared her throat.

'And I'm not saying he's not best for you. I'm just saying that for the moment, don't commit yourself to anything. He might not be successful.'

'Ha! He'll be successful, believe me!' A little snort of satisfaction. 'He's always successful.'

'Then if you're right, you can afford to wait a little. It won't take long for Thorfinn to make up his mind, and he might only have been here a few days but I've seen the way Bjorn looks at you. Just be prepared to shift, if need be.' She made it sound quite reasonable. Sigrid made a face.

'That's not what I want –' came the younger voice.

'What you want? You're just a girl – you have no idea how these things work. Happiness has nothing to do with some girlish nonsense. If you want power –'

'Power? Isn't that what you lost? Threw away?'

'Don't you dare speak to me like that, girl! At least I had that power – had it for years.' There was a pause. Sigrid was stuck, frozen to the spot. Cheese, she thought, she was here for cheese. The older woman drew a deep breath. 'Now, get back into the hall and see if you can employ your charms on Bjorn. Find out all you can about him: what he likes or doesn't like, what he fears or doesn't fear. How he really stands with Harald Hardrada.' She drew breath. 'Leave the other alone for now: if he cares enough he'll be all the more eager after a bit of neglect. And don't say anything definite to either of them until we know which direction the wind is blowing.'

There was a sharp sigh of frustration and annoyance, then a step on the stone floor. Sigrid backed into the shadows as Thordis strode out of the preparation room: even as she went, Sigrid could see her trying to smile, to unclench her teeth, to lift her eyebrows. Sigrid checked to see that her own expression was as empty as could be before she popped back into the doorway. Cheese, she thought.

'Cheese,' she said with unaccustomed brightness. 'Is there any more?'

And she watched as the expression on Rannveig's own face folded shut again, from intense intelligence to blank dullness in a flash.

'Cheese,' she said, 'cheese. Of course – here we are.'

V

Rannveig walked out of the room past Sigrid, head lowered, leaving Sigrid to snatch at the heavy cheese dish and try to balance it. Sigrid's eyebrows rose to the border of her headcloth, and she grinned to herself in the privacy of the room. Rannveig's plotting days were not over, then: the interesting thing was that she felt she had to hide it.

And evidently Sigrid had been right: one of the nephews had caught Thordis' eye, presumably when they lived near each other in Kirkuvagr. The little settlement was growing in both size and importance as a trading place, and from all she had heard it was nearly as big as the settlement on the Brough. She knew what trading places were like, how certain merchants could somehow rise on a wave of clever selling, good contacts, a little daring, perhaps, and become as important as a warrior without ever raiding or holding an axe. In Heithabyr they had taken some pride in it. Now she wondered if that clever selling and a little daring, on the part of Thordis, anyway, might spoil her own business success. She had never been very skilful at either.

But if Thordis was keen on one of the nephews (which one?) or if Rannveig steered her daughter towards a useful alliance with Bjorn, would that be better or worse? The wife of the lord of Buckquoy would need fine clothes and furnishings, and would be able to pay for them, but if she chose to and had the skills, she might well simply make her own. Rannveig had always seen the benefits of passing the work on elsewhere: it freed time for her own machinations, and also gave her the chance to act like the powerful lady of the hall. Sigrid wondered if she would advise her daughter to do the same, and if her daughter would take her advice. It did not seem as if relations between mother and daughter were particularly good, at present. Yet if Thordis married the next lord of Buckquoy, presumably Rannveig intended to benefit from that arrangement, and not simply bask in the reflected glory of her daughter. Was Rannveig trying to re-establish her power by proxy?

Sigrid hefted the cheese dish – the soapstone rectangle must have come from Hjaltland, and almost weighed more than the mountain of cheese that had been perched on it – and took it back out to the hall, still thoughtful. Contrary to her mother's insistence, Thordis was down at the end of the hall, talking with one of Bjorn's men – the one with the rather nice blue braid on his shirt. Sigrid was sure that braid was their topic of conversation. No doubt Thordis had found herself a new customer, while Sigrid was sweating under a tray of cheese.

The feast was a subdued one, as befitted a funeral. When the bulk of the food had been eaten or cleared, and the cups had been filled again, one or two of his hird spoke poems in honour of Einar – most of them dated back to when he had been a mighty warrior, but there were one or two more recent compositions. One was by Foldar, Oddr's son, a man not much younger than Sigrid, tall but with the extra weight of a man who had not spent the summer raiding as he should. The hird applauded him especially enthusiastically, and Sigrid gave him a sharper look: was he their chosen representative, their preferred leader? His verses were not skilfully made, but they were sincere, and Sigrid and Helga, who had found themselves an empty bench at the back of the hall to rest their legs, each wiped a tear from her eye at the thought of an age over and done with.

Bjorn's crew behaved themselves very well in a strange hall, despite consuming between them enough food and drink for a whole fleet of warriors, and gradually settled down in sleeping places for the night, helping to shift the tables and benches out of the way. His close men joined him at the top of the hall, waiting to see where they were going to sleep. Sigrid saw Ketil and his men watching to see if Thorfinn would direct arrangements. She was curious to see who would go where: those nephews, Varin and Sigvat, had not yet shifted from their seats as if they had every intention of taking over the hall at once. Bjorn could go and sleep in the longhouse – that would probably be his now, and no doubt that would suit Rannveig's plans if she and her daughter were still there. Sigrid felt a mighty yawn surge up, and shook herself, and caught Helga's eye.

'I'm for home and my own bed at last,' said Sigrid. 'Are you coming, or are you staying here with Hrolf?'

Helga sighed.

'I'm coming,' she said. 'Hrolf can stay if he wants to.'

Pleased to have the company for the walk, Sigrid pulled her cloak tight about her and headed out into the damp autumn night, lighting a torch to take with them. They could probably walk the path without it, even in the dark, but it was a comfort, and would ensure that Sigrid had a fire when she reached home, in case Gnup had let it go out. A cold, damp longhouse was not a welcoming thing, even when it was home.

Ketil watched Sigrid and Helga disappear into the night. They both looked tired: he had barely seen them stop all evening. All the women had now gone except for Rannveig and that woman with her – her daughter, apparently. He had not realised that Rannveig had a daughter, but it was clear the woman was not Einar's child, and seemed, surprisingly, to be unmarried. Hovering with her mother, waiting to see what further hospitality would be required of her, she made a handsome figure. She had Rannveig's dark colouring but stood taller, with a fine figure and a gown that Ketil was sure Sigrid would admire. He had not noticed the woman – Thordis, wasn't it? – gossiping much with the other women like Sigrid and Helga, or even the unmarried ones like Oddr's daughter Frogunn. Perhaps she was shy of strangers. He found he doubted that.

He noticed Bjorn trying to catch his eye, and went over to see what he wanted.

'Ketil, wasn't it?'

'That's right. Can I help?'

'Just settling in,' said Bjorn with a grin. 'Some fine lasses around here: a man might think of staying a while!' He cleared his throat as Ketil said nothing. 'The lass with the dark hair – who would that be, then?'

'That's Rannveig's daughter.'

'But not Einar's, no? She's not my sister?' Bjorn was suddenly anxious.

'No, not Einar's. A man called Svein, I believe.'

Bjorn's great shoulders relaxed.

'It's good to be here,' he said. 'Even though I missed seeing my father, it's good.'

'What made you come?'

'Ah, well.' Bjorn fumbled at his throat, and produced, on a leather thong, a longish, pale tooth. 'See this?'

Ketil looked more closely. The tooth was about a finger-length, yellowish, with some dark marks along its side. Runes ... he tilted his head to read them. F U T H A R K, was all it said. Meaningless, on the surface.

'A charm?'

'My amulet. I got it in the north – a bear's tooth. They know about bears up in the north, you know. They told me I have a bear spirit, guiding me.' He nodded, eyes bright and solemn. 'It's true. The bear spirit told me to come here. I saw it in a dream.'

A bear spirit. Ketil had heard of the people of the north with their strange, ancient beliefs. He wondered what Thorfinn would make of that.

Thorfinn was giving directions, which Ketil hoped would be taken well.

'Bjorn, since you have a number of men to look to and they are all already here, you will take the hall tonight,' Thorfinn announced. 'Arrangements over your longhouse we can discuss tomorrow: there is no rush, and Rannveig will have to find somewhere to stay if you take it over.'

Rannveig had her head bowed as was her habit these days. Ketil could not see her face to judge her reaction. It would be hard for her, no doubt, to give up her lovely home – if Bjorn had been her own son he would have had to look after her. Thorfinn barely looked at her.

'Varin, if you can stand,' Thorfinn went on, and Varin leapt at last to his feet to prove that he had held his drink. Sigvat had already stood respectfully at his side. 'Varin, you and your brother can come back to the Brough with me.'

Ketil almost smiled at the look of confusion on Varin's

flushed face. Did that mean he was not to be given Buckquoy? Or did it mean that he was Thorfinn's honoured guest, more suitable for his company than Bjorn?

Sigvat was more philosophical.

'Thank you, my lord, we shall be glad to. Come on, Varin – lean on me,' he added kindly. But Varin shook him off, guided himself with both hands around the table and went to stand by Thorfinn and glare, from that position of authority, at Bjorn.

'I hope you enjoy your brief stay with us, Bjorn,' he said. His tone alone might have been taken as a challenge.

'I'm sure I shall,' said Bjorn amiably. A man his size could afford to ignore a challenge. 'It's a comfortable hall. We'll all be very happy here.'

Sigvat glanced quickly at his brother, then seized him by the arm.

'Come along, now, Varin, we can't keep my lord Thorfinn waiting.' He flashed a smile at Bjorn and the ghost of a bow, and rather than keeping Thorfinn waiting he hurried Varin out of the hall before Thorfinn had shown signs of leaving. Thorfinn watched them go, a look of distaste about his mouth. He turned back to look slightly past Rannveig until she bowed her head and left, taking Thordis with her, off to the back of the hall where they could return to their longhouse – Einar's longhouse. Thorfinn's expression was bland as he looked back at Bjorn. Bjorn had also watched as the women departed, though much less blandly – it was obvious that Thordis had caught his eye.

'I'll talk with you over the next few days. You're your father's heir, no doubt,' he said, 'when it comes to his personal possessions. But I imagine what you do about them will depend on whether or not I grant you authority here, at Buckquoy. If I do not, there can be little for you here.' He spoke firmly, not admitting any disagreement, but Bjorn did not look the kind to disagree. The big man smiled and nodded.

'No reasonable man could ask you to make that decision right away,' he said. 'You'll have plenty of candidates about you here, no doubt, or up on the Brough. I'd like fine to see the buildings up there, if I may.'

'You may indeed,' said Thorfinn, and now he was pleased. 'Come and see me tomorrow. For now, good night.'

Thorfinn nodded at Ketil, and Ketil and his men followed him out of the hall into the darkness. A gesture to Alf and a couple of torches were lit, letting the men light the way for Ketil and the Earl.

'How was Westray?' Thorfinn asked.

'Mostly all right,' said Ketil.

'Problems?'

'One case still unresolved. We brought a pig back with us, a young sow.'

'Really? Where is she?'

'With the swine on the Brough.'

'Good.'

The wind caught the torches and spun the flames into fine golden yarn, trailing sideways. It required practice to derive any benefit from their light and not lose hair. They stepped out on to the landspit that joined the mainland and the Brough, the harbour down in the darkness on their left, the sea crashing on invisible razor rocks on their right. Ketil wondered if he imagined that the spit was narrower now than it had been when he had left for Westray. Ahead lights glinted, at the gateway to Thorfinn's stronghold and at some of the buildings beyond. Many from the Brough would have been at Einar's funeral, but had left earlier and were now snug in their own longhouses. The guards at the gate saluted Thorfinn, and nodded at Ketil and the others, knowing them well. They passed into the shelter of the path that rose towards the buildings, and the wind, dropping from their ears, left a numb silence behind. Thorfinn paused and asked the nearer guard,

'Two men come in just now?'

'Varin and Sigvat? Aye, my lord. They've gone on up to the hall.'

'Good enough.' Thorfinn turned towards his own longhouse, and led Ketil into the lee of the hall itself where they could talk for a moment. 'Well?'

'I have met Bjorn briefly before, my lord. He's popular. His men like him, and so, apparently, does King Harald.'

'Has he turned and become Harald's man, do you think?'

Ketil shrugged.

'It's always a risk, when hostages are exchanged so young. I think he enjoys his life at Harald's court – fine clothes, a good little warship, some excitement. I hear he's been raiding with Harald.'

'Raiding?' Thorfinn queried, though Ketil was sure he already knew.

'Down into Danish lands. Harald's quarrel with Sweyn.'

Thorfinn nodded.

'He'd have liked that, no doubt. I wonder how he acquitted himself?'

'I can find out, my lord.'

Thorfinn smiled, his lips dark in the torchlight.

'No doubt. It's what you're good at.'

It was almost a dismissal, but Ketil suspected there was more. After a pause, Thorfinn asked,

'And the other two?'

'Less appealing, at first acquaintance,' said Ketil cautiously. Thorfinn snorted.

'They thought I would be impressed if they came straight through Buckquoy and up here to pay their respects to me before they went near their uncle's body.'

That was not the kind of thing that pleased Thorfinn, as no doubt Varin and Sigvat now knew.

'They do seem very young, my lord. Is Einar's brother still alive? I don't believe I have met him.'

'Olaf? No, he's been dead a few years. He was a merchant, chiefly, in Deerness. Those two young fools know how to pose with an axe, but I doubt if they have ever used one in anger.'

'They've been in Kirkuvagr – it has not been without its troubles, my lord.'

'No … true. Perhaps I misjudge them. See if you can find out a bit more about them, though, Ketil.'

'In Kirkuvagr?'

'If necessary, yes. It's not that far.'

'No, my lord.'

'And the other thing.' Thorfinn shuffled a little, less sure of himself. 'Rannveig.'

'Aye, my lord?'

'And that daughter of hers – good looking woman. Why isn't she married?'

'No money, perhaps?'

'There would be men who would take her for her looks

alone, no doubt, if she works hard and has a sensible head on her shoulders. Odd. But what I want to know is – can I trust Rannveig? Is she up to something?'

'What should she be up to, my lord?'

Thorfinn hissed out a sigh of frustration.

'I don't know. I don't trust her, that's all. Nor, I think, does anyone else, which may be our best defence. But I'm sure she's up to something.'

'That might be harder for me to discover, my lord,' said Ketil. 'I think a woman would be better placed to find out.'

'Well, I can't ask Ingibjorg,' said Thorfinn. Ketil pictured Thorfinn's wife, the woman Sigrid called Sheep-face. No, he would not ask Ingibjorg either. 'She and Rannveig were friends. All she would do is weep and wail about betrayal. She won't speak to her anymore, which is of course quite sensible.' Ketil wondered again at Thorfinn's apparent devotion to Ingibjorg. But Thorfinn had another solution for him. 'Ask Sigrid. She'll probably know,' said Thorfinn. 'Go and see her tomorrow. Then see what you can find out about those two nephews, and about Bjorn's fighting skills. I don't want someone in charge at Buckquoy who can't defend the place. It's our line of defence on the land side. I don't want someone hostile there, but it would almost be worse to have someone useless. And as for someone loyal to King Harald …'

'I'll find out what I can, my lord,' Ketil assured him.

'Good man. Good,' said Thorfinn. 'I'll go back down to Buckquoy tomorrow, maybe set up some exercises. I'll bring the nephews.' He seemed about to say something further, but instead took one of the torches and headed off on his own to his longhouse door. Ketil and his men, lit by the other torch, went to the hall where presumably Varin and Sigvat were already settled, and hoped for a decent night's sleep.

The following day was dull, but dry, and despite the autumn chill Ketil was not surprised, when he crossed the landspit back to Buckquoy and climbed up to Sigrid's little longhouse, to find her seated on the ground outside her door, her back to the doorpost and legs outstretched. One foot was booted, but the other was bare and a loop of wool around her big toe held her work taut as she twisted and turned the little bone tablets that made the patterns, and shot the weft back and forth next to them.

'Nice,' he said, cocking his head to try to make out the pattern. It was a broad band, rich with colour, patterned with leaves and leaping hares. 'A commission?'

'Yes – maybe my last one,' said Sigrid. Before he could ask why, she added, 'I can offer you cold water or hot water, or a stale flatbread. Or all three. What would you like?'

'I'll leave you the flatbread,' said Ketil with a smile, though even stale bread was useful. 'Cold water would be very welcome.'

Sigrid released her toe and limped, half shod, back into the longhouse. In a moment she was back with a cup of water. It tasted fresh and sweet.

'I've been at the hall all week,' she explained. 'No food in the house – I think when Gnup had finished what there was, he went up to Helga's and persuaded the children to feed him. And there's no ale, for two men came in the other day to order gifts for their wives, and finished the barrel between them.'

Ketil sat with his back against the longhouse wall and stretched his long legs out in front of him, taking in the view of the bright green pasture, the Brough and the sea on either side. He almost felt as if he were home. This outlook, a welcoming cup of cold water and Sigrid complaining – familiarity, at least.

Sigrid settled again, this time with some nailbinding that she did not have to concentrate on.

'How was Westray? I hear you brought back a pig.'

'We're not keeping it. We just didn't have time to ensure its safety.'

Sigrid gave a snort that might have been a laugh.

'I hope the men behaved themselves.'

'They usually do.'

She sighed.

'Yes, you're right, they do seem sensible. Even Geirod.'

'Even Geirod. He's one of those people that always seems grumpy, yet in their hearts they are really quite kind.' He felt Sigrid turn to look at him, and deliberately stared out to sea.

'There are a lot of them about,' Sigrid conceded at last. Ketil smiled.

They sat for a moment in silence, as Sigrid plied the bone needle about the wool in her hand, and added several rounds to what was evidently a length of winter hose for someone smallish – Helga, perhaps, or Gnup.

'So who do you think Thorfinn's going to choose?' Sigrid asked at last. 'The big fellow, or one of the unappealing nephews?'

'I was going to ask you what you thought,' said Ketil. 'You've seen more of the nephews than I have.'

'You haven't fought with them at all?'

Ketil shrugged.

'I suppose they would have been Einar's men if they had fought at all, but I don't remember them. I only saw Einar occasionally then. Their father's a merchant, apparently.'

'In Deerness, yes, I'd heard. He died a couple of years ago, I think. The two lads have been spending time in Kirkuvagr.'

'And Rannveig's daughter was also living in Kirkuvagr?'

'Yes,' said Sigrid, and he noted a little tension around her jaw. 'Thordis.' He waited, but she said nothing else. Evidently she was struggling to hold back some sarcastic remark.

'She must know the nephews from there, I suppose,' he went on eventually.

'I imagine so.'

'Why was she there, and not with her mother? Is her father dead?'

'Yes, long ago, before Rannveig married Einar. I think Thordis stayed with her father's family. You know Rannveig was from Kirkuvagr originally, don't you?'

'Yes, I remember. Odd that she should not stay with her mother.'

Again, Sigrid said nothing, but concentrated on the nailbinding that she could probably do in the dark.

'She's a very handsome woman,' Ketil pressed on. 'Takes after Rannveig, of course. I wonder if she's as intelligent?' He paused, but there was no reaction. 'She looks intelligent. I'm surprised she's not married.' Another pause. There would be a way, he knew, to provoke Sigrid into speech. He was almost there. Looks, intelligence, what could it be? 'I hear,' he tried carefully, 'that she's good with weaving and such. Is that right?'

It worked. Sigrid wrenched the nailbinding from her thumb and flung it out on to the wet grass.

'What have you heard?' she snapped. 'Or are you already

buying your own braid from her?'

'That's not –'

'Because if she's as wonderful as she says she is,' Sigrid scrambled to her feet and snatched up Ketil's cup, 'then stale flatbread and cold water is all I'll have to live on for the rest of what will probably be my very short days!'

VI

'All right,' said Ketil, not moving. His guess had hit the mark. 'Tell me about her.'

Sigrid bit her lip.

'Apparently her tablet-weaving is remarkable, and she's going to make sure everyone in Buckquoy and Birsay will be her customers, now she's settling here.'

'What, even Helga?' asked Ketil.

'You know Helga. She's been a good friend to me, but she loves new, different things. If she likes the look of Thordis' work she'll find it very hard to resist, friend or no friend.'

'There must be others who would be loyal to you – assuming that her braids are better than yours, which would surprise me.'

Sigrid, who had been staring down the hill with her arms folded tight about her, glanced round at him, taken aback by the compliment.

'Anyway, who told you her braids were wonderful?'

'Well …'

'Evidence? Proof?' he nudged.

'Um …'

'She told you, didn't she?'

Sigrid nodded.

'She's one of those confident people – you just believe them,' she said miserably. 'And her customers would believe her, too. They probably won't even look at my braids: they'll just order hers.'

'Why is she going to stay here?'

Mind clearly on braiding, it took Sigrid a moment to answer. She picked up her nailbinding, making sure the needle had not slipped off the end of the wool, and came back to sit beside him.

'That's a good question,' she said at last. 'I suppose when she first said it, I assumed she was here to keep her mother company now she's a widow. But the pair of them don't seem to get on that well.'

'Thordis looked very attentive to Rannveig over the last few days,' said Ketil.

'In public, yes,' Sigrid agreed. 'The dutiful daughter. And you're right, she's very handsome, and I'd say she's intelligent, too. Perhaps they are too alike.'

'Have you heard why she is not married?'

'No. Some gossip reaches us from Kirkuvagr, of course, but I was barely aware of her existence, let alone her history. Even Helga doesn't know.'

Ketil considered.

'Did Thorfinn send you to find out more about her?' Sigrid asked.

'Yes. He thought you would know.'

Sigrid looked more pleased than resentful, then said reluctantly,

'Ingibjorg might know more.'

'Thorfinn said Ingibjorg and Rannveig no longer spoke, and that Ingibjorg would be upset if he asked her about Rannveig.'

'They don't speak, no. But they were friends. She might know more about Thordis, and why she lives with her father's family rather than her mother. And she probably wouldn't be upset if I asked her – I mean, she wouldn't want to show that she was upset, which would make it easier.'

'Would you really go and ask her?' Ketil knew how little Sigrid liked Ingibjorg. Sigrid sighed.

'I would if I had to,' she said. 'Why does Thorfinn want to know about Thordis, anyway? She's not one of his options for the hall.'

'No,' said Ketil, 'but he wants to know if Rannveig is plotting. You can see his point. If you want to give someone an important position like that, you don't want to find out when it's too late that there's something going on in the background.'

'And he doesn't trust Rannveig.'

'Who does, now?'

Sigrid made a face, acknowledging his point.

'Well, he's right to think she's plotting, but whether or not it might affect his choice is a different matter.'

Ketil's eyebrows rose.

'She is?'

'I overheard her last night when I went out for more cheese. Accidentally,' she added with emphasis. 'I wasn't even thinking about her. Or Thordis, at the time.'

'What's she plotting, then?'

'Thordis' continued presence in Buckquoy,' said Sigrid sourly. 'Of course, that's not her emphasis. Thordis seems to be interested in one of the nephews – and I think it's true, I saw her watching their arrival and her whole expression changed.'

'Which one?' asked Ketil. 'Varin or Sigvat?'

'No idea,' said Sigrid. 'I can't say I noticed either of them pay any attention to her. Perhaps it's a one-sided business.'

'So Rannveig is plotting to have one of the nephews take over the hall, is that it?'

'As to that, I'm not sure,' said Sigrid. 'I don't know that she has any influence or power left to make that happen. What she is doing is trying to stop Thordis from making any commitment to one of the nephews before we know who Thorfinn will choose, and trying to find out more about Bjorn – Rannveig maybe reckons that Bjorn might be a potential husband for Thordis, if he's successful.'

'And that would allow Rannveig to stay on, of course,' said Ketil thoughtfully. 'With influence through Thordis.'

'Well, it might, if it worked,' said Sigrid with a grin. 'I can't say that Thordis sounded too co-operative. And, if we wanted evidence about her relationship with her mother, I'd add that she said that Rannveig had no right to ask her to do anything like that now as she had taken no interest in Thordis up to now.'

'Which makes me wonder again what Thordis is doing here.'

'I know. Unless the people in Kirkuvagr simply became fed up with her and wanted her to go.'

Ketil looked at Sigrid, and she smiled again.

'Well, I'd want to get rid of her. I just wish she would go somewhere else.'

'Not until I've found out more about her. Whether it's relevant for Thorfinn or not, I'm intrigued. There seem to be more questions about her than facts.'

Sigrid nodded.

'Anyway, apart from that what are Thorfinn's plans? Do you

know?'

'He is trying to find out more about Bjorn and the nephews,' Ketil told her. 'He's asked me to do some digging.'

'But you knew Bjorn in Trondheim, didn't you?'

'Not really. As a hostage from Thorfinn's hird he was much more important than me. I've never heard much against him, though: his men like him and he was popular at the court. He seems to have spent some time up in the far north, too – he has a protective bear spirit, apparently.'

Sigrid met his eye, and they both raised their eyebrows.

'Is he married?' Sigrid asked suddenly. 'That would spoil Rannveig's plans.'

'Not that I know of,' said Ketil. 'I talked with some of his men last night, and they didn't mention a wife.'

'Find out! Never mind bear spirits. It's important: wives buy cloth and braids and dye.'

'You could marry him yourself: that would solve all your problems,' said Ketil, and then wished he had not. 'I take it the nephews are not married, either.'

'No. Helga might find out more about them: she has her eye on Sigvat.'

'Thorfinn wants me to go to Kirkuvagr to see what I can discover,' he said. 'He's anxious that Varin and Sigvat have no battle experience, while Bjorn has fought with King Harald.'

'He's not expecting them to go raiding, is he? When was the last time that Thorfinn set out in his warships?'

'Nevertheless, it's hard to judge a leader who has only sold – whatever it is their father sold – for a living. Particularly when Buckquoy is so important to him defensively.'

'True,' said Sigrid, daughter of a merchant herself, but widow of a soldier.

'Then again, he was wary when he heard that Bjorn was a fighter.'

'Fighting for whom?'

'For King Harald, of course.'

Sigrid's eyes widened.

'Oh, yes. I can't see Thorfinn liking that. I mean, officially he's Harald's man, but …'

'Indeed,' said Ketil. 'It's easy to be Harald's man when

Harald is in Norway and Thorfinn is here. But otherwise, no.'

'No. So where is King Harald fighting these days? Ireland?'

'No. He's raiding along the Danish coast.'

Sigrid looked at him quickly.

'Because of King Sweyn?'

Ketil nodded. News always travelled fast: even a widow in her little longhouse could know much of what was happening in the world, if she took an interest. Sigrid laid down her nailbinding for a moment: she appeared to be picturing the Danish coast, as if feeling her way back there again.

'I hope they don't go near Heithabyr.'

He nodded again.

'Me, too. But anyway, Thorfinn's other concern is to find out just what Bjorn's fighting experience is, and if he's any good at it.'

'Just in case.'

'Just in case. As I say, I began talking with his men last night –'

'And there was I thinking you were marking the death of Einar Einarson, and enjoying a good meal.'

'Opportunities need to be seized.' He almost smiled.

'Particularly when you work for Thorfinn Sigurdarson,' she added lightly. Then she frowned a little. 'Do you ever feel you've missed some?'

'Some what?' he asked, not quite sure what she meant.

'Some opportunities. Things you might have liked to do. Places you might have wanted to go.'

'I've been to many places,' he said, but he still thought he might be misunderstanding. Perhaps she thought so, too.

'Well, I mustn't keep you,' she said, curling her feet up under her to stand. 'You have all your questions to ask, and I have to finish that bit of braid, even if it's the last one I do.'

'It won't be,' he said firmly. But he stood, too, shook out his cloak, and gazed down towards the hall at Buckquoy. 'I don't believe Thordis will be any threat to you.'

Sigrid only managed about her own foot's length of the complicated braid before she was interrupted again. Helga came skipping – and yes, it almost did look like skipping – round the corner of the longhouse and at once perched beside her on a handy rock, worn smooth by similar visitors over the years.

'Help yourself to water,' said Sigrid. 'I need to get on with this.'

Helga grinned and bounced up again, spending a little more time than necessary inside the longhouse. She was more than familiar with it.

'Sigrid, have you no food in the house at all?'

'I have a flatbread,' said Sigrid, trying to sound as if that would be sufficient for at least a week.

'Good thing I brought you some more,' said Helga, swinging her pack from her back and emptying out some parcels. 'Bread, and here's some dried meat and a few onions, enough to start a stew this evening. I hear Gnup's been up at our place.'

'Yes, sorry about that. He should have come to the hall and told me –'

'Don't talk nonsense! He was quite right to come to his neighbour's. And I'll have a commission for you when you're finished with that braid, so you can consider it payment in advance, if it makes you feel any better.' She stood and eyed the braid, much as Ketil had earlier. 'Hares? Lovely! That's such a pretty pattern. Who's it for?'

'It's for one of the women I knew in Shapinsay last winter,' Sigrid explained. 'She sent word a couple of weeks ago, but it took me a while to work it out.'

'Thordis should see that,' said Helga. 'I'm sure she's never made anything like it. Anyway,' she continued briskly, as if suddenly aware that she was treading on dangerous ground, 'how are your nettles coming along?'

'The first batch is in the house,' said Sigrid. 'Drying out.'

Helga glanced towards the house again in alarm.

'Didn't you say you'd gathered several armfuls?' Sigrid nodded. 'Isn't that a bit ... inconvenient?'

'They don't sting any more,' Sigrid explained. 'That all goes when they're soaked. Well, mostly – sometimes I miss a bit.'

'Goodness,' said Helga. 'So how long will it take before you can weave with them?'

'It depends how long it takes them to dry out,' Sigrid explained, then nodded at the sky where the grey clouds again talked of rain. 'In this weather, it could be months.'

'I'm looking forward to seeing it. What are you going to make with it?'

'I'm not sure yet,' said Sigrid. 'I just wanted to have it to hand.'

'It would make a lovely shirt,' said Helga thoughtfully.

'It would, if there's enough of it,' Sigrid agreed, 'but I'm not weaving a shirt for any man just yet.'

'Just yet?' Helga raised a conspiratorial eyebrow. 'Who do you have your eye on, then? Bjorn? Sigvat?' She sat back. 'Not Varin, I beg you, or I shall never visit you again!'

'None of them,' said Sigrid. 'I'm quite happy where I am. As long as I have work to do, and am able to do it.'

'Ah, yes – my commission,' said Helga, abandoning the hopeless task of finding Sigrid a new husband. 'Well, I came by this recently …' She rooted in her pack, and brought out a bundle of unspun wool, dyed a good even blue. 'I wondered if I might get hats for the boys from it? It's lovely and soft, but I think it might wear well.'

'Nailbinding?' Sigrid asked, giving the wool a close inspection. It was clean and with a good long staple, longer than their own sheep usually produced.

'Yes, if you would.'

'Where did it come from?'

'From … well, somewhere along the Danish coast, apparently.'

Sigrid glanced up at her. Helga's face was bland, but her fingers were busy knotting themselves together. She saw Sigrid noticing, and a tiny smile tugged at the corner of her mouth.

'Helga, did this come from a raid on the Danish coast?'

'He may have mentioned something like that, yes. I'm not entirely sure. Our conversation was … um, wide-ranging.'

'Was it indeed.' Sigrid considered, still fingering the wool. 'I thought I saw you going home last night?'

'A person can leave home after they've gone home,' said Helga, a little defensive. 'I made sure the children were all right and then … then I thought I might like a little walk.'

Sigrid sighed: she had no wish to know all the details. But one question did strike her.

'It wasn't Bjorn, was it? Not Bjorn himself?'

'No!' Helga laughed. 'Bjorn was far too busy sorting things out in the hall. No, it was one of his men – very nice, very –'

'Enough!' said Sigrid, trying not to laugh. 'I'll work your wool, Helga. Just don't tell me anything more about how you got it, please!'

Helga was laughing, too.

'Sometimes I worry about you, Sigrid. You have to find yourself a good man. You're taking far too little interest in such things!'

'Well, when Thordis takes over all my customers maybe I'll have time to concentrate on finding a husband,' said Sigrid, more lightly than she felt.

'I'm sure Thordis will find a husband long before you need to worry about your customers,' said Helga, growing more serious.

'Have you heard anything more about why she isn't married?

'Not a thing. I was mostly talking with Bjorn's men and his crew last night, so I haven't heard any Kirkuvagr claik. Why is it bothering you?'

Sigrid pursed her lips, taking a moment to check her braid for mistakes. She would not, she thought, say anything about Ketil. Mention of his name always made Helga sillier than usual.

'I just wondered if Rannveig was up to anything. You know what she's like: she was always clever.'

'But that all stopped when Einar found out about her.'

'I doubt he stopped her being clever,' said Sigrid drily. 'He just stopped her doing anything with that cleverness. But look, now: Rannveig is a widow, and Bjorn is to inherit the longhouse she lives in. He's unlikely to want to inherit her, too.'

'She's his stepmother: he has a duty to take care of her,' Helga objected.

'And do you think that's where Rannveig wants to be? A dependent of her unknown stepson?'

Helga frowned.

'It doesn't sound like Rannveig, certainly. But she could … I don't know, advise him, the way she advised Einar?'

'Don't you think that whoever takes over Buckquoy, Thorfinn will make sure they know all about Rannveig's past?'

'Then how could she possibly be plotting?'

Sigrid hesitated. Helga was usually discreet – she had to be able to keep her own secrets, anyway – but Sigrid liked to take a moment before she passed on interesting details like this. Nevertheless, she told Helga exactly what she had overheard when she went to fetch the cheese. Helga looked gratifyingly intrigued.

'So she wants to use Thordis to make the link with whoever gets the hall,' she said.

'If Thordis co-operates. And there's one mildly interesting thing that seems to me to come out of what Rannveig said,' Sigrid went on.

'What's that?'

'Rannveig clearly thinks that there are no other candidates for Buckquoy. It's either one of the nephews, or it's the Bear. And I don't think she trusts the Bear.'

That only Einar's nephews and his son were being considered for Buckquoy would not have been well-received down at the hall just at that moment.

Ketil had gone on to Buckquoy hoping to continue his conversation with Bjorn's men, but had found the place almost deserted.

'They all woke up with sore heads,' said a broad lass with freckles and a cheerful smile. 'Bjorn took them down to the harbour to take his boat out down the coast for a bit, brighten them up.'

'So it's all locals here just now?'

'That's right.' She set down the heavy stack of soapstone dishes she had been holding, and wiped her hands on a cloth. Ketil remembered her from the previous evening, a friendly face amongst the women serving. 'Are you here from Thorfinn? Did he want to call Bjorn up to the Brough?'

'No, no, I was talking with some of the crew last night and said I might come and see them today.' It was always a bit of an effort for Ketil to make himself sound chatty, but the girl seemed happy enough.

'Come in, anyway,' she said. 'We're just redding up now that the last of the men are up and about. From all I hear, Thorfinn's coming down later anyway with Varin and Sigvat, so we'd better look our best!' She glanced behind her at a sound, then called, 'Hey, wait, a bit over this way!'

She strode off to help one of the men shift a long table back to its usual place. Ketil went to give them a hand, but it was done before he could move.

'Aye,' said a voice almost at his elbow, 'and that's just an example of the family.'

He glanced down. Oddr, who had for a year or two been Einar's chief counsellor, was at his side, nodding in satisfaction at the freckled girl.

'Your daughter?' Ketil asked, trying not to stare at Oddr's moustache. There seemed to be more of it than ever.

'That's my lass, my Frogunn,' said Oddr. 'A fine lass, strong as an ox – and not married yet, should you be interested. And if that's my daughter, you can imagine what my son Foldar must be like.'

'I'm not sure I've met him,' said Ketil. He hoped that the son had not followed his father's example as regards facial hair.

'You'll have seen him last night, though,' said Oddr. 'He made that poem about Einar – a very fitting tribute to his late leader.'

Ketil remembered him. On the whole, he thought, Frogunn looked more warlike.

'Oh, aye,' Oddr went on, 'he's a lad of all the talents, my Foldar. He'll be taking Thorfinn round later, you know, to see all the hall and its assets. He's known them from a lad – can put his hand to any weapon, knows all the best lines of defence. And he can fight, too! You take him on later and he'll show you.'

'I might do that,' said Ketil. He had no wish to grow rusty, and Thorfinn would want to know of any promising warriors about the place.

'Oh, aye, he's a grand lad, my Foldar,' Oddr went on. Really, that moustache was astonishing. It was as though he had shorn a sheep and decided to drape the fleece over his top lip. Ketil almost missed what Oddr said next.

'You wait till he's leader here – then you'll see! Aye, Foldar's the man to take over Buckquoy.'

VII

Ketil was taken aback, but then considered. It was not unreasonable, after all, that Einar's own hird should hope, if not assume, that their new leader might be chosen from amongst them. He wondered if this was a collective decision, to push Foldar forward, or if it was just ambition on Oddr's part. He should probably try to find out, and let Thorfinn know that there was another candidate for him to consider.

The trouble was that if there was a local candidate, it was not going to make it easy for Thorfinn to impose an outsider like Bjorn or the nephews on the hall.

And it was always just possible, he conceded, that Foldar was a better candidate than he looked.

He searched about the hall, and found a few familiar faces in the shadows, lingering, as so often, at Einar's expense, or at the expense of his successor. There was Hrolf, Helga's husband, and Afi, the large boatbuilder, propped at a table and discussing the ways of the world. There, at least, Ketil had an excuse to make conversation. He went over.

'Good morning, Ketil! You're about early!'

Not really, Ketil thought, but he nodded.

'Lots to do,' he explained vaguely. 'Have you had a chance to look at my boat, Afi?'

'Oh, is there a problem?' Hrolf asked. 'That's the trouble with these nippy narrow boats – sometimes they go too fast for an inexperienced man to handle.'

Ketil ignored that remark: Hrolf had never much liked Ketil, and he did like to be the expert on everything. Ketil noted that he was as neatly turned out as ever, his clothes all newly made and prettily finished. Helga kept him well, probably by buying Sigrid's wares.

'It's just a couple of planks,' said Afi, reassuringly. 'It won't take long once I get down to it. I thought I'd spend tomorrow doing repairs: there's a new boat I'm working on, but I'm waiting for some timber for it.'

'Will there be timber for mine?'

That was the strangest thing Ketil found about the islands – so few trees, therefore so little timber. Always having to calculate how much one might need, how long one might have to wait for it to arrive.

'I've a few short pieces will do very nicely,' Afi told him. 'If you're in a real hurry I could make a worse job of it, but I know you like your boat.'

'I hear Bjorn's already out on the water today,' Ketil said. 'Now that's a very neat ship.'

'Oh, yes, isn't it?' Afi grinned, waving his huge hands in a ship-like shape. 'Those lines – and just that angle of the curve in the prow – ooh ...' He drew in a long, whistling breath. 'That's some boat builder. I'd like to meet him.'

'I haven't seen it yet,' said Hrolf tartly, as though he had been deliberately left out.

'He'll be back later,' said Afi casually. 'He just took a tour down the coast, maybe as far as Hamnavoe in this wind,' he added, knowing the wind even indoors. 'Just looking about him.'

'Planning,' said Hrolf darkly.

'You don't like him?' asked Ketil.

'I barely know him,' said Hrolf.

'That's the problem,' said Afi, nodding solemnly. 'He seems all right, but we'd rather have someone we know.'

'Do you know the nephews?'

'Varin and Sigvat?' Hrolf looked at Afi. 'Not much more than we know Bjorn, anyway.'

'Does that mean that the hird has someone else in mind? One of you?'

Hrolf smirked.

'I have no wish to push myself forward ...'

'Oddr's son Foldar is keen,' said Afi, and Hrolf's smirk became disgruntled. Ketil imagined that no one else wanted to push Hrolf forward either.

'How do other people feel?'

'He's a good lad,' said Afi, 'though a bit young. He hasn't

much experience.'

'Of fighting?'

'Of anything, really.'

He and Hrolf both sighed.

'That's the trouble,' said Hrolf. 'The experienced men are too old, apart from Afi and me, and the ones with the energy are too young. I don't think Foldar's ever been on a raid.'

'You're right,' said Afi sadly, 'he hasn't. That's the trouble: we haven't been away for a good while.'

Not something any of you seemed to object to when you were lazing around Einar's hall, Ketil thought to himself. Oh, they had trained, certainly – Ketil knew from experience that Hrolf was a good swordsman, and Afi was terrifying in a fight – but apart from the odd skirmish they had had little to do for the past few years. Ketil was fairly sure Bjorn would change that, if he were put in charge. The Buckquoy men might even find themselves following Harald's ships and harrying the Danish coast – it would have been commonplace a few years ago, but Einar had never been so far for a long time. Varin and Sigvat were less obviously keen – if the Buckquoy hird wanted to continue with their quiet life, one of the nephews might be better for them.

'But I suppose if Foldar were chosen, you'd accept him as your leader?'

'Well, yes.' Both men shrugged, as if an alternative had not occurred to them.

'And if the hall went to someone else?'

Hrolf and Afi looked at one another again.

'I suppose we'd have to, wouldn't we?' said Afi, not too reluctantly. Ketil was not surprised: Afi was the kind to make the best of most things. But the expression on Hrolf's face was much less generous. Ketil wondered what Hrolf thought he might do instead.

'Did Bjorn take all his men with him?' he asked at last, looking about him for strangers. It would have been odd for Bjorn to leave all their baggage unattended in a relatively strange place. Hrolf, businesslike again and keen to show that he knew what was going on, pointed towards the door.

'He left two lads here, and I think they went outside a while ago,' he said.

'Aye, they wanted to take a look about the place,' said Afi. 'I would, too, if I thought I was going to stay any length of time.'

'Spying,' muttered Hrolf. Afi ignored him.

'Peedie things, the pair of them. They come no higher than my chest. It'd be like Bjorn having a couple of pet mice: I wonder how many times he's lost them?' He laughed, like a great pair of bellows with a slow puncture. 'Aye, well, I'd best get back down to the harbour, or there'll be no seaworthy boat to be had. I'll put yours to the top of the list for tomorrow, Ketil, aye?'

'That's good of you. Thank you.'

Afi heaved himself to his feet, and Ketil could almost hear the bench sigh with relief. He blocked the doorway briefly, then vanished, off to his work.

'And I'd best go home and see if my wife needs me for anything,' said Hrolf, and cast a swift glance at Ketil. Hrolf's trust in his wife might have been misplaced, but he had the opposite problem with Ketil: he always seemed to suspect him of designs on pretty Helga. It might have made Ketil laugh if it had not been quite so irritating – it made Hrolf an unpredictable ally at crucial moments. They walked together to the door, though, when Hrolf had fetched his soft woollen cloak and pinned it exactly with a silver pin, checking the folds with a careful hand. Outside, Hrolf set off for his longhouse up the hill, while Ketil scanned the infields and outfields for two small strangers of northern origin.

There was plenty for a couple of visitors to look at, around here. Einar's hall had its own brewery, pig sties, dairy, smithy and bathhouse, several longhouses rolled into the folds of the land like moths in abandoned cloth, a number of storehouses, a practice yard for fighting and sports, and a paddock with a couple of horses Ketil knew quite well. If the men had wandered further, they could have taken the path east along the coast towards Kirkuvagr, or south towards Hamnavoe where Bjorn might have gone this morning. The Hamnavoe path would take them past the harbour and the settlement there, while Kirkuvagr's road had even more in the way of longhouses and boat nousts and the strange circular dwelling houses of the old people. Ketil, in Thorfinn's employ, was growing to know the islands better every season. He wondered if he would ever be free to go north again, to where the land was not so dangerously flat and where trees grew abundantly, yet the pastures were rarely so vivid a green against the blue-grey sea, the cattle rarely so fat, the crops rarely so rich. He would never make a farmer, but he could appreciate the worth of these islands, sometimes, when he could see them through the mist.

Ketil circumnavigated the hall, taking in the other buildings and casting long looks further afield, but it was only when he had returned to the practice yard at the front of the hall that he found the two men Afi had described, perched on the wall and looking out towards the Brough. It was the two he had spoken with the night before.

'What do you think, then – a good inheritance?' he asked.

The two men started, and turned to greet him. They must be quite at home now, Ketil thought, or they would have been more wary of someone approaching them from behind. The little chatty one – Atli, Ketil remembered – grinned in a friendly fashion when he saw who it was.

'Aye, you find us abandoned this morning!' he joked. 'Guarding everything while our friends take a trip down the coast.'

'You'll be sorry to miss that,' said Ketil.

'Ach, the Bear's taken them out to clear their heads,' said the quieter one – Egil, that was it. 'He knows we're a bit more responsible than that, and we don't want to be there with the youngsters spilling up their guts over the sides all the way to – is it Hamnavoe?'

'That's the place he said,' Atli confirmed, a twinkle in his eye. 'Oh, it's a fine thing to be young and foolish – until the next day!' He turned his attention back to the prospect in front of them. 'Aye, it's not a bad bit of land. Very green,' he added. 'My family are farmers. I'd be thinking about foot rot, looking at a bit of pasture like that.'

Ketil shrugged.

'I'm sure some of the locals will know better than I do.'

'You're from a military family, then?'

'Aren't we all?' Ketil gave a brief laugh. 'Traders, though, mine were.'

'Oh, aye? Whereabouts?'

'Heithabyr.' He caught the two men glance at each other. 'Norwegian trading family, part of the Norwegian community there.' He had no wish to be mistaken for a Dane, not just at the moment. Not that he looked like one.

'Aye, well, if you're Thorfinn's man, then that's good enough for me!' said Atli, jumping down off the wall. He was not as short as Afi had implied – just shorter than Afi. 'Now, are there plans for the day? The Bear said they'd not be long, if the wind favoured them.'

'I think Thorfinn was going to come back later,' said Ketil. 'He'll want to talk more with Bjorn.'

'He does a lot of talking, that Thorfinn,' said Atli.

'He needs to know who he's dealing with.'

'Easier to fight them. That tells you who you're dealing with, and a lot faster, too.'

'He might do that, too.'

'When's he going to make up his mind?' asked Egil, still perched on the wall. The other two leaned on it, looking out and down the hill.

'It can't take long,' said Atli. 'It's obvious the Bear's ten times the worth of those two lads put together.'

'There might be other possibilities,' said Ketil, more to avoid giving his opinion than anything else.

'Other possibilities?' Egil repeated quickly. 'We weren't told about that. Others?'

'Relax, Egil!' said Atli easily. 'Whoever it is, how likely is it that they are a better prospect than the Bear?'

Egil made a face and nodded, clearly accepting this as a fair point.

'What if he's not Thorfinn's choice?' Ketil asked. 'The longhouse would still be his – would he stay?'

For once Atli did not reply straightaway. The possibility must not have occurred to him.

'Stay here? Under someone else's leadership?' he tried slowly. Egil scowled.

'Doesn't seem likely,' he muttered. 'But then, the whole thing doesn't seem likely. Thorfinn's bound to choose the Bear.'

And considering the options, Ketil felt that he had to agree.

Helga turned up again at Sigrid's place just as Sigrid and Gnup were finishing their midday meal – almost entirely contributed by Helga.

'The men are to fight!' she said. 'There's going to be fighting practice down at the hall!'

'What, Einar's hird?' Sigrid stopped herself just in time from making a dismissive remark – after all, Hrolf was one of Einar's warriors, in theory.

'Well, them, yes. But Bjorn's men, and the nephews, too.'

'That will be a bit uneven. A whole longship crew against Einar's two nephews?'

'Oh, Thorfinn will add some men to make up the numbers, no doubt.' Helga's eyes were shining in anticipation. 'There'll be bouts of different kinds. Maybe wrestling! Come on, come and watch!'

'Do you want to go, Gnup?' Sigrid asked. The boy was studiously wiping every trace of stew from his plate with his last piece of flatbread, with evident delight.

'I wouldn't mind,' he said after a moment. 'Though there's the neeps to bring in.'

'The neeps aren't going anywhere today,' said Sigrid. 'Go on, have a keek. Whoever wins might be our new leader.'

Gnup scrambled to his feet and went to sort out whatever work he was to abandon.

'Aren't you coming, Sigrid?' Helga pushed.

'I've plenty to do here,' Sigrid objected.

'Come on,' said Helga. 'It'll be fun! And the light will go here soon, anyway. There'll be torches lit down at the hall, and you know you can spin without looking anyway, so leave your weaving for today and come and watch!'

Helga, able to afford good lamp oil, had no idea how dark Sigrid's longhouse could be in the evenings, and how she dreaded the shorter days of winter. And Sigrid had seen enough violence to do her. But it was hard to resist Helga's enthusiasm, and anyway, there was a good chance that she, and the other women, might be needed to deal with injuries. And there might be food, though that seemed greedy after she had just had a good meal. She sighed, and went to fetch her cloak.

'It'll be a real test for Bjorn's men,' Helga chattered as they took the path to Buckquoy, Gnup behind them. 'They went down towards Hamnavoe today, and Hrolf reckons they'll have had to row back.'

'He'll probably still do better,' said Sigrid. 'He just looks like a man who wins.'

'Doesn't he?' Helga agreed, though it seemed to please her more than it did Sigrid.

'Are you sure they're back, if they went south this morning?'

'If they're not, we'll be there and ready when they arrive. Isn't this exciting?'

Sigrid considered that she might have put in an hour's work before the excitement, but it was too late now. And anyway, she could see from here that quite a crowd was gathered in front of Einar's hall, and that evidently Bjorn and his crew had already returned.

The crew did not seem tired: instead they had a refreshed, wind-blown look to them, just ready for a bit of a skirmish. Thorfinn, with that broad authority he always seemed to carry, was walking away from Bjorn across the practice ground to where Sigrid could see Varin and Sigvat standing with a group of local men. Bjorn was gathering his crew about him, already issuing directions. Sigvat had turned to assess the local men, while Varin stood, fists on hips, glaring at Bjorn. Sigrid thought it was unlikely to have much effect on the big man. Sigvat evidently agreed, for he patted Varin on the elbow and turned him to face Thorfinn and receive instructions.

'There's a space there by the paddock wall,' said Helga, pushing Sigrid on and into the paddock. Experienced watchers flocked to this spot, where you could duck quickly down below the height of the wall if the fighting became a bit too wild. The horses had already wisely trotted to the far end, out of range.

They found a spot where the wall was high enough for protection but low enough that they could comfortably lean on it. Sigrid already had her spindle out when she spotted Ketil's men amongst the crowd allocated to Varin and Sigvat. Skorri was wriggling his arms into his chain mail, but he managed somehow to fold the back of it up into his collar. Alf, the tall, skinny one with the dreamy air, watched Skorri struggle for a moment, then stepped across to disentangle him with a few deft tweaks. Skorri jumped up and down on the spot to complete the task, jiggling the fine mail into place. Sigrid was glad she would never have to wear a garment like that. She noted that Alf preferred a padded undercoat with a mail waistcoat and belt. Was it any lighter? It looked as if it would stop an elk, and it certainly transformed a thin man like Alf into something much more intimidating. Where was Geirod, the third of Ketil's men? She looked about her, then found him crouched on the same side of the paddock wall as she was, settling that yellow dog of his.

'Geirod!' she called. 'Do you want to bring your dog over here? I think he knows me a little.'

Geirod grunted, and brought the dog over to sit at Sigrid's feet.

'Thanks.'

'What's his name again?'

But Geirod was already off, stamping along by the paddock wall to the place he could swing himself over and join the preparations.

The sound of blades against whetstones sang through the air: this might not be a real fight, but every man knew he had to keep his blades fresh, particularly in the damp air of the islands. Many pulled on leather gloves when their blades were ready, some with a fishscale layer of wooden slats on the back to make them even stronger. She remembered sewing a set for her husband, long ago, and wondering if they would catch on things. Not everyone favoured them.

It looked as if Thorfinn wanted to begin the day with a general fight involving everyone, rather than individual contests. Sigrid wondered if Ketil was to fight, or if he were off doing Thorfinn's business elsewhere. One never knew with Ketil. She had always assumed he was not a very good fighter, and that that was why Thorfinn had him making enquiries and finding things out. Yet the evidence she had seen in the last few years seemed to indicate that he actually was quite skilled. It constantly surprised her.

Now some of the men were tipping helmets on to their heads, another thing Sigrid was sure she would hate. They looked hunched under the weight now, the quilted or mail skirts protecting the backs of their necks. Fewer of them were recognisable as individuals. A real battle must be desperately confusing, she thought: how would you know who to kill? Or who was about to kill you? The shields with their badges would help, as long as the fighters managed to hold them. For now they had propped them against their legs, waiting until the last moment to take the weight. Fighting, she thought, must be about economy of effort. You had to let your enemy tire themselves out before you did. But the sheer effort of struggling into and then just standing in all that gear – that would tire her out before she had even lifted a weapon. She would have no hope.

Yet here were forty men, armed and armoured, and ready to begin.

VIII

It was half-exercise, half-competitive. But with Thorfinn watching closely, and two or more candidates for the hall involved, the competitive half was likely to dominate.

Sigrid guessed that the two opposing lines did not arrange themselves opposite one another so tidily in a real battle. Thorfinn, who chose to oversee the event on foot, examined both sides closely before backing clear, and giving the signal to attack.

Bjorn's men instantly ran hard at the locals, smashed through the shield wall in seconds and flattened three or four of the men, gently enough, just to show that they had won. Thorfinn sighed, and shouted for a retreat.

'Well done, Bjorn,' he called. 'The element of surprise.' He looked across at Varin, but Varin and Sigvat were in urgent conversation. Sigvat waved over a few of Thorfinn's men as well as, Sigrid noticed, some of the Buckquoy hird. Oddr's son, Foldar, was amongst them. At the back of the locals she saw Ketil, standing with his sword drawn, looking if anything quite detached from what was happening. Skorri spat on the sandy ground, and Alf weighed a spear in his hand as if trying to determine its quality before buying.

'Are we quite ready?' asked Thorfinn, a little tartly. Sigvat looked at Varin and muttered something. Varin nodded.

'Aye, my lord,' he said. Thorfinn gave the signal.

Bjorn was not foolish enough to use the same tactic twice in a row. This time his men advanced more slowly, edging across the practice ground as the locals tensed behind their shield wall. Sigrid saw that each of the front shield bearers had braced themselves with a long leg to the back, their bodies turned almost sideways to present a harder target. But Bjorn's men had their spears low, aiming for the vulnerable points of the wall where the round shields no longer overlapped, and the thighs of their opponents were less well-protected. After a moment of unbearable tension, Bjorn's men charged again, and once the long weapons had done their work the long-handled axes came out, prising the remaining shields from the hands of their owners or reaching helmets and shoulders over the top of them.

But this time the local men were fighting back. Huge Afi used his shield as a battering ram in the centre of the line, and followed by Sigvat and Foldar, the latter's face already running with blood, they ploughed through the front rank of Bjorn's men, trampling two or three underfoot. The rest of the locals who were still standing followed, a wedge that broke Bjorn's little army in two and scattered the men. The wedge split and the locals were fighting confidently on two fronts now, back to back. Bjorn's men sagged away as Thorfinn shouted the retreat, and the locals cheered.

'I'd better go and see to Foldar,' said Frogunn, who had arrived unnoticed beside Sigrid. 'Brothers are such a responsibility!'

Hrolf seemed uninjured, though pleased with himself, wiping off the blade of his axe as though he had slaughtered dozens. Helga and Sigrid watched, in case they were needed, as Frogunn put a pad of cold cloth to her brother's nose, and Thordis made sure, it seemed, that Varin and Sigvat were unhurt. Sigrid was interested to see that Rannveig was tending to the wounds at Bjorn's end of the practice yard.

Frogunn returned to the safer side of the paddock wall.

'He'll need that sewn later,' she said. 'He's not really a fighter, Foldar. I think I'd be more use out there than he would. I might enjoy it more, too!'

It was true that Foldar, who barely looked grown up though he was older than Frogunn, seemed a little nervy as the locals took their places again to face Bjorn's crew. A few men sat out now with those in the paddock: there had indeed been spear wounds to thighs, which could be very nasty, and Geirod, nursing one hand, came to claim his dog back from Sigrid.

'Two more rounds,' he told them, 'then there'll be some

individual combat.'

'What have you done to your hand?' asked Helga. Geirod made a face.

'Used it to barge through Bjorn's shield wall,' he said, and the dog followed him mournfully away.

'I don't know why they do the big fight first,' said Helga, watching him go.

'Weeds out the weaklings,' said Frogunn. 'Like Foldar, bless him. They should let us out there: we'd show them!'

The third bout had started, and Frogunn was watching with keen interest. Foldar seemed to have taken a blow to the head, and was very unsteady on his feet, his face still smeared with blood. But the locals were holding their own, generally. Varin seemed to be talking to the men, planning his attack, and they seemed willing enough to follow. Bjorn relied more on charging into the fray or shouting at his men as they fought, always with a huge grin on his face.

It did him no good in the third bout, for Varin reversed his tactics, allowed his own shield wall to collapse in the middle then surrounded Bjorn's men as they hurtled through. Skorri himself casually gave Bjorn a good dunt on the helmet, and Bjorn stumbled and went down with a mighty thump that jarred everyone's teeth.

Thorfinn called again for the retreat, and this time Sigrid had to put aside her spinning and join Helga and Frogunn in staunching and binding up wounds. The practice ground was growing messy, gouged and stained, and one of Bjorn's men had a broken leg where Afi had accidentally trodden on him. Afi carried the man gently off the field, apologising every step of the way.

For a while it looked as if Bjorn himself had broken his arm in his fall – there were a couple of other men already with arms strapped up – but after some examination Rannveig declared it was only bruised, and Bjorn, beaming, lifted it high to encourage his men. Varin, still uninjured, was striking a pose close to where Thorfinn had established himself, while Sigvat moved amongst the locals, talking. Sigrid, tending to a fighter's calf and noticing Sigvat pass her yet again, wondered if he were too nervous to stand still.

The final round was the hardest fought yet. The men were barely tiring, except a few of the older ones from Einar's hird, but Bjorn's crew wanted another win, and they were determined to get it. For a while the din was relentless, metal on metal, grunts and shouts, feet pounding the sandy ground and men tumbling down. Thorfinn's keen gaze seemed to be everywhere. The densely-packed men could barely be distinguished from each other: it was a knot of leather and mail, blades and helmets and flailing limbs. The fight surged briefly across the practice ground towards the paddock wall and the crowd backed away, shouting warnings, but the nearest men elbowed themselves away from the wall again and the fighters, huddled together like one great beast on its erratic track, stumbled back towards the hall. Thorfinn moved out of its path, still watching closely. Then, as if at some unheard signal, the whole thing broke apart, men fell to the ground and others staggered off, panting, and in the middle of it Bjorn and Varin stood, shoulders heaving, facing each other with axes in their raised hands.

And Thorfinn stepped forward, and called for the retreat.

Ketil checked about him before stepping back from the fight: there could be as much damage done through carelessness when people relaxed as from deliberate intent, he thought, glancing at Afi's victim. He took a moment to look over his sword before he sheathed it: he had only used the flat, but there was always the chance that he had accidentally nicked someone, especially in that last struggle. But it was clean, and in a moment he felt the satisfying hiss and rattle of it returning to the scabbard.

'We'll take a rest, briefly,' Thorfinn called out to Bjorn and Varin – the two men had moved abruptly away from each other as Thorfinn had stopped the fight. Bjorn glanced back at Thorfinn and nodded, his grin a little forced. Rannveig, Thordis and the women of the hall were already bringing out ale and a little meat. The fighters found themselves seats where they could, on the walls or against them. Ketil, seeing that Skorri and Alf were quite happy, was about to go and check on Geirod and his injured hand when Thorfinn caught his eye and summoned him over. Thordis brought them both ale, with a winning smile which they both ignored.

'Well?' asked Thorfinn.

'A little surprising,' said Ketil. 'It was about to get nasty at the end, there.'

'Yes: I think I stepped in just in time. I don't want to make them into enemies. What did you think, up to then?'

'Bjorn is clearly used to his own men, and they to him: they have established habits of fighting and that was what they did, stuck to their usual patterns. Perhaps they would be more imaginative in a real battle - perhaps this was just because they knew it wasn't serious. I don't know.'

'Yes, I was not as impressed as I expected to be by Bjorn. Perhaps his responsibilities under King Harald are not as extensive as I had assumed.' Thorfinn pondered for a moment, his gaze deliberately away from any of the candidates, though Ketil noted that Varin and Sigvat at least were watching them closely. They were too far away to hear, though. 'And the brothers?'

'By contrast, better than I had expected. Varin assessed the situation, learned from each bout, and instructed the men clearly.'

'You took no part in the matter?'

'As you suggested, my lord. I kept my mouth shut.'

'One of the reasons I employ you,' said Thorfinn, nodding approval.

'My question there, though, my lord, is what Sigvat's role was. Varin barely spoke with the men except to issue his orders. Sigvat, though, was everywhere, and I believe that before each bout he talked intensively, but privately, to Varin. It's possible that the ideas are Sigvat's, along with the ability to gather information and assess a situation, but he's allowing Varin to assume the role of leader.'

'Varin is the elder.'

'Sigvat would know he would have a fight on his hands to be granted Buckquoy over Varin's head. But it may well be to his advantage to have Varin in the high seat after all.'

'Interesting … if you're right, then if anything happened to Sigvat and Varin held Buckquoy, he would be a useless leader – or worse, perhaps, open to the influence of some other instructor.'

'But for the moment I think they should be considered together, my lord. Whichever head was behind it, it was a better head than Bjorn's.'

Thorfinn puffed out a sigh.

'I don't know whether to be pleased or disappointed that there is no local candidate,' he said, his voice carefully low. 'You'd think there would be somebody, but at the same time it's going to be hard enough to decide without a third – or fourth – man involved.'

Ketil cleared his throat.

'There is a local man, my lord. I thought you might already know, as I heard he was to show you over the property today.'

'I think it's Oddr's son that'll be showing me around. I don't know why Oddr couldn't, but I shan't miss him – self-important old fool. But who is the candidate, then?'

'Oddr's son, my lord.'

'Really?' Thorfinn frowned, and looked about the practice ground. 'Is he here, then? I'm not even sure I know his name, or what he looks like.'

'He's the one over by the wall there – you can't see him just now, for his sister is attending to his injuries.'

'He was fighting?' Thorfinn was surprised.

'A little, my lord.'

Thorfinn's look sharpened.

'You mean not very well, don't you?'

Ketil shrugged, a kind of apology to the absent Foldar.

'He split his nose in the first bout, then had a crack on the head in the second, so I don't believe he had much chance.'

Thorfinn tutted.

'Father Tosti, who has read of such things, tells me that the Romans believed a leader should not only be skilled, but should also be lucky. Father Tosti suggests, and I agree with him, that we might now read that as being blessed by God. Do you think that Oddr's son is blessed by God?'

Ketil touched the cross at his neck and considered.

'In many ways, perhaps, my lord. But I don't think the blessings include skill in battle.'

'Hm,' said Thorfinn. 'Then why bother to stand forward?'

'I can't say, my lord. The hird wants at least one of their own men to be considered, which is not surprising. Perhaps there was no one better?'

'Or no one they could all agree on?' Thorfinn suggested. Neither was an option that boded well for the hird. 'One thing to be said for Bjorn,' Thorfinn said. 'He'd bring a lot of new blood into the hall. It could do with it.'

He stood straight and looked about him, at the uncared-for buildings, at Foldar squatting miserably by the wall, at Hrolf and Oddr, smug in the doorway, at Rannveig and Thordis taking round the ale jugs.

'I should have done something about this place long ago, when Einar started to fail,' he said sadly. 'But I could not bear to put the man aside. We had fought together for so long, and I respected him. Him and Rannveig. And these have been peaceable times, these last few years. But there is no defence here: the best of these men are unpractised and untrained, and the worst are old and damaged and lazy. If King Sweyn appeared tomorrow in the harbour with ten – five – fighting ships, we would fall by sundown. I need this place strong, and secure, and loyal to me.'

'Then we need more evidence for you to make the right choice, my lord.'

'We do indeed.' Thorfinn flung off his moment of anxiety, and waved Hrolf and Oddr off the hall's low step. 'Right!' he called. 'Time for more fighting!'

The cheer that went up might almost have been enough to reassure him. Almost – but Ketil, looking from Varin to Bjorn to Foldar, found he was more anxious than he had been when the day had begun.

Sigrid preferred watching the individual fights. The fighters' skills were more evident, the details more obvious, and there were fewer injuries to tend to. She managed to wind quite a length of yarn around her spindle during the first few bouts, where Thorfinn picked up to four men from amongst the fighters and set them against each other with knives, swords or axes, or even with hammers. The work was delicate, but there was a great deal of laughter, some applause, and a bit of excitement in the watching. Geirod had returned with a bandage around his hand and sat with the yellow dog to see the fighting, raising his ale cup when Skorri managed a particularly elegant defeat of one of the men Ketil had been sitting with at the feast. Sigrid glanced over at Ketil to see his reaction, but Ketil seemed unmoved. Sigrid had seen him talking with Thorfinn, and wondered what new tasks Thorfinn was setting him. And what Thorfinn was planning. After the way Varin and Bjorn had fought, she thought, Thorfinn's plans might have changed.

She was considering sharing this thought with Helga, when she noticed that Helga was standing differently and tweaking at the neckline of her dress. Evidently there was a desirable man nearby.

Sigrid sighed: there would be no sense from Helga till the man had gone. She turned to see who it was.

Sigvat, Varin's brother, was making his way amongst those who were watching from the paddock, stopping for a moment here, chatting and pointing to the fighters there. If Sigrid was any judge, he was trying to get to know the Buckquoy hird, trying to make friends. It made sense, she thought, but why was it Sigvat, and not his brother? Not expecting Sigvat to talk to her, particularly as she was standing next to Helga, Sigrid looked about for Varin to see if he was also trying to gather support.

'Have you seen Varin?' she asked Frogunn, who had returned to perch next to her again.

'He's over there, with Thorfinn,' said Frogunn at once. 'I think he's done well today so far, don't you?'

'Better than I expected,' Sigrid agreed. Yes, there was Varin, though it did not look as if Thorfinn was paying him any attention. Varin just wanted to be seen near him, she thought. She preferred Sigvat's strategy.

Rannveig and her daughter were also near to Thorfinn, though that was more likely because they wanted to be close to the hall to distribute ale, food, and treatment for injuries. At that moment they were idle, though. Thordis sat by her mother, but her hungry gaze seemed to be focussed on Varin. Sigrid wondered if Rannveig had any chance of redirecting Thordis' interest towards Bjorn, even if only to find out more about him. It really did not look like it.

'I hear you're Sigrid,' came an unfamiliar voice next to her, and she jumped. It was Sigvat. What had he heard?

'Your husband was my uncle's man, I believe,' he said with a smile. 'A good warrior.'

Up to a point, thought Sigrid.

'I'm glad they say that,' she said. Glad, and a little surprised.

'And you live up over yonder?'

'I do.' Why had he been asking questions about her? Or was he working to find out all about Buckquoy? 'And you are from Deerness, I'm told. Did you know your uncle well?'

Helga beside her chuckled nervously. Sigrid wondered if Sigvat might take the question as a criticism – why had they not seen him visit more often? – and then decided she didn't care if he did.

He was a handsome man, though, and she could quite see that Helga would not want to annoy him.

'My father was not well for several years before he died,' Sigvat was saying, 'and so no, we did not come to Buckquoy as often as we might have. Einar came to see us a few times, though, over the years. We knew him better when we were boys.'

'He was a good man,' said Sigrid.

'He was. And a fine warrior, in his day.'

They kept a respectful silence for a moment.

'The fighting went well earlier,' said Helga, keen to be in on the conversation.

'Ah, yes. You're Helga, Hrolf's wife?' Sigvat must have been asking lots of questions. Sigrid almost laughed when she noted the wariness in Sigvat's eyes. He had had answers, too, it seemed. Helga gave him one of her particular smiles, the ones that made her look almost like a modest, respectable wife.

'That's right. I live up yonder, too.' She waved a hand, but kept her eyes on Sigvat's face. Just giving him directions, Sigrid thought. Helga might have gone on, but Frogunn had other interests.

'That Bjorn and his crew are good fighters,' she said to Sigvat, who turned to her in surprise. 'Do you think you can beat any of them?' Her smile took the edge off the challenge, and Sigvat smiled back.

'I think some of the Buckquoy men are skilled enough, and then we have a few from Thorfinn's own hird. But much of it will come down to luck, you know. Bjorn talks of his bear amulet – let's see how powerful it really is.' He fingered the curl of the lead amulet at his own neck.

'Sigvat!' came a shout. 'Sigvat, come on! Your turn!'

'Oh!' said Sigvat, and with a nod to Sigrid and Helga he hurried off. Sigrid thought he seemed just a bit relieved at his escape.

Though his relief might have been brief. Sigvat had been drawn to fight Bjorn.

'Oh, knives!' said Frogunn. 'That'll be interesting.'

'Nasty, too,' said Helga. 'They always seem to make more mess with knives than they do with swords or axes.'

'They take the swords and axes more seriously,' Sigrid suggested.

'Bjorn will have a much better reach,' said Frogunn,

assessing the two men like a warrior herself. 'But Sigvat will be much lighter on his feet. Hm – hard to tell who might win this one!' She settled herself with evident delight against the wall, freckled elbows firm on the flat stones. 'And they've both been busy – they'll be too tired for a long fight.'

As it turned out, Frogunn was right about that. The fight was very short indeed. In fact, it was hard to see exactly what had happened, for in a moment Sigvat was face down in the sand, and Bjorn was on his knees, clutching at the haft of Sigvat's knife, plunged deep into his shoulder.

IX

There were as many different versions of what happened as there were people watching. Some said that Sigvat had gone straight for Bjorn's shoulder like a thing possessed. Others said Bjorn had unexpectedly turned and caught the blade which had been aimed elsewhere. Then had Bjorn lashed out in fury and punched Sigvat on the side of the head, or had Sigvat tripped and fallen? There was certainly a bruise on his temple – Sigrid had seen it herself – but it was a shapeless blotch, and told them nothing, any more than the pain in the jaw he was nursing.

'Are you sure you don't remember?' Ketil asked. Sigvat went to shake his head, then stopped, and looked up at Ketil sideways trying not to move at all.

'I have no idea what happened. The last thing I remember is facing Bjorn and wondering which way he was going to attack. Then I woke up in here.'

'Here' was a bedspace in Einar's hall. They had thought it best not to move either man too far. Frogunn wrung out another cold cloth, and gently replaced the one around Sigvat's neck, supporting his head and chin. Sigrid was preparing more bandages.

'Oh, well, at least it was even,' said Helga, who had been quite attentive to Sigvat. Ketil thought perhaps Sigrid was staying for Sigvat's protection.

'I wouldn't want to blame Bjorn, anyway,' Sigvat went on stiffly. 'If it was him, it was probably just a reaction to the pain, if he hit me at all.'

'Doesn't know his own strength,' murmured Helga. 'More broth?' She held out a tantalising spoon, but Sigvat waved it away. Ketil sighed, and crossed the hall to see Bjorn.

The great Bear was swaddled in blankets and furs in a bedspace twice the size of Sigvat's. Sigvat's blade lay, coated in blood, on the floor nearby, and Bjorn, clutching his bear tooth amulet, was breathing hard as Thordis pressed down on the wound with all her strength. The padding under her hands was already dark red.

'Ketil,' said Bjorn, looking up as if desperate for a distraction. His teeth were gritted as if they would never part. 'What a fuss, eh?'

'How's the arm?'

'Oh, if we could get it to stop bleeding …' Thordis put in. Bjorn shot her a sideways look of admiration.

'If anyone can sort it out, it'll be this girl here,' he said. 'I have every confidence in her.'

'I'm sure she's very competent,' said Ketil. Thordis beamed.

'How's Sigvat? Is he all right?' Bjorn seemed genuinely concerned.

'Do you remember what happened?'

'No! All I remember is a pain in my arm, and then I fell down. I must have caught him somehow as I fell. Has he come round?'

'He has. He can't remember anything either.'

Bjorn frowned.

'Well, someone will have seen. But if he's all right it doesn't matter so much, I suppose.'

If they were both prepared to leave it, then Ketil had no further interest in the incident. He heard someone light-footed come up behind him.

'Thordis, what are you doing here? Isn't there someone else who could be doing that?'

It was Varin. Thordis looked up at him, hands crimson.

'Varin! Mother told me to …'

'I'm sure there are other women. Those two over there, attending to Sigvat – they've probably finished now. Go and tell them to get over here, and you come with me and wash your hands.'

To Ketil's surprise, Thordis did exactly as she was told.

'Helga! Could you help, please?'

Helga hurried over, eyes wide at the mess of Bjorn's shoulder but happy to take over from Thordis. With hardly a backward glance, Thordis left the hall in Varin's wake. Ketil looked back at Bjorn.

'So that's her name,' Bjorn said, a little breathless – though it may have been from the pain. 'Thordis …'

'Oh, this is still bleeding!' cried Helga. 'I don't think I'm as heavy as Thordis. Ketil, you have lovely strong hands - you'll help, won't you?'

But Sigrid was already beside her to add pressure to the wound. Between them they managed to stop the oozing blood, bandage the shoulder firmly, prop Bjorn more comfortably on his bedding, and remove all the stained cloths from around him.

'I'll take Sigvat's knife back,' said Helga, 'after I've cleaned it, anyway.' She plucked it delicately from the floor and left the hall. Bjorn settled back, closing his eyes. There was a worrying, grey look about him.

'I'll stay with him for a bit,' said Sigrid. 'He's lost a good deal of blood, to judge by that mess. He shouldn't try to do too much for a while.'

She looked tired, Ketil thought: she would probably prefer to go home to her own bed.

'I can sit with him if you like,' he said. 'I'm sure he'd prefer a comely attendant, but ...'

'If you can get that Thordis back that would be perfect,' Bjorn interrupted, opening his eyes a crack to make his point. He slumped back again. Sigrid turned back to Ketil with her eyebrows raised. Ketil met her gaze.

'Now there's a thing,' she said.

'But Thordis has gone out – at Varin's bidding,' said Ketil in a low voice. There was no reaction from Bjorn: he did seem this time to have fallen asleep.

'So it's Varin?'

'I should say so.'

Sigrid made a face, and said,

'He was ignoring her before, despite her best efforts.' She looked down at Bjorn. 'Perhaps he thinks he needs to try a little harder, in the face of competition?'

Ketil shook his head.

'Too complicated for me,' he said. She grinned.

'I should think so. You just stick to the simple task of hitting other people and ducking when they try to hit you.'

'That's not always straightforward,' he said, with a nod at Bjorn. 'Were you watching? What did you see?'

Sigrid shrugged.

'It all happened too fast. I don't know if either of them intended harm.'

'They're both happy to let it lie.'

'Then let it lie. There's enough trouble in the world without digging out more to poke sticks at.'

He nodded, very much inclined to agree. It was just that he had a feeling, somehow, that the event had greater significance than it seemed just now.

It was next morning before Sigrid realised she must have left her spinning somewhere down at Einar's hall, in the confusion as they treated Sigvat and Bjorn. She had been working on other things, so by the time she clipped on her back cloak and set off she hoped it was late enough that the men sleeping in the hall would be up and about, the doors opened and the place aired. It was not always pleasant to visit a busy hall first thing in the morning.

In fact, most of the men seemed already to be outside, stretching and rubbing their tired limbs after yesterday's exertions. Oddr and his son Foldar stood by the paddock wall, regarding the practice ground dismally. Sigrid suspected they were reviewing Foldar's performance the previous day. Foldar had had his nose stitched, and it was about twice its usual size. He looked utterly miserable.

There was no sign of Bjorn or Sigvat, about whom she also intended to ask, and as she was fairly sure she had left her spindle in the hall itself, she took a deep breath and went inside.

Sigvat was seated on a bench, the bruise on the side of his head turning a fine shade of purple. Helga was seated beside him, holding a cup, and they both smiled as Sigrid appeared.

'How are you this morning, Sigrid?' Sigvat asked.

'Never mind me, how are you?' she replied.

'Could be worse,' he said, though she could see how little he moved his jaw as he spoke. It was tied about with bandages, but it clearly still hurt. 'I can still drink ale.'

'We kept him here last night rather than him going back to the Brough. That knock on the head was a bad one.'

'Happy enough not to move too far,' Sigvat agreed.

'Now Rannveig has made him some of her spiced wine,' said Helga, with a significant look at Sigrid. Rannveig was well-known for her skills with herbs, including ones that dulled pain. 'But he says he doesn't like the taste.'

'Drink it down, nevertheless,' said Sigrid firmly. 'It's not there for you to enjoy!' She turned to Helga. 'Is Hrolf all right? No injuries?'

'None, I'm pleased to say,' Helga told her. 'His chief complaint was that while Thordis was checking him over, she tried to sell him one of her braids.'

'Did she?' Sigrid was alarmed.

'Oh, don't worry: Hrolf knows well enough that I do the buying in our household. I just wonder who else she's been talking to, though?'

'Anyway,' said Sigrid, pulling back from annoyance, 'Any other injuries?'

'Well,' said Helga, still frowning, 'apart from Foldar most of Einar's men – I mean – well, what else can we call them yet? – most of Einar's men are fine.'

Too lazy to get into the fight, thought Sigrid, but she kept it to herself.

'And what about Bjorn? How was his night?'

Helga nodded across the hall to the great mound of blankets and furs that concealed Bjorn.

'He's still asleep, I think. He was snoring a while ago, fit to be heard in Lervig.'

'I was not!' came a muffled voice from within the mound. 'I never snore!'

A hefty, tousled head emerged, flushed, from under the blankets. Bjorn was already grinning.

'Good morning, Bjorn!' Helga called. 'How is your shoulder?'

The grin turned to a scowl.

'I'm sure I've had worse,' he said, 'but I don't know when.

How are you, Sigvat?'

Sigvat raised a hand in acknowledgement.

'Bit sore,' he said, indistinctly.

'Did I break your jaw?' Bjorn looked crestfallen.

'Well,' said Sigvat, whose face was certainly puffy, 'let's just say it's broken. I'm sorry about your shoulder – it wasn't intentional.'

'I know that,' said Bjorn, smiling again. 'Let's have another go when we're feeling better, eh?'

Good heavens, thought Sigrid. No sense at all.

'Here to help, Sigrid?' Frogunn was bustling past with a broom, sweeping the detritus of the night towards the door.

'Here to find my spindle. I think I left it here yesterday.'

'Oh, it's over here,' said Frogunn. 'I thought it might be yours, but I wasn't sure. You do spin a lovely thread, Sigrid.'

'Thank you,' said Sigrid. 'Thanks for keeping it safe.' The spindle had been left on a hanging shelf at the side of the hall, out of harm's way. Frogunn was a sensible girl. Reluctantly, for she wanted to go home, she added, 'Can I give you a hand while I'm here?'

'You can help me move this table back,' said Frogunn. It seemed to be one of her regular jobs, rearranging the tables. No wonder her forearms were broader than her brother's.

Sigrid and Helga took one end, and Frogunn the other, and in a moment or two the tables were back in their daytime pattern, the benches tucked underneath. Rannveig had always kept a tidy hall. Thordis would too, no doubt, if things worked out the way Rannveig planned.

'And would you mind taking those blankets outside and giving them a shake?' Frogunn asked her. 'I'll take these pots away for scrubbing. Helga's keeping an eye on the wounded.'

As long as they're handsome and muscular, thought Sigrid, laughing to herself. Helga had not been so attentive when Geirod had injured his hand, and the man with the thigh wound, who had a face like a troll, was lying abandoned at the back of the hall, grumpily attended by one of his fellow fighters.

Sigrid took the bundle of blankets out to the paddock wall and began shaking them out, spreading them over the wall for a little air while it was not actually raining. The wind snatched at them, billowing them up, and she stooped to find stones to weigh them with. When she stood again, she noticed two figures approaching from the direction of the Brough. A little closer, and she could make out that they were a man and a woman, moving with the ease of youth but in no hurry to get anywhere. Courting, she thought at once, and arranged her stones on the blankets. When she had finished, she looked back to where the couple had made little progress towards the Buckquoy hall. Still, screwing up her eyes she could make them out a little more clearly. It was Thordis and Varin.

Hm, she thought to herself. That's not going to please Rannveig.

She watched for a moment – there seemed little danger of either Thordis or Varin noticing her. Varin had definitely ignored Thordis when the nephews had first arrived. Was he trying to focus on pleasing Thorfinn? Or had he now thought of some reason why he should be more attentive to Thordis? Was it that, seeing Bjorn paying attention to her, he found her more attractive – Sigrid was not sure that she could explain that to Ketil, but it was often the case – or was he being strategic, forming an alliance with Rannveig? Sigrid blinked at how her own mind was working. She had not recognised till now how little she instinctively trusted Varin.

Thordis, however, seemed to have no trouble with him. As they gradually approached the hall, Sigrid could clearly see how much of her attention was focussed on Varin. But when Sigrid considered, she was not wholly sure if it was devotion or – was it wariness?

Making sure the blankets were firmly weighed down, she turned her back on Varin and his admirer, and went back into the hall.

'Was Thordis here last night?' she asked Helga quietly. 'And was Varin?'

'Not Varin, no: he went back with Thorfinn. Thordis stayed in the longhouse with Rannveig,' said Helga definitely. 'She came in now and again to help with the wounded.'

'Good,' said Sigrid. For some reason, she felt that Thordis slipping off to spend the night with Varin would be disastrous just now. But disastrous for whom? She tried for a moment to decide, then dismissed it. Quarrels at a hall affected everyone in the hird, and therefore in the area. They were best avoided, by everyone.

Back in the hall, she went to make sure that the man with the thigh wound did, in fact, have all he needed and brought him a little of Rannveig's wine to ease the pain. There was no sign of infection in his wound, and she sat with him for a few minutes to allow his friend to go out for a breath of air and a visit to the privy. When the friend came back, she stood up with her spinning to go.

Thordis and Varin appeared at last at the door, a frown on Thordis' face. Varin abandoned her and went to see his brother, but Thordis wheaded to sit by the fire. Bjorn waved Sigrid over to him with his good hand.

'That's Thordis, isn't it?' he whispered. 'I wasn't dreaming?'

'That's Thordis,' Sigrid confirmed.

'Is she married to Varin? Betrothed to him?'

'Not that I'm aware of,' said Sigrid, 'but she knows him from Kirkuvagr.'

'Is that where she's from?' It seemed to lend some kind of exoticism to Thordis: he followed her with his eyes as if afraid she might slip away without him knowing. 'Kirkuvagr?'

'A settlement along the coast – trading settlement.'

'Interesting …' Bjorn watched Thordis, but not so closely that he did not notice when, a little while later, Varin rose, nodded goodbye to his brother Sigvat, and left the hall without bothering to say anything to Thordis. Bjorn gave a little smile, then called out to Thordis.

'Thordis! I wanted to thank you for looking after me so well when I came in yesterday!'

'Oh … you're welcome,' said Thordis. She looked over to where Varin had been, then scanned the room for him.

'Come here and tell me about yourself,' said Bjorn. 'I'm sure your company would be better for me than any medicine.'

Thordis' expression was interesting, Sigrid thought. She was still looking for Varin, but perhaps remembered her mother's request – and she was obviously flattered by Bjorn's attention. Thordis liked attention.

She knelt down by Bjorn's bedspace, and touched his bandages confidently. They seemed to meet with her approval, and she sat back.

'A skilled nurse, then,' said Bjorn. 'And a handsome

woman. A wife?'

'Not yet,' said Thordis, with the least glance at the hall door.

'A daughter, though.'

'Of Rannveig, yes.'

'Of course. And what else?'

'A skilled weaver,' said Thordis, with unassailable confidence. 'My braids are the best in the islands.'

'Oh, I'm not sure that's true.'

Sigrid jumped as Helga stood up next to Sigvat.

'Sigrid here weaves the finest braid I've ever seen,' said Helga, stepping forward. 'And I've seen braids from everywhere.'

She nodded firmly at Sigrid. Sigrid longed for a giant to pop his hand through the roof lights and snatch her away. She knew she was scarlet.

'I don't think so,' said Thordis with a smile. 'I've never heard of her. Touching that you should stand up for your friend, Helga, but there's no need.'

'No, there really isn't,' muttered Sigrid.

'Perhaps we should have a weaving competition,' said Bjorn with a laugh. 'You women can line up on the practice ground and show us what you can do!'

'I'd win,' said Thordis simply. 'Though of course practice is valuable for anyone – at any level.'

'Sigrid's weaving is lovely.' Frogunn had reappeared from the back of the hall, arms folded. 'I've never seen anything like it, either. The patterns are just wonderful.'

'Um, thank you,' Sigrid murmured.

'I'm sure they're very … that they have a certain charm,' said Thordis, with what she may have thought of as a kindly smile.

'Oh, Thordis, why?' Sigvat spoke suddenly. It clearly hurt. 'Why do you always go on like this?'

'Like what?' she demanded. 'I am the best braid weaver in the islands!'

'Um, well, if you are,' said Sigrid, despite an urge to run from the hall and never go back, 'then you choose the best customers, and I'll get on with what's left, if that's all right.'

'Sigrid!' said Helga crossly. 'You know you're better than she is!'

'I don't, really,' said Sigrid. 'And I can do other things, too

… and there's the farm …' The farm could barely keep her and Gnup, and of all the things she could do with wool braid weaving brought her the best returns by far. Except for the elaborate hangings for Thorfinn's hall, and she could not see Thordis employing her to make a similar set at Buckquoy.

'There! She has a farm,' said Thordis, as smug as if the farm had been a midden. But already Helga had Sigrid by the elbow and was steering her out of the hall. In a burst of movement, Frogunn followed, helping to hustle Sigrid across the practice ground and back to the paddock wall. It was starting to rain, and Sigrid began to fold the blankets she had left there to air.

'Sigrid, what were you doing? Stand up for yourself!' Helga shook her elbow, then, with Frogunn, started to help with the blankets.

'There's no point, Helga. Whoever our new lord is at the hall, Thordis is here to stay. If I let her have the best work, she might deign to let me do the rest. If I try to fight her, I might as well find somewhere else to live.' She thought for a moment, then said out loud what she had thought earlier. 'Quarrels are best avoided by everyone.'

'But …'

'Varin says she's always like this,' said Frogunn. 'That's why she's never married.'

'Quarrelsome?' asked Helga.

'Full of herself,' said Frogunn. 'She's the best, and she won't allow anyone to disagree.'

'Varin said that?' asked Sigrid, smoothing the last blanket on to the pile. 'Then he doesn't like her?'

'Varin? No!' said Frogunn. 'He and I were talking yesterday and he was telling me all about life in Kirkuvagr, and I asked him about her – you know, I wanted to see what he would say. So that was what he said.'

'Better get these inside before they're soaked,' muttered Sigrid, though she was thinking. Another layer to Varin's sudden closeness to Thordis – he didn't even like her. Or was he protesting too much?

X

'I don't want to go back inside,' said Sigrid, 'not just now.'

'No, I agree,' said Helga. 'Particularly if you're not going to stand up for yourself. But I'll tell everyone what she's like. No one round here is going to want to take her braids when they can have yours. I'll stick with yours.'

'Thank you, Helga,' said Sigrid weakly.

'I'll take those blankets in, then,' said Frogunn. 'I don't like her either – and I won't have her braids, Sigrid – but I do have more work to do. Did you leave your spindle in there again? I'll fetch it out for you. Wait there.' She beamed at them both, wound her freckled arms around the blankets and headed back to the hall door. As she reached it, she backed out of the way of someone coming slowly outside.

'Sigvat!' cried Helga in alarm. 'You shouldn't be on your feet yet!'

Sigvat made his way tenderly over to them and leaned on the wall.

'I can't stay in there with Thordis telling everyone how wonderful she is,' he grunted. 'Damnation, this hurts.'

'Shall I fetch you more of Rannveig's wine?' Helga asked, a concerned hand on his arm. He went to shake his head but stopped himself.

'No, it's making me dozy,' he said, 'and then I won't sleep tonight. It's good to get some fresh air.'

'Don't let yourself get chilled,' said Helga. Sigvat almost smiled.

'You're a good nurse,' he said.

They stood in silence for a moment, Sigvat staring out towards the sea and the Brough, and the women either side of him, watching the hall.

'Is she a good braid weaver?' Sigrid could not stop herself, though her voice came out very small.

'Not as good as you,' snapped Helga loyally. Sigvat leaned back so that he could look at both of them without turning his head.

'She's all right,' he said. 'I don't know what your weaving is like, but if you're doing well here you're probably better than her. She's not the first one I would go to in Kirkuvagr, though that's not what I would tell her to her face. She can have a nasty temper when she's crossed.'

'There, you see?' said Helga. 'Not even the best in Kirkuvagr, let alone the islands. You'll be all right.'

'Well ...' said Sigvat. 'You don't want to make an enemy of her. I've known Thordis all my life, on and off, and she's never been a comfortable person to know. She's clever, mind, and there's no denying she's a fine looking woman, but I couldn't live with her and I don't know any men that think they could.'

'Your brother Varin was very friendly with her earlier today,' Sigrid said before she could stop herself.

'Varin? Was he?'

'It looked that way,' said Sigrid. 'I saw them walking back from the direction of the Brough together, as if she had gone to meet him.'

'Well!' said Sigvat, eyebrows high on his fair forehead. 'That's odd. He's always done his best to avoid her. She seemed keen on him at one point.'

Sigrid was sure that Thordis was still keen on Varin, but this time she managed to hold her tongue. Sigvat seemed genuinely surprised at his brother's behaviour. Perhaps she had been mistaken.

Sigvat was frowning now.

'Varin's quite good with the charm if there's something he wants. Perhaps he thought ...' He tailed off, as if he realised he, too, was about to say more than was wise.

What Varin wanted was Buckquoy, of course. Was there something else?

Ketil and his men had spent the night in the hall at Birsay, which was as close as they came to a home. Rising early that morning, as was his habit, Ketil cut through the settlement to where Thorfinn's pigman looked after the animals, and found Skorri already propped against the flag wall, checking on the Westray sow.

'That was a day yesterday, eh?' Skorri said, turning at Ketil's approach. The lights had been out by the time Ketil had returned to Birsay last night and they had had no chance of conversation.

'Full of events,' Ketil agreed. 'I saw you bring down Bjorn at the end of that skirmish.'

'Surprised myself,' Skorri admitted. 'I don't think I did him much damage.'

'If you did, the single combat was worse. I wonder if he'll lose the use of his arm.'

Skorri whistled, shocked. The Westray sow looked up at him, then returned to her trough.

'She's already escaped twice. What about Sigvat?'

'Broken jaw, bad head.'

'Miserable.'

'He is.'

'Varin wasn't hurt, though.'

'No, I don't think so.' They reflected. Had Varin been lucky – blessed by God? Or had he just dodged the fighting?

'Wolf,' came a voice from behind them. Alf and Geirod had found them, along with the yellow dog.

'No,' said Geirod.

'Fenrir,' said Alf.

'No,' said Geirod.

'How's the hand?' asked Ketil. He wondered if Alf would ever run out of suggestions for the yellow dog's name.

'It's all right,' said Geirod, lifting it briefly.

'Shouldn't try to get through a shield wall by punching the shields,' said Skorri in mock disapproval. 'Three broken fingers! What use is that?'

Geirod scowled at him, but said nothing.

'We'll go to Kirkuvagr tomorrow,' said Ketil.

'I thought you wanted to go today?' asked Skorri.

'I did, but today I want to be in Buckquoy.'

'I don't know why,' said Skorri. 'If you ran down there the air's so thick with tension you'd probably knock yourself out.'

'Love and ambition,' sighed Alf, always the poetic one.

'Ambition, aye,' said Skorri. 'Whatever way Thorfinn decides, there'll be trouble. Did you see the way Varin looked at Bjorn at the end of that fight? Nasty.'

'What about Foldar?' asked Alf. 'Take the middle ground, Varin goes back to Kirkuvagr and Bjorn to Trondheim, and everyone's happy.'

'Did you see the way he fought yesterday?' asked Skorri in disbelief. 'An invading child on a donkey would walk right over him.'

'He was unlucky,' said Alf generously.

'He was that,' Skorri agreed. 'No, Thorfinn will never choose him, if he has any sense. And Thorfinn has plenty of sense.'

Ketil let them talk, as was his habit. It was often useful. But now he turned back to Alf.

'Love?' he queried.

'Bjorn for Thordis, and Thordis for Varin.'

'And Varin for himself,' added Skorri. They all nodded at that one.

'And Thordis is Rannveig's daughter,' Ketil added. His men had not been here when Rannveig had betrayed her husband, but it was fresh enough in Ketil's mind. Rannveig had not, apparently, had much to do with her daughter's upbringing, but was Thordis as little to be trusted as her mother? That remained to be seen.

'She's a fine-looking girl,' said Skorri, and again, they all nodded. It was interesting, Ketil thought: he had heard it said several times, and each time there had been a hesitation, a silent 'But ...' after the words. Why did no one like Thordis? Why was she not married? Perhaps he would find out in Kirkuvagr tomorrow.

'Storm,' said Alf suddenly. Skorri and Ketil looked at once to the sky, but Geirod, realising what Alf meant, said,

'No.'

'That damned dog,' said Skorri. 'Will you not give it a name?'

'Not "it",' said Geirod sulkily. '"Him."'

'Give him a name, then.'

But Geirod said nothing, and Skorri gave up.

'You can stay here tomorrow, Geirod,' said Ketil, 'and rest your hand.'

'Aye, you'd be no use with sail or oars,' Skorri agreed.

Geirod shrugged, which Ketil took for agreement.

'There might be something you can do here or at Buckquoy – we'll see. I'd better go down there soon and find out how the injured are.'

But just then a boy came skidding round the corner and called out,

'Ketil Gunnarson! My lord Thorfinn wants you!'

'Aye, you'll not be going down to Buckquoy just yet, though,' said Skorri.

'No,' said Ketil, and followed the boy.

By the time Ketil had given Thorfinn the latest information on the injured men – particularly Bjorn and Sigvat – and by the time Thorfinn's wife Ingibjorg had interrogated him on the subject of Rannveig, and Thordis, and Bjorn, and Westray, and what she was supposed to do with an extra pig in the sty (that she almost certainly never visited), and by the time she had made him wait and eat a midday meal – it had begun to rain, the tiny persistent droplets caught and hurled by the wind against the back of his head as he strode across the landspit towards Buckquoy. Better than in his face, he thought. At least this way he could see clearly. He rested his hand on the hilt of his sword, kept dry under his cloak. It made him feel a little better.

He was going with the intention of finding out more about Bjorn and perhaps about Foldar, though he had a feeling there would be little to learn about him. Perhaps, he thought, he might even have a word with Thordis about Varin and Sigvat, if they had known each other in Kirkuvagr? They must have, surely, for it was a small settlement still, and the shared link with Einar must have brought them together at least occasionally. And to judge by last night, when Varin had summoned Thordis and she had obeyed, at least now there was some kind of connexion between them. It did not look as if Bjorn had much hope of success if he tried for Thordis, unless Thordis had a weak spot for injured warriors.

He wondered how Bjorn's shoulder was. The cut had been deep, dragged down a little, too, as Sigvat fell. Had it been deliberate? How far would Varin and Sigvat go to make sure Varin claimed the hall? How far would Bjorn go to beat them? The closer he drew to Buckquoy, the more uneasy he felt.

The midday meal was over, too, and the women were tidying up. Some of Einar's hird were, as usual, asleep, but Bjorn's men had gone out for a walk, undeterred by the rain. Bjorn was seated on a bench with his back against the wall, a thick fur protecting him from any jagged stones. Sigvat was sleeping. Ketil nodded to Bjorn, looked about for Bjorn's two men that he had spoken with before, and instead found himself meeting the eye of Frogunn, who greeted him with a bright grin.

'Good day to you!' she said, friendly as ever. 'Are you here from Thorfinn? Is he coming again tonight?'

'No, he'll be at the Brough tonight,' said Ketil.

'Will you be staying? We've only just finished our midday meal, but it won't be long before we'll be getting the meat on for this evening. I don't think the hall has been this full for years!'

'Do you like it?'

'Oh, yes – plenty to do, and lots of people to talk to,' said Frogunn.

'You're Oddr's daughter, aren't you?' he asked.

'That's right.'

'So your brother is Foldar?'

Frogunn made a wry face, and Ketil gave her a brief smile.

'That's right, poor fellow,' she said.

'How is he today?'

'Sore, and a bit confused still. But I think he'll recover. His head and his nose, that is: his pride might take a bit longer.'

'He was unlucky,' said Ketil.

'He was. And, to do him justice, he didn't really want to be there. He's not much of a fighter, bless him. It was our father's idea.'

That Ketil could believe. He had not had much to do with Oddr, but the man was as self-important as his whiskers were voluminous. He would have known he was too old himself to be considered, but he should have realised that his son was too young. And too inexperienced.

'Are you disappointed?' he asked her. 'Would you like him to be in charge here?'

Frogunn laughed.

'I don't think so! He would take a deal of looking after, and I work hard enough here as it is! And if anything happened … if we were attacked … well, then, I'd take his armour and his weapons and go out to meet them myself. It would be more useful.'

Her eyes shone with laughter. Ketil's mood was almost lifted.

'Anyway,' she said, 'stay and eat with us tonight. You don't look as if you eat nearly enough.'

'I'd be very pleased to stay,' he said, and meant it. He looked about him, at Sigvat sleeping and Bjorn with a bored expression. 'Is Thordis about? There's something I wanted to ask her.'

Frogunn's gingery eyebrows rose.

'She's just popped over to the longhouse to fetch braids to show Bjorn,' she said, though there was a tightness in her voice that had not been there before.

'Is Varin around?' Ketil had not seen him on the Brough this morning. Frogunn's face lightened, and whatever the problem was with the braids seemed to vanish.

'Yes, I think he's outside somewhere. I can find him for you if you like.'

'No, don't worry. I'll wait for Thordis.'

'Up to you!' she said, her grin returned, and she strode off to the back door and vanished. Ketil went to sit beside Bjorn.

'How's the shoulder today, then?'

'Oof, not so bad that I don't want to sit up and be about things!' Bjorn complained. 'Everyone's telling me to rest.'

'They're probably right. I know it's frustrating.'

'It certainly is. I'm sure I've had worse before and recovered well enough.'

'Worse than that? That must have been bad.'

'Oh, aye, I had a sword blade through my leg! Here, look.' He pulled up the tails of his tunic and tried to undo his trousers one-handed, but he had to give up, irritable.

'Can't do anything with that arm,' he grumbled. 'Sword went straight through, you see, but came straight out again. They said I'd never walk again, I'd lose the leg, get infected, but no! Fit as can be.'

'Impressive,' said Ketil.

'Then there was the axe in my back. Just hit the bone the wrong way – wrong way for my attacker, that is – and I was fine. Had to lie on my stomach for a week or two but, well, when you have company that's not so bad!' He elbowed Ketil heavily with his good arm, and Ketil nearly fell off the bench. He wondered what woman would want to lie with Bjorn – it seemed a dangerous business. 'It's the Bear Spirit, you see,' said Bjorn in a lower voice, leaning towards Ketil's ear. He grabbed his bear's tooth. 'The protector. I know, it sounds like the old beliefs, but if God made bears, too, then why not bear spirits? It's all part of the same thing, isn't it?' He nodded solemnly. 'Varin knows, too. I've seen him holding his own amulet.'

'Here we are!' Thordis paced elegantly across the hall, fully expecting every eye to be on her. She glanced around briefly, and Ketil wondered if she were checking for Varin. But she came over to Bjorn and Ketil, trailing a handful of colourful braids. 'These are my favourites. But I've done so many!'

Of course – Thordis' braids, that had had Sigrid so worried. Ketil almost did not want to look at them. He was not sure if he wanted them to be good or bad – if they were bad, and still found more customers than Sigrid's, she would be even more unhappy.

'Oh, let me see,' Bjorn was saying. He ran the braids through the fingers of his left hand, perhaps deliberately drawing Thordis a little closer to him. 'Thordis, these are wonderful! You are tremendously skilled.' He squeezed her hand briefly, gazing more at her than at the braids. Ketil braced himself, and took a look.

The braids were, as far as he could judge, all right. They were neatly worked in smooth wool. The patterns were simple, though, and as far as he was concerned, the colours were not very pleasing. He could honestly say that he preferred Sigrid's, and believed them to be much more skilled. He breathed a sigh of relief. Thordis seemed pleased with Bjorn's approval – in fact with every word of praise she seemed to glow more - and lingered, talking over the details. Ketil felt he was achieving little, and left the hall to find someone who could tell him something useful.

Until it was time for the evening meal, he wandered about Einar's property, having a word with one of his hird here, or with one of Bjorn's crew there. The crew had enjoyed yesterday's fights, and hoped there would be more: they were on the whole confident that Bjorn would mend soon. 'He always does!' was a frequent response, leaving Ketil wondering just how often Bjorn was injured. He was a distance away from the hall door when he noticed Sigrid arrive, with Helga, to help with the evening meal – with so many guests the women of the hird would always be needed. Sigrid did not look happy, but no doubt she had left behind some urgent woolwork. Helga seemed to be urging her on.

It was dusk when the men began to go back indoors, faces and hands washed, ready to eat and drink. Ketil lingered at the back of the hall, allowing others to go and find places nearer the front and watching to see who sat with whom, or avoided someone else. On the whole, Bjorn's crew still stuck together, and the hird – some of them with a resentful touch to their smiles of greeting – stayed in one group, too. Sigvat had woken and had gingerly taken a place near the high seat, but not too close. Bjorn, too, was near it on the other side. Foldar was far away, down the other side of the hall. Without Thorfinn there, no doubt the high seat would remain empty tonight. Not even Varin –

But at that moment, Varin arrived, strode to the head of the hall, and took the high seat for himself.

There was a gasp. Ketil found his hand, under his cloak, was back on the hilt of his sword. Half of Bjorn's crew stared, aghast, at Varin, and the other half turned at once to Bjorn to see what he would do – and what he wanted them to do.

But Bjorn, settled as comfortably as he could be on his bench, laughed, and shook his mighty head.

Some of his crew laughed too, a little nervously. Others frowned, not sure what was happening.

'Good for you, Varin!' Bjorn called, his voice like amiable thunder. 'Take what you can get, while it's available. That's right!'

And he leaned back a little on his bench, so that Varin could see past him – could see that beside him on the bench, evidently quite at ease, was Thordis.

'Sitting there expecting to be waited on,' snapped Sigrid later to Ketil. The temptation to spit in the wine before she had poured it into Thordis' cup had been very strong, only that she did not like to see food and drink go to waste. Ketil had probably noticed: he was always noticing things you didn't expect him to. 'Like a bride at her wedding feast.'

'I think that she and Varin would be very well matched,' said Ketil unexpectedly, but he was right.

'Doesn't look as if that's happening,' said Sigrid. 'No, she'll hang on until she knows who's going to win, and then that's the man she'll go for. And we'll be stuck with her, and I'll have to move to – to – back to Heithabyr,' she finished, unable to think of anything further in her bad temper.

'Her braids are nowhere near as good as yours,' Ketil offered.

'Doesn't matter,' said Sigrid. 'If we both stay, I'll have her over the cliff in a week.'

'Where's she gone, anyway?'

'Privy, I suppose. All that wine has to go somewhere.' Sigrid struggled to keep her annoyance out of her voice. 'I wish she would hurry up. I want to go myself, and if I meet her out there in the dark I might not be responsible for my actions.'

'She's been a while, hasn't she?' Helga remarked, overhearing them. 'I don't think she's there at all: she probably went out with Bjorn. Or Varin,' she added, uncharitably.

'Well, they've both been out,' said Ketil.

'I'll have to go,' said Sigrid, setting down the jug she was carrying.

Thordis was not in the privy. Sigrid made swift use of it herself, and stepped outside, feeling the light misty rain on her hot cheeks. She would have to get over this, she thought. She knew too well that anger like this took up too much time, too much strength, and she needed both just to make a living and survive.

She stretched, her back tired from standing and carrying food and drink all evening. The horses in the paddock across the practice ground were uneasy. She felt the skin prickle on the back of her neck.

She moved over to the paddock wall, scanning the field, but there was no sign of an intruder. But an odd, out-of-place smell came to her, familiar from the privy, wafting unpleasantly up from the ground below. She leaned over the wall, using the faint fingers of light from the torches by the hall door, and saw first two legs sticking out, leather-booted toes pointing upward. A skirt, pleated blue. And a dark-haired, uncovered head, flopped forward. She had found Thordis.

XI

'Thordis?'

The voice behind her nearly made her go over the wall.

'Who's that?' she snapped, though her words were not as steady as she would have liked.

'It's Rannveig. Have you seen Thordis?'

'It's Sigrid here … Rannveig, I've come upon her by accident … it doesn't look as if she's …'

'What are you talking about? What's going on?'

Rannveig strode over to where Sigrid was standing and looked about her – then her gaze dropped to the feet on the other side of the wall.

'Thordis!'

Rannveig was over the wall in a moment and kneeling by her daughter.

'I'll go and get –'

'You'll go nowhere where I can't see you!' Rannveig told her abruptly. 'Stay there. Thordis! Oh, Thordis!'

'But we need to fetch – well, torches, at least. You can't possibly see properly there.' Why did Rannveig want her to stay?

Rannveig stood, undecided.

'Go and get a torch and bring it straight back. I'll be watching you.'

Confused and self-conscious, Sigrid walked back to the door of the hall. Before she lifted a torch, though, she leaned in through the doorway. Alf, Ketil's man, was near the back of the hall.

'Alf!'

Alf turned at once, recognised her and came over. She would not have to shout.

'What is it, Sigrid?'

'Tell Ketil we need him. Something's happened. Quietly,

though, Alf – we don't want everyone outside.'

'Sigrid!' Rannveig's voice was angry. Sigrid hurried back out into the darkness, and lit her torch from one by the hall door. In a moment she was back with Rannveig, holding the torch over the wall. Rannveig snatched it.

'I told you not to leave my sight!'

'I sent Alf for help,' Sigrid explained.

'You should have told Varin. Varin's the one you should have told,' Rannveig said, and Sigrid could hear her teeth starting to chatter. 'Oh, Thordis! What's going to happen now, you stupid woman? I needed her!'

Sigrid, still shocked and baffled, thought it was a very odd lament of a mother for her child.

'She is dead, isn't she?' It was a harsh question, but if Thordis had just passed out from drink, or had a knock on the head, this was all a bit premature.

'Yes, she's dead!' Rannveig cried out, and Sigrid could hear her control slipping.

'Who's dead?'

Ketil had joined them, soft-footed, with Alf in attendance. No one else had appeared from the hall.

'It's Thordis,' said Sigrid. Rannveig was clutching her sleeve now, not letting her move.

'My daughter is dead!'

'How?'

'You need to fetch Varin. Varin will know what to do,' Rannveig insisted.

'I think Ketil knows what to do,' said Sigrid. The torch light showed a disparaging look on Rannveig's face.

'Yes, but Ketil will take your side. Varin will not.'

'My side in what?' asked Sigrid.

But Rannveig was watching Ketil closely. Ketil had swung himself over the wall, and was crouched by Thordis. The torch's flicker played over delicate fingers as he lifted her heavy head, touched her throat, and examined her hands. Despite the endless sigh of the wind, Sigrid heard him catch his breath.

'What is it?' she asked, not receiving a reply from Rannveig.

'She's been strangled, by the look of it,' said Ketil.

'See?' said Rannveig. 'See?'

'See what?' asked Sigrid. 'I don't understand what you're talking about, Rannveig.'

'You did it! You did it, you stupid woman!'

'I did not!' Sigrid went cold. 'I never touched her! What on earth makes you think I did it?'

'It's braid!' shouted Rannveig. 'It's braid wrapped round her neck!'

And staring down at Thordis' body, Sigrid could see the dark strip of braid cross Ketil's pale hands as he looked up at her.

The hall was subdued.

Thordis' body had been removed to Rannveig's longhouse, where she had insisted on attending to it herself with her women – her right, of course, but Ketil would have liked someone he trusted to have been able to take a look. Sigrid was out of the question, and even Helga, apparently, did not meet Rannveig's standards, as a friend of Sigrid. The best Ketil could do was to move the braids to one side a little as he, Skorri, Alf and Geirod, the last left-handed, carried Thordis to the longhouse: under the braids Thordis' white throat was bruised black and rubbed red. He had already seen that her fingernails were torn and bloody, yet there were no scratches around the marks on her neck. Thordis had not scrabbled to pull away the braid: she had scratched at her killer.

When Rannveig had dismissed them, they had returned to the hall and Ketil went to find Varin, taking him over to where Bjorn sat before giving them both the news at the same time. It was not ideal for judging their reactions, but it prevented one squabble, at least.

'Thordis? Are you sure?' Bjorn was stunned. For a moment his mouth worked, but no words came out. His eyes were stretched wide in shock. 'But she was here only a moment ago!'

'Sitting by you,' Varin spat. Bjorn clutched at his bear's tooth, while Varin, watching him, had wrapped his arms tight about himself like a little boy needing comfort. He glanced over at Sigvat, who nodded slightly. Varin looked on the brink of saying more, when Ketil pulled him up.

'You'll need to tell people. Rannveig's laying her out in the longhouse: you can't have any singing tonight, or you'll disturb them. You'll need to say, before people start.'

Bjorn had slumped down in his seat, trying to absorb the news, while Varin, chin jutting as though he were forcing himself to stay calm, made the announcement to the gathered men.

Silence fell in the hall. Deaths and injuries even in mock fights were everyday stuff. But a woman killed just outside their hall, by an unknown murderer – that was a different matter. Varin surveyed them for a long moment, caught in sudden shock.

'Does anyone have anything to say about this?' he asked, with an authority that surprised Ketil. 'Does anyone want to declare this as a just killing?'

A just killing – self-defence was the usual reason. Could Thordis have been a danger to anyone? He tried not to look across to Sigrid: a danger to one's livelihood did not usually count.

No one spoke. Several seemed nervous, but it was probably fear of saying the wrong thing into the silence. After an ominous moment, Varin sat down, and leaned across to murmur something to Sigvat. Sigvat looked cross, but one layer of tension was broken.

Apart from Rannveig and her women, no one had left the hall that Ketil could determine, but with Rannveig's women absent, working in the longhouse, and Sigrid and Helga sitting in a corner, silent, no more food and drink seemed to be forthcoming. A couple of the older women sat with them, glad to get the weight off their feet, whatever the reason. Frogunn emptied the last of her jug of wine into Varin's cup, and retired to sit with Sigrid.

'What are you going to do, sir?' asked Skorri, more formal now they had a task to face. Ketil's three men were by the door, observing as the hird and Bjorn's crew talked quietly among themselves.

'Good question,' said Ketil. 'At this stage of the evening, everyone is in and out, moving about. It will be almost impossible to work out who saw her last, or where.'

'Was she already cold?'

'Cooling.' He watched Skorri make a face. 'She hadn't been dead long.'

'And the braids …'

'Round her neck. Looped right round, and pulled tight.'

Alf coughed gently.

'Whose braid was it?' he asked. Ketil met his eye.

'Her own, I believe. I'd like someone to take another look,

though, in case I'm wrong. I don't know if it had been made for anything specific. I'm no expert, but I think it was one of the ones she was showing to Bjorn earlier. It was a red and black pattern.'

'To Bjorn?' Skorri brightened. Ketil knew he liked Sigrid. 'So where were those braids in between? Did Thordis take them away or did Bjorn keep one?'

'She could have dropped one, or he could,' Geirod put in, broadening the field reluctantly. 'Anyone could have a bit of braid.'

'We'll have to find out if all of Thordis' were accounted for, and where she put them.'

'What was she doing over at the paddock wall?' Skorri asked. 'That's nowhere near the privy.'

'Someone might have called her over there. Or she might have arranged to meet someone.'

'Where it's more private than the hall,' Skorri nodded, liking the answer. 'That might mean Bjorn.'

'Or Varin,' Ketil suggested.

'Or someone else, that she thought was Bjorn or Varin,' said Geirod, pleased with himself. 'That would confuse things.'

'You're always the one that makes things more difficult,' Skorri complained.

'I'm not,' said Geirod. 'Things just are difficult.'

They reflected on that happy statement for a moment.

'Thorfinn's not going to like this, is he?' said Alf thoughtfully.

'No.' Ketil did not much like it himself. And as for the two chief competitors for the hall, Varin had shifted from his high seat to sit with his brother, their conversation intense, while Bjorn himself was still sagging in his place, his face white with shock. He was so still that Ketil watched him carefully for a moment, checking that he was breathing.

'What's going on there?' Skorri asked suddenly. Ketil looked past him as he turned. Einar's hird, mostly seated over to their right and including, for now, Varin and Sigvat, were – what were they doing? For a moment it was hard to distinguish. Faces were grim – well, they would be. Limbs shuffled on benches. There was a muttering, and it seemed to Ketil that while the bolder ones were looking straight across at Bjorn, the rest were deliberately staring the other way, making their point.

'There's going to be a fight,' said Alf with a sigh, just as Varin launched himself, knife drawn, across the table and directly at Bjorn.

Bjorn's men were quick to defend their injured leader. There were angry yells. Ketil saw the men he had spoken to, Atli and Egil, running behind the benches to reach him before Varin did. But Varin had support, too: Hrolf and Oddr were on their feet, and Hrolf, roused, could be a dangerous man. Foldar, appalled, followed them. When Ketil glanced round, he saw that the women, including Sigrid, Helga and Frogunn, were already gone, the hall door open behind him.

'Should we try to stop it?' Skorri asked. Ketil considered. Twenty of Bjorn's men. A dozen of Einar's hird. Three of them. There was courage, and there was good sense.

'Let's leave them to it,' he said. 'We can pick up the pieces later.'

'Good idea,' said Skorri, and Ketil ushered them out of the hall and into the wet night.

'They went home,' said Frogunn as the men emerged from the doorway. 'Sigrid and Helga and the others. And I'm not going to hang round for long.' She stood with her broad arms folded, as if holding them responsible for all that was happening. She had a father and a brother in there: she had a right to be cross.

'Fair enough,' said Ketil. Shouts, grunts and thumps rumbled from the hall. 'Before you go, though, I wouldn't mind if you shared some sensible thoughts with us. Did you see anyone acting oddly this evening? Anything Thordis did or said that might have roused someone to kill her?'

Frogunn paused, frowning, as a particularly violent clatter came from inside the hall.

'That'll be Einar's shield down off the wall,' she remarked when the echoes had subsided. 'I hope they're going to clear up after themselves. Did I see anyone acting oddly? I don't know that I did. It felt like an ordinary night – except without Einar, and with half the hall full of Bjorn's men.'

'When did you last see Thordis?' Despite his misgivings, Ketil thought that if anyone had taken note of anything useful it might well be Frogunn.

'I'm not sure. After the food was finished, anyway. I think the last time I noticed her was when Bjorn decided he was going to out to the privy, and she tried to stop him because she said he would do his arm some damage. I don't know what she thought he was going to do if he stayed in the hall.'

'Was that the first time he had left the hall this evening?'

'Yes, I think so. He's hard to miss, being so big.'

'So she was definitely inside while he was outside.'

'Yes, and later Varin went out, and Sigvat too, and I'm sure she was in the hall both times. I'm not sure who else I noticed … well, Father was in and out a good bit, and I think Foldar went out for a while. But he was back in before Rannveig went out, I'm sure.'

Loyalty, thought Ketil, so perhaps not reliable. She was as protective of her menfolk as a warrior would be of his women.

'Did any of them leave the hall again, then, while she was outside?'

'Varin didn't,' she said at once. 'Nor did Sigvat. I know because I noticed how white he was when he came back in the first time, and I thought I'd ask Foldar to go with him if he headed out again, in case he fell over. Bjorn … actually, Bjorn went out a couple of times, I'm sure, after that first time. While Thordis was out? Hm – perhaps.'

That was really only the leaders, though, Ketil thought. Would Frogunn have noticed everyone in Bjorn's crew wandering in and out? Even everyone in Einar's hird? She had not mentioned Hrolf, for example, nor big Afi, nor several others.

'And Thordis herself?'

'Did she annoy someone enough for them to kill her?' Frogunn laughed. 'She certainly annoyed me! But I can't think of anyone in particular. And certainly not Sigrid.' She stopped and stared at him, emphasising the point. 'Not Sigrid, I'm sure of it.'

'That's … that's good to know,' said Ketil, taken aback at her conviction. But Varin, when he had announced the tragedy, had not mentioned how Thordis had died. And Rannveig suspected Sigrid because of the braids. So why was Frogunn so keen to tell him that Sigrid was innocent?

'Anyway,' said Frogunn, wrapping her shawl around her shoulders, 'I'm not waiting here to patch up tonight's share of the wounded. They can do it themselves. Good night, Ketil!' she said, and with a wave disappeared off round to the back of the hall, presumably to Oddr's longhouse. Ketil called goodnight after her, and turned back to his men. The clatter and shouting from the hall had barely diminished.

'Alf, take a look. See how they're doing.'

Alf stepped across to the hall door like a speeder-legs, knees high, feet barely touching the ground, as though he might disturb the men inside. As he touched the door, a knife hit it, handle first, and clattered to the floor. He toed it out and stuck it in his own belt, though the removal of one weapon was unlikely to make much difference.

'I think they're still busy,' he said, returning to the others.

'You'd think they might be tiring by now. On full stomachs and all. Einar's lot, anyway.' Skorri scratched his head thoughtfully.

Ketil nodded.

'I don't think yesterday was enough to tire them out.'

'Maybe we should just leave them to it – go back to the Brough,' said Skorri. It was what Ketil was thinking. They would do no good here until things had calmed down. He only hoped that no one would be killed before they could give him useful information about Thordis' death.

Someone would need to speak to Rannveig, but not now, not while she was preparing her daughter's body for burial. And Helga, too: she always knew some tidbit of gossip that might be useful. But most of all he wished he had had the chance to speak to Sigrid before she had left. For a moment he stared up into the darkness in the direction of Sigrid's longhouse, the place invisible in the rain. He imagined Sigrid, glum over the fire, Gnup the farmhand wondering at her new sorrow, the cat and the cows shifting in the half-light of the economically-lit dwelling. He would go and see her tomorrow. Otherwise, knowing Sigrid, she would convince herself that he was sure she had killed Thordis, and not speak to him at all.

Skorri, Alf and Geirod were waiting, with the yellow dog propped against Geirod's leg.

'Come on,' said Ketil, 'let's settle down over there. I want to see the end of this.'

Ketil's imagination, for once, had been fairly accurate.
Sigrid was leaning over the fire in her longhouse, trying to

draw its heat into her bones. The cows were indeed shifting a little in the dark lower end of the house, lending a drowsy warmth of their own to the darkened air. Gnup, though, was curled up asleep in his own bedspace, the cat using him as a nest. Sigrid had managed not to disturb them when she arrived home.

She knew she would not sleep if she went to bed cold, but she did not want to revive the fire at this time of the night, rousing Gnup and using up precious fuel. She stared instead in to the luscious red of the embers, seeing Thordis lying against the paddock wall, feet sticking out. Braids. Braids around her neck. But whose? She had not been able – barely been allowed – to see them. Were they hers? And even if they were, could there possibly be any clue – anything that might convince anyone apart from Rannveig – that she had killed Thordis?

She went over, more than once, everything she could remember from that evening, every time she had stepped outside the hall, whether for food and drink or outside the main door. Every person she had talked to and what they had said. Every time and place she had seen Thordis. They had not spoken together, anyway: in fact, she had done her best to avoid the girl after what had happened earlier. And she and Rannveig didn't speak much now anyway. Sigrid had mostly talked with Helga and Frogunn, and with the men they were serving.

Everyone had left the hall at some stage, she was sure. Everyone had been drinking – except perhaps Ketil, who was oddly abstemious – and even the injured had hobbled out by necessity from time to time. It had been a big event when Bjorn had eventually stood up and gone out – Thordis had tried to persuade him not to, she remembered, so she had been there at that point – but Sigrid herself had been more concerned about Sigvat, who was still a bit wobbly, and the man with the thigh injury, who had only managed with two sticks and a friend helping him. At least Bjorn had the use of his legs.

So yes, she could say that pretty much everyone had been outside at least once, but as to who might have been outside at the same time as Thordis – that was another thing. If Thorfinn wanted Ketil to find out more about the killing, and he probably would, since he had ordered Ketil to do such work before, then she did not envy Ketil his task.

And would Ketil take her side, as Rannveig had said?

They were friends, she supposed. They had been, long ago, in Heithabyr. But if Ketil thought she was guilty … she was not at all sure that Ketil would allow himself to be swayed by mere friendship. She shivered. She would have to make sure that Ketil did not think she was guilty.

And as for Thordis, then, who wanted to see her dead?

She had not made many friends in her short time in Buckquoy, that was certain. But even Sigrid, who had perhaps more to lose from her arrival than anyone (as far as Sigrid could see, anyway) had wished her gone, rather than dead.

Or that's what she told herself, as she hunched beside the slumbering fire.

XII

With the dawn, Geirod kicked Alf and Skorri awake. It took a wise man to know they were Alf and Skorri, wound about as they were with their cloaks and snuggled against the paddock wall like maggots. The yellow dog yawned and stretched.

'Hawthorn,' said Alf, disentangling himself and yawning in turn.

'No,' said Geirod. 'Ketil's here.'

'How long did they go on?' Skorri sat up, flicking the dew off his cloak.

'Fire's lit. Come inside,' said Ketil.

He led his men back into Einar's hall. It looked as if a storm had ripped through it, or trolls. Tables were overturned, benches had been broken, wine was splashed across the flag floor and bread had been trodden into it, and, as they had heard, Einar's shield, once hung high on the wall, lay on the floor with a few extra dents in it. A couple of men sat by the fire, poking it into life and rubbing their hands over it. They barely glanced up when Ketil and his men came in.

'Who won?' murmured Skorri, trying to see who was conscious.

'Hard to tell,' said Ketil. 'Someone's going to be in trouble with Rannveig, though.'

There was a movement over to their left, and a cup rolled dismally across the floor. Someone groaned, then swore. Then came a great upheaving, and from under the wreckage of several benches Bjorn emerged, his face haggard. He looked at Ketil, grabbed at his injured right arm, and swore again, with emphasis. He surveyed the hall.

'That was a bad one,' he grunted.

'Where's Varin?' Ketil asked. There were a few responses, none of them friendly, but then he had been a bit loud.

'Who wants to know?' Varin stuck his head out from behind the high seat, and recognised Ketil. 'Oh, it's you. What is it – does

Thorfinn want me?'

'Probably not,' said Ketil. 'Are you injured?'

Varin stood, and shook himself. There was blood on his face, but not much – it seemed to come from a scratch just above his hairline.

'No,' he said, 'I'm fine.' He, too, looked about him. 'That got out of hand.' A little smile curled about his lips. Ketil resisted the urge to slap him.

'Bit of redding up to do,' said Bjorn, clearing his throat.

'Yes, you have,' said Varin. 'We'll leave you to it.'

He straightened his shirt and strode down the hall, past broken benches and sagging bodies, and headed out into the morning. If he expected his men – Einar's men – to rally and follow him out, he must have been disappointed. One or two peered at him from squinting eyes and bruised faces, but barely anyone stirred.

'I'll help,' came an indistinct voice, and Sigvat emerged from behind a table, the bandage for his jaw somewhat askew. He tried rearranging it, and winced.

'Aye, we'll all do it, lad,' said Afi, checking his teeth warily. They seemed to be in place. His boat-building eye surveyed the wreckage. 'Shame about these benches, though. That was good wood – it'll need mending.'

'I'm not sure Rannveig will be in much of a position to organise this today,' said Ketil, 'and I'd be surprised if she has managed to set the bath house fires going. I think we should make as much of a clearance as we can before she comes in.'

Bjorn, tousled and weary, shook his head, and single-handed righted the table next to him. Big Afi, not to be outdone, carried a couple of the broken benches outside for fixing. Gradually the hall came to life: bundles left in corners raised their heads and opened their eyes, and counted their injuries as they set to, slowly, to sort out the mess they had made. Once the furniture was straight and the men had shifted, or been shifted, out of the way, a few of them sheepishly found hot water and a means to scrub the flag floor where it was stained with spilt wine, sprays of blood and the occasional pool of vomit. You could not say that they worked with enthusiasm, but they were dogged, and eventually they had all earned their place by the fire and in the queue for the bath house.

'I'm surprised there weren't some of them killed,' said

Skorri, waiting in the line. It was he who had organised the hot water for the floor, and his fingers were reddened with scrubbing. Afi and Bjorn had between them lifted Einar's shield back on to its hook on the wall, at least until the local smith could knock out the new dents. Alf and Geirod were piecing together the parts of broken benches in the hope of efficient mending.

'It'll have kept Rannveig awake, no doubt,' said Ketil. It was too early yet to call at the longhouse. Rannveig had ignored all the fuss and not shown her face at all. Skorri shook his head.

'Shameful,' he said.

'It helped relieve the tension,' said Ketil.

'Aye, between Bjorn and the others. But what about Varin? And barely a mark on him!'

'Hm, marks,' said Ketil, suddenly thinking of Thordis' bloody fingernails. 'Keep an eye open for nail scratches on anyone's neck or face,' he said. 'But we might have bother proving it was not from the fight, now.'

'True,' said Skorri, tutting. 'Ah! At last.'

The hot bathwater was like a healing miracle after a night in the ditch and a couple of hours cleaning and tidying. Ketil submerged himself entirely, holding his head under the water for as long as he could manage, then scrubbing himself vigorously. A shave and drying off and he was ready to face the day, even in yesterday's shirt. It was just as well, for the first person he saw as he emerged from the bath house was Thorfinn, striding towards Einar's hall and staring at the battered men and broken benches.

'What's been going on here?' he bellowed, as Ketil hurried over to intercept him.

'My lord.'

'This isn't the aftermath of the fights yesterday, is it?'

'No, my lord, there was a fight in the hall last night.'

'Between Bjorn's men and Einar's hird?'

Ketil shook his head, then shrugged.

'Sort of. More between Varin and Bjorn, my lord.'

'I'm flattered they are both so eager to take on Einar's place,' said Thorfinn grimly.

'There was more to it than that, my lord. It was more to do with Thordis –'

'Rannveig's daughter?'

'Yes. She's dead.'

Thorfinn, who had clearly had some comment ready about either Thordis or Rannveig, stopped with his mouth open, then shut it fast. He eyed Ketil as if suspecting him of an inappropriate joke.

'Dead? How?'

'Strangled,' said Ketil shortly.

Thorfinn continued to stare at him.

'Who did it?'

'Unknown, my lord.'

'Anyone nearby? Who found her?'

'Sigrid.'

Thorfinn scowled and looked away, tapping his fingers on the hilt of his sword. He gave a sharp sigh.

'When?'

'Last night. The feast was well under way. There had been tension between Bjorn and Varin –'

'What a surprise.'

'Varin took the high seat, but Bjorn took Thordis – to sit with him, my lord. As far as I know it was no more than that.'

'Yet,' said Thorfinn, and Ketil nodded agreement. Bjorn had looked quite ready to take things further. As had Thordis.

'And Varin took the high seat, eh? No one challenged him to it?'

'Apart from Bjorn, I don't think anyone else is politically strong enough. And Bjorn was playing other games.'

'I'd like to knock their heads together,' Thorfinn muttered fiercely. 'I don't suppose either of them could have killed Thordis? Or was there someone else with reason to?'

'I wouldn't say she was popular, my lord,' said Ketil, 'but there's no one obvious. Either Bjorn or Varin could have killed her, but so could almost anyone in the hall. Her absence wasn't noted for a while, and it was the time of the night when everyone was in and out.'

'Of course …' Thorfinn swore softly to himself. 'Where is the body?'

'Rannveig took it into her longhouse.'

Thorfinn swore again.

'I suppose I'll have to go and see her. Come with me.'

It was an order, but Ketil could not help feeling there was

just a hint of desperation about it.

'Come on, Sigrid, wake up!'

Sigrid's head jerked up as her elbows slid from her lap.

'Ouch! Ow!'

'Sorry!' Gnup stood cheerfully beside her. He was annoyingly happy in the mornings, something Sigrid regarded as unnatural. She tentatively stretched, wondering if her limbs would ever work again. Why had she let herself fall asleep sitting by the fire?

'I was worried about you, sitting there,' said Gnup brightly. 'I thought you'd been turned to stone.'

'You weren't worried, you just wanted to get the fire going,' Sigrid grumbled.

'It would help you, too,' he said. 'Warm fires are good for old bones.'

'Old bones? You cheeky little –'

But Gnup was off, running outside with the hens, letting in the morning's damp air. Sigrid muttered to herself before she remembered just why she had slumped so hopelessly beside the fire last night. Thordis – and Rannveig.

If she closed her eyes she could see Thordis' long legs sticking out into the paddock, her slumped dark head, and the look on Ketil's face when he felt Thordis' cold hands – hands skilled in weaving braids, hands that would weave braids no longer. For a moment she looked at her own worn hands and saw their mortality, and for a moment she wondered, as she had wondered before, if it was all worth it. One day she would be gone, and what would she leave behind? A few tatty braids, that was all. A wave of pity, for herself and for Thordis, swept over her, and she allowed a tear or two to trickle down her face before wiping them away. It would not do for Gnup to see her crying.

And already Gnup was back inside, with some dried seaweed for the fire.

'Not a bad day out there!' he said. 'The sun's trying to break through the haar.'

'Good,' she said, making an effort. Gnup sat opposite her, and poked the seaweed into the embers, blowing on them gently. Sigrid stared into the glow, but as the flames grew and flickered and he added peat, she sensed that Gnup was watching her. Eventually she gave in, and met his eye.

'What's wrong, Sigrid?' he asked, kind eyes anxious. He was barely half her age, but sometimes he seemed so much older.

'Do you know who Thordis is?'

'Thordis? Do you mean Rannveig's daughter? Tall, full of herself?'

'That's the one.' Sigrid stopped her smile before it could appear. She sighed. 'She's dead.'

Gnup's lips formed a perfect O.

'How did that happen?' he asked warily. Sigrid frowned. Did he suspect her so quickly?

'Someone strangled her,' she said flatly. 'Rannveig thinks it was me.'

There was a heavy pause. Gnup poked the fire.

'And –'

'No! It wasn't me!' she snapped before he could ask.

'I wasn't going to say that!' said Gnup, affronted. 'I was going to ask who you thought did it!'

'Oh.' Sigrid cleared her throat. 'Well. Um, I don't know, really.'

'You and Ketil will sort it out,' said Gnup confidently. 'You always do.'

Sigrid cleared her throat again. It didn't seem to work.

'What if Ketil thinks I did it?'

'Does he?'

'I don't know.' Her voice wavered, and she shut her mouth fast.

'Bet he doesn't,' said Gnup firmly. 'Go and ask him. He'll tell you.'

'I don't want to go down there today. I don't want to see any of them.'

Gnup nodded.

'Fair enough,' he said. 'Well, then, think about my question. If you didn't do it – which of course you didn't – then who did? Who wanted to?'

'Lots of people, I should think,' said Sigrid with feeling.

Gnup tilted his head to one side.

'Are you just saying that because you wanted to? Was she

really that unpopular?'

Sigrid considered. Was she being unfair? Probably.

'No, you're right. Not really. I mean, I don't think Helga liked her. Or Frogunn. But Rannveig must have cared for her, and Bjorn was growing to like her.'

'Oh, was he?' Gnup had seen Bjorn, and been impressed. His principal ambition was to grow tall. 'Then do you think that might be why she was killed? Something to do with Bjorn?'

'It's possible … Then there's Varin.'

'Varin from Deerness?'

'Yes, Einar's nephew. But I don't think he was really interested in Thordis until Bjorn began to pay her court. Then he gave her more attention.'

Gnup laughed.

'How silly! But which one did she like? Or did she like either of them?'

Sigrid managed to smile at him. He was not entirely grown up yet.

'I'm not sure. She started by liking Varin, or it could maybe have been Sigvat, but she was certainly sitting with Bjorn last night. To make Varin jealous? Maybe. Was Varin jealous? I don't know. Varin likes to be in charge.'

'Pff,' said Gnup. 'Varin's useless. He'll never be in charge of anything.'

'What do you know about him?' asked Sigrid, surprised.

'He came to stay with my family one winter – I was quite small.' Gnup was still quite small, so this was hardly indicative. 'He and Sigvat. I didn't like either of them.'

'They get around. Thordis knew them in Kirkuvagr.'

'Did she? Well, maybe she annoyed them there.'

Or maybe she had annoyed someone else there, Sigrid thought.

'We don't know very much about Thordis – she had only just arrived, really,' she said. 'She said she could weave good braids, but I hadn't seen them yet. She lived with her uncle and his family – her father's brother. Why with them and not with Rannveig, her mother?'

'Not everyone wants to live with their family,' said Gnup wisely. He himself had been very glad to be taken in by Sigrid.

'True. But then there's the other question: why is she not married? Handsome girl, intelligent, I'd have said the family were probably well enough off – yet there she is.'

'Not widowed?'

'She doesn't – I mean didn't – cover her head.' Thordis' dark hair once again appeared in her mind's eye. She was glad it had concealed the dead woman's face.

Gnup was thinking, evidently.

'She wasn't killed in the hall, was she?'

'No – even Einar's hird might have noticed if that had happened.'

'Outside?'

'Just across the wall into the paddock. At least, that was where I found her.'

'Hm. And it was dark?'

'Oh, yes. And lateish in the evening.'

Gnup shrugged.

'Almost anyone could have crept out and done it, couldn't they? Argued with her, maybe, and lost their temper.'

'Bjorn or Varin, if they pushed her too far and she resisted.'

'Obviously someone's going to have to ask them about it,' Gnup agreed. 'But you can't do that. Well, you could, but you might not get very far.'

Sigrid nodded. That much was true: she could not see Varin sitting down with her to tell her what he truly thought of Thordis.

'And you don't want to go down to the hall anyway,' Gnup continued. She gave him a quick look. He seemed to be leading up to something.

'No … but I have plenty to do here …'

'Tablet-weaving, though, eh?' said Gnup, and there was definitely a light in his eyes now. The last time he had looked like this it was because he had thought of a new way of keeping track of a particularly independent old ewe who would lamb in the most obscure places. Sigrid hoped he was not comparing her with the ewe.

'Yes, mostly.

'And you can carry tablet-weaving with you, can't you?'

'Carry it where?' she asked slowly.

'To Kirkuvagr, of course! Where else are you going to find the answers to all your question about Thordis?'

'Me, go to Kirkuvagr?'

'Why not? You've been before.' He made it sound as if she was there once a month.

'I don't have a boat. And I don't want to go to the harbour for someone to take me. I can't afford it, anyway.'

'You can walk. It takes less than a day, doesn't it? If you left now you'd be there before dark.'

Sigrid hesitated. Gnup was good about the farm, but what if something went wrong? And it was a busy time, even with their small harvest.

'I can walk there in a day, but I couldn't be back again. I'd have to stay overnight.'

'You'd find somewhere.'

'I don't know anyone there.'

'All the better. You could go to stay with Thordis' uncle, and then you'd be perfectly placed to find things out, wouldn't you?'

'I don't think ...'

'And the thing is,' said Gnup, with the air of a man spotting the winning move on a king's table board, 'if Rannveig starts saying you killed Thordis, where would you rather be? Here or Kirkuvagr?'

'Or Trondheim?' added Sigrid, with feeling. 'But wouldn't it look as if I was running away?'

'I'll tell anyone that asks that you're away on business. Visiting a customer.'

'A customer in Kirkuvagr? But all the people in Kirkuvagr that wanted braid bought it from Thordis, didn't they?' She stopped, considering. Had they really? Were her braids that popular? She wanted to know. And she wanted to know why Thordis, lovely, talented Thordis, was not married, and why she lived with her uncle.

'Are you sure you can look after the farm while I'm away?' she asked.

'As long as you don't ask me to do anything with those nettles,' he said, 'I'm sure I can.' It was the confidence of youth, but suddenly Sigrid was prepared to trust to it. He had done it before, and Helga was only up the hill.

'All right, then.' She stood, and shook out her shawl with a flourish. 'All right. I'll go.'

Ketil was impressed. Thorfinn had so far managed to find

three separate things to delay his visit to Rannveig's longhouse.

'Tell me again about Varin taking the high seat,' said the Earl, propping himself against the paddock wall after he had insisted Ketil show him where Thordis had been found. Ketil did so: there was really not much more to the story than that. Thorfinn gave one of his irritable sighs. 'The man is an upstart,' he said. 'How does he think that's going to help him? What did Sigvat do?'

'Nothing much. He's still nursing his broken jaw,' said Ketil.

'Of course.' Thorfinn stared about him, desperate for another distraction. 'Oh, there was a man up at the Brough looking for you.'

'Really?' Ketil was indeed briefly distracted. 'A local man?'

'No, I don't think so,' said Thorfinn. 'I hadn't seen him before.'

'Did he say what it was about? Or where he was from?'

Thorfinn looked torn between declaring that he was not Ketil's messenger boy, and prolonging the conversation by any means.

'I didn't speak with him myself, you understand,' he said, a little lofty. 'But Ingibjorg said he had a Westray look about him.'

Ketil frowned. What was a Westray look? He hadn't much faith in Ingibjorg, but there was always the chance that one of the Westray men had followed them to the mainland and wanted to reclaim his pig. Or kill it.

'I'll tell Skorri,' he said.

'You could go and do that now,' said Thorfinn.

'No, my lord, I would not wish to detain you any further. You'll want to be seeing Rannveig.'

'Yes … Has Afi had a chance to mend your boat?'

Ketil struggled to keep his face bland. Thorfinn had never before expressed any interest in Ketil's boat – in fact, it was a surprise that he even knew it had been damaged.

'Not yet, my lord. I think he might mend those benches first. They were sorry they had done anything to cause more distress to Rannveig, with her daughter dead.'

'Rannveig …' Thorfinn pushed himself away from the wall, leaned his hand on his sword hilt, then deliberately moved it away. The name seemed to taste bad in his mouth. 'Rannveig. Yes. I had better see her. Come on, then.'

XIII

Thordis' body lay at the head of the longhouse in a sleeping space, with a fine blanket covering her to her chin. Rannveig, almost invisible, knelt with her head lowered by her daughter's side, her headcloth drooping to hide her face. When she heard Thorfinn's voice at the door, she rose slowly to her feet and came forward to bring him wine. He took it, but Ketil was sure he would never raise the cup to his lips.

'I am sorry to hear of your daughter's death,' said Thorfinn formally. 'It is a sad occasion.'

'My husband, and now my daughter,' murmured Rannveig. 'My only child …'

'Has anyone declared this death? Has anyone claimed responsibility?'

'No, my lord. I have not heard anything.'

'And was it told? Was the news brought? The hall would have been the nearest house – did someone come in and announce it?'

Anyone wanting a death for which they had been responsible not to be counted as murder had to go and tell someone fast. Ketil knew that Sigrid had not brought the news to the hall – had not had the chance, presumably – but then she had not killed Thordis.

'No one announced it, my lord,' said Rannveig humbly. 'Yet Sigrid Harald's daughter was standing over my daughter's body when I found it.'

Thorfinn's face tightened in a frown, as if it were news to him.

'Sigrid Harald's daughter?' He turned to Ketil. 'Your Sigrid?'

Hardly his Sigrid, he thought.

'That Sigrid, yes,' he said. Thorfinn turned back to Rannveig.

'You don't think Sigrid killed her, do you?'

'Sigrid was jealous of my daughter, my lord.'

'Jealous?' Thorfinn looked baffled. 'Why would she be jealous of Thordis?'

Rannveig lifted her face towards them: she was still a very striking woman, Ketil thought – and could assume a look of injured innocence with great ease. He shook himself. It was too easy, with all that had happened before, not to trust anything Rannveig said, but perhaps she had a right to be heard. After all, she was quite right – a husband and a daughter, in a very short time. And a murder. She had suffered, no doubt.

'My Thordis was a skilled wool worker, my lord. Sigrid – poor Sigrid, how could she help it? – feared for her livelihood when my daughter seemed likely to stay in Buckquoy.'

Thorfinn was still scowling.

'Woollen braids? Thordis wove braids, is that what you're saying? And Sigrid thought she would lose her customers?'

'That's right, my lord. Poor Sigrid,' Rannveig repeated. 'She probably lost all control in her frustration.'

Despite his lecture to himself about listening to what she had to say, Ketil felt a strong urge to shake her. Sigrid had no need of Rannveig's pity.

Or had she? Had something happened between Sigrid and Thordis? If Thordis had been as annoying as her mother … And Sigrid was not the most patient of women.

'Show me her injuries,' said Thorfinn at last. Rannveig bowed her head again, and led the way over to her dead daughter. She lifted the blanket from Thordis' bruised throat. The braids had been removed, but there were two distinct lines around the neck, just the width of the braids Ketil remembered. Thorfinn gestured to Rannveig to bring a lamp closer and both men studied the bruises carefully. Ketil could see no marks of anything other than the braids. Thordis' hands had been washed and her fingernails trimmed neatly: he would tell Thorfinn later about the blood. There were, as he had thought, no scratches on her neck. She must have scratched her attacker.

'Did you see Thordis leave the hall last night?' Thorfinn asked, still not quite meeting Rannveig's eye, as though she would bewitch him.

'No, not at all. She was attentive to our guests at all times,' said Rannveig innocently.

'But she must have gone outside at least once,' said Thorfinn.

'I didn't see her go out. I know she was in the hall for most of the evening, then I tried to find her and couldn't. Someone said she had gone to the privy and I went outside to look for her – and found her.'

'Why did you try to find her?'

She blinked at Ketil's question.

'What?'

'You said you were trying to find her – I wondered why?'

'Oh ... a matter of where she had put another couple of cheeses.'

'Odd,' said Ketil.

Rannveig looked at him with an edge of hostility.

'Why should that be odd? We were tending to our guests.'

'Food is hardly so urgent at the latter end of the evening,' said Ketil. 'But you went outside to look for her. Why didn't you just wait until she was back? You would hardly expect her to take long.'

There was an instant where a number of expressions seemed to flicker over Rannveig's face. He could not quite catch any of them before she settled on distraught.

'My daughter is dead! Maybe, maybe in my heart I knew she was in danger – a mother always knows! My daughter is dead!'

She tossed her head back, hands thrust upwards in despair, her breathing hard.

Thorfinn seized Ketil by the arm.

'Come on, let's go,' he hissed, and almost shoved Ketil out of the longhouse.

'I can't bear that woman,' he said, once they were clear.

That much was obvious, thought Ketil.

'There's something more going on,' he said.

'You mean the way she's blaming your Sigrid?' asked Thorfinn.

'That's part of it, my lord,' said Ketil. 'But why did she follow her daughter outside? Did she have a reason to be worried about her? I don't think she was that close to Thordis, but she probably had plans for Thordis' marriage.'

'That would be only natural. But what age was Thordis?' Thorfinn asked. 'She should have been married off long before now, surely?' He cast a sideways glance at Ketil: his own daughter's marriage was still causing him some embarrassment.

'I don't know,' Ketil admitted.

'And the people who brought her up – her uncle in Kirkuvagr, wasn't it?'

'That's right.'

Thorfinn thought for a moment.

'Probably best you go and see them. Break the news, if Rannveig hasn't already sent off her ravens to tell them.' He made a face. 'I'll talk to Bjorn, now.'

But before either of them could make another move towards the hall, they were stopped by a cry of greeting.

'Thorfinn! My lord.'

Thorfinn turned, and Ketil saw Varin approaching, strutting like an eager cockerel.

'My lord, I'm glad I've found you. Very bad news, I'm afraid: Thordis Svein's daughter is dead, murdered. And I'm convinced that, if Bjorn himself did not do it, then one of his men killed her at his instruction.'

His handsome face had assumed an expression that was seven parts anxious concern, and one part a smug satisfaction that he could not quite conceal.

'Really?' said Thorfinn. 'That would be bad, indeed. What makes you think that Bjorn saw to her death?'

'Well, if you'd seen him last night, my lord – he was well aware how much the woman meant to me. He obviously killed her to undermine me – not that that would work, of course!'

'Hm,' said Thorfinn, 'interesting. A motive, anyway. And have you any other information that would show me that Bjorn was responsible?'

'Other information?' Varin had clearly not expected to have to provide anything more than his own word for it. He seemed baffled.

'Yes – did they leave the hall together? Did she tell you she was afraid of him? Did – oh, never mind,' said Thorfinn, 'I'll go and ask him myself.'

'What happened your hands, Varin?' Ketil asked. Varin, eyebrows raised, glanced down at his palms, then turned them over. The backs of both hands were scraped raw.

'Got them trapped under a bench by one of Bjorn's men last night – but of course I freed myself!' he said. The wounds fitted the account, Ketil thought, but were they hiding something else?

Varin, though, had his mind on other things. He watched as Thorfinn stamped across to the doorway of the hall. Varin looked like a man who had attacked with a knife only to find his enemy had a spear. Whatever he had intended, his conversation with Thorfinn had not gone according to plan.

Sigrid cast one more look about her longhouse, and tightened the strings on her pack. Gnup was hovering nearby.

'Are you sure you'll be all right?' she asked him for the fifth time.

'You've left me here before,' said Gnup. 'I won't do anything stupid the moment your back's turned. If I have a problem I'll go and talk to Helga. And you're not planning to be away any length of time. You went to Shapinsay last winter!'

'That was the winter,' said Sigrid. There was, on the whole, less to go wrong in the winter.

'Go on, Sigrid: you'll enjoy it! Well, you'll enjoy not being here if Rannveig comes, anyway.'

'You're right. You're right, I know.' She sighed, and swung her pack on to her back. A change of clothes and plenty of wool. She would find out, anyway, what kind of braid was popular in Kirkuvagr.

She turned her back deliberately on everything else in the longhouse, made for the door, and turned right, not allowing herself any hesitation. Only when she had almost reached Helga's longhouse did she turn back and wave. Gnup was standing watching, making sure she took no detours. With any other young lad she might have suspected mischief, but she knew Gnup cared for the farm as much as she did: it was in safe hands. The only thing that was really holding her back was herself.

She marched, facing straight ahead, past Helga's longhouse and on to the path for Kirkuvagr.

Thorfinn's eyes darted about the hall, checking for the detritus of last night. Ketil was pleased to see that almost everything was now straightened and clean, and the injured were almost all washed and bandaged. Another couple of broken limbs, he noted, and evidently some cracked ribs and bloody skulls – he hoped no one would decide to chance an attack on Birsay just now.

'Where's Bjorn?' Thorfinn asked, more to himself than to Ketil. After all, the Bear was quite easy to spot, seated on a creaking bench and leaning back against a table, a great mound of fur and fine cloth. It took a moment for him to respond.

'I'm here, Thorfinn!' he called, with nothing of his usual cheerful smile. He struggled to rise to his feet, and Thorfinn waved him down.

'Stay there. How's your shoulder?'

'It was fine last night, after a jug or two of wine,' said Bjorn, making an effort, 'but I can feel it again this morning. Never mind – I usually mend quickly.'

'Good. No further harm from last night's disagreements?'

Bjorn made a face.

'A few bruises, certainly.' Ketil noticed a new bandage around Bjorn's hand, and wondered if it had met with Varin's drawn blade, but Bjorn evidently did not want to make a fuss. 'Just one of those things, I suppose: some people have short tempers when they've had a bit to drink.' Ketil waited for him to take advantage, blame Varin for the fight – he would have had every right to do so – but Bjorn just heaved a weighty sigh. 'A good feast, though: and if there's anything I can do to help fix the damage, just say. Just say.'

'I heard,' said Thorfinn, 'that it all started off with some bad news?'

Bjorn's broad face was fixed, but something happened behind it, almost as if a part of him had fallen away. Bjorn's great hands seized each other amongst the fur on his cloak. He swallowed heavily.

'Thordis,' he said at last, though his voice did not seem to be working properly. He coughed, and swallowed again. 'Aye, Thordis. They tell me the lass is dead.'

He moistened his lips, looking anxiously at Thorfinn, as if maybe Thorfinn could tell him it had all been a mistake, a sorry rumour. Yet there was no real hope in his eyes. Had he been to the longhouse? Ketil did not think so, but Thorfinn was ahead of him.

'Have you gone to see her body?' he asked, his voice fairly gentle.

'I haven't,' said the Bear. 'I didn't think ... the family'll want ...'

Thorfinn gave a little shake of the head.

'Did you see much of her yesterday evening?'

'Yes, she sat – she sat near me.'

'What, all evening?'

'Well, I suppose ...'

'Didn't she help with the serving?'

Bjorn was looking embarrassed.

'No, I don't think she did, much.'

Thorfinn frowned, and Bjorn added hurriedly,

'It was good to have her company. She was kind enough to spend her time with me.'

'So you'll have noticed when she went outside, then.'

Bjorn managed a shrug.

'I think she went outside a few times. I mean, she must have, mustn't she?' He looked at Thorfinn, then past him at Ketil. Ketil raised his eyebrows noncommittally, and Bjorn's gaze scuttled away.

'Did you go outside with her?'

'No!' It was almost convincing.

'Or at the same time as her? You know, by chance,' said Thorfinn, making an effort to be encouraging. But Bjorn did not look comforted.

'No, never! I was never outside with her. I mean, maybe she happened to come outside while I was outside and I never saw her, maybe, but I don't think so. I didn't see her. I only spoke to her inside the hall, with everyone else. That's where I saw her.' He nodded, his great head beating up and down for slightly too long, with slightly too much emphasis. Thorfinn gave one of his sharp sighs.

'Well, then ... did you see anyone else heading out with her? Or following her out? Or acting strangely at all?'

Bjorn's head turned from nodding to shaking, but with a little less certainty.

'No one went out with her – I'd have noticed that. But following her? I'm not sure, really. Once she was out of sight I wasn't looking, and it was crowded and busy. People were coming and going all the time. No one came up to me and said they'd seen her, certainly. Not until that fellow, Ketil, he came in and told Varin and me. I didn't believe him. I still can't take it in. She was sitting by me, and then she was gone, and then he says she's dead. I don't really understand at all.'

He turned a plaintive gaze on Thorfinn, and for a moment Ketil half-thought Thorfinn was going to pat the big man on the shoulder and tell him everything would be all right. But Thorfinn stared at him for a moment, then spun on his heel and left the hall, drawing Ketil after him with a jerk of the head.

'I went in there assuming Varin was talking nonsense,' said Thorfinn, 'and now I'm not so sure.'

'Thordis spent the evening virtually on his lap,' said Ketil. Thorfinn nodded.

'He must have noticed something. Or done something.' He folded his arms, standing feet apart as though steadying himself on his warship, and drummed his fingers on his elbow. 'Useless pair,' he spat at last. 'I don't trust either of them.'

'No, my lord.'

'Rannveig says Sigrid did it, Varin says Bjorn did it, and Bjorn can't believe it happened. I don't believe him when he says he wasn't outside with Thordis, whatever the circumstances. What about Varin? Could he have been outside with her?'

Ketil shrugged.

'Probably. The only thing is that if Varin wanted her dead, for whatever reason, he would have had to do it himself. The only person who might have acted on his behalf is Sigvat, and I don't think he's up to killing anyone at the moment. If Bjorn wanted her dead, then he had a whole hird he could have ordered to do it for him.'

'Making it much harder to find out who actually did it,' muttered Thorfinn.

'Or much easier, my lord. One man can keep a secret, but two rarely can.'

Thorfinn made a face.

'We can hope,' he said.

They stood by the paddock wall, just above where Thordis'
body had been discovered. Ketil found himself picturing the scene:
someone luring Thordis there perhaps for a moment of intimacy, or
the pretence of one. Loss of temper, loss of control, or something
planned? A moment's violence, then leaving the woman propped
against the wall out of sight, hopping back to return to the hall and
the feasting. Then Sigrid appearing, poking her head over the wall,
seeing the feet, horrified at what she had found …

'I don't know enough about this Thordis,' said Thorfinn. 'I
barely knew Rannveig's first husband or his family. Go to
Kirkuvagr and find out about them, as I said. Break the news. And
on your way, since you'll be taking that path – if you're walking and
not sailing – call in and see if Sigrid's all right. I don't like to think
of her sitting miserable in that longhouse, thinking everyone's
listening to Rannveig accusing her.'

When Earl Thorfinn suggests you walk, you walk. And
anyway, big Afi had not yet mended his boat.

Ketil took Skorri and Alf with him, with small packs of what
they might need for a few days in Kirkuvagr and a little food for the
journey. He wondered if Sigrid would have to scrabble around for
some food or drink to give them when they called, and felt guilty:
she had little enough.

But there was no need. Her longhouse was empty.

Ketil walked around the corner of the house, and found Gnup
in the infield, perched on a messy roo of gathered stones, whetting
his knife. The bygg waved pale in the breeze, ready for harvest.

'No, she's not here,' said Gnup firmly. 'She's away.'

'Away where?'

Gnup shrugged.

'She said she had to see a customer. Wool stuff, you know?'
Man to man, sure that Ketil would understand no more than he did.

'When will she be back?'

Gnup shrugged again, even more vague this time.

'Not tonight, anyway,' he said, and tested his knife on his
thumb, a clear message that he had better things to do. Ketil
considered. Gnup was generally friendly towards him – and a little
in awe of him, which was no bad thing. Yet he was not telling Ketil

the whole truth.

'Right,' he said to Alf and Skorri, 'let's go on to see if Helga's at home.'

Helga was more often out and about than Sigrid, but on this occasion they caught her at home, putting the finishing touches to the midday meal for her children.

'Sigrid's away? She never said!'

She seemed genuinely surprised as she waved them to places around the fire and handed out bowls. Skorri and Alf brightened.

'You were there last night, at the hall,' said Ketil. 'Did you see Thordis heading outside?'

'She wouldn't have been missed,' said Helga with a shake of her pretty head. 'Don't know who she thought she was, sitting there while the rest of us worked.'

'Was she generally popular amongst the women?' Ketil asked.

'No, she was not. Didn't you hear what she said to Sigrid? Ha!'

'What did she say to Sigrid?' asked Ketil, trying to keep his voice even.

'Oh, insulted her braiding. Her braiding! Sigrid's the best tablet-weaver in the islands! Have you seen Thordis' braids? Have you?'

'I think so,' said Ketil. He did not mention that he had seen them wrapped around Thordis' throat.

'Ordinary,' said Helga with emphasis. 'Dull.'

'I don't imagine Sigrid was too pleased about that!' said Skorri with satisfaction.

'No, she wasn't!' said Helga. 'Mind you, she was calmer than I would have expected. If it had been me I'd have taken that girl outside and stuck her head in the water butt! I'm surprised Sigrid didn't slap her. She must have been furious.'

Helga talked on, but Ketil was no longer listening. How far had Thordis driven Sigrid? For it seemed like a perfectly fitting punishment for a woman who had mocked someone else's braids to be throttled with her own – by the person whose braids she had mocked.

Outside again, Skorri wiped his mouth thoroughly on the

corner of his cloak and scowled ferociously.

'I hope she's not going to go round saying that kind of thing down at the hall,' he said. 'That's not going to do Sigrid any good at all.'

'And with Sigrid not here to defend herself, either,' added Alf dreamily. 'Aye, it's not looking so good.'

'Don't say that!' said Skorri in alarm.

'Well, if Sigrid killed Thordis I'm sure she had good reason to,' said Alf.

'Well, yes, but –'

'Skorri,' said Ketil, 'you're going to go back to Buckquoy and make sure that Sigrid is not condemned in her absence – or in our absence. See what you can find out about Bjorn and Varin and what they were doing last night – and anyone else who was out and about when Thordis was outside.'

'Aye, sir,' said Skorri promptly. 'I'll do that with a will. And if I find Sigrid?'

'If you find Sigrid, tell her to be careful. Alf,' said Ketil, 'you and I are going to Kirkuvagr.'

XIV

It was a good time for travelling on foot.

Sigrid had brought a skin of milk with her, fresh from the cow, but she had left what bread there was for Gnup. Along the way she sated her hunger with blaeberries, tucked in amongst their leaves on the hillsides, and some of the last soft thistle cheeses she found along the path. The air was damp and fresh on her face and arms, but the rest of her was well wrapped up against rain and wind, her best headcloth tight across her brow and her back cloak covering a warm shawl. She had her Sunday overdress with her, too. Who knew how smart the people of Kirkuvagr might be? It was possible that she might need to make a good impression, either for now or to secure custom in the future.

Her boots were old but comfortable with thick hose inside them, and she tramped steadily, a small figure making her way inland and south, away from the coast and its constant toing and froing of boats. Water was never far away, though: she skirted inland lochs where standing stones, it was said, went to bathe under the moon, and where waterfowl lifted in clouds at the least disturbance, sometimes circling and forming great arrows to head off on their mysterious journeys. Some seemed to be heading, like her, to Kirkuvagr. She wondered what they hoped to find there.

It had been a while since she had walked to Kirkuvagr, but as it was harvest time there were plenty of people about to ask for directions, and at one point near the middle of the day a kind woman with a face like a battle shield drew her into a crowded longhouse for some broth and a welcome round of bread. She and the woman sat outside for a little afterwards, scanning the Bay of Firth and talking about wool – the woman liked the braid she was working on, and showed her some of her own work before settling down with her nailbinding for a bit of claik. Sigrid paid for the hospitality with every snippet of news she could think of from Birsay and Buckquoy, to satisfied nods from her hostess.

'Aye, Einar Einarson! I mind him when I was a lass – gey tall, was he no? And him dead and all!' As if being tall could save you, Sigrid thought. 'And now his wifie's lass gone too? Och, the poor quine!'

'Did you know her? Or her mother?' Sigrid asked. 'She was a fine, handsome lass, if you'd seen her passing through here.'

The woman thought hard for a moment, looping quick stitches over her thumb and off, over her thumb and off.

'I don't know that I did. Rannveig, now, I seen her. She was frae Kirkuvagr, was she no? Did I know she had a daughter?' She pondered, examining her own memory.

'It would have been her first husband's daughter, a man called Svein? I don't know anything about him, except he has a brother in Kirkuvagr still.'

'Oh, aye, I know now who you mean! We're no far frae Kirkuvagr here, and mind, it's fair growing, that place! And the lass lived with them, that's right.'

'What's the uncle's name, then?' asked Sigrid. She had been sure she would discover it when she arrived, but to have the information in advance would be useful.

'His name's Ljotr,' said the woman confidently. 'Ask anyone and they'll tell you where his longhouse is – near the harbour, with a big shed beside it for all his goods. He's probably the wealthiest merchant in the place!'

'Oh, I hadn't realised,' said Sigrid. That might explain why Thordis had stayed there, instead of with an aging warrior in quiet Buckquoy, however close it might be to Thorfinn's court. 'But I'd better get going, now, if I want to be there before night. Thank you for your hospitality.'

'Thank you for the news!' said the woman, and they parted with friendly smiles.

'His name's Ljotr,' Ketil told Alf as they strode out along the path that followed the line of the coast. Ketil missed his boat. 'He's a merchant, apparently.'

'Oh?' Alf took in the information, though he often looked as if his mind were somewhere else entirely. 'Do you think there's any danger there?'

'I think it's unlikely,' said Ketil. 'We're going to tell him about his niece's death, and ask him to tell us a bit about her.'

'Was there any dowry with her?' Alf asked, and Ketil knew he should have posed the same question before now.

'There must have been something, but I imagine it wasn't much. Otherwise why was she not married?'

'I didn't like her,' said Alf. 'I wouldn't have taken her on, whatever the dowry.'

Ketil looked at him in surprise. It was unusual for Alf, a very charitable man, to make such a statement.

'Why not?'

'Something about her,' said Alf vaguely. 'A man wants a comfortable longhouse to come home to. Not just one with a handsome face in it. If you see what I mean. Could you see yourself comfortable with Thordis?'

Ketil tried to imagine it, picturing the longhouse he knew best, Sigrid's, with Thordis there at the end of a hard-working day. A handsome face, yes, but a calculating smile. Was that the problem? Had Thordis Rannveig's tendency to plot, without Rannveig's charms? He thought back to the times he had had any conversation with Thordis, and realised he had not trusted her. But had that only been because she was Rannveig's daughter? The taint of association? Perhaps ... His mind returned to Sigrid's longhouse, this time with Sigrid in it as usual. A more comfortable image – Alf was right. He shook his head and returned to considering Kirkuvagr.

Sigrid reached Kirkuvagr before she had expected to – not because she had walked faster than planned, but because there were new longhouses to this side, creeping up the hill and away from the harbour, extending what could be called the settlement. But it was still not the sprawling trading town she had half-feared as she had heard more about it: it was nowhere near the size of Heithabyr when she had last been there, or the sad remains of Kaupang that she had seen in Norway. She wondered what Heithabyr was like these days. She had left no close relations there to send her news.

The woman by the Bay of Firth had been quite right to say that Ljotr's longhouse was easy to find, down by the harbour with two kvarrs floating nearby like calves to a cow. She had almost been wrong, though, when she had said it had one big shed, for it was very close to having two.

Building work was progressing at speed at the back of the longhouse as Sigrid approached, the flag walls near enough complete and a wooden roof – wooden! And none of it driftwood – was being erected over it. A stout man with coarse blond hair and beard stood, elbows on hips, supervising the work with a ferocious grin on his face. Sigrid, suddenly nervous, decided to make for the longhouse instead and see if there was a wife inside.

'Hello?' she called, poking her head around the leather curtain that kept out the coldest sea air. Inside, a thin woman leapt to her feet in surprise, and hurried over to her.

'Yes? Come in,' said the woman, almost forgetting to allow her past.

'Are you Ljotr's wife?' Sigrid asked. 'Is this his longhouse?'

'That's right, yes. Who are you?'

'I'm Sigrid Harald's daughter, from Buckquoy,' said Sigrid, 'and I'm afraid I think I may be bringing you bad news.'

'Oh!' said the woman, and retreated quickly to the fire as though she felt safer there. 'Buckquoy? By Birsay?'

'That's right. Einar Einarson's place, till very recently.'

'Oh,' said the woman again. She must have guessed something of her news. She swallowed. 'Is it Thordis? Is she … is she in trouble?'

'I'm very sorry,' said Sigrid, and went to seat the woman gently in what seemed to be her accustomed place. 'Thordis is dead.'

'Oh,' said the woman again. Then, after a moment, 'Are you sure?'

'I found her,' said Sigrid, 'and Rannveig knows, too. When I left Thordis was – was being tended to in Rannveig's longhouse.'

The woman was silent. Sigrid looked about for something to give her, some hot wine, perhaps. This woman must have brought Thordis up, treated her as her own daughter, presumably: she must be in shock. But her relationship with Rannveig would be complex, then, perhaps? Maybe Sigrid should not have mentioned her, but she wanted to reassure the woman that Thordis was in safe hands, being cared for. The woman would probably want to travel back to Buckquoy to see Thordis before the burial. There would be other family members to tell, too, apart from Ljotr – cousins, presumably, perhaps other aunts and uncles. Sigrid had no idea how large the family might be here. Or if Rannveig, who had hailed from Kirkuvagr, had other relatives of her own in the area. Sigrid's head, which had been dulled all day, suddenly buzzed with possibilities and people. But the woman sat silent.

'What's your name?' asked Sigrid at last.

The woman looked up in surprise.

'Hrefna,' she said, as if the taste of the word were unfamiliar in her mouth. She chewed her lips for a moment. 'So she's not coming back? Thordis, I mean.'

'Oh,' said Sigrid – her turn. The woman must be wanting. 'No,' she said slowly, clearly, 'Thordis is dead. She won't be coming back.'

Hrefna's shoulders seemed suddenly to relax.

'Oh, well, then,' she said. 'Dear me. That's a shame.'

Sigrid blinked.

'I'm sorry – what did you say?'

'I said it's a shame. Rannveig will be disappointed.'

'No,' said Sigrid – the woman was more than wanting. 'No, Rannveig's there, she knows that her daughter is dead.'

'Yes, I know, you said. Rannveig will be disappointed. She'll have wanted to marry Thordis off to her advantage, no doubt.' Hrefna sighed. 'Such a clever woman, Rannveig. But not very nice, I always thought.'

'Ah,' said Sigrid, reassessing Hrefna again. 'Um, didn't you like Thordis, either?'

'Not particularly,' said Hrefna quite as if she were saying she was not partial to onions. 'We had to take her in, of course: her father was Ljotr's brother, and Rannveig had her own plans. But she was never a very nice girl, you know?'

'Nice' seemed to be an important word for Hrefna, a mark of quality.

'Did she give you trouble?' asked Sigrid, sympathetic.

'Not so much trouble,' said Hrefna, now tending to the pot on the fire as though nothing much had happened that day. 'There were no boys trailing round after her, nor actual disobedience. She was lazy, certainly. She thought all this was beneath her.' She gestured to the cooking pot.

'Even wool work? Braiding?' Sigrid could not help asking.

'Oh, no, she liked that. That suited her very well. But cooking and cleaning, looking after the animals – that was not something Thordis could bring herself to do.' Hrefna's mouth turned down, with old resentment. 'Sorry, who did you say you were again?'

'Sigrid Harald's daughter. I live at Buckquoy and I was there the night that Thordis died. Last night,' she clarified, though it seemed much longer ago.

'Did someone send you here to tell us?'

'No, I came of my own accord.'

'Well, that was kind. Did you know Thordis well? I mean, she hadn't been there long, but were you … friends?' She used the word as if she were not used to associating it with her niece.

'We were acquainted. You know what it's like: the women run around with the food and the drink and we gossip when we have a moment. Rannveig was organising it, so the rest of us helped as usual. And Thordis …'

'Did she work as well?'

Sigrid thought hard, torn between honesty and wanting to paint Thordis in a half-decent light for her family. But she could not actually recall Thordis doing any of the hard work. Last night, when she had sat herself down beside Bjorn and done nothing – that was just the next stage.

'She worked hard finding new customers for her braids,' she said in the end, the braid uppermost in her mind anyway.

'New customers?' Hrefna echoed in surprise. 'Was she thinking of staying at Buckquoy?'

'I think she was considering it,' said Sigrid. Hrefna met her eye at last.

'So we would have been shot of her anyway …' she murmured.

There was a noise at the door, and Hrefna sprang up just as she had when Sigrid had come in. This time, though, she seized a cup and filled it with warm wine, and scuttled to the door where the man Sigrid had seen supervising the building work outside was now flinging off his cloak and shaking the dust from his boots. He took the wine cup, and sniffed the air.

'Is the meal ready? The men are hungry, and we have guests coming.'

'Oh! Nearly, Ljotr, nearly.'

Hrefna had shrunk to half her former size, while Ljotr towered over her, that odd ferocious grin splitting his beard. His bright eyes scoured the longhouse, and of course spotted Sigrid.

'Who's this?'

'She's brought bad news, Ljotr, sad news. Thordis –'

'What about Thordis?'

'She's dead, Ljotr,' said Hrefna, and Sigrid could have sworn that Hrefna ducked out of reach. She had seen that flinch before – done it herself, too. She felt herself tense.

But Ljotr did not strike out. He frowned, great bristling eyebrows spiking like hedgehogs. He turned to Sigrid.

'How did this happen?'

Sigrid straightened her back and lifted her head high – not much use at her height, but it made her feel better.

'She was murdered.'

He struck fast, but she had been ready, and spun away just enough out of his reach not to feel the full force of the blow. She heard a squeak from Hrefna, quickly smothered, and saw her wide eyes as Sigrid scrambled to catch her own balance. She headed for the door.

'Where are you off to? Get back here!'

'I'm not your wife – you don't even know my name,' snapped Sigrid, turning in the doorway. 'If you can't keep your great stupid hands to yourself I'll tell you no more about your niece.' She flashed another look at Hrefna: she knew from experience that if she left, Hrefna would likely bear the brunt of Ljotr's anger, but there was little she could do to prevent that – Hrefna had to look after herself.

She turned to go. Ljotr stepped across the flag floor, reaching to seize her arm, and she jerked clear – and walked straight into someone coming into the longhouse.

'Ha!' said Ljotr, and pulled her back out of their way. 'Here are our guests. Hrefna, these are important men, come here from Birsay – from Thorfinn's own court!'

And even as she tried to shake free from the tight grip on her upper arm, Sigrid blinked in surprise. For there, in the doorway, were Ketil and Alf.

It took Ketil a moment, in the confusion, to see who Ljotr had tugged out of their way.

'Sigrid?'

'You know this woman?' Ljotr was gripping Sigrid's arm tightly. Ketil could not imagine why.

'He's my brother,' said Sigrid, unexpectedly. Ljotr's hand dropped at once.

'This is your sister?' he demanded, though Ketil noticed that he looked a little wary. His great bright eyes darted back to Sigrid again.

'Ah, yes. Yes, that's my sister,' said Ketil firmly. 'She was to meet us here – I just hadn't expected to see her so soon.'

'Well,' said Ljotr, dropping Sigrid's arm and rubbing his hands together as though dusting them off, 'you are all most welcome. Hrefna, this is Ketil Gunnarson and his man, come from Birsay with tidings for us. You must make them welcome.'

Hrefna hurried to produce hot wine for the guests, then, as the men settled about the fire, she worked at the meal, just coming to its completion. More men appeared, Ljotr's builders, presumably, whom Ketil had seen outside. The low seats along the centre of the room filled with easing shoulders and stretching legs, and rough hands freshly washed. Ketil was aware of being hemmed in by strangers, not a situation he much liked. There was an uneasiness about the place, he thought. He wanted to ask Sigrid what was going on, but for now that was impossible. Sigrid was doing her best to help the wife, who looked as if misery was second nature to her. Exactly what had been happening just as they had arrived? And why was he suddenly Sigrid's brother? He had not yet broken the news of Thordis' death to Ljotr, but perhaps, if Sigrid had been here for a while, their hosts already knew.

Best to get the meal over first, he thought, and the builders out of the way. Then they could concentrate on talking about Thordis.

'Where are you from, then – Norway?' Ljotr asked as his wife filled his bowl.

'Yes, though I was brought up in Heithabyr,' said Ketil.

'Heithabyr!' Ljotr's bright eyes lit up. 'I've been there a couple of times myself. What trade is your family in?'

Ketil pictured his brother Njal, his father Gunnar, chiselling and shaping, the air sweet with woodshavings.

'Cup-making,' he said shortly.

Ljotr nodded.

'A good trade. People always need cups. A few eerie-orums down the handle and the women'll buy a new one, too, just to be different. Aye.' He seemed to be debating with himself whether or not to go into the same business, then came back to Ketil. 'Ah, but Heithabyr! That's a fine place. The harbour! My, the ships! Goods in, goods out, traders in every corner, not a thing you could imagine from any part of the world that you can't buy: that place fairly hums with life! I liked the wooden pathways, and all. Keeps the merchandise out of the mud. Aye, that's what we need here in Kirkuvagr. A bit of planning, a bit of vision, get ourselves known in the world. Whatever your market, it can always be bigger and better. That's what I'm going to tell Thorfinn.'

It made a degree of sense, Ketil thought. He wondered what Thorfinn would think of it. The next step in the building of his kingdom? A good source of revenue? Or asking for trouble: a vulnerable entry point for who knew what in a world where alliances changed and kings fell? Take Norway and Denmark: not that long ago Harald Hardrada and Sweyn had been like brothers, and now Harald was toying with the Danish coast, aided by the great bear Bjorn. Ketil would not have liked to have seen the wide firth beyond Kirkuvagr's shore filled with ships, either Norwegian or Danish, just now.

'Yes, I can see you're a man with his eye to the future,' said Ketil at last, feeling that some kind of admiration was called for.

'I certainly am. And you've come from Thorfinn's court, so you can tell him what my plans are. He'll like them, I'm sure. I can go myself and explain, if he wants. Or he can come here. We'd like that.'

The last time Ketil knew Thorfinn had been in Kirkuvagr it had indeed been to fight off an imminent attack. Ketil felt that was not auspicious.

'I'll make sure he knows,' he said.

For the rest of the meal, Ljotr talked of trade, clearly expecting a man born in Heithabyr to know all about it, or at least to be interested. Now and again he waved Hrefna to bring him some piece of merchandise from around the longhouse, inviting Ketil's appreciation of some piece of cloth or woodwork or metalwork from Russland or Saxony or Greenland – Ketil lost track of what was from where unless he recognised it himself. It occurred to him that through all the conversation this merchant so keen on constructing his own empire here, had not mentioned an heir – but then, he supposed, he had not mentioned Thordis, either, nor even told them what his wife was called. The wife and Sigrid sat in the shadows, silent. Ketil thought Sigrid must be fit to burst by now: he had rarely known her quiet for so long.

At last, though, when the builders had said goodnight and gone off with instructions already for the morning, Ljotr sat back and drained his wine cup, holding it out to his wife for more, and fell silent. The two other remaining men were clearly his underlings, and did not seem to be going anywhere.

'I'm sorry to say I have come bearing bad tidings,' said Ketil into the sudden quiet. 'Your niece, Thordis, who went to Buckquoy to see her mother Rannveig: she is dead.'

He heard a small gasp, and wondered if it was the wife upset at the news, or Sigrid's way of saying he should have broken the news more gently. But Ljotr did not seem particularly shocked: Sigrid must have got here before him.

'I'd heard,' said Ljotr. 'How did that happen, then?'

'She was killed outside Einar's hall, during a meal.'

'Killed?' Now Ljotr did look surprised – and annoyed. 'Killed? Well, what was Varin doing to protect her that she got herself killed?'

'Varin?' Ketil queried.

'Aye – he has a responsibility! They're betrothed!'

XV

Skorri, obedient to Ketil's instructions, walked back down to Buckquoy with a full and contented stomach and an uneasy mind. How was he to protect Sigrid from rumours and gossip? Worse still, how to protect her from charges of murder? He was a sociable man, but he was not sure how to direct conversations, or even how to make people give him information the way Ketil did. It wasn't that Ketil was chatty, certainly: you wouldn't go to him for a gossip, a bit of claik over a cup of ale. But he had a way of saying nothing that seemed to make people want to fill the silence, and that worked well for him. Skorri doubted that he himself could do the same thing. He might just have to work out what to do as he went along.

Apart from protecting Sigrid, he tried to sort out his other purposes in Buckquoy in Ketil's absence. He was to find out where Bjorn and Varin had been through the evening – perhaps the easier part of the job – and try to see where everyone else was any time Thordis was outside the hall. That would be trickier. No use him going and talking to Bjorn or Varin himself: they wouldn't look at someone like him. That was another thing about Ketil. He might just be a cupmaker's son from Heithabyr, but there was something about the way he stood that made people think he might be someone important. A natural commander. Skorri knew that he himself was a natural second in command: he could get the men at the bottom to do things, and when it was Alf and Geirod, whatever their shortcomings, he could work with them as a team. But to take control, take the lead, decide what was to be done on any kind of grander level – or talk to high heidyins – that was not his role, and he knew it well. That was best left to Ketil.

So who would he talk to, then?

He remembered a couple of fellows Ketil had spoken to himself, a couple of Bjorn's men – they had seemed a reasonable pair, and about his own rank. He could talk to them, if he could find them. The trouble was that most of the men had had drink taken, even if they were not wholly fou. How much would they remember, even from only last night? The only sober people, apart from Ketil, would have been the women. And at the thought of talking to strange women, sober, Skorri quaked.

He would have to find those two fellows instead.

He eventually found them at the back of the hall, amongst the injured from last night. Egil seemed fine, though his left eye was swelling nicely. It had not diminished his appetite for he had found a plate of apples from somewhere and was working his way through them. Atli, whom Skorri remembered Ketil had described as more talkative, was in a worse state.

'Bashed his ribs,' said Egil, spraying a delicate arc of apple fragments over Skorri's sleeve. 'Sorry. Table fell on him.'

'Sore,' Atli acknowledged, trying hard not to breath. Someone had bundled cloth around him though as bandaging it did not look particularly comfortable or useful. Something green and oozy had been slapped about his chest: from the smell it was a dockan poultice for the bruising.

'Good fight, though, eh?' Skorri said encouragingly.

'Oh, aye,' Atli tried to nod. 'I've no notion who won, mind.'

'No ...' Skorri looked about the hall, remembering the damage. 'Hard to tell.'

'Is Bjorn all right?'

'I told you he was up and out,' said Egil, swallowing a lump of apple.

'Aye, but what does that mean? The man's got more injuries on him than an old target.'

'Aye, but he's always up again the next day,' said Egil, admiration rich in his voice.

'It's a strange kind of luck,' Skorri remarked.

Atli and Egil nodded loyally.

'Bear's luck,' said Egil.

'It works for us,' Atli whispered.

'Did he stay in the hall all last night?' Skorri tried. 'I mean, was he fit to be up and about through the feast? I thought he could barely sit upright before it.'

'Aye, that's him,' said Atli, managing his breathing a little better. He shifted, and winced. 'You think he's on his death bed and then he's up and laughing. I wish I had his gift just now – I could do with a bear spirit guarding me!'

'He's smitten with that lassie, mind. Or he was,' said Egil, his tone turning grim.

'The one he was sitting with?' asked Skorri.

'The one who's dead,' said Egil.

'Aye, that's shaken him, no doubt,' Atli agreed. 'I hadn't seen him so taken with a lass for a long time. And it looked as if she was as keen, didn't you think?' Egil grunted, and Atli, irresistibly despite his pain, chatted on. 'I mean, I wondered at the time would he even stay here because of her, even if Thorfinn didn't grant him the hall. But I was sure she would be coming back with us if he didn't stay.'

'So it was serious for him, you reckon?' Skorri was pleased with the way things were going.

'Oh, aye!' Atli's eyes widened. 'Aye, that's a fact. Knocked sideways, our Bear.'

An idea struck Skorri.

'Would that have upset any of your crew?' he asked. 'I mean, would anyone have resented him giving her all that attention?'

Egil turned a stern face on him.

'Do you mean would any of our crew have killed her? Is that it?'

'Our Bear's woman? Atli echoed. 'Killed her? No one would dare!'

'It was just a thought,' said Skorri quickly, trying to make it sound as if it really didn't matter. Egil was glaring at him. 'I mean, someone killed her, and hasn't declared it, so …'

'So you thought it might be one of the strangers,' said Egil, ominously.

'It could have been anybody,' said Skorri quickly. Egil was making him nervous.

'Aye, but –'

'Did you see the woman go out of the hall at all?' said Skorri. 'Maybe you saw someone go out at the same time? One of the locals, maybe?' he added, a little desperately.

Egil, only a little appeased, looked down at Atli.

'I don't know all their names,' said Atli. 'And everyone was in and out.'

'The woman went out twice only,' said Egil, 'if that helps.'

'Did she? That is useful,' said Skorri. 'And you mean the second time was –'

Egil nodded.

'The time she didna come back.'

'Right …' Skorri wondered how Egil was so sure, but he was not keen to ask.

'Aye, she went out the back once,' Atli agreed. 'As if she was looking for more food, or something like that. I think the other women weren't too pleased with her!'

The other women … that would include Sigrid. Skorri did not want to pursue that.

'So she came back, and went back to sit with Bjorn,' he suggested, and Egil nodded.

'That would have been not long before they started clearing the dishes,' said Atli. 'It was a while after that that she went out again.'

'Bjorn had already gone outside,' said Egil suddenly, then looked as if he would snatch the words back. Atli flicked a glance at Skorri.

'That's right,' he agreed again, making a gift of their honesty. 'Bjorn had gone out, and I remember thinking the woman looked as if she was at a loss, there on her own, then she got up and went out, too.'

'Someone came up to her first, though,' said Egil suddenly, more to Atli than to Skorri.

Skorri held his breath. This would be the kind of a time that Ketil would just wait in silence, he thought. Could he do it? He dug his nails into his palms.

'That's right,' said Atli. 'I remember looking over and I couldna quite see her past someone – someone with his back to me.'

His? Skorri wanted to say. Was he sure it was a man? He bit his lips hard.

'And I remember I was thinking that there'd be a bit of a crush at the privy, for your man Afi, the big boatbuilder fellow – he's one I know the name of – he'd just gone out not long before that.'

'Afi?' The word burst from Skorri before he could help

himself.

'Aye, Afi,' said Egil, turning back to Skorri. 'He was definitely outside when the woman went out. Maybe he's the person you should be asking about what happened her.'

And his tone, and his face, made it clear that that was round about the end of the conversation.

But Afi? Skorri thought as he made his way out of the hall, seeking fresh air to think in. Afi? He was a gentle, amiable man. But throttling a woman was something he would be more than capable of – if he had a good enough reason.

Thordis and Varin? Betrothed?

Sigrid was taken aback. If anybody had asked her, she might have said that Thordis was very keen on Varin – or Sigvat - but that Varin had no interest in Thordis, and the idea that there might be anything official arranged, between them or between their families, had never occurred to her. But then she remembered how angry Varin had been when Thordis had gone to sit by Bjorn – was that the justifiable anger of a man whose legal agreement looked as if it might be at risk? Or was he simply jealous?

'I'd have expected Varin to be keeping an eye on her. How did someone come to kill her?' Ljotr was angry, though Sigrid would have said it was not the anger of a man who had lost a beloved niece – more that of a trader who had just watched his kvarr sink with the cargo. She half-wished he would try hitting Ketil, just to watch Ketil hitting him back. But then, men like Ljotr didn't hit other men, not that way. Mostly, anyway.

Hrefna, ignoring the conversation, refilled the men's dishes and returned to sit quietly beside Sigrid. Sigrid kept quiet, too. In this household, she was sure, she would hear much more by listening unobtrusively than by asking questions – at least until after the men had gone.

'How did Varin and Thordis meet?' Ketil was asking – and not a bad question, either. It was something she wanted to know, too. 'Isn't Varin from Deerness? Is he a trader, too?'

'His father was a trader,' Ljotr said. The mention of trade seemed to soothe him. 'Varin and his brother have taken over his business, but Varin is more ambitious than that. He's a good man – he'll go far.'

As long as he keeps Sigvat on his side, Sigrid found herself thinking. She had the impression that Sigvat was the one who thought about things. Varin just liked to be seen to be important.

'More ambitious than trading?' Ketil raised his eyebrows, as if such an idea were unlikely.

'Deerness is a backwater,' said Ljotr. 'This is where the future will be. Defensible, but welcoming. A bay for safe anchorage, a well-protected, sheltered harbour, the hub of a kingdom that stretches in every direction. Varin knows that, but he wants more – stronger links with Saxony, with lands to the south, with Norway, perhaps even with Denmark when things quieten down. War is no friend to trade, you'll know that.'

'That's very impressive,' said Ketil humbly, though Sigrid thought it all a bit vague. 'How has Varin built up such excellent foreign contacts?'

'He's been to Heithabyr too, when he was a boy,' Ljotr explained. 'And Trondheim. He says he's met King Sweyn of the Danes, and I see no reason to disbelieve him.'

Really? Sigrid thought.

'You must have been delighted to make so good a match for both your families,' said Ketil. Sigrid blinked at him from her corner. Ketil could be quite a good questioner, it seemed.

'Well ...' Ljotr's smile widened with pride. 'When you say both, yes, indeed. After all, if he's going to take business far and wide and bring it back here, he needs to know that there is a place fit for it. So obviously he allied himself with the most powerful merchant in the settlement. He could see from the start that the match would be to his significant advantage.' He nodded, pleased with himself. 'Oh, yes, that was a good day!'

'And was Thordis pleased with the arrangement?' Ketil asked. Ljotr blinked.

'I should say so. Why wouldn't she be?'

'Ah, so she was ambitious, too?' Ketil almost smiled, making it sound like a compliment.

'Of course she was.'

'Presumably she was her father's heir? His only child?'

'That's right.' Ljotr nodded.

'And yours? Have you children?'

'Why do you ask?' Ljotr's grin was taking on that hard look

again.

'Only to estimate to what extent someone might have been envious of Thordis – of her good fortune, her looks and skills,' said Ketil with surprising smoothness. 'After all, someone has unfortunately killed her, and no one has come forward to declare the killing. So we must try to find out for ourselves who might have done this dreadful deed, and why.'

'Why do you have to find out why?' Ljotr growled. 'No sense in that: just find out who and I'll kill him myself.'

'Finding out why might help us to find out who,' Ketil explained peaceably. It took a moment for Ljotr to work this out, then his brow darkened.

'Was she interfered with?' he demanded.

'No.'

Ljotr's frown became more puzzled.

'How was she killed?'

'Strangled,' said Ketil shortly. No mention of braids, Sigrid noticed.

'So no accident.'

'No.'

Ljotr bent his head, fiddled for a moment with the lace of his boot.

'Did Varin do it?' he asked, his voice unusually quiet.

'We don't know.'

'Could it have been because of me? Traders, merchants, we make money and so we make enemies – is there a chance?'

'Who do you know in Buckquoy? Or Birsay? Did anyone from here travel there recently?'

But Ljotr was shaking his head.

'I don't much know anyone there. Names, of course, and I've met people coming from there. There's a combmaker on the Brough I've met a few times …'

Sigrid knew who he meant – an unsociable man, who nevertheless would have had no reason to walk down to Buckquoy and throttle Thordis – they were unlikely even to have met.

Unlike Sigrid herself, who had met Thordis and who had quite a good reason for throttling her. She wondered if anyone had told Ketil about what Thordis had said to her. Or what Rannveig had said. Had he heard? Had he – she swallowed hard, so that Hrefna glanced round at her, concerned. Had Ketil followed her here to take her back to face Thorfinn, accused of murder?

Once again, it seemed to ease Ljotr to talk of trade, and merchants he had known about the islands and farther afield. He gestured to Hrefna to refill their cups, and stretched out by the fire. Hrefna removed the food from the fire, laid out some more bread and cheese for the men, and retreated to the corner again.

'Do you want some?' she asked Sigrid quietly, inaudible under the men's conversation. Ljotr was asking Ketil about Heithabyr. She filled Sigrid's bowl with the dregs of the broth, and poured the rest into her own bowl. It was sludgy and lukewarm, with burned bits through it, but Sigrid was not in a position to object. Hrefna settled down beside her again, watching her husband warily.

'You know him?' she asked, nodding at Ketil. 'He's your brother?'

'Thorfinn's man,' said Sigrid, ignoring the second part. 'He'll find out what happened to Thordis.' She paused, still going over all she had heard. 'Was Thordis really betrothed to Varin?'

A small smile flashed over Hrefna's miserable face.

'We thought we were going to be stuck with her for good. Ljotr tried to marry her off to the best men around – and then to the less good men, and so on. But, well, perhaps it was fate, for she and Varin seemed made for each other.'

'She was in favour of the match?'

'When she saw how important Varin was, yes, indeed.'

'And Varin – was it purely business? Or was there an attraction, too?'

Hrefna frowned.

'She's – she was a handsome girl. And strong.' She shrugged, as if that was all that was to be said.

'And she made good braids.'

Hrefna looked sideways at her.

'Is that what she told you?'

'That's what she told everyone in Buckquoy,' said Sigrid.

'Ah, well,' said Hrefna, and fell silent.

Ljotr was a noisy drinker: he did not sing or shout, but his voice grew louder, as if he had trouble hearing himself, and he occasionally snapped out a sharp laugh – increasingly unconnected with the conversation. His two assistants, apparently well used to it, drank and talked fairly normally though all their conversation was the trade in Kirkuvagr. Sigrid found she was growing sleepy. Where was she going to find a bed for the night? Hrefna had not offered.

Whatever might happen later, she was going to avail herself of the privy now, anyway. The men were absorbed in their talk, and Hrefna's only role seemed to be to continue to fill up the cups. Sigrid pushed herself slowly to her feet, trying not to attract attention, and slipped outside.

The privy was easily found, but once she had finished she felt a strong reluctance to go back inside. Instead she found herself staring out at the glinting grey light on the bay, the dark headlands wrapping it about, the last silver gleam of the sky. She was not sure how long she stood there, her mind letting go of all the business of the last few days, but at last she heard a soft footstep behind her. She froze, then relaxed as she heard his voice.

'Are you coming back inside? I had a fear I might find you lying in a ditch, throttled with your own braids.'

'Not funny, Ketil,' she said sternly, but she smiled nevertheless. Not that he was likely to be able to see her. 'Anyway, he's a horrid man and she hasn't offered me a bed for the night yet. I might have to go and look for that ditch.'

'I'm sure they'll fit you in. I think we're staying, anyway.' He followed her gaze out across the bay. 'What don't you like about him? Do you think he's telling us everything about Thordis?'

'I see no reason to doubt anything he's said, except that I didn't have the impression they were betrothed. But it sounded like a business arrangement, anyway.'

'It often is.'

She wanted to tell him that Ljotr had struck her. But what would be the point in that? Some men just did.

They stood in silence, as the light faded gradually across the water. The wind threw tiny waves on to the shore and let them fall back, toying with them. Ketil's cloak shifted.

'Do you miss Heithabyr?' he asked suddenly.

'Heithabyr?' She looked about, as if expecting to find they were there. Could this place really become a trading centre like Heithabyr? 'I don't think I do. I have no family left there. It was … well, it was crowded and noisy and smelly. I like it here, on the islands.' She looked sideways at him. She could not see his face properly now. 'What about you? Do you miss it?'

'I miss my brothers,' he said. 'Of course, one of them isn't there any more – he's off somewhere. Who knows where. Perhaps they say that about me, too.'

'He's a priest, isn't he?' She remembered Ketil telling her when they had first met again. 'But Njal's still there, isn't he?'

'Njal and his wife, and their boys. Could be more children now, I suppose. I'd like to see them again.'

She had no idea what to say. For a moment longer, they watched the last of the day vanish from the sky, then turned, wordless, and went back inside.

XVI

Skorri was cleaning his axe.

It did not particularly need cleaning, being honed to perfection only this morning as was part of his waking ritual, but it gave him something to do outside the hall while he waited to find someone he thought he could talk with. It looked natural, he thought. And it made him feel better.

He had discounted Varin, as far too important to talk to a mere second-in-command. Or at least he thought he was. A seasoned follower of other men, Skorri was not sure he thought highly of Varin. He preferred leaders whose opinions of themselves were about the same as Skorri's opinion of them, or even a bit lower. And if they did have to think highly of themselves, they needed to show some evidence of competence. Varin had not impressed him so far.

He had wondered about Sigvat, Varin's younger brother – he could talk with him, he thought, as one second-in-command to another. Sigvat seemed friendly, had gone about trying to get to know the men allocated to Varin in the mock fights. Skorri had even seen him talking with some of the women, making connexions, having a laugh. He hadn't done more than nod and grin at Skorri, but Skorri had not felt overlooked: it was more, he thought, that Sigvat had seen he was competent and had no need to offer him instruction or encouragement. It had almost been the nod and grin of equals, but somehow it was not quite. Somehow … and Skorri could not quite put his finger on it, but that nod and grin had just been a little out of joint, like when your hose was not quite straight in your boot and whatever you did you couldn't find a crease or a hole but you knew that in a while your foot would start to hurt.

Skorri cleaned delicately round the wood where the metal of his axe met the haft, scraping with the tip of his knife blade. There was always the chance that something had got stuck in there since early this morning. It was important to set a good example to the men – well, to Alf and Geirod. Not that they needed it when it came to looking after their weapons. Alf tended to his as if they were works of art, while Geirod applied his usual resentment to cleaning weapons as easily as he did to everything else. Except the yellow dog, of course.

He wondered where Geirod was. Not that he wanted him around while he was trying to talk to people. Geirod made people uneasy. It was a bit of a gift.

People came and went around the hall door and he watched them as he cleaned and fiddled, looking for someone from whom he might glean some information. There was Oddr, for example, one of Einar's senior men, but Skorri wondered if he would actually know anything useful. He was one of those people who thought they knew everything so no one bothered to tell them anything. And there was Hrolf, Helga's husband – Skorri had never thought Hrolf was very bright at all. They might well talk to Skorri, both of them, but should he try to find someone more likely to be useful first?

He would have to have something to show for his time when Ketil came back. Ketil was not likely to stay too long in Kirkuvagr – though it was possible he would have to go on to Deerness to find out more about Varin and Sigvat, perhaps. But he could, instead, be back tomorrow evening. And what, if he was, could Skorri tell him?

He glanced up again from his unnecessary work and saw a young man wander round the corner, go to the door of the hall, hesitate, and turn away. Skorri summoned his name to mind and called out,

'Foldar! Come and have a seat for a bit. How are you doing?'

The young man swung round in surprise at the voice, saw Skorri and frowned, not sure for a moment who he was.

'I'm – I'm all right, thanks.' He ventured over and sat down, a little unsteadily.

'I'm Skorri, Ketil's man. Ketil Gunnarson,' he added, for Foldar's frown looked painful and he wanted to relieve it. 'My, that's a fine nose you have there!'

Foldar tried a smile, and winced.

'My sister stitched it for me. I don't think needlework is really her best skill.' His face was mostly blue, with some parts marked out in black for greater effect. Skorri was not quite sure he could call to mind what Foldar had looked like before the fights –

ordinary and inoffensive was the best he could manage – but he was certainly not improved. 'But at least I can blow my nose now. Though it still hurts.'

'It was a grand fight, wasn't it?'

'I don't remember much of it. Something landed on my head, I think.'

'Aye, well, that's how it goes,' said Skorri, philosophically. 'Have you done much fighting before?'

'Not really. I went to Kirkuvagr a while ago with Thorfinn when they thought Kalf was coming, but they left me to guard the ship. I didn't much like the look of what was going on on the shore, mind you.'

As a candidate to take over Einar's hall, Foldar did not seem strong.

'What about the fight in the hall last night? Were you in that, and all?'

'Only by accident.' Foldar shuddered. 'I don't even know what happened there. I mean, you could see Bjorn was upset when we heard about Rannveig's daughter's death. I didn't think Varin was that bothered, until he suddenly attacked Bjorn.'

'There was drink in the matter, of course,' Skorri nodded sagely.

'There was, but what was Varin doing? He wasn't anything to do with Thordis, was he?'

'Aye, but maybe he was trying to align himself with Rannveig and the locals, you know?' Skorri suggested. 'Make himself look like the local candidate, make Bjorn look like the outsider?'

'Oh!' This idea seemed to appeal to Foldar. 'I see – so it was like a deliberate thing? A kind of strategy, to do with who takes over from Einar?' Skorri nodded: the boy was not as idiotic as he had feared.

'Well, it's possible.'

Foldar considered it further, breathing a little noisily through his mouth. Skorri put his axe away and began cleaning his knife, which also did not need it.

'I don't really want to take over from Einar,' said Foldar. 'I'd rather just look after the farm. It's what I do, anyway, while my father spends his time in the hall.'

'Your father's Oddr, isn't he?'

'That's right. He likes all this political stuff. It was his idea that I should try for the hall, but I don't want it really. It would please him, though.'

'I'm sure it would,' said Skorri neutrally. 'You were sitting quietly taking note of things last night, and you seem like an intelligent man,' he added, now thinking that might indeed be true. 'Did you see Thordis heading out? Did you see anyone else go out who might have witnessed her death?'

Foldar shook his head.

'I spent a fair bit of time outside myself,' he said, 'but not round the front of the hall. It was too noisy in there. I just leaned on the wall by the pigsty most of the time. I didn't see anyone round there – except the pigs. I like the pigs.'

Pigs, thought Skorri. He should really go and check on the Westray sow.

'Ah, there you are!'

A woman had emerged from the hall, strong-looking, hair red and loose, and well freckled about the face and arms. She was heading for Foldar, and Skorri had the impression that for an instant Foldar tried to hide behind him.

'My sister – the one who can't sew,' he muttered to Skorri. 'Aye, Frogunn, I'm here! What did you need?'

'I thought you were coming into the hall for your midday meal once you'd finished with the animals,' she said. 'Good day to you, Skorri!'

She knew his name? Skorri was instantly nervous, though the woman seemed remarkably cheerful and not at all predatory. He mumbled a greeting. No wonder Foldar had seemed reluctant to go into the hall.

'I'm here now,' said Foldar, pushing himself to his feet, but Frogunn seemed inclined to linger, looking down on Skorri thoughtfully.

'Is Sigrid all right? Have you seen her?'

Skorri was confused: Ketil had told him to make sure any suspicion of Sigrid was quashed at Buckquoy, but should he say that she had gone away to see a customer? Would that look as if she had bolted? He tried to think of something vague – as vague as Gnup who had given them the news.

'I haven't seen her, but I think she's busy with people wanting her braids,' he said. Braids? But that would look as if she had customers now because she had disposed of the competition, or would it? He felt himself blushing. He liked Sigrid, but women in general he found quite … well, what could you say to them? And Frogunn was the kind you had to say something to. She clearly expected it.

'People wanting her braids?' Frogunn echoed. 'Good for her! Her braids are much better than Thordis' were, anyway. If you see her tell her I'll pop in to visit her when I get the chance. She has many friends here, tell her!'

'I will.' At least Skorri could agree to that. 'And now,' he said, tucking his knife into his belt, 'I'd better be going. I have a pig to see to. Good to talk with you, Foldar. Good to see you, Frogunn.'

'A pig?' asked Foldar, as Skorri began to walk away. It was clear where his interests lay.

'Aye. A Westray sow. I've been neglecting her.' He turned again to go, and heard Frogunn's delighted laughter follow him as he headed down towards the landspit to the Brough. Was she mocking him?

But thoughts of Frogunn and her alarming friendliness slid away from Skorri as he walked. The boats down by the harbour distracted him easily, as he remembered the damage to Ketil's boat and his silent wrath. Working for Ketil could have its disadvantages, he thought. It could be less worrying when a man struck out, shouted, swore – Ketil was not a man given to shouting. Or swearing, either.

Skorri yawned. Maybe he was getting too old to spend the night in a ditch, too. Or, well, too old to spend the night in a ditch and not feel the consequences the next day. And all that clearing up at the hall at Buckquoy – that had been hard work. But the bath had been a very fine one, he admitted, and he really wasn't that stiff. Still, it would be good to have a fine supper in Thorfinn's hall this evening, and a good night's sleep in a proper space, indoors, with maybe a fur or two around him. That would be fine.

The wind gave a final whip to his cloak as he stepped off the landbridge and into the gateway of Thorfinn's Brough settlement. The guards, well used to him, nodded him through, and he made his way round the back of Thorfinn's fine new hall, and beyond the chapel and the raw structure of the monastic quarters, to where Thorfinn's pigs were kept beyond the immediate dwellings. Not greatly to his surprise, he found that Geirod, nursing his bandaged hand, was already propped against the wall, the yellow dog at his feet.

'How is the sow?' he asked.

Geirod grunted what was probably intended as reassurance of some kind, and nodded down at the pigs beyond the wall. There were about a dozen altogether, and it took Skorri a moment – and the pigman pointing with his stick – to spot the diminutive Westray sow amongst the others. She appeared to be holding her own, and had her share of a mound of food scraps.

'There's been no fighting,' said the pigman, though he must have expected some, 'but I've been out after her three times. I've better things to do with my time than chase your pig. Are you thinking of breeding off her?'

'She's not mine,' said Skorri. 'She's here for her own safety, that's all. Just till we get things sorted out on Westray.'

'Don't know how you'll sort things out on Westray if you're here,' said the pigman, looking for problems.

'We have to sort things out at Buckquoy first.'

'Aye, and you're no at Buckquoy either,' grumbled the man. 'Am I just here to take in any stray pigs you might find?'

'You just said she'd been no trouble,' said Skorri reasonably.

'Aye, she hasn't,' said the pigman. 'But I can't be tholing all these people wandering about asking me questions. I'm Thorfinn's pigman, not his gate guard.'

Skorri looked at Geirod. Geirod was not the kind to bother with idle chatter, or asking questions, but one never knew.

'Do you mean him?' he asked. The pigman glared at Geirod.

'No, he just stands there, never a word out of him. It could be worse,' he conceded. 'And the dog behaves himself. No, it's the fellow looking for Ketil Gunnarson.'

'Here?' Skorri was surprised. It was not the first place he would have thought of looking for Ketil.

'Aye. Twice he's been,' he added, as though that was completely unheard of.

'I suppose it wasn't anyone you knew?' Skorri asked

tentatively.

'Never seen the fellow before in my life. The first time. Second time,' he nodded ominously, 'I knew his face well.'

'Was he from Westray?'

'How am I expected to know? Unlike some people, I don't have time to ask questions all day!'

'Fair point,' said Skorri, though the man's time seemed mainly to be taken up leaning on his stick and watching the pigs. 'But if I could have one more question, please – does anyone guard the pigs at night?'

The pigman looked at him in blank disbelief.

'Guard the pigs? From what?'

'Well ...'

'I bide in that house there,' said the pigman, pointing again with his stick – a bit aggressively, Skorri thought – 'and if I hear the pigs I come out and see to them. Thorfinn's got guards on the gate. Do you think the King of Norway's going to climmer up the cliffs and run off with my best boar under his oxter?'

'When you put it like that ...' Skorri admitted. 'I suppose not.'

Nevertheless someone unfamiliar had been here, asking for Ketil, even if he hadn't immediately made off with the sow. Skorri could have described either of the Westray men involved in the dispute, seen whether the pigman could match either of them to his stranger, but he had a feeling that the pigman would not be co-operative. He nudged Geirod and nodded to him.

'Want to come into the hall and see if there's any food?'

'Aye,' grunted Geirod, and glanced down at the dog. 'Come on, you.'

'You know, if you don't come up with a name for that dog, Alf will never leave you be.'

'No,' said Geirod.

'Well, then.'

'I'm not ready yet.'

'Alf will think of a name and start using it.'

'He'll not!' Geirod looked horrified, a hand going out to the dog's head at once. Skorri laughed. Alf would not be so cruel.

Skorri spent the rest of the day doing his best to talk with anyone who had been around the Buckquoy hall yesterday – chiefly the fighters Thorfinn had lent to Varin and Sigvat for the bouts – to see if they had anything to say about Thordis or who might have wanted to kill her. Most had not even noticed her, it seemed. He came up with almost no new information at all: only one man, who had stayed late for the supper having no family to go home to, had noticed that the big boatbuilder Afi had at one point looked uncharacteristically disturbed, and had then gone outside.

'Disturbed? Afi?' Skorri was surprised. Afi was the calmest of men unless he had inadvertently caused harm to another.

'Well, is disturbed the right word? I'm not sure,' said the man, his head on one side as if it might help him to think. 'Not disturbed – maybe he looked as if he had a job to do. Determined? Is that a better word?'

'Drunk?' Skorri tried, though perhaps only because it also began with that 'D' sound.

'Oh, yes, probably. Weren't we all?

'Distressed?' It could happen – he remembered Afi breaking that man's leg.

'Hardly distressed, no.'

'Distracted?'

'No, quite fixed on something.' The man pondered, tapping his bare chin with one finger and staring across the hall as if he could picture the scene. 'But distant, you know?' He thought for another moment, then nodded. 'No, I like determined. That was what he was. Determined.'

'Daft?' Skorri offered, but this time under his breath. 'Thanks,' he added, out loud. He would probably have to go and question Afi. He might just ask him to sit down, first.

But as the day's light slipped away to the west, he grew more concerned about matters closer by.

'I'm thinking about that sow,' he said to Geirod at last.

Geirod nodded.

'And the stranger asking for Ketil. I think if he came back for the sow he could be away with her, and the pigman would never know. He would just think she had escaped again.'

Geirod shook his head.

Skorri eyed the side of the hall where he usually slept. There were indeed a couple of furs there, good ones that he had worked hard for – he liked fine things. Not suitable for taking out into a muddy ditch. He went to the door of the hall, and squinted outside into the dusk, but he did not have to see clearly to feel the soft rain on his face and hands.

'Odin's bloody beard,' he muttered to himself, and went back to Geirod.

'Come on,' he said, 'we'd better go and spend the night by the pigs. Aye, this is the life,' he added morosely, but Geirod, by contrast, almost seemed cheerful at the prospect. Skorri glared at him as they wrapped their cloaks about them and, followed by the yellow dog, headed out into the fragrant night by the pigsties.

In Kirkuvagr, Sigrid was also settled for the night, and with about as much enthusiasm, sharing a bedspace with Hrefna. She supposed she should be grateful for a comfortable bed, anyway, in a warm longhouse. She could not help sensing that Hrefna was, if anything, relieved at the arrangement. Ljotr had the main bed splendidly to himself at the end of the house, and Ketil and Alf, and Ljotr's men who lived there, were arranged down the sides of the room, in the shadows, hidden behind curtains. Sigrid wondered if Ketil was sleeping easily. She herself had no wish to disturb Hrefna, but if she had not been sharing the space she would have been tossing and turning.

If Varin and Thordis were really betrothed, why did he ignore her? Presumably because it was just a business arrangement, on his part, anyway. Not on hers, Sigrid would have sworn, from that look she had seen on Thordis' face when Varin and Sigvat had arrived with Thorfinn that day before Einar's funeral.

But then Thordis had gone and sat by Bjorn, and Varin had not been at all happy about that. Because he actually did care for her, or because it offended him?

Sigrid had a feeling that Varin cared little for anyone but Varin.

But she was sure Thordis cared for Varin, too. Why had she gone to sit by Bjorn? Was it just because her mother had told her to?

Rannveig, plotting in the background. Rannveig, come to life again at the prospect of renewing her power, her influence, her connexion with the man in charge at Buckquoy hall. However reluctant Thordis had been to comply, that must be the answer. Rannveig, sitting at the king's table board, moving her pieces to her own, ultimate advantage.

XVII

'What are we up to today, then?' asked Alf. He was passing the time until Ketil decided by tossing his knife back and forth between his long, bony fingers, letting it spin in complex patterns high in the air in between. He seemed to be doing it without much thinking about it. It was the kind of thing that unnerved Skorri quite often.

'I'm toying with the idea of Deerness,' said Ketil, without raising his voice. They were standing much as he and Sigrid had stood last night, gazing out at the bay, just far enough away from the longhouse door for a private conversation. Ljotr made the house feel crowded just on his own, even though his men were already outside and working about his warehouse. The bay was busy too, this morning: the soft rain and tireless wind wrapped themselves about a whole flock of ships, coming and going or steady at anchor, most of them broadbeamed kvarrs, all of them with a busy air. Ljotr's trading centre seemed to be thriving already.

Though Ljotr's was the largest warehouse, it was not the only one: the shore was lined with buildings that were clearly designed more for trade than for living in, and even since Ketil had been here last the settlement had grown, expanding over the flattish land by the bay. Over to the east of the settlement, along the shore from them, was the chapel that had given the place its name, and Ketil could see that it was also busy, with men and women going in and out. It was not a church of Thorfinn's construction, but the Earl would be pleased.

And Varin and Sigvat had come to Kirkuvagr because the trade was busier than in Deerness. Was it worth going to Deerness to find out more about their background? Einar's brother's sons, and Einar's brother was dead, too. Was their mother alive? Was there more to discover there? It would be the best part of a day's walk, more if they could not find good directions, and the same back again, then another day on to Birsay and Buckquoy again – a good part of three days when no doubt there was information to be found at Buckquoy itself, or more happening. And what would Sigrid do while they walked to Deerness? She would not be keen to return to Buckquoy on her own, to face Rannveig's accusations – though Skorri would no doubt protect her. Ketil found himself making a face. Skorri had a soft spot for Sigrid. He was not sure how Sigrid felt about Skorri, but no doubt she would feel more kindly towards him if he saved her from Rannveig's attacks. He considered that for a moment. He was not altogether happy about his second-in-command forming associations with his friend. It did not seem quite sensible.

Sigrid could wait here till they came back, then return to Buckquoy with them. But as she clearly did not feel comfortable near Ljotr, Ketil doubted she would want to - nor was he too willing to encourage her. And anyway, things went wrong, sometimes. He and Alf might not end up coming back by Kirkuvagr at all, and then no doubt someone would have to send a message to her to come back on her own, and that would not please her, either.

Or she might go with them to Deerness.

It could work to his advantage, he told himself. Often she thought of questions that had not occurred to him, and obviously there were some people who would talk more readily to a woman than to a man. But if anything happened – and things did, even in Thorfinn's well-regulated lands – he continued in his silent debate, he and Alf could take care of themselves – much more easily if they were not also trying to protect Sigrid. And then there was the question of what people might think. A woman, even a widow woman, travelling about with two men to whom she was not related ...? Would it harm her chances of a second marriage? Assuming she wanted one, that was. Assuming Thorfinn found her someone he approved of. Assuming ...

'Another fine day in the Ljotr household,' came a sigh from

behind him. He looked back over his shoulder. Sigrid was wrapping a shawl about her shoulders, and looking faintly sick. 'He wasn't impressed by the speed of her wine delivery last night,' she explained. 'He's already knocked her to the floor once.'

'I wonder if he beat Thordis?' Ketil asked.

'Probably,' said Sigrid without hesitation. Something about the way she suddenly hunched her shoulders caught his eye. He touched her arm.

'Has he hit you?'

'Yesterday, just before you arrived.' She moved slightly so that his hand fell away. 'He's that kind of man. Are you going on to Deerness?'

Ketil opened his mouth to reply and closed it again. Were they? Or was he going to stay and pick a fight with Ljotr? Sigrid's brother, as they had claimed he was, would have every right to protect her. But she was staring straight at him, demanding a reply to her change of subject.

'I'm not sure how much more I need to know about Varin and Sigvat that I cannot find out from them, or from those around them, at Buckquoy,' he said.

At that, the longhouse door slammed shut, and they turned to see Ljotr striding off along the shore. Instinctively they distanced themselves from him even as he moved away, edging round the house towards the warehouse. Ketil found himself ensuring that Sigrid was ahead of him, away from Ljotr. For a brief moment he saw himself sprinting after the man, slipping a knife between his ribs ... no, probably not the best idea.

Outside the warehouse, the men who had spent the night in the longhouse were shifting barrels, rolling them noisily along the paved yard towards a boat at the shore. Ketil could see why Ljotr might want wooden paths.

'What do we know about them?' Sigrid asked as they went. Alf, sheathing his knife, had followed them, glancing over his shoulder at Ljotr's departure.

'Not much,' Ketil admitted. 'I'm not even sure if their mother is alive. Younger brothers? Sisters?'

Sigrid was shaking her head.

'I have no idea. The only one in Buckquoy who knew much about them was probably Thordis, and she's not in a position to tell us.'

'I heard Sigvat say they were on their own,' Alf put in helpfully. 'But I haven't heard anything else.'

Ketil gave Alf a nod of approval.

'But is it important? Do we need to know more about them?'

Sigrid made a face.

'I'd be more interested to know about this betrothal. That makes no sense to me at all.'

'You said it must have been a business arrangement,' said Ketil. 'Then it seems to make sense.'

'Not really ...

'Between Thordis and that lad? That was all business!'

It was one of Ljotr's men, ready to take a break between barrels now that the master had gone out. He folded his arms, and looked them over with a friendly air.

'Definitely business? On both sides?' Sigrid still looked dubious.

'Oh, aye,' said the man. 'I've known Thordis since she was so high.' He did not bother to indicate an actual height. 'Little madam. And everyone knew it. It took Ljotr to find a man from outside Kirkuvagr to make an agreement – and even he didn't rush into it.'

'What did you know of Varin and his brother?' Ketil asked, still not keen to walk to Deerness. 'Why were they here?'

'It's right what the master says,' said the man. 'They were merchants, looking for more business. That Varin's two-thirds ambition.'

'What's the other third?' asked Alf, interested.

'Vanity,' said the man at once. 'Varin's chief concern is Varin.'

Ketil saw Sigrid nodding to herself.

'Is he a successful merchant?'

The man made a tutting noise.

'He thinks he is,' he said. 'Sigvat's more the one with the ideas, if you ask me. And he's better at talking to the customers. If they'd gone off to beg an audience with King Harald – or King Sweyn, or both, or the Pope himself like Thorfinn did – it would have been Varin doing the swaggering round the court, but it would have been Sigvat telling him what to say.'

'Interesting,' said Ketil. That was very similar to his impression of what had been happening on the day of the mock fights. He was glad to have it confirmed.

'They were all set to make off for Trondheim, when word came that their uncle had died. And that was that – a fast boat to Birsay to make their homage to Earl Thorfinn. He'll see through them, though: he's not a stupid man, is he?' He beamed, sure of agreement.

'Well, no,' said Sigrid, 'but –'

'So when you say,' said Ketil quickly, trying to save Sigrid from herself, 'that the betrothal was business on both sides, do you think Thordis could have been drawn to another man easily enough?'

Sigrid blinked at him. He hoped it was for his perceptive question, rather than in irritation. The man laughed.

'Depends which other man, doesn't it?'

'I suppose it would, yes,' said Ketil, and he had an idea he knew which one – but this time Sigrid interrupted him

'It was Sigvat, wasn't it?' she asked, almost stumbling over the name in her hurry.

'Aye, it was!' said the man, surprised. 'That's right. She was betrothed to the one brother, but it was the other one she fancied. I always said it would end badly,' he added in satisfaction.

The news was enough to make Ketil determined to abandon thoughts of Deerness – he could always go back, preferably by boat – and want to return as soon as possible to Buckquoy, and to see the brothers Varin and Sigvat himself more closely now that he knew more about them. Left with the choice of staying at Ljotr's inhospitable house or trying to find somewhere else safe and welcoming, Sigrid sighed.

'I suppose I'll go home, too.'

'You're coming with us?' Ketil asked. He would have to talk to her about Thordis, what she had seen, what she had done. He needed her to be where he could find her, but if she came with them that would be even better. And talking while walking was always easier than talking sitting still.

Sigrid, on the other hand, had no particular wish to talk. As they set off her head was feeling very tangled. For one thing, she felt bad about leaving Hrefna, even though she did not particularly like the woman and knew, in any case, that there was little she could do to help or protect her. It was hard to know whether or not Hrefna even cared: she had shown little emotion at the news of Thordis' death, and had not even seemed ashamed when Ljotr had struck out at Sigrid. And to an extent, although Sigrid's husband had been nowhere near as bad as Ljotr seemed to be, even after his injuries made him so angry, Sigrid could understand Hrefna and her blank servitude.

And then, for she could torture herself with thoughts of Hrefna and the past as a distraction all morning, if need be, there was the matter of returning to Buckquoy and Rannveig's accusations, and trying to explain things to Ketil on the way. Perhaps he would not ask her ... no, that was ridiculous. He would have to ask her. For a moment, she was tempted to run back to Kirkuvagr's busy harbour and jump on a boat. But then, would they conclude that she was indeed Thordis' killer? She had run away already.

And who had killed Thordis? With her own braids?

For the second morning in a row, Skorri woke in a ditch, wrapped in his cloak. Geirod had poked him in the shoulder, and the yellow dog was sitting over him, watching with interest. Whatever Geirod's peculiarities, the yellow dog, who had suffered at the hands – and feet – of his previous owner, was growing more confident and less inclined to spend his days hiding behind Geirod's legs. Skorri sat up, groaning.

'Nothing,' said Geirod, without bothering with a greeting. 'Sow's still safe.'

'Good,' said Skorri, rubbing his bristling face hard. The bleak light of morning looked cold, safe and undramatic. 'Maybe we didn't even need to be here.'

Geirod grunted, which could have been agreement or not. The dog sat back and scratched. Skorri felt that as a conversation, it lacked something.

'The pigman will be up soon,' he went on. 'You go on and see if there's hot water in the baths, if you want. I'll stay here till his door is open.'

Geirod and the dog turned and wandered off to Thorfinn's

public bath house, over by the cliff edge, out of Skorri's sight. He could smell no smoke, so it was unlikely that the fires were up to much yet, but he just wanted a bit of time on his own to waken up and think about the day, and what Ketil might want them to do. Thought came slowly in the morning: he must be getting old.

He propped himself against the wall of the pig enclosure, listening to the small contented snufflings from the pigs waking inside the sty, his eyes half-closed against the wind, his thoughts wandering. So when a figure slipped from the back of the pigman's longhouse and ducked under the far wall of the enclosure, he was not even sure he had seen it.

Sigrid's feet, with their local knowledge, had taken her on the inland route back towards Birsay, away from the coastline that Ketil had apparently followed.

'We like the sea,' said Alf. He was drifting along several paces behind them, as if he had nothing in his head but stories and music – indeed, he had a bone pipe with him from which he occasionally drew a few notes, as though the music was bubbling in his head and sometimes had to burst out – but Sigrid had the impression that he was keeping his eyes open, all the same, just in case. She supposed that was what life was like for Ketil and his men, in most places they went: Thorfinn's representatives, who might find out things about the locals that might not necessarily please Thorfinn, could not always sleep easily or walk safely. She thought about her lonely longhouse, with just her and Gnup to keep an eye on everything, but yet where she had always felt safe even alone, and felt rather sorry for Ketil.

'This way is shorter,' she said, and waved over to the left of their path. 'And you can look at the lochs, if it makes you feel better.' Why was she taking the shorter way? She should have delayed going home for as long as possible – or perhaps it was better to get it over with. Those lochs were coming into view now, as she kept their route to the flatter lands to the west of the hills. Strange places round here, she always thought, though somehow comfortable enough. But no reason to linger. She found she had pulled ahead of Ketil slightly, and in two long strides he caught her up.

'Gnup told us you'd gone to see a customer,' he said. Sigrid gave a little nod, approving of Gnup.

'I'm sure he did,' she said.

'It was not that convincing,' he said. 'Why did you run away?'

'Run away? I went to see where Thordis had lived, to find out more about her.'

'Hm,' said Ketil, and she knew he only partly believed her. Which was reasonable.

'And I wanted to get away from Buckquoy. From Rannveig. It's not –' she tried to find words that did not sound ridiculous – 'it's not very pleasant to be accused of murder.'

'Did you do it?' Ketil asked, matter-of-fact.

For a moment, she could not think what to say. She could protest, accuse him of not trusting her, complain that he believed Rannveig – Rannveig! – over her, an old friend. But instead she turned and met his eye.

'No, I didn't.'

'Good.'

Was that all?

'I didn't like her, though. And you know about the braids. Helga will have told you, I'm sure.'

'Her braids are not as fine as yours.'

'That doesn't matter. She could persuade people that they were.'

'Are you trying to tell me you had a good reason to kill her?'

She looked sideways at him. There was an almost-smile on his long face.

'I'm not sure it was a good reason,' she admitted, 'but it was certainly tempting.'

'Well,' he said, 'if you did not kill her, then do you know who did?'

She frowned.

'You know what a hall is like at that stage of the evening. Well, you were there. Could you have said who was in and who was outside at any given moment? Did you notice if she went out alone or went out with someone else?'

'No,' he said, 'I don't think I did. But someone might have. And you were outside – did you see anyone else outside? Or see anyone definitely inside?'

She had already gone over it in her head – several times.

'As to anyone definitely inside, I'm not sure how long she had been dead – she was still almost warm when I touched her, but I think anyone I met could have been out and in again. Except maybe ...' She hesitated, but she had to be fair. 'Except Rannveig herself. I'm sure she had been in the hall for a while. She was busy with some bundle of sacking, off near the side door, and I don't think she could have gone outside without me noticing just then.'

'Well, that's something,' Ketil conceded. 'Rannveig did not murder her own daughter.'

She was not sure whether or not he was being sarcastic.

'There were people outside,' she went on. 'People by the privies, and I suppose one or two out for a breath of fresh air. I thought I heard someone being sick, you know, the usual.' She frowned, caught by a sudden thought as she tried to picture what she had seen as she left the hall and walked towards the paddock wall. 'There was someone big ... let me think, could it have been Afi? Over to my left as I came outside. You know where the paddock wall turns and runs ... well, away towards the harbour and the Brough?'

'The south side of the paddock.'

'Yes, that would be right. The south side. There was a big man standing there.'

'You're sure?'

'I think so. I could just see an outline, so whether he was facing the paddock or the harbour I'm not sure I'd have known.'

'Definitely Afi?'

'From the size ...'

'Not, for example, Bjorn?'

'Oh,' said Sigrid, feeling foolish. 'Well, now you come to mention it, it could have been Bjorn.'

'Interesting,' said Ketil. 'Bjorn or Afi.'

Skorri, now mostly awake, was creeping around the outside of the pig enclosure, keeping low to avoid being seen by whoever it was on the other side. His knees were killing him.

Which of the Westray men would it be? The big one or the small one? He had not liked the look of the big one at all, but the small one had had a wiry look to him, and was maybe stronger than he appeared. Which of them would have been desperate enough to travel over to Birsay and steal the sow back? How had they got past the gate guards? Thorfinn would not be pleased – if some little farmer from Westray could wander in and up to his Brough, who else might find it just as easy? He would have to report it to Ketil.

He reached a corner of the wall, and eased himself forward to look round it while showing as little of himself as possible. He wished he had had his woolly hat to pull on: it was dark grey in colour and squashed down his hair so that his head was less obvious. It would also have kept him warmer last night.

And as it turned out, it might have offered him some protection from the blow that now fell on the back of his head. That was his last thought as he fell forward and the grey light of dawn swirled and darkened around him.

XVIII

It was growing duskish when they saw the lights of Buckquoy in the distance, and of the settlement on the Brough beyond.

'Are you going straight home?' Ketil asked Sigrid, as Alf headed into the Buckquoy hall. Sigrid gazed longingly up the hill to her own darkened longhouse. If Gnup was in residence, Ketil thought, he was at least not holding a feast in Sigrid's absence. Sigrid's thoughts might also have been running along the lines of food. She turned reluctantly towards the hall, too.

'I have to face it some time,' she said, squaring her shoulders. Ketil had a moment's qualm: apart from her assurance that she had not killed Thordis, they had settled nothing on the way back. He should have asked her what had happened when Thordis had confronted her about the weaving – or whatever it was that had happened. Somehow he had not managed to find his way to the subject. And now they were back amongst the people involved – apart from Thordis, of course – and it would be harder to get her to talk about it. And without that account, he was not sure how to counter Rannveig's accusations – assuming they could be countered.

He was about to walk with her into the hall when Alf came out, a puzzled look on his face.

'No sign of Skorri or Geirod. Or the dog,' he added. 'Weren't they supposed to be here? Questioning people?'

'They were,' said Ketil. He was less concerned than Alf

seemed to be: he expected his men, particularly Skorri, to show some evidence of independent thought when he was not there. But Alf looked worried.

'No one has seen them since yesterday, apparently,' he explained. 'Skorri talked with some of Bjorn's men, and then someone says he talked to Foldar for a bit – that's the fellow with the split nose,' he added, in case Ketil had not realised. Ketil nodded. 'And then he disappeared, and as for Geirod, he hasn't been seen since just after we left.'

'They could have gone to talk to some of Einar's men in their own longhouses,' Ketil suggested, though Alf's anxiety was beginning to have an effect. 'Hrolf up yonder, maybe, or Afi, or Oddr.'

'Oddr's in there,' said Alf, 'and so's Hrolf. He's not in either of their places, and they say he hasn't spoken with them yet.' Alf had moved fast in the few moments he had been inside the hall.

'And Afi?' Afi, the big boat-builder. Had it been him Sigrid had seen at the side of the paddock? Or Bjorn?

'No, Afi's not there just now.'

'He can't be mending boats in this light,' said Ketil. 'But maybe he's finishing up down at the harbour. Let's go down and see if he's there. Sigrid?' He looked about him, but she must already have disappeared into the hall. Ketil went to the doorstep and took a good look inside.

Einar's men and Bjorn's crew were gathering again for supper. Ketil sensed no animosity between them, even after that fight the night before last: many of them still bore bandages but the two groups seemed to be mixing amiably enough. Bjorn himself, subdued, sat to one side on his heap of furs, staring at the floor while one of Rannveig's women – Frogunn, Foldar's more impressive sister – redressed his shoulder wound. Sigrid, her back to Ketil, stood for a moment a little way in from the entrance, looking about her, not sure of where to go. Frogunn must have noticed a little movement out of the corner of her eye, and turned.

'Sigrid! You're back! Excellent!' Frogunn called, and Sigrid hurried over to her, relief sagging her stiff shoulders. Ketil, content, retreated into the dusk outside.

'Come on,' he said, and Alf followed him down the path to the harbour that was tucked into the side of the landbridge, sheltered from the wind if not from the damp air. For a moment Ketil hoped that Afi might possibly have been working on the damage on Ketil's own boat, but he tried not to be too optimistic. Afi was a busy man.

As if to prove the point in his mind, Ketil spotted Afi almost immediately, still at work by the light of a lantern as large as Ketil had seen, though in keeping with the build of the man himself. Careful not to cast his own shadow, Afi was aligning two lengths of beautifully shaped wood, worked into the precise form for the place they needed to fit. Pale curls of shavings danced on the stones at his feet, and even against the sea-scent Ketil could smell the sweet aroma of worked wood, flinging him back into memories of his childhood, of his father scooping shavings out to make the wooden cups he sold, the wooden cups his brother now made, that his nephews would probably make in their turn. He could feel the warm, forgiving material between his hands, his long thumbs resting on the smooth curves of a cup, touching the carving of a handle, sliding into the bowl, smelling the rich fragrance. He was no use at working wood himself, as his father had found, but it did not mean that he could not understand it and see how it wanted to be.

But no: his wood was already worked, to shield him from axe blows, to guard his sword blade, to bear him over the waters – that last best of all. And to watch Afi tending to those sweet lines as he eased the new wood into the old, that was very fine.

'Hi? Who's there?' Afi must have heard their steps on the stones, but he took his time turning to see them, letting his broad hands finish their task first. 'Oh! Ketil, it's you. I thought you were off to Kirkuvagr, or points further east?'

'We took the ill news to Thordis' uncle,' Ketil said, 'but there was nothing else to keep us there beyond that. Tell me: did you see anything that night? Anything that might help us find out who killed her? Someone said, I think, that you were outside about that time, but some distance away.'

'I was, and all,' said Afi, with a half-laugh, less amused than rueful. 'Chilling my bones for no good reason.'

'Why was that, then?'

'Ach,' said Afi, laying down his wood and leaning against the boat, 'someone brought me a message to say I was wanted outside, that Rannveig wanted a word in private. Well, aye, she's been quiet enough this last couple of years, but when Rannveig sends you an order you just go and do it, don't you? I mean, she was Einar's wife and all.'

'And did you see Rannveig, then, outside?'

'I did not,' said Afi. 'I waited an age – getting cold, aye? – and then I gave up and came back in. Mind, I suppose she just might have come out and not seen me.'

'Would you not have seen her?'

'Och, I came over this side, up the hill there, and stood looking down here. I mean, if I have to be outside anyway, I'd rather be thinking about boats. I just passed the time thinking of one – that one there, if you can see it – that I'm making for a lad down the way there, his first proper boat. And you know what kind of boat that's going to be – he'll remember it all his life, if it's done right. So there I was, thinking about that, and when I thought I was going to freeze to the paddock wall I gave up and went back to the hall. But I think that must have been about the time they found the poor lassie, for I heard some kind of a cry out and I saw you, I think, going over to the wall by the hall. But I was that cold I just went straight inside before I could do anything else. I'd have come to help if I'd known.'

'That's all right,' said Ketil. 'Who was it gave you Rannveig's message?'

Afi's great face twisted into a scowl.

'I canna remember. I had a bit of wine inside me, you see, and someone just came up and spoke over my shoulder, nearly out of my sight altogether. I had the idea it was one of Bjorn's fellows, but I could be wrong. It was almost like he said "Off you go, away out and wait for Rannveig," and I just went, see? And now I'm wondering if it was some kind of a joke, and Rannveig never sent me the message at all, and someone just wanted the laugh of seeing me go and stand outside in the cold for half the night. There's folk like that,' he added innocently. It would never occur to kindly Afi to do such a stupid thing. Ketil nodded, though he was beginning to wonder if it had just been a harmless joke.

'So did you see anyone else about? – oh,' he added, catching sight of Alf's face, angular in the lamplight, 'and has Skorri asked you any of this already?'

'Skorri? I haven't seen him today. No idea where he is. So no, he hasn't asked me. And did I see anyone else? I was too cold coming back, and I had my back to everything around the hall while

I was waiting. No one came past me there. On the way there ... I'd have to think. I don't remember anyone. But I was looking for Rannveig. I definitely didn't see her. I'd have remembered that.'

'I think he was telling the truth,' said Alf. Their long shadows had faded as they left the lantern light: they had stayed silent until then. 'I don't think he saw anyone.'

'I think you're probably right,' said Ketil. They trudged the steep path that would take them more directly up to the Brough with the guard at its gateway: it required a degree of concentration in this light not to go over on an ankle. 'The question is, did someone deliberately lure him out there, and if so why, and if so who? What use would it have been to have Afi outside just at that point? He could have seen the murderer.'

'He could,' Alf agreed. 'And him such a big man, he might have knocked him down before he had the chance to do anything.'

'A big man ...' Ketil repeated. 'A big man, just like Bjorn. In fact, when I suggested Bjorn Sigrid was not sure which of them it was ... What if someone told Thordis Bjorn was waiting for her outside, and had Afi out there to lure her further out, away from the hall?'

'Aye,' said Alf, after a little thought, 'that might work. As long as she knew that Bjorn wasn't in the hall, though.'

'That Bjorn wasn't in the hall ...' Ketil repeated again, filtering the words through his mind. 'But if Bjorn was not actually in the hall, where was he?'

The guards at the gate nodded them through, looking forward to the end of their duty for the evening. The door of the hall was open, letting a pool of light spill across the flags in front of the building, encouraging visitors to enter. Ketil and Alf made their way over, and the moment they were inside Alf gave a huff of relief.

'There they are!'

At the side, tucked into the heap of their bedrolls, were Geirod and his dog, and Skorri, looking somewhat sorry for himself. He tried to struggle to his feet when he saw Ketil arrive, but Geirod shoved him back down, tilting his head so that Ketil could see the bandage over it.

'What happened?'

'It's my fault,' said Skorri at once, and he looked miserable. 'One of the Westray men – I don't know which – came back and and took the sow.'

'All the way here for the sow?' Ketil could not keep the surprise out of his voice.

'It looks like it. I caught a glimpse of someone and tried to follow them, but they must have come round behind me.'

'And hit him,' said Geirod with grim satisfaction.

'And hit me.' Skorri nodded, but quite gently. 'But then the yellow dog found me.'

'I told him to!' said Geirod proudly, 'and off he went and did!'

'Tracker?' suggested Alf at once.

'No,' said Geirod.

'Leave it, Alf,' said Ketil. 'Well done, Geirod. Why were you up here, anyway?'

'We thought the sow might be in danger,' said Skorri, keen to recover some of his credit. 'We spent last night by the pig enclosure, but they came at dawn, just after I had sent Geirod away to warm up.'

'But you don't know which of them it was?'

'I didn't get more than a glimpse,' said Skorri.

'I didna see him at all,' said Geirod.

'How did they get on to the Brough?' asked Alf.

'And more to the point, have they got off again?' asked Ketil. 'The answer to either question is something Thorfinn is going to be quite interested in.'

'Oh, yes!' said Skorri, wide-eyed at the thought. 'Aye, that's a fair point.'

Skorri insisted on coming with them when they went to find the gate guards. His head was painful still, and he had quite a chill from lying by the pig enclosure's wall, undiscovered, for longer than was sensible at this time of year – and with no hat. He had a rag permanently under his nose, and a damp look to his whiskers, and his eyes were bleary. But he was determined to find the man who had thumped him and taken the sow.

They met the guards just as they came off duty. At first they were resentful at being challenged, thinking that Ketil was finding fault with them, but as Ketil explained the situation they took more of an interest in it.

'Aye, there was a man that came looking for you,' agreed the smaller guard, bristling black hair sticking out from under his warm hat – he must have been keeping cosy under his helmet. 'A youngish fellow. Had your name, and all.'

'He said nothing about a pig, though,' said the larger man. He was bald, and apparently did not feel the cold. His bare arms could have done duty as the gate on their own. 'I like pigs, me. I'd have remembered.'

'I suppose he wouldn't say he was here to take the pig,' said Skorri, whose temper was understandably a little short. 'But has the same man left again?'

'No, not that we've seen,' said the smaller guard. 'But he arrived yesterday. There would have been time for him to go yesterday.'

'Except he only took the pig this morning, just after dawn,' said Ketil.

'We started on the gate at dawn,' said the smaller man. 'No, then, he didn't come through today.'

'So either he has found somewhere to hide until he works out a way of getting back through the gate –'

'That'll never happen!' said the big man.

'Or he's found a way of getting himself and the sow off the Brough without coming through the gate. And that's what we need to find out.'

'It's dark now,' said the smaller guard helpfully.

'We still need to find him,' said Ketil. 'We definitely don't want him around the Brough for another night, and if he's going to try to escape, this is when he might well do it. And I'd like to stop him.'

'Aye, that's right,' said the big guard. 'Nobody gets off the Brough without our say-so.'

'No one at all,' agreed the smaller man.

'We'd better get some torches and start searching, then,' said Ketil, and led the way back up to Thorfinn's hall.

In the hall, with torches ready to light, Ketil gave directions to his small search party – a larger one might well have allowed the Westray man to slip through in the confusion, particularly now it was dark. Skorri was unable to tell him which Westray man it was, but the fact the man would be in the company of a small and friendly sow would probably give him away. Ketil caught the guards' brief longing look across at the supper pots being brought in to the fire.

'Sorry, but I think it will be a late supper tonight.'

'Aye, well,' said the smaller man. 'If we get him it'll be worth it. We'll just have to tighten our belts!'

And they seized a torch each, and set off into the night.

'We'll start by the old houses,' said Ketil into the wind.

'They'd be a good place to hide, and they're not far from the pigs,' Skorri agreed.

'Good thing it's not a stormy night, then,' said the larger guard. 'We've bets on when the rest of the ruins are going to go into the sea. I mean, half of them is away already.'

'What's the betting?' asked Skorri.

'Let's try to go quietly,' said Ketil, and they all fell silent.

All the preparation, however, seemed to fall a little flat when, only a little while later, Geirod's dog yelped with delight and nipped around between the bath house and the cliff. When they followed, they found a little man huddled against the back wall of the bath house, with a small black sow clutched tightly in his arms.

'Thorthr,' said Ketil. 'I see you've found your neighbour's sow.'

Thorthr, in the torchlight, reddened.

'You'll just give it back to Ozzur!' he objected.

'How were you going to take her home, then?' Ketil asked, for the benefit of the gate guards.

'I have a boat down at the harbour!'

'Well, we didn't think you were going to swim,' muttered Skorri, still cross.

'And how were you going to get to the harbour?'

'I was waiting for the guards to go off the gate,' Thorthr said, though the look he was now giving the guards was a dubious one.

'This is Thorfinn's brough,' said Ketil. 'The gate is never unguarded.'

'Aye, well,' said Thorthr. 'I know that now.'

'Come on, back to the hall.' Ketil nodded at his men. Skorri picked up the sow, though you could see his head hurt as he bent down, and Alf hauled Thorthr to his feet by his elbow. Geirod saw to the yellow dog, who was extremely excited at his own success. Ketil saw Alf open his mouth, and lifted a hand.

'No,' he said, sounding like Geirod himself. Alf looked innocent.

Ketil followed his men, and the guards came up beside him.

'See, the thing is,' said the smaller man, 'that might be your pig man from Westray.'

'It is,' said Ketil.

'Aye, well, good, good,' said the man. 'Thing is, he's not the man who was asking for you.'

Ketil stopped.

'Are you sure?' Who would be asking for him by name?

'Oh, aye. The man that asked for you, he was younger.'

'In this light ...'

'And he had a burn down the side of his face.

'Oh.' Thorthr, however unappealing, was unscarred.

'Just thought we should say. In case you come across another fellow.'

'Thank you.'

They reached the hall. Thorfinn would not want to deal with Thorthr and the sow before he had his supper, not now. Ketil directed Alf to take Thorthr round to the building where they could lock in anyone likely to make a bid for freedom, and told Skorri to return the pig to the sty and warn the pigman.

'I could stay on guard there again,' said Skorri, and coughed mightily.

'I don't think so,' said Ketil. 'Let the pigman do it. It's his duty. Make sure he understands that.' He turned to Geirod. 'Your dog has done a good job again. Thank you for that.'

Geirod gave a wordless nod, and stooped to pat the dog's ears with his unbroken hand. Ketil thought he heard him whisper something, but in the wind it was hard to hear.

The guards were already in the hall, eager for their food. Ketil and Geirod followed, and since the meal had started, Ketil went to speak quietly to Thorfinn about the pig and its thief. But Thorfinn greeted him as though he had been looking for him.

'All well in Kirkuvagr?' he asked.

'Aye, my lord. Trade is busy, and the place was peaceful.'

'That's good to hear. And Rannveig's connexions there?'

Ketil raised an eyebrow.

'Not completely straightforward, my lord.' Making sure that no one nearby was able to overhear, he told Thorfinn quickly about Ljotr and Hrefna and their attitude to their niece Thordis, and gave him the news of the betrothal between Thordis and Varin. Thorfinn sat back in his high seat, thoughtful.

'That young man is not really to be trusted, is he? I thought not.' He considered. 'Right, well, good work. You didn't go on to Deerness, then?'

'I thought it best to get back here for now, and talk to Varin again. And we have some information about Afi, too, which I wanted to pursue.'

'Afi the boatbuilder? Surely he was not involved?'

'I don't think so, my lord.'

'Right ...' Thorfinn stared off down the hall for a moment, then said, 'There's news for you, too, Ketil. A messenger. Where did he go?' He glanced up and down the hall, then seemed to pick out a face. 'You there! Come here, will you?'

A young man, not much above middle height and walking wearily, approached Thorfinn's seat and bowed. He had a handsome face, but when Ketil caught a glimpse of the side angled away from him he saw that the man had been badly burned, and not long ago.

'My lord,' said the man, and even in those two words Ketil recognised his way of speech, and knew that this was not to be good news.

'This is Ketil Gunnarson,' said Thorfinn. 'You said you had news for him.'

'Yes, my lord,' said the man, and turned to Ketil. There was a wariness now, as well as a weariness.

'It's something from Heithabyr, isn't it?' Ketil heard the words coming from his own lips. The man nodded, grateful that Ketil had done a little to make his task easier.

'It's Heithabyr,' he said, 'and a message from your brother Njal.'

Thank goodness, Ketil thought: Njal was not dead.

'Heithabyr is burned,' said the man. 'In his quarrel with King Sweyn, King Harald sent fire boats into the harbour. The whole town is wood, you know that. The whole town ...'

XIX

'But my brother is alive?' asked Ketil. Heithabyr, burning. All that wood – his brother's workshop, too, all wood.

'Njal is alive,' said the man. 'But his wife and the boys ...'

'The boys ...' Ketil remembered them, fair-haired lads already cutting themselves on Njal's wood tools. Njal's wife, hard-working, broad and happy. The workshop, their father's workshop, that too. And all of Heithabyr.

'I had no idea,' said Thorfinn. The man must have kept the news for Ketil. 'Ketil, this is ill news indeed. I am sorry for your loss. May God be with your brother's family.'

Ketil bowed his head briefly, acknowledging Thorfinn's words. Then he bowed his head again, not sure what to do.

'This was King Harald?' Thorfinn wanted to make sure.

The man cleared his throat, fingers dancing briefly around his burned face.

'Harald's man,' he said. 'Bjorn Einarsson. That was the one that did it – the Bear.'

Ketil heard Thorfinn's quick intake of breath, but it meant little to him.

'Thank you for bringing the news,' he said to the young man, though he would rather have struck him. 'Perhaps we can talk later. For now ...'

He made his way out of the hall, feeling the floor unsteady under his feet. Outside the air was cold and wet. He stopped, and drew breath. Then he made his way round the hall and up, and into the chapel behind. For a moment he staggered in the doorway and caught his balance on the wall. Then he took two strides inside, sank to his knees, and felt the numbness overwhelm him.

'I thought you'd run away!' said Frogunn cheerfully.

'Sigrid wouldn't run away,' Helga retorted. Sigrid thought it might be best to let her think that. And had she really run away, anyway? Had she not just gone to Kirkuvagr to find out more about Thordis? Of course she had – otherwise it would not have been so easy for Ketil to persuade her to come back home. That was not to say that she was not keeping an eye open for Rannveig. But then, it was usually a good idea to keep a wary eye out for Rannveig.

'Where did you go, then?' Frogunn was not to be put off. She had left Bjorn, now tended and fed, in his heap of furs, and for a moment glanced back at him.

'He's barely moved since the fight, you know,' she murmured. 'Thordis' death really seems to have knocked him sideways.'

'He barely knew her,' said Helga.

'Maybe that's why!' Sigrid suggested, and the other two laughed. 'But I mean,' said Sigrid, 'it's easier to be all sentimental about someone when you've only just met them. When you get to know them, then you might feel differently.'

Frogunn made a face.

'Well, that doesn't make me look forward to marriage.'

'Oh, marriage is all right, Frogunn,' said Helga easily. 'I'm very fond of Hrolf. He's a good provider.'

Sigrid raised her eyebrows, and Helga laughed again.

'Oh, we shouldn't be laughing so much,' she said, 'not with Thordis' burial in the morning. We should be in the longhouse with Rannveig, I suppose.'

They exchanged looks, none of them enthusiastic. Sigrid was not even sure that Rannveig would want her there.

'Where are Varin and Sigvat?' she asked, looking around. 'Have they given up their bid and gone home?'

'No, no!' said Helga at once. 'That would be too easy. They're in the longhouse, though.'

Frogunn sighed.

'I'll go over shortly, then, and see if Rannveig needs anything. I have to check Sigvat's bandages anyway – he's still in a lot of pain.' She hesitated for a moment, as if trying to think of a good excuse, then lifted a freckled hand in farewell and headed for the hall door.

'Did you run away?' Helga asked. 'You went without saying anything. Gnup was very secretive.'

'I wanted to find out more about Thordis,' Sigrid said, perhaps a little too quickly.

'And did you?' Helga settled back against a table, always ready for a gossip. Around them the preparations for a quiet supper were almost complete: there would be no singing or verses with Thordis lying dead in the longhouse. Even Bjorn's crew looked subdued.

'I found out one or two things,' Sigrid admitted. 'She wasn't married because they hadn't found anyone to take her. Her uncle's a successful merchant, right in the middle of things in Kirkuvagr, but he's a horrible man – and of course Thordis was ...'

'Was very much Thordis,' Helga helped out. 'Was there any other family?'

'The uncle's wife, but she didn't like Thordis much. I think that Thordis considered herself a bit above helping around the house or learning about food and such. Braids were her pastime.'

'Sad,' said Helga, nodding. 'She wasn't even very good at those.'

Sigrid gave a half-smile at Helga's loyalty. She was a good friend.

Thordis plonking herself down beside Bjorn might not have been unusual then, she thought. If Thordis was used to ignoring women's tasks, expecting other women to do them, she might not even have thought to help serve the supper and the drink. But it had been quite a choice, to ignore Varin, her betrothed husband – who was also on the high seat, so she would have looked quite the lady seated by him – to go and snuggle up to Bjorn, the outsider. What had she been up to? Was she making an estimate of which man she thought might be successful, or was she an instrument of her mother's, doing what she had been told to do, finding out about Bjorn? Sigrid frowned to herself, remembering. If anyone could make people do things, invent strategies, plan and plot, it was Rannveig. But surely Rannveig would not have killed her own daughter, destroyed that instrument – would she? And if she had not, then someone had very seriously damaged her plans. What would she do now?

She looked about to see if they were needed yet to serve food, and took in once again the dejected mountain that was Bjorn in his nest of furs.

'Do you think he'll get over this?' she asked Helga.

'Oh, yes. He's bound to,' said Helga lightly.

'Why is he not in the longhouse, too? Paying his respects?'
Helga shrugged.

'No idea. He looks as if it would take the last of his strength,
doesn't he?'

Sigrid watched the great man for a moment, but he could
barely be seen to breathe.

'How is Varin taking it?'

'Oh,' said Helga, disgusted, 'it's all about Varin. How he's
been deprived of his woman. I'm not sure how he makes out that she
was his, but maybe we all are. How Bjorn had her killed just to spite
him – or possibly someone from here who resents his success and
wants to drive him out. He hasn't named names, but he's been eying
Oddr and Foldar with what I think he thinks is a threatening look,
but to me it's more as if he's been eating bad fish. If Thorfinn lets
Varin take charge of the hall, I think I might take Hrolf and go to
live on Hoy.'

'You'd miss the Brough.'

Helga grinned.

'Yes, probably. And what would Hrolf do? But can you
imagine having Varin here all the time?'

Sigrid twisted her mouth in unhappy agreement.

'Well, we'll see,' she said.

'Would you stay?'

'Where would I go? Back to Heithabyr? I've no family left
there.'

'But it's a market. You could find customers.'

'For that matter I could try somewhere like Jorvik, start
afresh.' She sighed. 'I'd rather stay here. In the end I didn't much
like living in a market. I like it here. And as long as Thorfinn doesn't
start demanding more taxes, I can just about afford it, too.'

'Oh, Sigrid! You're back!'

To her surprise, Helga's husband Hrolf looked quite pleased
to see her. She smiled encouragingly.

'Yes, I was only away for a night.'

'No doubt finding out more about this business, knowing
you!' he said. He had been a handsome man, and was still a skilled
fighter, but she noticed that he was running a little to fat. He looked

prosperous. 'Have you collected any interesting information?'

'Well,' she said, thinking. She was not sure that she wanted everyone to know yet that Thordis and Varin had been betrothed, at least as far as her family were concerned. Nor that Thordis' affections had lain elsewhere. The men of Einar's hird were the worst gossips in the islands. 'Well, it helped me to remember more about the other night, anything I saw when I went outside, before I found poor Thordis.' Poor Thordis. She did feel almost sorry for the girl. After all, someone attacking her must have come as a great shock: she could not have thought herself so hated.

'And was there something that you saw?' Hrolf was clearly interested, but not anxious – he must feel that no suspicion was likely to fall on him.

'I saw a large man over by the paddock,' said Sigrid. 'Well over to the left, where the wall turns. Nowhere near the body.'

'That must have been Bjorn,' said Hrolf confidently.

'Why do you say that?' Sigrid asked.

'Oddr saw him go outside, not long before Ketil came in to say Thordis was dead.'

'Are you sure?' Sigrid was surprised. Surely this would have been common knowledge by now, but perhaps while she had been away such things had been discovered. They would certainly have been gossiped about.

'Yes,' Hrolf laughed. 'He's not a man to miss, is he? And Oddr says he didn't look too pleased. You see,' he said, settling down for the story, 'what Oddr says is that he saw someone go over to him and have a word – one of his own men, I think, for it was no one Oddr knew, he said. Mind you, Oddr's eyes are going. He was watching the boats coming into the harbour the other day and he thought one of the kvarrs was a warship!'

'But he definitely saw someone talking to Bjorn?' Sigrid asked, otherwise Hrolf would be off on stories about boats until dawn.

'Oh, yes. Well, Oddr says this fellow, the one that was talking to Bjorn, pointed to the door. Oh, Thordis had already gone out, of course. I should have said that: Oddr said that Bjorn was sitting on his own and Oddr saw she was gone but assumed she was away to the privy. And Bjorn was looking for one of his furs, because Oddr thought that was where Thordis had gone, at first, to fetch it. Anyway, whatever this man was telling Bjorn, it looked as if he was talking about Thordis, or at least something outside, and Bjorn looked over at the door, and after a moment listening he got himself up and went out after her. Or after whatever it was. And he did not look pleased, according to Oddr. Though of course Oddr is an old gossip.'

'Did he see Bjorn come back?'

'He did – well, in fact I did, too. He can't have been out for long, for he was back by the time Ketil came in to say Thordis was dead.'

'When you say out for long ...' Sigrid remembered the slight warmth of Thordis' leg. How long had she been dead?

'Not ages, you know? Not half the evening. That would have been noticed, wouldn't it? With Bjorn, anyway.'

Sigrid had not seen what had happened to the large figure in the distance after she found Thordis. It was more than possible for the man – Bjorn or whoever – to come back round and into the hall. Had Bjorn killed Thordis and then, taking a moment to recover, gone to stand away from the body, over beyond the paddock wall? Or had that been Afi the boat builder, and Bjorn had been somewhere else instead?

'Why on earth would Bjorn kill Thordis?' demanded Helga, realising the way the conversation was turning. 'You could see he was smitten with her. It was a wonder he had let her go outside on her own at all, even to the privy.'

Sigrid's head was scrambling over that, too.

'What if he thought she might have betrayed him? Perhaps that she was outside with someone else?'

'Who, though? It was a wonder that one man liked her,' said Helga waspishly.

'Varin?'

'Varin didn't like her.'

'Varin started the fight when he accused Bjorn of killing her, though.' And Varin, though he might not have liked her, still had some claim over her if they were betrothed. She was his link to the most important merchant in Kirkuvagr. At least they could be sure that Varin had not killed her.

'But ...' Helga's pretty face was wrinkled with a frown, not happy with the picture Sigrid had offered. 'But Thordis would not risk what she was starting with Bjorn, would she?'

'Thordis didn't strike me as very clever,' said Sigrid. 'I mean ... well, clever in some ways, perhaps, but I don't think she knew, as Rannveig knows, how to play people off against each other. She might indeed have gone outside to speak to Varin. I don't think,' she said carefully, 'that Bjorn was the target of her affections. Just of her ambitions.'

'Harsh,' said Helga, but she nodded. 'That would be very like Rannveig.'

'I think it was Rannveig's idea.'

'Of course.' Helga sighed. 'It's a bit of a mess.'

'Or is it?' Sigrid wondered. 'Is it, in fact, much easier now that Thordis is dead?'

It was odd to eat in the hall with all the hird and with Bjorn's crew but without, now, either Einar or Rannveig, or even Thordis to represent her mother. The women had served supper so many times there that they needed no direction, but still there was an emptiness about the place. Sigrid half-expected Varin to come in from the longhouse just to take his seat at the head of the hall, but he must have managed to resist the temptation – it perhaps served his ambitions better to be seen to attend Thordis' corpse. At that thought, Sigrid stopped and told herself not to be so cynical. But there was something about Varin that brought it out in her.

The hird and the crew were less demanding than usual: their appetites were not diminished by the tragedy that had occurred, but perhaps wariness of another fight made them all drink less. Bjorn hardly touched anything. He looked utterly miserable.

'I wonder,' said Frogunn, standing with Sigrid and watching him from the dark edges of the hall, 'if maybe someone killed her to get at Bjorn? Someone who just wants to drive him away, and not let him take the hall?'

'Varin?' asked Sigrid.

'I don't necessarily mean Varin,' said Frogunn quickly. 'Just someone who doesn't want Bjorn in charge. There must be others besides Varin. I don't think he would have done it, would he? I mean, he was upset when she went to sit by Bjorn, wasn't he?'

Sigrid glanced at her.

'Well, yes,' she conceded. 'And maybe you're right. But

who else specifically did not want Bjorn to take charge? Who was against him so much that they would think nothing of murdering someone who had nothing to do with it?'

'She didn't really have nothing at all to do with it,' said Frogunn sensibly. 'She's Rannveig's daughter.'

'Is there another apple anywhere?' called a man nearby. Frogunn hurried off to find one, leaving Sigrid lost in thought. It might not be a mess, but it was certainly a tangle – in her mind's eye a tangle of yarn was something one could disentangle, while a mess meant you'd spilled the broth on it. She still had hopes of working out the answer here, rendering the solution clear. But how? She wanted Ketil: she needed to talk it all over with someone she trusted. Not that she did not trust Helga, but when it came to something like this ... Talking with Helga was just not the same, she concluded.

He would be at the burial tomorrow, no doubt. She could speak with him then.

But for now, what had they found out? Bjorn had been outside when Thordis was killed, and had gone out looking cross – well, according to Oddr, whose eyesight was unreliable. Oddr was Foldar's father, of course ... and Oddr, and others, wanted Foldar for the hall. Could Oddr or some of Einar's old hird be so keen to keep the hall to themselves that they would kill Thordis to drive Bjorn away? Had Frogunn – Oddr's daughter, Foldar's sister – been trying to tell her that just now? Surely not. Frogunn had seemed quite casual about what she was saying. But that did not stop it from being true. And if a few of Einar's men were working together to drive Bjorn out, it would be hard to discover exactly what had happened. They could quarrel amongst themselves like anyone else, but they would defend each other against an outside enemy – or against Thorfinn, if he was doing something they didn't like.

So had Bjorn killed Thordis, perhaps out of jealousy, or had Bjorn been tricked into going outside so that it would look as if he could have killed Thordis? Had Bjorn fallen for Thordis, or was he just trying to annoy Varin? Was Thordis attracted to Bjorn, or was she just obeying her mother? Or was she also trying to annoy Varin – it did seem like something people might want to do – since she was stuck with him when she really wanted Sigvat? And how did Sigvat feel about that? Was he as fond of Thordis as her uncle's workman had said she was of Sigvat? He had not said. Sigrid should have asked. She tried to think what Sigvat's reaction had been to Thordis' death, but she could not remember: she had been distracted by Rannveig's accusations, and by the reactions of Bjorn and Varin. Had Ketil spoken with Sigvat? She would have to find out. Maybe she should go up to the Brough to find him.

She checked herself. At this time of night? That would be silly. She could easily wait till tomorrow. She would see him then.

It felt like a long time to wait.

Her eye was caught by a movement on the other side of the hall, behind the men at the tables. Bjorn was emerging from his furs, shaking them off and standing, as if he would reach the roof of the hall with only a little effort. He was huge, even bigger than Afi. No wonder they called him the Bear. She thought for a moment he was going to take his place, belatedly, at the table, but instead he barely glanced at the remains of the feast, and made for the hall's door. It occurred to her for a moment to worry about him, for his expression was so unhappy she might have thought he was thinking of drowning himself, but it was more likely he was off to the privy.

One or two men watched him go, expressions unreadable. Could the hird want him gone? And if so, would they then turn on Varin?

And just as his name passed through her mind, there was a great shout at the door, and Varin rushed inside, face smeared with blood.

'He's attacked me! Bjorn attacked me! He's a murderer!'

And he fell dramatically to the floor.

XX

'Oh, heavens,' said Frogunn, hurrying over with a cloth and a dish of warm water. 'Can you sit up?'

Varin did, hastily, and shuffled himself backwards out of her reach.

'No, no, I'm sure it will be all right. A minor injury.'

'Yes, but the blood,' Frogunn objected, following him on her knees, trying not to spill the water.

'I'm sure I can manage.'

'Let me – you've had a shock.'

'I was only worried,' said Varin, attempting to draw himself up more effectively, 'that I might strike him back too hard and do him some damage. When someone comes out of the dark like that and attacks a fighter, they're taking quite a risk.'

Sigrid choked back a laugh, for at that moment Bjorn, looking like a bit that had come away from one of the peaks of Hoy, appeared in the doorway, bewildered. Varin sank back and wisely fell silent.

'I think I might have hit someone,' said Bjorn, almost as apologetic as Afi could be. 'Someone came round the corner a bit fast and I just lifted my fist ...' He showed them: his right knuckles were indeed a little bloody.

'Well, we can wash them, too,' sighed Frogunn, tucking her heels under her and standing up. In a moment she had wiped Bjorn's knuckles clean, and Helga, with one of her particular smiles, had fetched him a cup of wine. Bjorn seemed immune to the smile but he took the wine, then noticed Varin, trying to arrange himself to better advantage on the floor.

'Oh, was it you I hit? Sorry,' said Bjorn. 'You took me by surprise.'

'See? He doesn't even know what he's doing,' muttered Varin, but Sigrid noticed that his accusations of murder had not been repeated. Bjorn nodded as if the matter had been settled to everyone's satisfaction, and taking his cup of wine he retreated to his heap of furs on the other side of the hall, looking as miserable as ever. Varin, deprived of his opponent, looked sulky, and gracelessly allowed Frogunn to kneel beside him again and clean his handsome face. She took her time over it: Sigrid wondered if she were enjoying making Varin cross, though now that he had permitted her he seemed to be taking some pleasure in the attention. He was, thought Sigrid, an irritating little child.

Varin's injuries were minimal, when the blood was removed, and he allowed Frogunn to fetch him some wine, too. She even sat by him for a little, in a valiant effort to improve his mood and ease over any tensions in the hall that could be eased over – no one really wanted a repeat of the fight two nights ago, particularly not the women.

In fact, the incident had been dealt with so neatly at the back of the hall that Sigrid reckoned most of the men had hardly noticed anything happening. Drinking and talking quietly amongst themselves, they barely saw Rannveig enter the hall by the back door, even when she had made her way to the centre of the hall before the high seat. She waited, straight-backed and silent, until all eyes were on her and all speech ceased.

'In the morning we bury my daughter Thordis,' she said, and her voice was clear even if it was washed of its old authority. 'I ask that all who wish to now should come to the house where she lies to make their farewells, and to watch with me until dawn.'

She bowed her head then, before returning to the door she came in by. The men in the hall did not follow her directly, but a few at a time they finished their cups, brushed themselves down and straightened their shirts, and headed out of the hall by the main door to go round to the longhouse. Helga, Sigrid and Frogunn, left almost alone, tidied up quickly, brushing the tables, disposing of leftovers, straightening benches and seeing to the fire so that all was ready for the morning, before they too prepared to go. Helga and Sigrid retied their white headcloths, and Frogunn ran her fingers through her hair and looped it back tidily. They nodded at each other, solemn-faced, and headed out into the night.

Sigrid's heart skipped a beat or two as she followed the other two into the longhouse. Would Rannveig throw her out? But no:

Rannveig was there at the door to meet her guests, and nodded at Sigrid just as she had at the others. Then, seeing that the maids were attending to everything, she drew Sigrid to one side.

'I am sorry that I tried to accuse you,' she said quietly. Sigrid felt her jaw drop, and shut her mouth quickly. 'I should not have. I don't believe you could have done such a thing, even with more reason.'

'Well ... I didn't, anyway,' said Sigrid.

'But I want to find out who did,' said Rannveig, her hand now on Sigrid's arm. Sigrid tried not to let the word 'claws' cross her mind. 'I need to find out what happened. Who hated her enough to do that?'

'She might not have been hated,' said Sigrid. 'She might just have been in someone's way.'

Rannveig, who had been about to go on, stopped and looked closely at her. There was a lamp almost overhead, casting odd shadows straight down Rannveig's face, making her nose and brows and cheekbones into a mountain range. It was hard to see her eyes.

'You have always been very clever about this kind of thing, haven't you?' she said.

'Um,' said Sigrid. She and Rannveig had not always seen eye to eye on such matters.

'No, you have. I might not have made it clear, but I admire that skill in you. You're a clever woman: we need to value each other.'

Rannveig thought she was clever? That was quite a compliment! Sigrid had no doubts whatsoever about Rannveig's cleverness, and to think that Rannveig might consider Sigrid even remotely as intelligent was very pleasant to hear. Very pleasant indeed. Sigrid tried to make her face look as if all kinds of wise thoughts were running through her mind. Then she thought of the shadows the lamp was throwing, and realised she probably just looked as if she had toothache.

'No doubt you already have some ideas about what happened my Thordis,' Rannveig was saying. 'They say you were away in Kirkuvagr, my old home – did you discover anything there?'

'That Thordis and Varin were betrothed, that was the main thing,' said Sigrid, remembering to be careful not to give too much away. At least this was something Rannveig would already know –

'Varin? Betrothed?'

Apparently not.

'How did she not tell me that?'

'It was purely a business arrangement, I think,' said Sigrid hurriedly. Rannveig would be hurt that her daughter had not told her something of that importance, of course.

'Well, of course it was,' Rannveig snapped. 'What else could it be? Though why my late husband's brother could not find a better match for his own niece I fail to understand. I give him the benefit of a rich bargaining piece, and he throws it away on Varin? Words fail me.' And for a moment, it appeared, they did. Rannveig stood, fists on her hips, glaring into the darkness behind Sigrid's head. It was a little unnerving.

'No wonder the little worm has been hanging around,' Rannveig muttered eventually. 'Well, now I know. Helpful. Thank you, Sigrid.'

'Mm,' said Sigrid. She had no wish to go back to the subject of her Kirkuvagr visit, for she would have to admit to Rannveig, who thought she was intelligent, that they had not discovered much else. 'Had you other plans for Thordis?' she asked, more to distract Rannveig than anything.

'Plans for her? I have no power any more to arrange things like that,' said Rannveig.

'Ideas, perhaps,' Sigrid amended, sure that Rannveig was still perfectly capable of making people do what Rannveig wanted them to do, right down to marrying her daughter if that was what Rannveig required of them. Thordis had indeed been a rich bargaining piece, and it was a little surprising that Rannveig had given her away.

'Naturally I wanted to see her in a position of influence. For her own good. Marrying a man with a place in the world so that she could feel ... useful.'

Sigrid tried not to smile. Useful was one word for it.

'Bjorn, then?' she could not help asking. But Rannveig did not immediately deny it. Instead her lips twisted in uncertainty.

'You don't think this is my fault, do you?'

'You mean did Bjorn kill her?'

'Did he?'

'I'm not at all sure I could answer that.'

Rannveig gave her a hard look.

'You mean you don't know yet?'

'That's what I mean, yes.' Sigrid was not enjoying talking to Rannveig. Her throat felt stiff, wary of letting out words that Rannveig could, somehow, make use of.

'What about your friend Ketil? Does he know?'

'I'm sure if he knew, Thorfinn would be dealing with the matter,' said Sigrid definitely.

'Huh, Thorfinn! What does he know?' said Rannveig.

'Well ...' Sigrid thought Thorfinn was a sensible man, for the most part.

'That's why I'm glad you're taking an interest in the problem,' said Rannveig. 'You can tell me what you find out. I want to know what happened to her – and whether or not Bjorn had something to do with it.'

'And if he had?' Sigrid knew the answer, but she had to ask.

'Then he will be punished,' said Rannveig, and turned back to her guests. Sigrid, for now, had been dismissed.

The night passed as such nights usually did. There was a little subdued conversation, some prayer – Father Tosti had arrived at dusk from the Brough – and a good deal of discreet dozing. There had been little reminiscing about Thordis and her life. Hardly anyone there had known her well enough, and if Varin and Sigvat had memories of her childhood, they did not share them. Varin claimed the place at Thordis' head, with Rannveig at his side, oblivious to Rannveig's rather patronising expression. Sigvat sat by the fire, still bandaged, talking awkwardly with anyone who sat near him, and listening to the conversations of others. Bjorn, who stayed in the background, sobbed almost all night.

One of Bjorn's crew near the door was the first to notice dawn creeping across the headland outside, and yawned and stretched and pushed the door open. It was the sign for everyone to rouse themselves – Sigrid was pleased to escape a crush between Helga and Frogunn who had both been sound asleep for ages – and stretch their legs before the party was assembled for the burial.

Sigrid, shaking out her headcloth outside and wondering if her overdress was clean enough, was the first to spot the party approaching from the Brough. Thorfinn and some of his men, coming to pay their respects before the burial. She squinted, and saw that Ketil and Alf were amongst the company. She ran her fingers quickly through her mess of hair, and bundled it back into the headcloth before the wind could rearrange it again.

'Good morning, Sigrid,' said Thorfinn from a short distance. 'All well in there?' He tilted his head towards the longhouse.

'As well as is likely,' Sigrid confirmed.

'Ingibjorg has sent an invitation to Rannveig – I'll have to deliver it,' he said, his mouth curving down at the corners. 'She thinks we should hold the funeral feast at the Brough, since the burial's up there.'

He puffed his fringe off his face, his standard sign of annoyance, and plodded past Sigrid to the longhouse door. Sigrid turned back to Ketil.

'Where are your other two?' she asked, searching behind him for Geirod and Skorri.

'Guarding the sow. Skorri was knocked out by the Westray man coming back for her.'

'Really?' Sigrid laughed, but there was something more in Ketil's face. 'What's wrong? Is Skorri badly injured?'

'It's not that,' said Ketil. 'I have had some ill news.'

At his gesture they moved away from the rest of the party. Sigrid glanced back at Alf: his long face was full of – was that sympathy?

'What on earth is it?' she asked.

'Heithabyr,' said Ketil. 'it's destroyed.'

'All of it?' Sigrid asked idiotically. Then, 'Oh, Ketil – your brother! Njal – is he all right?'

'From what I've heard,' he said, careful as ever, 'he's alive.'

'Thank the Lord.'

'But his wife, and the boys, are – are dead. And the settlement was fired. His workshop will have gone – all his wood.'

'The whole town is wood ...'

'You'd have thought,' said Ketil, 'the place was so damp it would not have caught, wouldn't you?' They half-smiled at each other: it had always been a joke in Heithabyr, the damp, all that wet wood right by the water. Then his face tightened. 'But it seems that Harald sent in fire-ships.'

'Harald?' Sigrid blinked, and threw a look back at the longhouse. 'When did it happen?'

'In the height of the summer,' said Ketil, meeting her eye as she looked back at him.

'The summer ... when, presumably, Bjorn was out with King Harald.'

'That's right,' said Ketil, and his voice was surprisingly even. 'Harrying the Danish coast.'

'Including Heithabyr. Oh, Ketil.'

'I'll have to go and see for myself. See if my brother needs help.'

'Of course,' she said, but for some reason the idea made her stomach wrench. Just the idea of it, perhaps. The idea of seeing Heithabyr, destroyed. She had not loved the place, but still - all those memories. Her parents, and their friends and neighbours. And Njal, a good man, a skilled woodworker. She swallowed hard.

'Once we have this business sorted out. That's what Thorfinn says.'

'And what Thorfinn says ...' She tried to make the comment light, but her throat hurt. Suddenly Ketil reached out an arm, and pulled her into a hug. Taken by surprise, for a moment she let herself take comfort from his strength, felt her tears soaking into his shirt. Then she wiped her eyes firmly, and stepped back.

'Better get it sorted out, then,' she said.

The burial took place at the chapel on the Brough. Whatever way Thorfinn had put the invitation to Rannveig, she had agreed: the women followed the bier as far as Thorfinn's hall, where Ingibjorg greeted them graciously, with loud commiserations for Rannveig. The men carried on up to the chapel, while the women settled down with spiced wine to await their return. Ingibjorg took Rannveig to sit with her at the top of the hall, while Sigrid, Frogunn and Helga, with others from Buckquoy, found spaces down near the back, out of the way. It was pleasant to be waited on for a change: they might as well enjoy Ingibjorg's maids bringing them their cups before the men came back.

'Did you see poor Bjorn?' Helga asked when they were settled. 'So sad!'

Poor Bjorn, who had set fire to Heithabyr, Sigrid thought. It was hard to picture it.

'He certainly seemed to have fallen in love with Thordis,' said Frogunn.

'Would it really have helped him take the hall, though?' Helga asked. 'I mean, she was sort of connected with Einar – oh, she was almost Bjorn's sister!'

'Almost, but not,' said Sigrid. 'I don't know who Bjorn's mother was, but Thordis certainly had a look of her uncle Ljotr about her, her father's brother. It would have been all right.'

'A waste of a fine man, if you ask me,' said Helga. 'I hope he gets over his loss quickly. We can't have him moping about, or Varin will step in and take the hall.'

'Would that be so bad?' asked Frogunn after a moment.

Helga and Sigrid looked at each other.

'I suppose he might improve with age,' said Sigrid, 'but I don't much like him at the moment.'

'At least he's from the islands,' Helga conceded.

'And he's Einar's nephew,' added Frogunn.

'And he's handsome,' said Helga.

'And he knows it!' Sigrid objected. 'But if Sigvat stays to advise him he might be of some use. If the men accept him.'

'I'm sure they would, once they realise poor Foldar won't do it,' said Frogunn. 'They'd sooner accept him than Bjorn. Bjorn's a real outsider.'

'Even though he's Einar's son?'

'He's practically Norwegian,' said Frogunn, then blushed. 'Sorry, Sigrid, I'd forgotten where you come from.'

'And Ketil, too,' said Helga, making Frogunn flush even more.

'I'm sorry! You've been here most of my life, Sigrid – I'd completely forgotten! It's a kind of compliment, really,' she tried to recover. 'You seem so much like one of us.'

Sigrid winced, but tried to smile. If Varin was young, Frogunn was even younger. But she was a capable girl, strong and sensible – she would be fine.

'I suspect Thorfinn would get on better with Bjorn,' she said. 'Unless it was proved that Bjorn killed Thordis, of course.'

'Do you think he did?' asked Helga.

'He was out of the hall when she was killed,' said Sigrid,

deciding she might as well talk about it. 'So were others, of course, but he might have found her with another man, or thought she was going to betray him, or ... well, some reason like that.' But that argued a moment of madness, she suddenly realised. But if someone had gone to the trouble of sending Bjorn and Afi outside, assuming that was connected, then the murder might have been more planned than that.

'Varin was out of the hall, too,' said Helga, suddenly. 'I've just remembered. You know you and Ketil came up and you were wondering where Thordis was, and Ketil said that Bjorn and Varin had both gone outside.'

Sigrid blinked at her.

'You're right! Of course he did. Now, apparently someone went up to Bjorn with a message and sent him outside, looking concerned, but I don't know who it was – it was your father that saw him, Frogunn.'

'Oh, that's a pity,' said Frogunn. 'My father can barely recognise me if I'm further away than his fingertips. He's getting worse.'

'Yes, that's a shame.'

'But why would Varin have killed her?' asked Frogunn, looking puzzled. 'I mean, if he was betrothed to her, surely he could just break it off if he didn't want to marry her?'

'Betrothed to her?' Helga echoed in surprise.

'Business arrangement,' Sigrid said. 'All the more reason to break it off and not be over-complicated about it. I wonder why he would, though? It was quite a useful arrangement.'

'Maybe he thought he had found a better option,' Frogunn suggested. 'Someone more useful to him.'

'That's possible,' Sigrid agreed. It seemed like exactly the kind of way Varin would think. But to kill Thordis just to get rid of her? That was messy, and required more effort than Sigrid would have thought Varin would bother making. Unless she had simply really annoyed him. Now that seemed much more likely.

Her gaze drifted along the hall as she sat, comfortably warmed by the wine. At the top Ingibjorg seemed to have run out of conversation and sat looking bored, while Rannveig kept her head down. Any minute now Ingibjorg would call for her twin boys to be brought so that she could show them off. The infants had just celebrated their first birthday and were independently mobile, and once they were in the hall they were very easy to trip over, or find their sticky fingers clinging to your skirts to haul themselves upright, or have to be dragged away from the fire. Ingibjorg thought they were angels brought to walk on the earth, and spoiled them horribly. No one else liked them very much.

What was Rannveig thinking, though? Was she mourning her daughter? Or regretting the loss of a piece to bargain with? Had she really not known of Thordis' betrothal? Had Thordis gone to flirt with Bjorn because her mother had suggested it, or had Thordis really felt attracted to him? Or did both mother and daughter share that love of power?

And why had Rannveig left her daughter with her brother-in-law, her marriage entirely in his gift?

XXI

Not long after that, the men who had attended the burial, just up the hill at the chapel, returned to the hall ready for food and drink. With a sigh, Frogunn and Helga went to help attend to them. For the moment, though, Sigrid caught Ketil's eye and they slipped back outside, taking the chance to catch up.

'How did the burial go?' Sigrid asked.

'Nothing out of the ordinary,' said Ketil. 'Tosti made the prayers, Thorfinn led the mourners, Varin appeared serious, Sigvat appeared sorrowful, and Bjorn wept.' His voice tightened on the last two words. Sigrid winced at the sound of Bjorn's name, and scowled. She had liked the man. Ketil had liked him. But to send fire ships into a wooden town, just to annoy King Sweyn ...

'He looked miserable,' Sigrid agreed. 'His men must be worried about him, you'd think.'

Ketil gave a sharp nod.

'I should speak with them – with the ones I know, anyway. The ones who raided with him.' He cleared his throat. 'Anything new just now?' The dusting of damp shimmered on his blue cloak and on his short-cropped blond hair. Sigrid leaned back against the wall of the hall, feeling the warmth of the wine and the fire creeping out of her. She shook her head.

'No, not really. I didn't talk except with Helga and Frogunn.'

'Foldar's sister?'

'Yes, she's a good lass. But nothing new from either of them, really.'

'So Afi and Bjorn were both outside,' Ketil said.

'Seems so. But I think we know where Afi was, whereas Bjorn was more vague.'

'Of course he was. And what possible reason could Afi have for killing Thordis?'

'Exactly. Rannveig, I'm sure, was inside.'

'Do you know about anyone else?'

'I've thought,' said Sigrid, 'but I'm really not sure. Helga remembered just now you noting that Varin was outside, just before I went out, too.'

Ketil nodded.

'I remembered that, too. But I'm fairly sure Sigvat was still inside. I noticed him trying to eat something that was not just broth, and that was just before Alf came to fetch me.'

Sigrid sighed.

'I'd love to know who told Afi to go outside, and was it the same person that sent Bjorn out?'

'If either person existed at all. It was Oddr who claimed to see the man speaking to Bjorn.'

'And Oddr's eyes are going,' she said. 'Frogunn confirmed that. She's his daughter, and she says he wouldn't recognise her an arm's length away.'

'Exactly.' Ketil stared past her for a moment. 'So assuming it happened at all, it could have been anybody. Even one of Bjorn's own men, told to do it to make it look as if someone had sent Bjorn a message.'

Sigrid tutted.

'They couldn't assume that everyone seeing them was as blind as Oddr,' she objected.

'Do you think the same person sent both of them outside? Bjorn and Afi?'

Sigrid thought about it.

'I'd say it's too much of a coincidence for it to be two different people, wouldn't you?'

He nodded.

'Then what was their purpose?'

'To cause confusion. Not just between Afi and Bjorn, but generally.'

'But the more people there were outside, the greater the chance of the murderer being seen, surely?'

'I'll tell you one thing, though,' said Sigrid, still trying to picture the whole sequence of events. 'If it was the murderer sending both men outside, then first, they were confident, and second, the whole thing was planned. No one was outside chatting to Thordis and then suddenly killed her on impulse.'

'I think you're right. But how does that help us?'

'It means,' said Sigrid, 'that we probably have fewer possible killers. It was someone who specifically needed Thordis out of the way, for a specific and strong reason. Now, if we knew why, it would help, but we don't. But we can assume, I think, that it has something to do with the hall, and who gets to take Einar's position.'

'Maybe ...' said Ketil, not quite so sure.

'It must be, surely.' She glanced around at the hall door: soon Ingibjorg would start ordering the food to be brought in, and she would have to go and help, and who knew where Ketil might have gone to by the time she was free again? 'Now, how would that work? She's betrothed to Varin, who is one of the competitors, and she's flirting with Bjorn, the other one.' She made a face. 'At least she has no connexion with Foldar.'

'That we know of,' Ketil put in.

'Bjorn appears to have fallen for her. For Varin she is just a business associate.'

'What about Sigvat?'

'Hm. We don't know if Sigvat cared for Thordis as much as Thordis cared for Sigvat, do we?'

'He hasn't shown much sign of grief. But then we also don't know definitely that Thordis cared for Sigvat,' Ketil reminded her. 'Only one person has told us that. And anyway, perhaps she fell for Bjorn as heavily as Bjorn has fallen for her?'

'What if Bjorn discovered she was in love with Sigvat? Or that she was betrothed to Varin?'

'That she had betrayed him, you mean? She was deceiving him?'

'Would that work?' She was suddenly unsure.

'Do you mean would that be reason enough for Bjorn to kill her?'

'Yes.'

'I have no idea. I thought I knew what kind of man Bjorn was, and now I'm not sure. Would it be reason enough for Varin to kill her?'

'I don't think so,' said Sigrid reluctantly. 'If it is just a business arrangement, and he feels she's let him down, he can just call off the betrothal. Why kill her?'

Ketil sighed, and stepped back to glance into the hall.

'Look, they're getting ready to say grace,' he said. 'We'll have to go. Let's –' she could see he was gritting his teeth – 'let's try talking to Bjorn afterwards, before he goes back to Buckquoy. He'll be on less familiar territory here: it might make him uneasy enough to talk to us more openly.'

'We'd better hope so,' said Sigrid, rolling up her sleeves ready to work. 'We can hardly make him talk by force. He could probably use your sword to clean under his fingernails.'

The meal seemed to pass painfully slowly. Ketil envied Sigrid, keeping herself busy running about with plates and jugs, and tried to concentrate on watching Bjorn, and Varin, and Sigvat, and Rannveig, and to try to work out if he could who might have benefited from having Thordis out of the way. Sigrid was right – if they only knew why, it would surely lead them to who. But they did not know why.

Thorfinn sat in his high seat with Ingibjorg beside him, graciously bestowing her hospitality on all. In fact, Ingibjorg seemed to be the only person enjoying herself: Thorfinn had his chin on his hand and a look of thunder on his face worthy of Thor himself. Ketil couldn't blame him. Replacing Einar should have been a fairly straightforward business, but the decision was far from obvious yet.

And even Ingibjorg, when her gaze occasionally fell on Rannveig next to her, seemed less than satisfied. Rannveig was not responding to Ingibjorg's generosity, and in fact had half-turned away, head low, apparently lost in misery. Yet Ketil could not shake the impression that she was instead watching the others in the hall – calculating something, planning something. Rannveig was always planning something. But what? Now that she had lost Thordis, was she being forced to redraw her battle lines?

Ketil had managed to find a seat near to Atli and Egil, the two men from Bjorn's crew he had spoken with before. Had they been there, at Heithabyr? He had to put that aside for now, persuade them to talk to him. He could not start by accusing them of destroying Danish towns. But since they had just come from Thordis' burial, it was not hard to start a conversation about her.

'Aye,' Atli nodded solemnly, 'he's cast down, right enough. I never saw him so smitten.'

'So this isn't a common thing with him? You know the way

some young people –'

'Bjorn's not like that,' said Atli. 'Whatever it was about her, it's hit him hard. I'm not saying I liked her much myself,' he went on carefully.

'No,' said Egil, in between mouthfuls, 'not at all.'

'But if she made Bjorn happy, that was the important thing. That and not interfering with him leading us, of course.'

'Of course.' Ketil considered. 'And now it might affect his leadership, mightn't it? If it makes him want to go home again, leave Buckquoy?'

Atli scowled.

'Who wants to settle down? I mean, it's fine here, but there's not that much for a fighting man to do, is there?'

Ketil thought he himself was busy enough, but he shrugged.

'Do you think he'll come to himself again, anyway?'

Egil set down his knife, and wiped his mouth with the back of his hand.

'He'd better,' he said, with finality.

'And that's a fact,' added Atli.

After a little longer Ketil left them, swinging his long legs out over the bench. He had diverted the conversation to reminiscences of raiding on the Danish coast, and while Atli and Egil had apparently enjoyed their anecdotes he knew he was waiting to hear of their attack on a wooden market town, on their fire ships and destruction. It was hard to concentrate on the death of Thordis and the appointment at Buckquoy with the fate of Njal and Heithabyr in his head, but he had to finish here, somehow, before he could leave.

He moved into the shadows at the sides of the hall, lost in wandering thoughts. Sigrid, he noticed, was taking a break on the other side of the hall, standing with a jug on her hip, talking with Helga but watching the guests. They were not far from Bjorn, slumped over the table, head in his hand, playing with a piece of flatbread and staring at the fire. As Ketil watched, a slim figure slipped along towards him and on to the bench beside him, touching his arm. It was Rannveig.

Ketil watched, curious. Rannveig's touch was easy, friendly – almost familiar.

His mind went back to what had happened the night of Thordis' death. Someone had sent Afi out of the hall, and had then been seen talking to Bjorn before he, too, went outside. And then Rannveig herself had been seen clearly staying in the hall, while outside someone strangled her daughter. Wasn't that exactly something Rannveig would do?

So why would Rannveig want her daughter dead?

'Look at that,' said a disgusted voice just in front of him. Ketil glanced down, and saw that he was standing behind Varin. Next to him was his brother Sigvat, battling his way through a bowl of broth. Even from behind you could see how his jaw was still swollen. 'Bjorn getting sympathy with a few tears. It's pathetic.'

'You're just jealous you didn't think of it,' said Sigvat indistinctly. He scraped the last spoonful from the bowl and carefully dribbled it into his mouth, and peered more carefully across the central fire at Rannveig and Bjorn. 'And I don't think that's just sympathy, do you?'

'What do you mean?'

Sigvat sat back and glanced around. Ketil, imperceptibly shifting back into the shadows, was almost invisible.

'Rannveig's not an old woman,' Sigvat murmured. 'What if a little chat about their shared loss turns into ... well, something more?'

'What?' Varin looked disgusted. 'Her?'

'It wouldn't be the first time an older woman has married a younger man, would it? And she's had a few years with our weakly uncle – she'll want a bit of excitement, won't she? And even if it's not that –'

'Oh, but that would be great!' said Varin, delight on his face. 'The two of them get married and he takes her back off to Trondheim, and I'm rid of both of them!'

Sigvat sighed heavily.

'Even if it's not that,' he repeated slowly, as if to the dangerously stupid, 'the two of them together would be a powerful force. Einar's son and Einar's widow – taking over Einar's hall?'

'Oh,' said Varin after a moment. 'Yes, I see. That wouldn't be so good.'

'No, it wouldn't,' Sigvat agreed. 'In fact, I'd say it was something that needed to be stopped. Wouldn't you agree?'

'Oh, yes!' Varin was pleased at that. 'But how ...?'

'Shh, not here,' said Sigvat, with another quick glance around. 'Later.'

'Oh, yes!' said Varin again eagerly. 'Yes! We'll talk later.'

Sigvat nodded slightly, then turned away from his brother. Perhaps only Ketil saw the look on his face – the look of patience just about to be lost.

'Did you see Rannveig and Bjorn?' Sigrid caught his arm with her free hand as he continued around the hall. They were in a quiet corner, beside one of the great barrels of water.

'Yes – I think we need to talk to him,' said Ketil. 'What if he killed Thordis because of something Rannveig told him? What if it was Rannveig's plot to get rid of her daughter from the start?'

'Rannveig's plot? The two words go together well,' she agreed, 'but why would she want her daughter dead?'

'Maybe Bjorn can tell us,' said Ketil. 'I suppose you'll all be going back to Buckquoy soon – let's try to catch him outside and talk to him.'

'He was definitely outside, and even if she didn't tell him to kill her, or trick him into it, he's still a possible murderer,' said Sigrid. 'You're right, we need to talk to him.'

'Any more of that wine?' called a man nearby. Sigrid sighed, hefted her jug, and went to attend to business. Ketil, moving slowly, continued around the hall. Rannveig was still talking to Bjorn, and he did not look as if he was going anywhere just yet. He had turned to face Rannveig, whose hand still lay on his arm.

'What's she up to?' Thorfinn asked when Ketil reached him. He had no need to name Rannveig.

'Not sure yet,' said Ketil. 'I'm keeping an eye on it.'

'She's always been trouble,' Thorfinn grumbled. 'I wish Einar had banished her.'

'Maybe better to have her where you can see her, my lord,' Ketil suggested. Thorfinn scowled.

'I don't like to feel I'm being manipulated,' he said. 'Whoever I choose for Buckquoy, I'll be wondering if I only did it because she somehow made me – and if she didn't, does she approve or will whoever it is be brought down within the year?' He shivered. 'I don't trust her,' he added unnecessarily.

When the meal drifted to a close, Ketil returned to the back of the hall, trying to find a good moment to corner Bjorn. But the Bear, swathed in his bearskin cloak, was on his feet and heading for the hall door before he had a chance to catch him. Sigrid hastily set down her jug and joined him, following Bjorn outside.

The moon was high, milk-white, oblivious. Ketil wondered what it had been like the night Heithabyr was fired, if it had lit the scene as Bjorn – could it have been Bjorn? – sent the flaming ships into Heithabyr's vulnerable harbour. Had he laughed? Had his men applauded him?

Bjorn seemed to sense that there were people behind him, and shifted off to the side, then took the path that went to the back of the hall, through the settlement, past the chapel, and out on to the open ground beyond. Sigrid and Ketil followed him discreetly all the way. At last Bjorn turned around.

'I'm sorry, did you need me? Only I wanted to find somewhere to be alone for a while.'

His eyes glinted moist – little wonder, for he seemed to have been weeping for the past night and day. More to Ketil's surprise, he was slurring his words. He must have decided to drown his grief.

'We just wanted a few words, and then we can leave you,' said Ketil. He noticed Bjorn looking oddly at Sigrid, perhaps wondering why she was there. He ignored that.

'A few words? Well ... go on, then.'

'About the night that Thordis died,' said Ketil. 'I heard that after she left the hall, you also went outside.'

'Me?' He considered. 'I was looking for my best fur – I couldn't find it at all. Funny, it turned up again later.'

'But did you go outside?' Ketil chose not to mention the messenger, if there had been one. He would see what Bjorn told them himself.

'I don't think I left the hall when she was outside,' said Bjorn.

'Someone saw you go.'

'What are you saying?' asked Bjorn, and his moist eyes seemed to harden. Ketil felt himself tensing.

'That someone saw you go outside when Thordis was outside – that you came back in, and that Thordis was then found dead. At the very least –'

He was going to suggest that Bjorn might at least have seen something useful, but Bjorn was too quick to hear.

'You're saying I killed her?'

'Did you?' Ketil asked, then held his breath. Sigrid was right: if Bjorn turned angry, Ketil had a slim chance of overpowering him. And Sigrid would have to run fast.

'How can you ask that?' Bjorn's voice was low, but ominous. 'How could you accuse me? The Varin thing, that was just stupid. I didn't mean to strike him, but if I had he would have deserved it. And of course I've killed people in battle – that's what you do, isn't it?'

And in Heithabyr? Ketil thought to himself. But now was not the time to mention that. He had to be calm.

'But a woman ... maybe, sometimes, by chance. I've always regretted it. If I'd killed,' he swallowed hard, on the brink of naming her – 'Thordis, if I'd killed Thordis by accident, you'd have found me by her body, willing her to live, you'd have had to drag me from her, you'd have had to stop me falling on my own sword to follow her. Believe me,' he turned burning eyes on Ketil, glinting in the moonlight. 'Believe me, I did not kill her, by accident or intent. Believe me.'

'Then who did it?' asked Ketil simply.

'I don't know!' Bjorn bellowed, and a cloud of screaming gulls lifted, alarmed, into the night. 'How can I know? All I know is she is gone, and all my good fortune with her!'

And he seized the bear's tooth amulet that still hung at his throat, broke the thong that held it, and flung it far into the darkness. Then he sank to his knees, and howled.

Ketil felt a hand on his elbow. It was Sigrid.

'I don't think we're going to get any more out of him tonight,' she murmured, almost inaudible against Bjorn's lament.

'I'm not sure it's safe to leave him.'

'What's he going to do? If he tries to kill himself, even between us we wouldn't have a chance of stopping him. If he throws himself off the cliff he'd drag us over with him. He can't go anywhere else.'

Ketil looked back at Bjorn. Sobs wracked the great man as he cried Thordis' name to the moon. Ketil shivered, and cleared his throat.

'A man that size won't take much harm from one night in the open at this time of year, wrapped up like that, too,' he acknowledged. 'And you're right, he can't leave the Brough unless he goes over the cliff.'

'Or knocks out both guards at once,' Sigrid added, 'but I don't think he's likely to try, do you? I think we should just leave him alone, and see what state he's in by daylight.'

'Well ... All right, then,' said Ketil. He was not sure how concerned he really was for the Bear's safety, when it came down to it. She was right: there was nothing much more they could do with him tonight.

Next morning they rose earlier than most of the previous night's guests. Sigrid wanted to see what a sober Bjorn might say, and Ketil seemed anxious to make some progress with the business. They left the hall together, blinking at the sharp morning light, and turned the corner to pass back through the settlement, assuming that Bjorn would be very much where they had left him.

'Unless he has gone over the cliff,' Sigrid could not help saying out loud.

'We'd have heard the splash.'

Sigrid smiled.

'But your question was a good one – and we still might need to ask it. If Bjorn did not kill Thordis, then who did?'

'You want it to be Varin.'

'I'd like him to be brought down a bit for something. It doesn't have to be murder,' she allowed generously.

'There he is – he hasn't gone over,' said Ketil, pointing ahead. 'I think he's asleep.'

'Face down like that, without his cloak wrapped round him?'

'He was drunk.'

'True ...' There was something not quite right, though. A dark stain on the grass around Bjorn's tousled head.

'Oh, no,' said Ketil, and approached the prostrate man carefully, walking, first, right round to his head, which was pointing away from them. Sigrid followed, and crouched down to see Bjorn's face more clearly. Ketil stepped in, and heaved on Bjorn's shoulder to try to tip him back.

'Oh, no,' Sigrid echoed. 'He's cut his throat instead.'

'No,' said Ketil. 'Instead, someone's cut his throat for him.'

XXII

Thorfinn himself, along with a selection of his hird, had followed Sigrid back up through the settlement to the broad hillside of the Brough. It was easy to see where they were to go: the mound of Bjorn's mighty body, with tall Ketil standing respectfully beside it, would have been hard to miss.

Thorfinn's expression, though, was difficult to read, as he marched solidly up the gentle hill. Sigrid trotted along beside him, trying to match his pace and watch him at the same time. Was he shocked? Angry? Relieved? Just annoyed? No doubt he was going to have to explain this to King Harald Hardrada, and Thorfinn did not like to be accountable to the King of Norway in any way. So yes, annoyed, certainly. But as for the rest, Sigrid could not make it out.

As they reached Ketil, Thorfinn drew a heavy sigh.

'So what happened?' he asked.

Sigrid scowled. She had already told him.

'We left him here around midnight,' said Ketil. 'He was drunk, and upset, and I could get no sense out of him. We wanted to question him about Thordis' death, because we had found that he was out of the hall when she died.'

There was a slight stir in Thorfinn's followers behind Sigrid at this news. Thorfinn's followers ... she turned to see exactly who had come with them. Yes, one or two of Thorfinn's men, obeying orders. Alf, coming to help Ketil. A couple of Bjorn's own men, their faces white with shock. Hrolf, of course – he had to be anywhere that something was happening – but not Oddr, whose feet could betray him in the mornings and had to be worked on. Foldar, possibly on Oddr's behalf – no doubt Oddr had sent him, for Sigrid doubted he had the initiative to head out on his own – and Varin and Sigvat. Varin was looking rather pleased with himself. Sigvat had the sense to look both saddened (whether that was genuine or not) and a little worried. Very reasonable, Sigrid thought: with Bjorn out of the way and Foldar so ineffectual, Varin must have thought his appointment to Buckquoy was certain. Sigvat was wise enough to see that that would make him the chief suspect.

'His throat slit from side to side,' Ketil was saying, the wind catching his voice. 'He was cold: it probably happened not long after we left him.'

'Could he have done it himself?' Thorfinn asked. 'Sigrid told me he was self-destructive.'

'We did think he might harm himself,' Ketil agreed. 'But no: his knife is over there, pushed into the turf. I don't know if it was deliberate, but someone has made it quite obvious that it was murder, not self-killing.'

'Could he have pushed it into the ground himself, and staggered on to here?'

'The blood says differently,' said Ketil, knowing his battle scenes. 'It's all around him here, where it would have been if it had sprayed out at once and he had fallen forward into it.'

Thorfinn nodded. Sigrid was impressed. It made sense.

'And it's definitely his knife?'

'It has his sign on it, the bear's head.'

'Should we be looking for someone with a lot of blood on them?' Hrolf piped up, wanting to show that he was a thinking man.

'I don't think so,' said Ketil, over his shoulder. 'If Bjorn was struck from behind, his own body would have shielded his killer. And I believe he probably was struck from behind, with the advantage of surprise, because – well, who could have done this otherwise?'

'If he had seen them coming he could just have swatted them away like a clegg,' Sigrid agreed. Most of the men nodded, Foldar in particular. 'This way even a smaller man could have done it, couldn't they?'

Thorfinn grunted agreement, surveying the great body thoughtfully.

'Varin, where were you last night?' he asked.

There was a good deal of shuffling amongst the men. Thorfinn's own men, and Bjorn's crew, subtly arranged themselves to prevent any hasty attempt to escape, with Bjorn's crew eyeing Varin in an unfriendly way. Hrolf and Foldar managed to shift further away, just in case.

'I was in your hall, my lord,' said Varin.

'All night?'

'I think I have witnesses to prove it!' said Varin, with great satisfaction. 'There was a very willing young woman who kept me company almost every minute!'

Sigrid blinked. Who on earth could that have been?

'You never left the hall?'

'Twice,' Varin conceded, 'but only for a moment or two each time. I was not going to leave such entertainment for long! I assure you: no one will say I had time to come all the way up here and do that.' He gestured with some disgust to Bjorn's body. One of Bjorn's men edged closer, not at all happy.

'Keep back, you there,' said Thorfinn. 'I'll have no more brawling. Justice will be done in the right way.'

The crewman shuffled a little away, clearly disappointed. Thorfinn turned back to the body.

Sigrid's mind ticked over the various women who had been in the hall last night. Not Helga, surely? Please, not Helga. But even Helga, even had she not disliked Varin anyway, would not have been so indiscreet as to keep another man company while her husband Hrolf was in the same hall, and Sigrid herself had been working alongside Helga and Frogunn for most of the evening.

'We'll have to bring a bier up here to shift him – six men, do you think?' Thorfinn asked Ketil.

'Maybe eight,' said Ketil. 'Depends on the men.'

'We'll do it, my lord,' said the crew man who had been told off by Thorfinn. 'We'll look after him. He was our man.'

'Bring him to my hall,' said Thorfinn. 'He may lie there until the burial, if that is your wish.'

The two crew men looked at each other, and one nodded. The other said,

'Thank you for the honour, my lord, but we think he should rest in his father's hall. Even though,' he conceded, eyeing the corpse in a more calculating way, 'it will be further to carry him, there and back.'

'That's up to you,' said Thorfinn, 'but of course you must do what you feel is right. Here is the priest: he will see to all that needs to be done.'

Father Tosti was hurrying up the hill, having been off saying his prayers when Sigrid had gone to the hall.

'Oh, that's dreadful,' he said at once, and went to crouch by the body. 'Dreadful. Poor man.' He began to pray, and most of the men bowed their heads.

Sigrid found it hard to concentrate on the familiar words. Ketil said Bjorn had been killed – by the same person who had killed Thordis? It seemed more than likely. So who had wanted them both dead? Varin certainly seemed most likely to want Bjorn out of the way. The Buckquoy hird might not have wanted him as their leader, but they could never have worked up the energy between them to kill him – besides, she would have thought that of the two they would rather have had Bjorn than Varin. Sigvat? What had he been up to while Varin was being entertained by some woman in Thorfinn's hall (who could it have been?)? Was Sigvat capable of killing Bjorn, even with the advantage of surprise, with his broken jaw and sore head? She could see how misshapen his jaw still was, how uneasily he moved. Her mind was galloping. Who had killed them? Who had wanted them both dead?

'Could Bjorn have known something about Thordis' death, and the killer stopped him from talking?' she asked Ketil later. They had waited on the damp, windy hillside until Bjorn's crew men had returned with their comrades, and with Afi, who had brought the bier and was attempting some anxious reinforcements with rope and bits of driftwood. It had taken three men to roll Bjorn on to the bier – corpses were rarely co-operative but everything here conspired against them, even the angle of the hillside at that particular point, and the new height of the bier's edges now that it had been strengthened. They arranged Bjorn's bear fur cloak over him delicately, closed his eyes, and covered as best they could the gash in his throat, and one man, tears running down his weatherbeaten face, brushed the mud from Bjorn's huge boots before they moved him any further.

Afi insisted on taking a corner of the bier at the back, so that he could watch the structure close to, which made it tricky for the other crew men to balance his height. Between them, though, they lifted the wooden frame with its terrible load, four of them each side, and began a slow, careful procession down the hill towards the settlement and the landbridge that would take Bjorn back to his father's hall at Buckquoy. Ketil noticed Sigrid wipe her eyes despite herself.

'If Bjorn had known anything, he would have said,' Ketil decided.

'What if it was something he hadn't realised he knew?'

'What could that be?' They were still on the hillside, not quite ready to return to the settlement yet.

'I don't know. I can't see his amulet, can you?'

'No. But I'll take the knife.' Ketil drew the bear-headed knife from the turf, and wrapped it in a cloth before tucking it into his belt beside his own knife. The blade was bloody at the top, but most of it had been wiped clean by the earth – a good, strong, long blade, made to do damage efficiently and well. Ketil wondered which of Bjorn's men would want it as a keepsake – difficult to say, when it had belonged to a beloved leader but had also been used to kill him. 'Come on, let's walk up to the headland.'

They had stood there before together, staring out to sea, sharing their thoughts on a problem. Ketil found it easier to think when he could see the horizon and the constant waves, if he could not actually be on the water itself. The wind whipped at his cloak and Sigrid's shawl and skirts. No one could overhear them here without them knowing, too. Sigrid peered over at the toothed rocks below.

'I did think we might find him there,' she said sadly. 'And I know it would have been a sin, but in a way it would have been less upsetting.'

'Did you like him? Do you think he might have settled in here?'

She pursed her lips.

'Better than Varin, I think. He was a bit ... You looked at him and thought oh, a great strong man! They'll follow him!' And clearly his men do – they seem devoted to him. But he was quite ... look at him, so upset about Thordis, whom he barely knew.'

'Was he as smitten by her as everyone says? As he said?'

'He really did seem to be. I'd have been surprised if he had told me he was only doing it to annoy Varin, for example. Very surprised. The way he looked at her ...' Her voice died away, and she shivered. 'Almost too much. Almost.'

'So could he have killed her?'

'I thought the same person killed both of them.'

'But could he have?' he persisted. Sigrid frowned.

'I do think he could. We thought so last night, didn't we?'

'In which case, his own death could be revenge, couldn't it?' Sigrid's frown deepened.

'But that takes us back to Varin, who had everything to gain then from Bjorn's death.'

'Who was he with?' Ketil had not noticed Varin's amatory adventure.

'I didn't see.' She shifted, perhaps warming her feet. 'Isn't that odd, though?'

'What?'

'That neither of us saw? We're both quite observant,' she said, and Ketil admired her generosity, 'and no doubt Varin himself was quite pleased with himself, finding a compliant girl – who on earth? – and right in front of Bjorn in his misery. Don't you think he would have wanted to make sure we all saw how successful he was being?'

Ketil glanced at her, then stared out across the waves, picturing the scene. Yes: Varin would have wanted everyone to know.

'You're right. I think we need to find out who she was, then.'

'And if she does exist – outside Varin's imagination – and she can tell us that he was definitely there all evening, where does that leave us?'

'Stuck, for now,' said Ketil, and turned to make his way back down the hill to the settlement.

'Gnup is going to hate me,' said Sigrid obscurely, and followed him.

Back at Thorfinn's hall, most of the men had disappeared for the day to the infields. Einar's hird and Bjorn's crew had all followed Bjorn's body back to Buckquoy, according to one of Ingibjorg's maids, Bolla. Helga and Frogunn, on whom Sigrid had been relying for a bit of gossip, had presumably gone with them.

'What about Varin and Sigvat?' Sigrid asked. Bolla made a face.

'Those two! Swaggering off after the Bear's bier as if they'd saved the day. They're off back to Buckquoy, too, as far as I know.'

'So you wouldn't be giving the hall at Buckquoy to either of them, then?' Sigrid settled with a grin beside Bolla's basket of wool, and lifted out a clump to start carding. The worst of the clart had already been picked off it, or else she had found it on a very clean branch. Ketil, Sigrid noticed, propped himself against one of the hall's pillars, arms folded, and seemed to disappear.

'Them?' Bolla sneered. 'I wouldn't miss them if they went off back to Deerness this very day.'

Sigrid paused, carding carefully, wanting to put the next question gently.

'Have they been difficult, at all? While they were guests here last night, for instance?'

Bolla's shoulders stiffened a little. She had had a bad experience only last year, a guest who had taken more than he was entitled to. For a long time Bolla had found it hard even to speak, or to eat. She looked much better now, but her eyes, Sigrid noticed, were still tense.

'No, not that I know of,' she said. For a moment there was little sound but the steady, rasping purr of the carding, the tick of the low fire, the gulls crying beyond the open hall doors, the wind and the sea a constant background, barely noticed. 'Groa might be able to tell you more,' Bolla went on at last, as if she had had trouble saying the words.

'Is she about?' asked Sigrid lightly.

'She's sorting apples in the store.'

'I'll maybe go and see her, when this is done. No sense in leaving it half-carded, is there?'

'Did I tell you I made fine hose at the back end of the summer?' asked Bolla. 'Thanks to you – I don't think I'd have had the patience otherwise. But look!' She drew up her skirts and showed Sigrid a very neat pair of hose in a soft brown that must have taken some blending from the right fleeces. They fitted beautifully.

'Oh, aren't they lovely?' Sigrid said sincerely, and talk fell to wool and nailbinding, until she had made two or three soft rollags of wool, ready to be spun.

'I'd better go and catch Groa,' Sigrid said. 'Before she goes off to something else.'

'She's an ambitious one, Groa,' said Bolla, taking the rollags from Sigrid. 'Don't assume she likes people, just because she gets on with them.'

'Thank you – I'll remember that.'

Sigrid felt Ketil catch up with her as she left the hall.

'What was that supposed to mean?' Ketil asked quietly.

'I'm not sure,' said Sigrid. 'Thank you for waiting, and not asking questions: Bolla's still not quite herself.'

'Yes, I'd realised that. But much better than when I last saw her.'

'Oh, yes.' For the second time that morning, Sigrid was impressed. Some men would not have taken such a thing into consideration at all. Ketil was a patient man.

The store round the back of the hall was rich with the scent of apples, though they could see that other vegetables were vying for space. It was a wonderful time of the year for food, even if you had very small fields, Sigrid thought, remembering how hard Gnup was likely to be working. Sacks of neeps vied for space on the flag floor alongside barrels of salt fish, and cheeses were stacked on stone shelves. Groa was on her knees picking through a basket of apples, selecting the ones that would have to be used quickly. She looked up in surprise when Sigrid said her name.

'Oh! I thought you'd gone home with all the Buckquoy crowd,' she said. 'Did you forget something?'

Sigrid looked at her. Despite her menial task, Groa's hair was elaborately arranged and the beads that crossed from shoulder to shoulder were – well, if not costly, at least fancy. The top hem of her dress was finished with a colourful piece of braid. Sigrid thought quickly.

'No, I didn't, but there's someone here who would like to talk to you. You remember Ketil? Thorfinn's second in command?'

'I'm not –' Ketil objected, then broke off as Sigrid trod on the arch of his foot. 'I'm not unwilling to talk with the girl,' he finished loudly, coming into the store properly. Sigrid felt his elbow poke her sharply in the ribs, but at least he understood what was required. And Groa was already on her feet, and rewarding Ketil's arrival with a very winning smile.

'Oh, yes,' she said, 'of course, sir!'

Ketil cleared his throat, and to her surprise Sigrid noticed that he smiled back. Not broadly, but enough, it seemed. Groa emitted what could only be called a giggle. Sigrid suddenly felt unnecessary, and stumbled back outside.

Of course she did not go far: she propped herself against the wall outside, despite the misty rain, and waited, trying to hear what was going on. Groa's voice was low, and Ketil was facing away from Sigrid. They were both hard to make out, but Sigrid could catch the occasional phrase.

'... sympathy, you know? After he'd lost his friend, that – that woman Thordis ...' Even though Groa was trying to be charming, it was clear she shared the common opinion of Thordis.

'... he treated you well? Because if he didn't ...'

'... very well indeed, until ... Servant? I mean to say ... Just walked away, and then ...'

'... That's a terrible way to behave. It sounds as if you're much better off ...' Ketil's voice faded still further, and Sigrid, straining to hear, was almost sure she could hear another, soft, giggle. She spun back to the doorway.

'Groa! I think Ingibjorg is calling you!'

Ketil almost backed into Sigrid, and Groa, with a backward smile for him and a curt nod for Sigrid, hurried past them and off to Thorfinn's longhouse. It did not do to keep Ingibjorg waiting – if she was there at all.

'Well?' Sigrid demanded, at the same time trying to hurry Ketil away back towards the hall. She had no wish to be at the store when Groa came back. Ketil followed her more slowly.

'Yes, she was with Varin. She says she was sorry for him, and that Father Tosti was talking to him but Varin was clearly bored, so she made him a better offer. But Varin made it clear this morning before he left her that she was only a servant, that he intended to do better and that she was of no further interest to him.'

'Bolla did say she was ambitious. You need to watch yourself!'

'Yes,' said Ketil, walking beside her now as they headed, by unspoken agreement, back to the landbridge to Buckquoy. 'Though perhaps more now since you threw me to her.'

Sigrid blushed, angry at herself.

'You're right. I shouldn't have. I'm sorry.'

She was walking into the rain, and did not notice him stop to stare at her in surprise.

XXIII

'I'm in a tangle here,' said Sigrid, 'and I'm happy to admit it.'

Ketil nodded. The wind caught at his cloak: it seemed to be rising. He could hear the sea before he saw it.

'Who wanted to kill Thordis and Bjorn?' he asked. 'The obvious answer is Varin –'

'Well, for Bjorn, anyway,' Sigrid put in.

'But that's the one he can't have killed.'

'Assuming Groa is telling the truth, and I think she was – but you were closer. What did you think?'

'I agree,' said Ketil.

'But Varin could have killed Thordis. But why would he do that?'

'Jealousy?'

Sigrid stamped along for a few paces before answering, as if she could beat the solution out under her feet.

'I suppose so.' She did not sound convinced. Ketil was not surprised.

He wondered how much longer this was going to take. Part of him was itching to be away, to go to Heithabyr and find out what had happened to his brother Njal. But even if Thorfinn had not required it, the other half of him wanted to get this sorted out. He did not like to think of Einar's old place in disruption and dispute, for the sake of Einar's memory and for Thorfinn's security. If there was also in the back of his mind a crumb of genuine concern for what might happen on these islands if there was any instability here – what might happen to the residents of Buckquoy, for example – he chose not to think about it.

'And what was Rannveig up to last night?' Sigrid was asking, though he assumed she was not really expecting a proper answer. 'Was she making moves towards an alliance with Bjorn? If so, does that mean she could not have killed him?'

'Could Rannveig physically have killed someone like Bjorn?' Ketil asked reasonably.

'He was attacked from behind, wasn't he? The element of surprise?' Sigrid considered. 'But could she have reached?'

'She could if he had been kneeling down,' said Ketil.

'As he was when we left him, true ... But why would she have done it? Surely what Rannveig wants is a return of her old power and influence. She's not interested in Varin – who would be? – but there's a chance that she could marry Bjorn, and once again be the woman in charge in Buckquoy. She might even bear him a child – she's not that old. Why would she kill him?'

'Revenge?' Ketil suggested. Sigrid stopped – they were nearing Einar's hall.

'Revenge ... for Thordis? Did she think Bjorn had killed Thordis?'

'He could have.'

They stood and looked at each other, reflecting each other's confusion. Sigrid's arms were folded close about her under the loose wings of her back cloak. She looked cold, and worried.

'We should get inside,' he said.

'Did Rannveig actually benefit from her own daughter's death?' she asked. 'It's possible, of course. If there was anything Thordis had from her father, that would come to Rannveig now. But I definitely can't see us going up to Rannveig and saying "Saw you flirting with Bjorn there last night – any chance you persuaded him to go outside the hall at Buckquoy and murder your daughter for you?" That doesn't seem likely to work.'

'Well, if we can't talk to Rannveig, then we need to talk to someone else,' he said, again trying to encourage Sigrid into the warm hall, out of the cold. She needed to go home, too, back to her farm and her work and her own longhouse, where she could be more content. She would never give up and go home while there were still questions to answer. He needed to finish this for her sake, too.

'We could talk to Sigvat, I suppose,' said Sigrid at last.

'When Rannveig was talking to Bjorn last night,' he said, 'Sigvat and Varin noticed. And were not pleased at the thought that Bjorn and Rannveig might edge Varin out.'

Sigrid's eyebrows rose almost to her headcloth.

'Of course they weren't,' she said, nodding. 'The question is, would they have done something to stop that happening?'

'Come on, then,' he said, 'let's get inside and make a start, before even more people start gathering for Bjorn's funeral.'

'Three funerals in only a few days,' said Sigrid, suddenly solemn. 'Rannveig might indeed feel unlucky – assuming she didn't cause the third one herself. Or,' she added thoughtfully, 'assuming she didn't cause more than one?'

And on that tantalising thought, she finally turned and went to the door of the hall.

Of course, it was a sombre place. Bjorn's body lay on a table in the middle of the hall, in state, much as his father had lain so few days ago. Sigrid still found it hard to connect the two men, but ifBjorn had tried to deceive in order to inherit Einar's place, it was no longer relevant.

And she had liked him, at least before they had found out about Heithabyr. It had been hard not to smile back at his cheerful grin, to feel friendship even though he had only been on the islands for the blink of an eye, and quite possibly had not even known that Sigrid existed. But she had felt that he might well have made a good leader, under Thorfinn's guidance. If it had not been for Heithabyr, she would have found him an easy man to follow. Who would they have now? Surely Thorfinn would have to look further afield. Varin would be impossible.

Bjorn's men were arranged mournfully down their side of the hall, and Einar's hird on the other side, as usual. She wondered how long it would have taken them to mix properly, but now, presumably, Bjorn's men would see to his burial, take his ship, and go home. It was a shame: they had certainly brought new life to the place.

Varin had taken a prime position amongst Einar's hird, of course, but she could see Sigvat nearer the back. There was no sign of Rannveig, which might give them the opportunity to talk more freely – except that it was so quiet, everyone would hear.

Sigrid and Ketil went, anyway, to pay their respects to Bjorn's huge body, and took a moment each to bow their heads in prayer. Sigrid stood for a moment, surveying the man properly for the last time. Rannveig's women had not finished their work and she could see clearly how the blood had marked his shirt at the neck and sleeves, where it had run when the initial bright spurt had subsided. The wound in his shoulder must have opened, too, and there was a blotch of blood there. It did seem that he had fallen forward after being attacked from behind, just as Ketil had worked out. And there – his knees were muddy, though whether he had been kneeling already, in his despair over Thordis, or whether he had sunk to his knees in death, it was hard to tell now.

If someone had crept up behind him – and in the wind over the Brough it could be easy enough to conceal your approach from someone whose mind was not entirely alert – if someone had crept up behind him and grabbed and slashed, in one quick movement, he would not have stood a chance, even with his size and strength. Sigrid could feel tears surge again in her eyes: such a waste. Surprising herself, she reached out and took Bjorn's nearer hand in hers for a moment, or at least laid her much smaller hand against it, rubbing her thumb over the cold flesh in farewell.

Then she paused.

'Ketil!' she murmured. 'Look!'

The back of Bjorn's great hand, under the sleeve of shirt and tunic, was scratched in long, deep lines. As if – Sigrid shivered – by the fingernails of someone trying very hard to fight against him.

Ketil saw at once what she meant, and moving at a reverent speed so as not to draw attention, he went to examine Bjorn's other hand, then returned quietly to Sigrid.

'Both,' he said.

Sigrid swallowed. Was this proof that Bjorn was Thordis' killer? She made herself examine the lines closely – bloodless, now, but deep. Would they have seen them before? Bjorn had injured one hand in the fight in the hall, but that had been a sprain, not a flesh wound, and left no mark now except a faint bruising around the wrist. Why had they not noticed? Who had bandaged him?

She glanced back at Ketil, and he nodded up to the top of the hall, where the side door would lead them out towards Rannveig's longhouse. Keeping to that solemn pace just as he had, she led the way past Varin's seat by Oddr, past the now vacant high seat, and off to where the food was kept, where she had heard Rannveig issue her orders to Thordis about keeping her options broad. It was a tight space, with Ketil there, too, but they hurried through now they were away from the mourners and found themselves outside again, between hall and longhouse.

'Thordis' killer?' Ketil said in a low voice.

'I don't know,' said Sigrid. 'There's been so much fighting going on – can we be sure?'

'No,' said Ketil, 'but it won't have come from the practice fights, anyway. Almost everyone wears gloves. As for the skirmish in the hall, who knows? Who bandaged his hand after that?'

'I was wondering that myself. I don't know.'

'We'll have to talk to her,' said Ketil.

'It won't do any good.'

'We can just ask her if she noticed the scratches. He's been laid out neatly enough, so she, or her women, must have been making a start, mustn't they?'

'I suppose ...' He was right. In all likelihood they had gone to get hot water and cloths to clean him down and prepare him for burial. She and Ketil had not been that far behind them, heading over from the Brough. She thought for a moment, half-aware of the clop of horses' hooves on the flags at the front of the hall, half-noting Ketil hear and turn to the sound. 'All right, then, come on. Let's see what she says. I suppose even if she tells us lies we might learn something.'

The horses must have stopped at the hall door: no one appeared round the corner. Sigrid led the way to the longhouse door, and tapped on the doorpost.

'Rannveig?'

They went inside. Rannveig and her women looked round to see who had arrived.

'Here to help?' asked Frogunn cheerfully. They were indeed shaking out cloths and finding the accoutrements for laying out a body – they must have been to hand, with both Thordis and Einar buried from this place so recently. In fact, Rannveig was now peering into a box as if she thought some particular ingredient was running low.

'I could,' said Sigrid, 'of course. I just wanted to ask

Rannveig something, when you have a moment, Rannveig.'

'Really?' said Rannveig, something imperious in her tone already that made Sigrid's knees shake. 'What's that, then?' Her look moved on to Ketil, standing silent by Sigrid's side. Sigrid was glad he was there. Rannveig folded her arms, pale fingers tapping briefly at her elbow. 'Oh, dear, is it something from Thorfinn?'

Ketil might not be intimidating Rannveig, but Frogunn and the other women seemed to sense some discomfort, gathered their equipment, and hurried out. Frogunn glanced back at Sigrid with a twisted smile and a raise of the eyebrows, as if to say she hoped whatever it was would go well. Sigrid made a face.

'Well?' said Rannveig, a little smile on her own lips. 'What is it? What would he like to find me guilty of this time?'

'I only wanted to ask, Rannveig,' said Sigrid, 'if you noticed Bjorn's hands when you started to lay him out.'

Rannveig froze. Only those pale fingers twitched, and were still.

'His hands?' she asked.

'Yes. The scratches.'

'It doesn't mean I killed him,' said Rannveig, her voice low. 'If that's what you mean.'

'I only wondered if you thought it was possible that Bjorn killed your daughter. And if so, when you found out – well, found the scratches, perhaps?' Sigrid stopped – she was probably saying too much.

'I only saw them when we brought him here,' said Rannveig, with grim defiance. 'That was the first time I saw them.'

'And did it make you think – because, after all, it wouldn't matter then, because he was dead anyway – but did it make you think that he might have killed Thordis?' Sigrid felt she was definitely babbling now. And anyway, it would be easy for Rannveig to answer that one. She might have had other reasons to think Bjorn guilty, and now she would not have to state them, would she?

Rannveig seemed to consider all this, too. She drew breath to answer – and at that moment, the longhouse door banged open.

'What's going on?' demanded a familiar voice. 'Rannveig, where's our niece?'

Ljotr, slamming the door back hard, strode into the longhouse, his wife Hrefna scuttling behind him. Sigrid saw at once that his fists were ready to strike, but Ketil was somehow already in his way, standing between him and both Sigrid and Rannveig. Hrefna, anxious eyes on Sigrid, slid round to reach her, evading danger neatly.

'Good day to you, Ljotr,' said Ketil evenly. 'Are you just arrived from Kirkuvagr?'

'I am,' shouted Ljotr. 'I'm here for Thordis' funeral. I go to the hall and ask if that's where the body is and some fellow with a moustache the size of Eynhallow Sound comes and tells me yes, it is, and he waves me into the hall, and what do I find? Some great lump of a man in furs, still covered in blood, lying on a table! Where's my niece? How is that man in her place?'

'That man is Bjorn Einarsson,' said Rannveig, though Sigrid noticed she did not really emerge from behind Ketil. 'My Einar's son. My daughter,' she went on, with a slight emphasis on the words, 'is buried already.'

'You should have waited for me!'

'I didn't know you were coming,' said Rannveig. 'And how long was I to wait?'

'I was held up waiting for a ship,' said Ljotr. 'Important business. But you should have known I would be on my way.'

'Come and sit down, Ljotr,' said Rannveig, and Ketil stood back a little to allow the man to pass, though he watched him carefully. 'Take a cup of hot wine. It's been – a busy time here, recently. When you are rested, I'll take you to where Thordis lies.'

'Well,' said Ljotr, taking the best seat by the fire, 'a cup of wine would be most welcome. And some food, too. The weather's getting up: it wasn't the easiest of journeys.'

'That's why the ship was late,' murmured Hrefna, nodding at Sigrid, not quite loud enough to be thought of as joining the conversation. She seemed to find some comfort in seeing Sigrid again. 'Was that really Einar's son? Einar was never that big!'

'That was him,' Sigrid said quietly. 'He died last night.'

'Oh, aye?' Hrefna seemed not to make a link between Bjorn's death and Thordis'. Ljotr must have heard her voice, for he scowled at her across the fire.

'And you two here, as well,' he said, nodding now at Ketil. 'You could have waited for us. We could have travelled together – more friendly, eh?'

'Sorry, we needed to get back,' said Ketil. He did not sit down, but leaned against a roof pillar, giving the impression of relaxing. Ljotr gave him one of those bristly, hard smiles again. Sigrid tried to disappear into the darker edges of the longhouse. She wondered if he had ever hit Rannveig, and decided that he had not. Rannveig had ways of dealing with her enemies.

Ljotr was now giving the inside of the longhouse a lengthy, considered assessment, and not with any great show of approval, though that smile still gripped his face. Sigrid had always admired Rannveig's home: it was not over-cluttered, like Helga's, but contained well-chosen, well-made items arranged in a practical way that was somehow very pleasing to the eye. It always smelled good, too: Rannveig was a fine cook, and skilled with herbs. But Ljotr seemed to be assessing how best to sell it to the highest bidder, and he did not seem to think he would do well out of it. His fingers on the cup Rannveig had given him were white about the knuckles, though he was clearly trying to look relaxed. Trying to keep his anger under control, Sigrid thought. It did not make her feel any more at ease herself.

'We buried Thordis yesterday,' said Rannveig. 'I suppose someone must have borne the news to you. I had thought this would be a good time for us, her here, helping me after Einar's death. She was settling down, talking of weaving, perhaps thinking of a husband – I note that you had not been successful in finding her one in all these years.'

'She wasn't an easy girl to marry off,' said Ljotr. 'Proud, and full of herself. Don't know where she got that from.'

'She had a good deal to be proud about,' said Rannveig. 'Maybe I made a mistake, leaving her in Kirkuvagr. There was no one of her quality there, not in that little trading settlement. I should have brought her here with me.'

'And we know why you didn't, Rannveig,' said Ljotr, disgust rich in his voice. 'We know why you left her with us to deal with.'

'She was a rich prize for you! No children of your own, but a useful niece to help you form business alliances!'

'Aye, and now she's dead,' said Ljotr. 'Go on, then, Rannveig, tell me. Did you kill her, too?'

XXIV

Rannveig stiffened, suddenly aware, if she had not been before, of the presence of not only Hrefna, but also of Sigrid and Ketil. Her dark gaze flickered quickly between all of them, catching a glint of the firelight. The mousy Hrefna, Ketil thought, was either stupid or knew why Ljotr was speaking this way: the question seemed to come as no surprise to her. Sigrid sat very still, trying not to be seen. Hrefna seemed to be half-hiding behind her. Ketil, propped against his pillar, simply kept his face blank, waiting to see what Rannveig would say or do.

'I did not kill her,' she said at last, her voice quiet but clear. 'She was my daughter.'

'You expect that to have any weight with me?' Ljotr demanded. 'Svein was your husband!'

Rannveig paled, shocked. She must not have thought Ljotr would go so far.

'Ljotr ... you promised ...'

'Aye, but Thordis is dead now. Didn't think of that, did you?' Ljotr's odd, fixed smile slid into a snarl. Hrefna glanced quickly at Sigrid, then back to her husband and Rannveig. Ljotr, almost as if she had reminded him of the others in the room, looked round at Ketil, jerking his head at Rannveig. 'Friend of yours, is she?' he asked.

'Why do you ask?' said Ketil.

'You'd need to know what she did. To her husband. My brother.'

Ketil waited. Rannveig seemed to be holding her breath, all the colour gone from her handsome face. Ljotr, sure now he had their attention, nodded.

'She was married to my brother Svein, Thordis' father. Then Einar Einarson came along, big fellow, warrior, you know? Pal of Thorfinn's. Svein was just finding his feet as a trader, working with me – everything was smaller then. We were small men. Einar's ship was in Kirkuvagr harbour, getting a new sail. And one day, Svein fell ill.'

'Yes,' Rannveig breathed, as though remembering. Ketil could not have said what the expression was on her face. Was there some regret there? Some sorrow?

'No one else was ill, just Svein. And she nursed him, of course. And he died.'

Rannveig shook her head suddenly.

'People fall ill and die, Ljotr.'

'Aye, they do. Handy, though, when they do it when their wives want to marry someone else, eh? Svein's barely in the ground when she's making up to Einar. And we all knew how clever she was with herbs and such. If you can cure with herbs, you can kill with herbs, can you not?' He nodded at Rannveig as if pronouncing judgement, and glanced at Ketil. 'She killed my brother – she near as anything you like admitted it to us. I doubt she'll be so stupid now. But that's why we took Thordis, isn't it, Rannveig? For Thordis' protection – my own brother's child!'

'I let you take Thordis because you had no children of your own,' said Rannveig sharply. 'Because she would help you make alliances for your trading. You were to have the marrying of her – I don't know why you held off so long.'

'You were pleased enough to see the back of her,' snapped Ljotr, 'off to start your new life with Einar Einarson! No need for a bairn in tow. No, she was safer with us.'

'You took so long to find her a husband – then you chose Varin! A conceited fool!'

'Varin was the only one that would take her,' said Ljotr. 'And he would have been useful to me, it's true. He would have done well enough for us. But then off you went and killed her, too.' The fixed smile scowled again. 'You waited a long time to do what we thought you'd do then. Was she in your way again?'

Rannveig's face twisted into a kind of smile now.

'You say I killed your brother with herbs – but Thordis was strangled. With her own braids.'

'So?' said Ljotr with a shrug. 'You're a nasty woman, Rannveig. No doubt you could throttle a girl.'

But, thought Ketil suddenly, it was a fair point. The damage

Rannveig had done in the past had all been with herbs. She had no need to risk being seen actually attacking someone. Unless, of course, she felt that any mysterious illness might indeed cast suspicion on her – or it was useful to her to open the field of suspects. He pressed his lips together in thought. This was not really helping them, revealing as it was.

'Why would I kill her, Ljotr? What harm could she do to me? If I had not wanted her alive I could, if your story is right, have killed her when, according to you, I killed my husband Svein. Why wait till now? Why kill, anyway, someone who might afford me companionship in my widowhood? Just when we were growing to know each other again ...'

For a moment, Ketil almost thought he could see tears in Rannveig's dark eyes. But if they were there, they were having no effect on Ljotr. He turned again to Ketil.

'You're Thorfinn's man. What are you going to do about this?'

Ketil pushed away from the pillar at last, and looked down at Ljotr and Rannveig.

'Nothing, for now. Unless you have proof of any of this.'

'It's obvious!'

'Thorfinn prefers to have something more than that,' said Ketil. 'But I'll certainly pass on your concerns. I'm sure he'll be interested.'

For a long moment, Ljotr stared down at the fire in front of him, teeth gritted. He must have been trying to think of any proof he might have, either concerning Thordis' murder or concerning his own brother's death – what, almost twenty years ago? If he had had proof, why had he done nothing about it at the time?

But at last Ljotr shook his head, a short, frustrated twitch. Ketil nodded to Sigrid, who at once headed for the door as though she had just been let off a leash. Ketil followed.

Outside Sigrid put twenty paces between them and the longhouse door, then sagged against the stone wall of the hall, fingers pressing between the slabs behind her.

'What do you make of that? I know it shouldn't surprise me, but I hadn't considered it, had you?' The words burst out of her as if she had been holding her breath all the time they had stood in the longhouse. Away from the tension, Ketil felt much the same.

'It might explain why Thordis was ... Thordis.'

'Yes ... what a life, eh?'

Ketil nodded, sorry for the girl, for her life and then her death.

'Living with her mother – Rannveig – who may or may not have killed her father, then moving to live with that man ... I wonder if Svein was just as violent? It could have been a good reason for Rannveig to prefer Einar.'

'Rannveig would just have divorced him. Or poisoned him, knowing Rannveig. She might have wondered how Einar would look on a woman who was divorced from her husband. But anyway, she's not like Hrefna,' said Ketil.

'No ... No, she's not.'

Sigrid looked away towards the sea. Ketil wondered if Sigrid were comparing herself with Hrefna and Rannveig. Why had she not divorced her violent husband and left him? Had she felt sorry for him? Or was it that her family was so far away – if she had left her husband, where would she have gone?

Sigrid leaned away from the wall again and dusted down her backcloak. They were out of the wind here but the rain found them in heavy drops.

'Do you think we learned anything useful there, though?'

Ketil shook his head.

'Rannveig did not admit to anything, and Ljotr has no proof. On either death. We don't know if she wanted to be rid of Thordis, and we don't know if she killed her. And there was nothing there that pointed to anyone else, either.'

'No, completely useless ... I'd better go and help prepare Bjorn's body. It'll take more than Frogunn to lift and turn him.'

Ketil almost smiled.

'A strong woman, Frogunn,' he agreed.

'Nice, too,' said Sigrid. 'I'd better go.' Yet she still hesitated, and he did not move, either. It was quiet there for a moment, just standing next to each other, thinking. Then he shook himself.

'I'm going to head up to the Brough,' he said. 'See if Skorri is all right, maybe deal with Thorthr.'

'Who?' Sigrid blinked.

'The man from Westray who wants his pig back. His

neighbour's pig.'

'Right ... It's an interesting life you lead, certainly,' she said, and patted him on the arm in encouragement. Then she gave a quick grin, and headed off round the corner of the hall to the main door. Ketil watched her go for a moment longer, then set off himself, back to the landbridge to the Brough.

It seemed harder than usual to make his way, cloak flapping, to Thorfinn's guarded gate across the spit of land. He was sure the sea was nibbling steadily at its northern flank, and the wind scoured it. The two guards on duty watched him dismally from their shelter.

'Aye, wind getting up,' one of them remarked usefully.

'Storm coming,' added the other, not to be outdone. Ketil had already seen the white dashes across the waves, smelled the scent of the storm as it threatened. He was glad, as much as it made sense, that Bjorn had wandered out on to the further reaches of the Brough last night, and not tonight. But then, perhaps if it had been tonight, even a determined murderer would have thought twice about following him. Or Bjorn himself would not have ventured so far.

He pictured the scene again when they had followed the Bear up that gentle hill. He remembered him ripping off his bear tooth amulet, and flinging it out into the darkness – all his luck must have left him then, if it had not before. Yet the amulet could not have flown far, surely – Ketil remembered the leather thong on which it had hung catching briefly on Bjorn's fur cloak as he flung it. He wondered where it had gone.

He needed a walk in the fresh air, anyway: the short distance from Buckquoy had not been enough to clear his head and let him reassemble the pieces of the last few days. He climbed up the few steps to Thorfinn's hall, then went past it, between the longhouses and up towards the chapel. Usually when you stepped between the buildings the sudden shelter made the silence ring in your ears, but now the wind was too strong and noisy, sweeping over the roofs and round the sharp stone corners of the houses. When he was clear of the buildings, Ketil made the effort to fight the wind over to the cliff edge, staring out to the north. To his right, the buildings almost met the edge of the land, leaving only a walkway around the outside of the bathhouse. They seemed precariously balanced when you saw the waves below. To his left there was proof of what could happen: the ruined buildings of the old people, the ones who had been here long before Thorfinn and his kin, were abandoned, half-consumed by the sea. The cliff rose gently with the rest of the headland, its soft reddish rock perched on the harder ridges of slanting boulders below, relying on their protection against the waves. Yet even as Ketil watched, a larger wave than the rest surged in and broke on those ridged teeth, and sucked itself back out to sea, tearing gouts of the cliff face with it. They had lost parts of the cliff in a storm before: it was wise not to build too close to the edge here, however strong the walls.

He stared out to sea for a while, leaning into the wind, feeling his eyes water. He could be out there now, heading for Heithabyr, looking for his brother. Safer well out at sea in a storm than close to land, where a casual wave could send you to the rocks. Safer still here on land, he thought, and surprised himself. Still, he could feel the surge of the waves under his feet, the dip and rise and lurch of the boat's timbers, the spray on his face ... soon, soon he would be there again. But something at the back of his mind was not quite as pleased at the prospect as it used to be.

At last he turned away from the tempting waves and let himself be blown back inland, almost running across the short-cropped grass where the sheep were still intently grazing, undisturbed by the weather. They would have seen worse, no doubt. They were avoiding, though, that dark patch of ground where Bjorn's body had lain last night: the storm would presumably wash that print away, and soon the sheep would graze just as thoughtlessly there.

Ketil staggered to a halt and looked about him. Was the place where Bjorn had died just about where he and Sigrid had left him, or had Bjorn moved before being killed? Ketil squinted at the marks on the grass, then up and around. In daylight it was difficult to remember. He looked back down towards the chapel, trying to remember what angle he had seen it from as they walked back down, leaving Bjorn to his private misery. Yes ... that was right. He spun back and saw that no, Bjorn had not moved far at all from where they had left him. He might even have sunk to his knees there and then, and stayed there.

A wave of guilt passed over Ketil at the thought of

abandoning the man there, so vulnerable. But he had wanted to be left alone, and Sigrid was right: there was nothing they could have done to help him without his cooperation. He was simply too big and strong. Unless they had come up behind him, unheard in the wind, and slit his throat. Someone had.

He glanced around once more to be sure of his bearings, then began a careful examination of the grass around Bjorn, starting with the direction in which Bjorn had cast his bear-tooth amulet. It was possible that his killer had dropped something, left some mark or sign inadvertently, that could help them to identify him – or her, he added to himself, thinking of Rannveig.

But though he searched until his ears were cold, and his fingers had lost all feeling, he found nothing. Not even Bjorn's amulet. He tried to picture Bjorn holding it out for inspection: it had been maybe the length of Ketil's little finger – smaller on Bjorn, of course. A paleish yellow, with the runes carved in double lines on one side. Bjorn had set such store by it, then. Ketil took a final sweep just a little further than he thought the amulet might have fallen, but there was still nothing but sheep droppings and stones and grass and dried blood. He sighed, and gave up, heading back to Thorfinn's hall to warm up by the fire and to tell Thorfinn yet more ill tales about Rannveig.

In Einar's hall, the central fire also burned bright, and so they had made sure Bjorn's body was some distance from it, just in case there were any delays before the burial. Even that short shift had required a dozen of Bjorn's crew along with big Afi, to lift Bjorn and the table and take them over to one side. His fur cloak alone, which had now been washed out and brushed to make the fur stand smooth again, had taken Sigrid and Helga between them to carry clear of the ground to the paddock wall for cleaning. Everything about Bjorn was giant-sized: it had been all Sigrid could do to keep Helga's remarks decent as, with the other women, they washed and wiped his body and clothed him again in a clean shirt, eventually folding his cloak around him. For Sigrid's part, she was more impressed by the number of scars Bjorn bore, old and new. It was indeed hard to say whether he had been a lucky man or not. But the newest scars, apart from the slice across his throat, had been those scratches on the backs of his hands, so neatly done that they almost looked planned. Sigrid remembered Thordis' bloody nails, and felt a surge of sorrow for the girl. What had she done, though, to drive a man like Bjorn to kill her? For nothing she had heard of the great Bear indicated that he was the kind of man who would hurt a woman deliberately. Not like some.

'Do you think the stories are true?'

Sigrid jumped as she watched two of Rannveig's women finally pull a linen sheet over Bjorn's damp face. Frogunn was staring at him, too.

'What,' asked Sigrid, 'the stories of all the injuries he survived? It certainly looks like it, doesn't it?'

'No, I meant the stories about bears,' said Frogunn, and she sounded almost anxious. 'That they die in the autumn, and come back to life in the spring?'

'I hope not,' said Sigrid firmly. 'I'm sorry he's dead, but I don't like the idea of people coming back to life, unless they're gods. That would be like a draug, wouldn't it? Neither dead nor alive? Not good.'

'Definitely not,' said Helga. 'What were those scratches on his hands? I saw you looking at them.'

'Oh, probably something from the fight in here the other night,' said Frogunn.

'They looked fresher than that,' said Helga. 'Could it be from when he was killed?'

Sigrid frowned. Helga could be right: the scratches had had a raw look. She stepped forward to the table again, and lifted the sheet carefully, shifting to one side to allow the lamplight to fall clearly on Bjorn's massive hand. Frogunn came to stand beside her. Yes, Helga was right. Sigrid had been distracted at the thought that they were a sign Bjorn had attacked Thordis, but they were more recent than that, surely. They were straight, but ended in little curls of white, raw flesh that would have dried quickly and crisped. But Bjorn had been attacked suddenly, from behind, with one blow of a sharp blade – he would have had no chance to scratch himself, or be scratched by his attacker, in that confrontation. Sigrid closed her eyes, scrunching them tight to try to remember. Bjorn's hands, as he lay face down in the grass of the Brough. Was she imagining it, or had they been uninjured?

'Yes, fresher,' said Helga, glancing at them again. 'They

probably scraped him on something as they tried to bring him here. You know how hard it was for us to lift and turn him: imagine trying to get him on to the bier up on the Brough!'

'Of course,' said Sigrid, not at all sure. She laid the sheet back down again sadly. Had someone tried to make it look as if Bjorn had killed Thordis? Condemning him when he could no longer defend himself? She shook her head, and went to sit down with Helga.

'I'd better clear these away,' said Frogunn.

'Sit down, Frogunn, and take the weight off your feet,' said Helga. 'Don't go round looking for work – it's exhausting to watch!'

'I just want to make the place look a bit tidier,' said Frogunn. 'Where shall I put these? No one's going to want them.'

'What are they?' asked Helga.

'Thordis' braids, the ones she was showing to Bjorn the day she died.'

Sigrid winced as she felt both women glance at her.

'Let's see them?' she said, holding out her hand.

Frogunn laid four or five longish braids over Sigrid's arm, all about right for the edge of a tunic. It was odd to make them without a specific purpose for them, though, as if she had only made them to show people. Sigrid wondered if, in fact, she had had any customers at all.

'They're really not very interesting, are they?' sighed Helga. 'Poor girl.'

'Neatly done, though,' said Sigrid, and they were. 'Maybe Rannveig would like them. Or her aunt and uncle – they're with Rannveig in the longhouse.'

'Or Varin might want one, to remember her by,' said Helga.

'Oh, no, I shouldn't think so,' said Frogunn quickly. 'No, don't give one to Varin.'

And to their surprise, Frogunn flushed bright pink.

'Frogunn?' asked Helga. 'Don't tell me you have your eye on Varin!'

'Me? No!' said Frogunn loudly, but it was about as convincing as any other protestation Sigrid had ever heard from a young woman about a young man.

'Oh, Frogunn!' said Helga, on a long, sorrowful moan.

XXV

'What?' asked Frogunn, but it was obvious she knew.

'I think it's time you went away for a bit, saw something of the world,' said Helga. 'Or spent more time down by the harbour when the trading ships come in. I'm sure Varin has a kind of exotic appeal – and he's certainly a good looking young fellow,' she added, in a tone that implied that she herself was above all that kind of thing – Sigrid almost laughed out loud – 'but there are plenty of fine young men to choose from without ... Well, without choosing him.'

'But I like him,' said Frogunn, a little petulant.

'Hm,' said Sigrid, poking Helga before she could say anything else. 'What is it you like about him, Frogunn?'

'Well, he is very good looking, it's true,' said Frogunn. 'And he's a good leader, and brave – did you see him tackling Bjorn in the mock fights? I think it was that day when I saw how he managed to avoid being injured, in all that mess, that I began to admire him. And some of his fights were very clever, you have to say! Getting his men to fall back and let Bjorn's men through then trapping them! That was clever, wasn't it? I've been watching mock fights since I was a girl, and I hadn't seen that before.'

That was probably, thought Sigrid, because she had only been watching them at Einar's hall, and even when Frogunn was a girl, not that long ago, Einar's men were growing bored and lazy and unimaginative. Helga was probably right: Frogunn needed to get away from Buckquoy and see a few more marriageable young men. She would be a good catch for most of them.

But something began to niggle at the back of her mind – something to do with Varin, perhaps? She glanced around. Frogunn looked as if she might experiment with sulking, but Sigrid doubted she would manage a sulk for long: she was not that kind of person. Helga's gaze had fallen back on to Bjorn's huge body, perhaps regretting a missed opportunity. Where was Varin?

She scanned the room. Varin was sprawled on a bench near the high seat, though for once had resisted taking it. Perhaps it had lost its appeal now that Bjorn was dead. She should really go and talk to him. But would he talk to her? He probably would if she were prepared to flatter him, but she was not sure she could face that. Anyway, it would be awkward to go and approach him when he was sitting so prominently amongst the mourners, lost in – well, contemplation of some kind. She wondered what went on in his head: the glory of Varin, and not much else, she decided uncharitably. He certainly looked quite pleased with himself.

Really, the idea of talking to him was very unappealing.

But over there, behind the tables, was Sigvat, sitting on his own bed roll, and looking a little out of things. The nearest men to him were all Buckquoy loyalists, Oddr and Foldar and their friends, cutting him off from his brother. Sigvat would be much easier to talk to, and, she told herself, just as useful. After all, he had made the effort to come and talk to Helga and her while they were watching the practice fights. He seemed approachable, and certainly brighter than Varin. She nodded to herself before she could change her mind, and went along the side of the hall towards him.

'Hello, Sigvat, how are you feeling? How's your jaw?'

'Oh! It's –' He touched it warily. 'It's a bit better, thank you.'

'Can I rebandage it for you? That dressing must slip very easily and it can't be comfortable.'

'That's very kind, but Frogunn did it not long ago, thanks. Holding me together nicely.' He was speaking a little more confidently than he had a couple of days before, though you could see it still hurt. His words were muffled, as if his mouth were still swollen. It looked puffy. She thought for a moment, then pulled up a stool and sat down next to him. He did not appear to find this odd, and she felt more confident, her back to the Buckquoy men and her voice reasonably low.

'Awful thing, Bjorn dying like that,' she said. 'Whoever you might think would be best for the hall, it's a tragedy.'

'Isn't it?' said Sigvat. 'Terrible.'

'And so soon after poor Thordis, too,' she went on. 'You'd known her a long time, hadn't you?'

'Since we were – well, not quite children, but young things, when Varin and I began travelling and went to Kirkuvagr,' Sigvat agreed. 'She was a handsome lass.'

'She was. I hear she and your brother were betrothed?'

Sigvat gave her a look that was half-hard, half-amused.

'I thought I saw Ljotr poke his face into the hall earlier! Has he been talking, then?'

'He's said a few things,' said Sigrid, offhandedly.

'No sense in denying it then: yes, Varin was betrothed to Thordis. A business arrangement.'

'But he intended to go through with it?'

'Of course – all the more once this question of Einar's hall came up. It was one thing to have that trade link with Ljotr, but quite another to have the bond with Rannveig, too, and of course if he takes the hall it will give him a higher standing with Ljotr anyway. It should work well.'

'Even without Thordis?'

Sigvat made a face.

'It would have been better with her.'

'Nicely organised,' she agreed lightly. 'And anyway, you were fond of her yourself, weren't you?'

'Me? Of Thordis?' His voice rose slightly in his surprise, and she felt, rather than heard, some interested movement behind her. Oddr, probably, eavesdropping. Sigvat must have noticed, and dropped his voice again. 'Not more than would be usual for a brother's intended wife,' he said. Sigrid, annoyed, could not make out how true this was.

'But she was fond of you, though,' she tried, but Sigvat was already following a new line.

'I mean, I didn't do it, obviously, but whoever killed Bjorn has done us a favour,' Sigvat went on. 'Revenge is ... I can't see Thorfinn approving, nor King Harald when he hears about all this, but I would have found Bjorn hard to face.'

Sigrid shook her head, momentarily confused by the turn.

'Sorry, what do you mean?'

'I mean after he killed Thordis. He should have admitted it and paid compensation. But not saying anything – well, it put all of us in a very awkward position.'

'I hadn't realised ... I mean, I must have missed something. When did everyone find out that Bjorn had killed Thordis?'

'Oh, all the men know that,' said Sigvat dismissively.

'Bjorn's men, too?'

'I don't know. The Buckquoy men, though.'

With whom you have tried to ally yourselves, Sigrid thought. But then, what else could they have done, in the circumstances?

'I didn't know that they felt that strongly about Thordis' death,' she said, without thinking much about it.

'Oh, no, now they know it was Bjorn of course they're angry!' said Sigvat, sitting up straighter. 'Coming here from outlands and killing one of their own!'

Since the men barely spoke to Rannveig anymore, and few of them had even known of Thordis' existence till last week, Sigrid felt that this was stretching things a bit. But sometimes it did not take much for one hird to fight another. Even so, how had they proved, even to their satisfaction, that Bjorn had killed Thordis? Was it the scratches on his hands? Would it lead to another fight in the hall? Maybe it would be best – lock the doors and leave them to it.

She shook herself, lowered her voice a little more and changed the subject.

'Tell me, has Frogunn been looking after you well?'

Sigvat smiled, and touched his bandage.

'Oh, yes: she's a great lass. Not everyone at Buckquoy has been so welcoming ... sorry, but you know what it's been like.'

'Yes, not ideal,' she agreed, a little vaguely.

'But Frogunn has made sure we have blankets and places to sleep and eat – and of course she's taken care of my injuries, in the absence of womenfolk of our own.'

'Have you mother or sister at home?'

Sigvat shook his head.

'Our mother died years ago, and we never had a sister.'

She made a sympathetic face, though she was a little surprised. The two brothers had struck her as the kind made by an over-devoted mother tending to their every need, particularly Varin.

'You'll have chatted with Frogunn, then – gathered news from her about the place, and the people?'

'Oh, yes: I like to find out about the people I'm living amongst.'

He had already found out about her and Helga before he came to talk to them, Sigrid remembered. Frogunn would no doubt have been a useful source of information, for she seemed to know everyone and was less complicated than Helga.

'And maybe told her a bit about yourselves, too? I'm keen for her to find out a bit more about the islands – she's lived too long just in Buckquoy, I think.'

'Yes,' said Sigvat carefully, 'yes, I have probably talked about Deerness and Kirkuvagr. They are interesting places – well, Kirkuvagr, anyway. Deerness is an old-fashioned place these days, I think. Kirkuvagr is where things are starting to happen.'

'Everywhere takes it in turn,' said Sigrid. 'And all about your family? Your late father, Einar's brother? Varin's betrothal? Your connexions with Ljotr? All this would be interesting and different for her. She has led a surprisingly sheltered life so far.'

'It doesn't seem to have done her much harm,' said Sigvat, coming admirably to Frogunn's defence.

'Not yet, anyway,' Sigrid muttered. 'Well, if there's nothing else I can do for you just now ...'

'I'm very well looked after, thank you!' said Sigvat cheerfully.

'Then I shall leave you in peace,' said Sigrid with a smile, and left him. She had plenty to think about.

Rannveig, being Rannveig, managed to cause to be cooked and served a very good midday meal for all in the hall. Ljotr and Hrefna apparently stayed in the longhouse – Sigrid did not go looking for them.

After the meal had been cleared, she sought out Helga.

'I'm going to have to go home,' she said. 'I can't remember the last time I slept in my own bed, and if Gnup has to bring in the whole infield's harvest on his own, he'll be claiming the land for himself. And I still haven't finished that braid.'

'You'll be back for the burial, though, won't you?' asked Helga. 'And you won't vanish off to Kirkuvagr again?'

'I have no plans to,' Sigrid reassured her. 'Anyway, Ljotr and Hrefna are here.'

'I saw them,' said Helga, glum.

'I wouldn't go near him, if I were you,' said Sigrid, and Helga shook her head emphatically.

'Not at all. Horrible man.' She sighed. 'I know all I've said, but poor Thordis, all the same.'

'Yes. Poor Thordis.'

She hurried away across the hill to make the most of the rest of the daylight. Gnup, as she had expected, was hard at work in the infield, gathering and binding armfuls of bygg, stooking them against each other to dry. He had a fixed, grim look, and when Sigrid stopped him he swayed on his feet. She felt terrible.

'Go and lie down,' she said. 'I'll finish here.'

'It's easier with two.'

'It is, but you've been managing on your own. I'll do the rest.'

She had already shed her best overdress and back cloak, and set to, sleeves bound flat against her forearms to protect her from the tough stalks. Gnup watched her for a moment, half-reluctant to give up and half too tired to move, then he left, staggering a little, making for the longhouse door. Sigrid hoped he had been eating well. She had brought back some leftovers from the midday meal at the hall for him, which, with some dried meat she had been paid with a few weeks ago, would make a stew for supper. If either of them was awake.

Gnup was indeed asleep when she slipped back into the house at dusk, feeling her way through the familiar darkness to the glow of the fire. She added fuel to make it dance higher, then lit a lamp and set to with the leftovers and the meat and a pot full of water, coming gradually to the boil. It could be left for a little: she slipped back outside, called and milked the two cows, and brought the bucket of foaming warm milk back in to stand it by the fire, ready for Gnup. The cattle would stay outside, tough enough for these autumn nights.

It was too late to start weaving now, and too dark, and her hands were tired with cutting and pulling and binding, her back weary with stooping and swinging. Gnup ignored the faint light and snored on: he had not even taken his boots off. She thought she should go over in her mind all she had learned today about Bjorn and Thordis, but it was too much to think about. She managed to wonder what Ketil was doing, and left all mental effort at that.

Mindlessly she added meat and vegetables to the boiling water, and watched them cook. She had some herbs to throw in, too:

she was not the best of cooks, but she could manage that. The broth began to smell quite good – good enough, certainly, for a couple of tired workers. She felt guilty again about Gnup. He was nearly grown, but she had left him with too much to do even so, all on his own. It was too easy to be distracted by puzzles and mysteries. She would have to be more firm with herself, and kinder to Gnup, or he might up and leave her for some gentler farmer. And how on earth would she manage then?

Gnup, his instincts finely honed, stirred himself just as Sigrid was about to wake him and wriggled over to sit by the fire.

'All done in the infield, thanks to you,' she said, spooning broth into his ready bowl. He grunted, took a hunk of bread from the leftovers, and worked hard at the bowl for a moment or two. Then it was empty, and he held it out for more, his cheerful smile just about back in place.

'You could have left me to it,' he said. 'I was nearly there.'

'You were – you were nearly dead on your feet, too.'

'Well ...' He tucked in to the second bowl.

'Animals all well?' she asked. 'I've seen the cows.'

'Aye, the lambs are all fit and fat, and the hens are grand and still laying well.' He nodded to a bowl of eggs nearby, saw the milk and filled his cup from the bucket to wash down the soup.

'What about the nettles? Did you fetch the last batch out of the stream?'

Gnup looked a little awkward.

'Yes, yes I did.'

'Are you sure?' she asked, allowing him time to modify his story. He took another draught of milk, and made a face.

'You were wrong, you know,' he said. 'They don't stop stinging when they've been in the water. But I've left them to dry, like you said.'

'How long did you leave them in the stream?'

'Long enough.'

'Not really, if they're still stinging. How long?'

'Well, I may have taken them out quite quickly,' said Gnup, still not quite meeting her eye. 'I had the harvest to get on with, and I didn't want to come back and find they'd been washed away.'

'They were held down with rocks!' She would have to try putting them back in the water soon, before they just – she was not quite sure what they would do, but they would not be broken down enough to work if they were still stinging. 'Where did you put them?'

'I couldn't think of anywhere else that was sheltered and not full of wool.'

'Where did you put them?' she asked again, a little more ominously.

'They're quite dry!'

'Where?'

'In the privy.'

'In the privy?' She took this in. 'Then where ...'

'I go up to Helga's quite often,' said Gnup, trying to sound offhand. 'And, well, there's the midden.'

'I don't fancy using the midden!' She wanted to be cross, but then she had left him with so much to do. 'Right, first light you can take them back down to the stream and put them back under the rock, and we'll see what we can salvage. It's too dark now to ... can we use the privy at all?'

'You can just about squeeze in,' said Gnup, always the optimist. 'You just have to remember to turn a particular way.'

'Oh ...'

She tried to put the idea to the back of her mind, to deal with when she had to, and mindful of looking after Gnup gave him more broth, and asked him what else had been happening about the farm.

Their talk grew slower as they finished the broth and the fire began to sink down. Gnup had brought in the hens, and taken off his boots, while Sigrid sorted out the fire and the dishes. They both braved the privy – at least, Gnup said he had – and Sigrid found that if she pressed herself hard against one wall and clung on to the stonework with one hand she was at least less likely to be stung. In a short time, such were the benefits of a simple life, the little longhouse was quiet and dark, and both Sigrid and Gnup were settled and asleep in their respective bedplaces, lulled by the familiar sough of the wind outside.

It was the cat that woke Sigrid, walking over her with miaowing persistence. She opened her eyes, but it was almost entirely dark. She reached out a hand for the cat, and felt its furry head.

'Not morning yet,' she told it. 'Go back to sleep. Or go and catch mice.'

She turned over, trying to ignore it, but somehow she was now aware of the sound of sheep outside. Noisier than usual, she thought, not just the usual night time signalling. She frowned. Could something have happened to one of the lambs? Well, yes, of course something could have happened: sheep were always going about looking for new disasters to happen to them. Sometimes she wished she had stuck with cows, like the rest of Buckquoy – but cows were not known for their wool. On the other hand, they were less noisy at night.

She jumped as a cow outside let out a surprised grunt, as if she had walked into something unexpected.

'What was that?' called Gnup.

'Something's out there,' said Sigrid, already scrambling to her feet and reaching for her shawl.

'A bear?'

'No,' she said, 'they don't come back to life until the spring.' She seized a twig and poked it into the embers of the fire, and quickly as possible lit a torch from it. Gnup was wide-eyed in the flickering light. 'Stay here,' she said.

'I should go first,' he protested, wanting to be the man.

'No, I need you to guard the house in case someone gets round behind me. After all, they could steal ...' She swept a look about the bare longhouse. 'The eggs,' she finished, on a determined note, and headed for the door.

Outside the wind caught her torch and she angled it to stay lit, at the same time trying to take in as much as possible nearby. A cow, presumably the one that had grunted, was staring over the wall at her, annoyed at being disturbed again. She heard footsteps, soft but quick, and braced herself for an attack, but the steps seemed to be going away. Not a bear, then – a human. But who?

There was a sudden creak, a rustling, and then a faint, surprised 'Ow!'

A few quick strides took her over to the privy, and she pulled the door open, holding her torch high.

Inside, caught up in the nettles, was Foldar, Frogunn's brother.

XXVI

Thorfinn's immediate lands on the Brough had more sheep than crops on them – an easy choice to make when the land ran with water and was scoured by the wind, and one had people who would send you grain in return for your general protection and overlordship. The men in his hall had not been much involved with harvest, unless they had family somewhere nearby and had gone to help. The hird in the hall were relaxed, but not particularly tired, and after their meal they were happy to sit and gossip and play board games and sing a little, though not too much, perhaps out of respect for Bjorn lying dead not so far away.

Ketil had left it till after the meal before he approached Thorfinn with what little news he had. Skorri, Alf and Geirod were scattered about the hall, listening to the talk of others to see what they could pick up, and no doubt spreading the odd bit of gossip themselves – probably pig related. Skorri had been keeping an eye on the Westray man periodically, and the sow, and was more impressed with the latter than the former. He was keen to tell the whole story, with comic emphasis. Alf was playing on his bone pipe for a group of attentive young girls, who would no doubt later tell him how much their group favoured Bjorn, or Varin, and why. Geirod sat with one or two companions, as silent as he was, thoughtfully emptying their cups every now and again. Something might come of it, but it was not clear what. Ketil left his bench and made his way round the outer edge of the hall, making for Thorfinn's high seat.

He had hoped that Ingibjorg would have retired to her longhouse by this time, but the twin boys were sleeping on her lap in a complex tangle, both rather too large now for it, and she was clearly unwilling to move.

'Evening, Ketil,' said Thorfinn, half-raising a cup to him in greeting. 'I take it Bjorn reached Buckquoy safely?'

'Just about, my lord.'

'And Rannveig has seen to his laying-out?'

'It was in progress when I left.'

'Good. Quite a job – no doubt some of Bjorn's own men will help with the heavy work.'

Ketil bowed his head. He hoped Sigrid had managed to get some rest: she had looked tired.

'Any progress? Do you think he and Thordis were killed by the same person?'

'It's still hard to say, my lord,' said Ketil. 'You can see why someone in Einar's hird, perhaps, or supportive of Varin, might want Bjorn dead. It's not so easy to see why they might have wanted to kill Thordis.'

'Did you find out any more about Thordis?'

'Her uncle Ljotr arrived at Buckquoy while I was there, from Kirkuvagr. We had wondered why Thordis might have been brought up in her uncle's household, and he made his side of the story clear: he said that Rannveig had murdered his brother – her first husband, Svein – and he had insisted on taking in Thordis for her protection.'

'Did he?' said Thorfinn, interested. 'Did he really? Why would Rannveig have killed Svein?'

'In order to marry Einar, he says.'

'I see.' He fell silent for a long moment. Ketil, out of the corner of his eye, could see Ingibjorg readying herself to plunge into the conversation, but before she could, Thorfinn spoke again. 'I'm sad to say I could believe it of her. What did she say?'

'She said she had handed Thordis over to Ljotr because he didn't have any children of his own, and he could use her to form a trading alliance.'

'Generous of her.' Thorfinn nodded, with just a trace of irony.

'Generous? Casting out her own daughter?' Ingibjorg could wait no longer. 'She's a terrible woman!'

'My lady,' said Ketil respectfully, 'I know you were kind to Rannveig. Did she ever say anything to you about her life in Kirkuvagr? Her first husband? Her daughter?'

'She never said much directly,' said Ingibjorg at once, 'but it was obvious there was a story to be told, if she would tell it. Not that I would make anyone tell a story they didn't want to tell, of course.'

'Of course,' echoed Thorfinn and Ketil, Thorfinn perhaps more sincerely.

'Anyway, anything she did say about that first husband was perfectly all right. I mean, she never complained about him, that I heard. Of course, if she'd murdered him she probably wouldn't complain anyway, would she? It might make her look suspicious.'

Ketil raised his eyebrows a little, surprised at Ingibjorg's clarity of thought – but then, she was not considered a stupid woman, merely a silly one.

'Very true, my lady. She's clever.'

Ingibjorg nodded agreement.

'Did she say much during Thordis' burial?' asked Thorfinn. 'You were good enough to take her in here and seat her beside you, my love.'

'She said barely anything,' said Ingibjorg, the disappointment lingering. 'It was hard to have any kind of conversation with her. I said I was sorry about Thordis, and she said she was, too. That was about all. We have grown apart – well, she has.'

'And of course you'd barely have had the chance to talk about Bjorn,' said Thorfinn, reasonably.

'No, of course not. But I'll tell you something,' said Ingibjorg. 'I saw her face when you came in with the news of Bjorn's death. And I'll tell you something,' she repeated, leaning forward to give Ketil the full benefit of her information, 'she looked as if her world had fallen in on her. As if everything she had planned had come apart. That's what she looked like,' said Ingibjorg, and sat back, nodding seriously. 'And whatever she'd said or done to me in the past, in that moment I felt so sorry for her, I could have cried.'

When Ketil had paid his dues to Thorfinn and Ingibjorg, he began a gentle circuit of the hall, casually taking in who was talking with whom, who was arguing, who was eyeing up which of the women serving the wine and ale. And which of the women was eyeing back. He always found this time of the evening useful: not everyone ate in the hall, of course, but by this time those who were there were comfortably in their cups, and able to give him all kinds of information, wittingly or not. He had mentioned the tactic to his men: Alf, he thought, understood it best, unobtrusively charming those around him in a way Ketil would never have managed. Geirod hovered like a dark cloud and put people off talking, and Skorri, who liked fine food and wine, tended to forget when to abstain. But Skorri was a good gossip, and it was to him that Ketil eventually made his way now.

'Anything?' he asked him, swinging his long legs over the bench to sit beside his second in command. Skorri leaned back against the table, looking around him as if to glean some extra information.

'Not much,' he said quietly. 'None of them knew Thordis, and they barely knew Bjorn. There's some teasing of Groa because she lay with Varin – fair enough, I'd say.' He nodded over to where Groa was topping up wine cups, but Ketil did not look round: he had no wish for her to think he was talking about her. She would hardly hear their conversation, for the noise between her and them, and all around the hall, was considerable. 'She's saying she was told he wanted her particularly to attend him, then later he told her she was beneath him. I mean, she was unworthy of him,' he clarified.

'She was told?'

'That's what she's saying,' Skorri confirmed.

Ketil thought back to his uneasy interview with Groa in the apple store. She had not mentioned being summoned by Varin – or by someone who thought she ought to attend Varin. Was this something new she had thought up, or had he asked the wrong questions?

'And then there's what they're saying about Bjorn, even though they barely knew him,' Skorri went on.

'What's that?'

'That someone killed him because he killed Thordis.'

'It's a possibility,' Ketil acknowledged.

'As far as half the men here are concerned, it's a fact,' said Skorri. 'They're saying it as if Thorfinn had condemned him himself. We're not that sure, are we?'

'No, not at all,' said Ketil. He considered. Who would have taken revenge for Thordis, even if they were sure Bjorn had done it? Varin? But he was with Groa. Sigvat on his behalf? But his jaw was broken – could he have done it? Rannveig? But if Ingibjorg was to be believed, and for once Ketil was inclined to believe her, then

Rannveig had been shocked by Bjorn's death. Was there anyone else who might have wanted to avenge Thordis? He was quite sure her aunt and uncle would not have bothered: they had not even hurried themselves to quit Kirkuvagr for her burial.

'Do they say why they think Bjorn killed Thordis?' he asked at last.

Skorri shook his head.

'I think the idea is that she wouldn't lie with him. Looking at her that night I'd have been surprised, myself. But on the other hand, Bjorn struck me as a man in it for marriage, I thought.' He looked uncertainly at Ketil, but Ketil nodded.

'I think you're right. That doesn't ring true to me, not with an important woman like Rannveig's daughter. He wasn't so drunk that he would have done something that stupid, and jeopardised his chances with Thorfinn, too.'

'Maybe he did make a mistake, and that was why he had to kill her, to stop her telling,' suggested Skorri.

But Ketil was remembering the story of someone going up to Bjorn and saying something quiet to him, something that made him head out of Einar's hall in Thordis' wake. Even if Bjorn had killed Thordis – and he had difficulty seeing it – it was someone else that was in control of this situation, sending people here and there. Sending Groa to Varin, sending Afi to stand in the cold, sending Bjorn out after Thordis. Who was it, telling everyone what to do? It sounded like Rannveig, but he had a feeling that this time Rannveig had been out-plotted. And who could do that?

He looked about the hall, wondering, even though the answer was more likely to be at Buckquoy. Groa was laughing with some of the other women. Ingibjorg had taken her sons and departed, leaving Thorfinn to talk with whom he pleased. Ketil saw the man from Heithabyr, the burn still shocking on his face, sitting in silence with his drink – Ketil should talk with him, but not yet. Near him, as though they had been speaking together but had run out of words, was Tosti, the little priest. Ketil left Skorri and worked his way round to Tosti, taking a seat beside him. Tosti grinned, and greeted him warily.

'Thought you'd be down at Buckquoy,' said Ketil. Tosti winced.

'I felt like taking a break from funerals for a bit. It feels like abandoning my duty, but surely between the Brough and Buckquoy there must be something else for a priest to do besides burying the dead?'

'You'd like to think so,' said Ketil, then nodded his head at the man from Heithabyr. 'Like talking to the injured and bereaved?'

Tosti's face fell.

'Oh, Ketil, I was so sorry to hear about your brother's family. It sounds a terrible thing, the whole business.'

'I'm going to go there once this matter is sorted out. Thorfinn has given me leave.'

'Good – I should think so. And your other brother, the priest – was he there, too?'

Ketil had not thought of that possibility.

'No one has said so. I pray not,' Please not, he said to himself. Please not him, too.

'Well,' said Tosti, 'and I hope this is sorted out soon for your sake, too. What on earth is going on, Ketil? It feels as if Einar's death – which was due and came as a mercy from God – set off something awful. All this rivalry! Poor Thordis – poor Rannveig!'

'It's been a hard week for her, certainly,' Ketil agreed. 'Though I do not think she was particularly close to her daughter.'

'Perhaps not, but it must have been a dreadful shock, all the same. I had a word with her last night, but she was never very easy to talk to – well, I can talk all I like to her, but I doubt she chooses to take much of it in,' he added frankly. 'And now there's word going round that Bjorn killed Thordis – tried to take her by force, then killed her.'

'I can see why you might be reluctant to go and pray over him, then,' said Ketil.

'Oh, I'll be praying all right. His need will be all the greater, if the rumours are true.'

'Where did you hear that, anyway?' Ketil asked.

'I'm not sure I can remember,' Tosti admitted. 'It was some time yesterday evening. I'll try and recall it, if you think it matters.'

'It might,' said Ketil. 'I'd be grateful. I thought I heard you were talking to Varin.'

Tosti frowned, thinking, then nodded.

'Oh, I was for a bit. Someone asked me to, saying he needed a word, but I'm not sure what that was about. I'd barely explained who I was – don't think he had noticed at the burial,' he added, self-deprecating, 'when that girl Groa came up and, well, she definitely has charms I don't possess!'

'I think she ended up regretting deploying them,' said Ketil. 'She didn't say that anyone had sent her to talk to Varin, did she?'

'No, I don't think that was mentioned,' said Tosti. 'It certainly wasn't a focus of the conversation, anyway.'

'No, I suppose not ...' Ketil shrugged, then something struck him. 'Wait, did you say that someone told you to talk to Varin?'

'Well, asked, yes.'

'Who was that?' Not that he held out any hope of a useful answer. No one ever seemed to know who had told them to do anything. Could this be yet another manipulation? He looked at Tosti, sitting neatly at the table, a peaceful, reliable person in the midst of a mess. Who had manipulated him?

'Who asked me to talk to Varin? I don't know why you're looking so dubious, Ketil. It was Frogunn, Oddr's daughter.'

'Frogunn didn't kill Thordis.'

It had not taken much to encourage Foldar back into the longhouse, and whatever he had been trying to do, Sigrid did not consider him much of a danger. He cut a fairly pathetic figure with his blackened, scarred nose, but his mouth had a determined line to it, nevertheless. He watched as Sigrid chivvied the fire back to life, and Gnup took up a post near the door, in case Foldar decided to try to run for it. Sigrid was not sure how useful Gnup would be – he seemed to like Foldar.

'Did you come all the way over here to tell me that?' she asked, allowing her crossness to sound in her voice. She was not quite sure why she had not just sent him home. But he was Frogunn's brother.

'I did,' he said firmly, 'and I did it because you were thinking that Frogunn might have killed her, weren't you?'

Sigrid pulled a pot of water over the youthful fire and subjected Foldar to a long, hard look. The idea had begun to cross her mind, but she almost did not want to say it, in case it made it true. She liked Frogunn, and thought her sensible. Or she had, until she had admitted she was in love with Varin. But people did fall in love with very peculiar – other people. People, in fact, were peculiar.

Even sensible Frogunn.

Her silence, though, seemed to be more intimidating than anything she might have thought of to say. Foldar swallowed noisily, more obvious as he was still breathing chiefly through his mouth. The noise in turn made him blush. He did look very young.

'Whoever killed both Thordis and Bjorn, it looks like someone who wants Varin to win, doesn't it? Especially now there are all these rumours going round that Bjorn killed Thordis.'

'There are?' Sigrid stopped herself with a nod. 'Of course there are. Go on.'

'I mean, it could be someone who wants me to take charge. But that's only really my father and Hrolf, Helga's husband. I don't think anyone else wants me to – least of all me,' he stressed. 'Really, I don't want it. And Frogunn knows that, so she wouldn't have been doing anything like that for my sake. Do you see?'

'I see that much,' Sigrid agreed.

'So the other man that might get the hall if Bjorn doesn't is Varin, isn't it? And today you found out that Frogunn's - she's a bit soft on Varin.'

Sigrid could not stop herself rolling her eyes, but she managed to bow her head over the water pot and hide it.

'On Varin!' Gnup exclaimed from his post by the door. 'And your sister Frogunn? Is she mad? The man's horrible!'

'Oh, I've warned her,' sighed Foldar. 'I love my sister dearly, I really do. She's strong and brave and she'd make a much better leader than me, usually. I'd much rather look after the cows – and she's good at that, too. She's just good at everything – but sometimes she's just not very clever.'

'You mean because she's fallen for Varin? I'd say so!' said Gnup. Sigrid remembered that Gnup had met Varin and Sigvat when he was a youngster, at his uncle's. Maybe she should have asked him more about that. She wondered if it would be useful, felt her eyes closing, then roused herself to listen to what Foldar was saying.

'Varin's got her running round after him and Sigvat, anything they want, and I don't think he's even looked at her twice. It's clear he has no feelings for her at all – she wouldn't be useful to him.' He gave a frustrated sigh, then stopped and glanced at Sigrid. 'But when I say anything they want, I don't mean killing. I mean, why would Varin have wanted Thordis dead, anyway? She was useful to him. She was Rannveig's daughter. He wasn't going to give her up lightly.'

'So in fact,' said Sigrid, sombrely, 'while Varin might not have asked your sister to kill Thordis – it would have been to Frogunn's own advantage to get rid of Thordis, wouldn't it? And what's more, she was physically capable of doing it, wasn't she?'

'Oh, yes,' said Foldar sadly. 'I've no doubt Frogunn could have managed either killing.'

'Well,' said Sigrid, feeling utterly miserable, 'since you came here to tell me she didn't do it, you're not making a very good job of it, are you?'

XXVII

Foldar stayed for the rest of the night, warmed by a hot drink but otherwise not much comforted by his evening's efforts. Sigrid was not happy, either. If a man who had come to tell her his sister was innocent had had such trouble proving it, the sister should be worried.

Once Sigrid had seen him and Gnup off, Foldar back to his father's farm and Gnup to milk her own cattle, Sigrid set up her tablet weaving – it felt like an age since she had last worked on it – and began to twist and turn the little tablets, reassured by the feel of them in her hands, letting her thoughts run free.

Could Frogunn really have killed Thordis? Or Bjorn? Or both?

Physically, yes – well, she could certainly have killed Thordis, and if Bjorn's death happened the way Ketil said it had, then she could have killed him, too. She was a big, strong lass, with muscular arms, ready to deal with heavy soapstone trays of cheese or an injured bull on her father's farm, either without blinking. She had been very interested in the practice fights, and keen to join in – she was certainly stronger than Foldar, which both of them admitted.

Did she have good reason to kill either of them? Sigrid made a face. Yes, sort of. Well, in that Bjorn was Varin's rival, so she could have killed him to help Varin take the hall, and Thordis then was Frogunn's rival, so she could have killed her to take Varin. She hadn't like Thordis very much, anyway.

But Sigrid was really struggling to picture Frogunn hating Thordis so much that she would kill her.

And the outcome of the hall business was so unclear anyway that it hardly seemed worth killing one of the candidates, did it?

Sigrid knew she was biased. She liked Frogunn, and had appreciated her support when Thordis had dismissed Sigrid's weaving – she glanced down at her own braid with a hint of pride.

She counted Frogunn as a friend, almost as much as Helga – and a good deal less silly than Helga could be. She really did not want to find that she was a murderer.

She turned the smooth bone tablets again, concentrating on the pattern for a moment, making sure she remembered the sequence correctly. The wind, strong again today, nipped about her bare foot, blowing mist over from the sea on one side of the headland to the sea on the other side: she could barely see the Brough or Einar's hall. Often, up here, one could pretend that the rest of the world did not exist. It was sometimes tempting.

The real question, she thought at last, returning reluctantly to the main problem, was whether or not Frogunn had had the opportunity to leave either hall, Einar's for Thordis' death and Thorfinn's for Bjorn's, at the appropriate time. Sigrid knew that she herself had spoken with Frogunn just before she had gone outside and found Thordis' body – in fact, it had been Frogunn who had told her that Thordis was outside somewhere. But had Frogunn been in all along? Or had she just come back in from outside herself, from killing Thordis?

And if she had, was she the person who had managed to send both Bjorn and Afi outside at the same time? If so, why?

She would have to talk to Helga, see what she remembered about that night. It was not so long ago, but so much seemed to have happened since that the memory was already fading. She needed to find out soon.

Then to Thorfinn's hall on the night of Bjorn's death, the night after Thordis' burial. Where had Frogunn been? She was not that sure. It had been busy, with all Thorfinn's hird there, all the Buckquoy crowd and Bjorn and his crew, and the man from Heithabyr with his burned face. So many injuries just now – his face, Foldar's nose, Bjorn's shoulder, Sigvat's jaw, Geirod's hand, and now Skorri's head, too. It was a good thing the women of the Brough and of Buckquoy were sufficiently skilled in their nursing. The thought of Rannveig's herbal concoctions sprang to her mind. Well, sometimes those skills went ways they shouldn't, that was true. But a bit of bandaging could rarely go far wrong, unless you turned a leg numb, or set an arm the wrong way so it always hurt and lost its strength.

Her mind was wandering, almost as if it did not want to

remember what Frogunn had been doing that night. She forced herself to concentrate. She thought she remembered Frogunn talking to Varin – not that surprising, now. She could see him sitting beside his brother, about halfway down the hall, perhaps not daring to sit too near the top in Thorfinn's hall. Then she had the impression that she had seen Frogunn talking to Tosti. Why would she have been talking to the little priest? She towered over him, but they were smiling together over something, Sigrid was sure. And that was before they had gone outside with Bjorn, wasn't it? Yes, of course. Would Tosti remember what Frogunn had done next? Would anyone know how she had spent the night? For there was a good chance that Bjorn had been killed once they were all in their beds, wasn't there? She should make sure of that with Ketil. He had touched Bjorn's body when they found him, where she had only touched it later, once it was down at Buckquoy, too late to be sure of how long he had been dead.

Those scratches on his hands ... Her mind leapt away from thoughts of Frogunn again, and back to those strange scratches. Frogunn could not have done that, anyway, she was sure. But Helga had pointed out how recent they were. Had they been there when they had found Bjorn's body? Again, something to ask Ketil. He was observant: he would surely have remembered something like that. Straight, sober lines, down the backs of his hands

Wait – the scratches had not run down his hands, not towards his wrists. They had run down to his fingers.

She tried to imagine fighting against someone throttling her with a braid. For a moment she laid down her own braid, and raised both hands to her throat, fingernails clawing over the imagined hands of her attacker. She turned them this way and that, but it did not make sense. She thought she would be much more likely to scrape the backs of her attacker's hands from the thumb to the other side, but if she really did make scratches like the ones on Bjorn's hands, they would run the other way, down to his wrists.

'Are you all right, Sigrid?' Gnup's voice roused her as he appeared round the side of the house. 'If you've a sore throat you shouldn't be out in this mist!'

'You're right,' she said, and unlooped the braid from her toe. 'You're right, I should be ... I have to go and see Ketil,' she said. 'You can manage on your own, can't you?'

And the look on Gnup's face gave her the usual pang of guilt, even as she grabbed her back cloak and shawl, and hurried off down the hill towards the Brough.

She had not reached the landbridge when she saw two familiar figures emerging from the patchy mist and striding across towards her, the tall, delicate shape of Alf and Skorri's more business-like sturdiness. They saw her about the same time and went to meet her, both smiling.

'Is Ketil back on the Brough?' she asked. 'Have you seen him this morning?'

'Oh, aye,' said Skorri with a shiver. 'We've seen him, but he's not on the Brough. He's gone for a swim: he'll be along here shortly.'

'He said he'd meet us here,' Alf added for clarification. 'In fact –'

'There he is,' Skorri finished, as they both spotted Ketil reaching the top of the path from the harbour. They went to meet him.

'Swimming?' Sigrid asked. His hair, what there was of it, did look wet. He nodded.

'Checking on my boat, too,' he said. Skorri and Alf, Sigrid noticed, looked a bit sheepish. Ketil glanced at them. 'Afi's nearly finished mending it.'

'Oh, grand. That's grand,' said Skorri, over-enthusiastic. There was a story there, Sigrid was sure, but she decided she would be wiser not asking what it was.

'Where are you off to?' Ketil asked Sigrid.

'Looking for you, in fact,' she said. 'Time to consult again, I think.'

'You have news?'

'Bits,' she admitted. 'Not much, but some of it is interesting. Did you know rumour has it that Thorfinn was about to have Bjorn punished for the death of Thordis?'

'Where did you hear that?' asked Ketil who, to her disappointment, did not look very surprised.

'From Foldar, and around the hall,' she said.

'The same rumour is going about on the Brough,' he said. 'Each time I hear it, Bjorn was nearer exile and the evidence was more definite.'

'Hm, evidence,' said Sigrid. 'Tell me, you looked at Bjorn's body up there on the Brough, when we found him. Are you sure you didn't see those scratches on his hands?'

'His hands?' Ketil frowned, clearly calling the moment to mind. She watched as he examined the memory, sure he could see it in detail before him. 'He had been kneeling. His attacker came from behind – probably a little to one side, to avoid standing on his legs – and slit his throat, quickly and effectively. Just one blow. He fell forward, dead before he hit the ground. His arms slumped by his side – he can't have tried to save himself with them. His left was a little forward, and his right straight along the line of his body. The left was palm down, the right palm up. I lifted both of them to see if there were any cuts that might have been made by him trying to fend off a blade. They were bare – no rings, but I never noticed him wear a ring – and a little muddy on the palms.'

'And the backs?' asked Sigrid, her own spine prickling. She had been right: he was observant.

'Not muddy. Clean. And not scratched.'

'I've been thinking about those scratches,' she said.

'What kind of scratches?' Skorri was as intent on the answer as the others.

'They looked, at first, as if someone had scraped their nails down his hands.'

'As if they were trying to defend themselves?' asked Alf. 'Thordis?'

'I think that was what it was meant to look like,' said Sigrid, 'but they're wrong. They're going the wrong way. Here, let me show you. Skorri, pretend you're trying to strangle me with a braid or a belt or something.'

Skorri hesitated, but Ketil nodded and he stepped up close to Sigrid, his hands hovering awkwardly.

'No, here, like this.' Sigrid shoved him into position. 'As if you're holding something round my neck, and pulling it tight.'

'It's not something I do every day!' Skorri protested, his face reddened.

'Now I'll scratch your hands, trying to tear them away. See? I'm scratching – sorry, Skorri, that was a bit sharp – down towards his wrists.'

'Unless he stands behind you,' said Alf, interested. 'Skorri, go and try to strangle her from behind.'

'But the natural thing would be to have the tails of the braid behind the body, then,' said Ketil. 'And they weren't, they lay down her breast.'

'He could have leaned over her,' said Alf.

'Awkward,' said Sigrid. 'But you see what I mean? Or the scratches would be sort of sideways.'

'And they aren't,' said Ketil, waving Skorri to leave his position. Skorri retreated in relief.

'They aren't. They go the other way, down to his knuckles. They're very regular, not like something that happened mid-struggle. And they're very fresh.'

'I think I should go and take another look,' said Ketil.

The hall was just as quiet as it had been the day before. Bjorn's corpse lay on the table, this time with a lamp lit at either end and Father Tosti kneeling by its side, accompanied by several of Bjorn's crew. One or two looked as if they had been there for a while. Alf went to join them, while Skorri looked about for someone to talk to.

Einar's hird were not all present yet – no doubt they would soon gather for the midday meal as they usually did. Sigrid noted that Hrolf was not there, nor Oddr, nor Afi the boatbuilder, but a few of the older men, less active in life, were already stretching their limbs by the fire and gossiping quietly. Skorri slipped in to sit with them, friendly, ready to listen to their newsan. As she followed Ketil towards Bjorn's body, Sigrid thought she heard the words 'Bjorn' and 'Thordis', and suspected she knew what the gossip was. The story was spreading quickly, as stories often do. Someone was trying hard, with the scratches and the rumours, to make it look as if Bjorn had deserved to die. The question was, was it someone who knew Bjorn was guilty and wanted to make sure everyone else did, too, or was it someone trying to distract attention from their own guilt?

Ketil, with a respectful nod at Tosti, had reached under the covering and lifted Bjorn's great hand out, awkwardly. He examined the scratches, just as Sigrid had remembered them, then tilted his head to tell her to follow him back outside.

'They look wrong, don't they?' she asked, as soon as they were clear.

'Yes. Who would have had the opportunity to do that?'

'Anyone who was attending to the body, I suppose,' said Sigrid. She had already asked herself the same question. 'Possibly the men who carried him here, though it's hard to see how one of them could have scratched both hands so neatly.'

'So more likely a woman.'

'The scrapes are not very far apart, either,' said Sigrid. 'As if whoever did it had small hands.' That probably excluded Frogunn, anyway, she thought with pleasure. Her hands were as big as a man's. But then the scratches could have been made one at a time.

Ketil turned, making for the paddock wall where Thordis' body had been found. Sigrid followed, a sudden vivid memory of those legs sticking out beyond the wall, the slumped head.

'What else were you going to tell me?' Ketil asked.

'I had a visitor last night,' she said. 'Foldar, Frogunn's brother.'

'The one with the split nose?'

'That's right. And the nettle stings.' She told him what had happened.

'You shouldn't have gone out in the dark to see who was there,' he said, surprising her. 'It could have been anybody.'

'What was I supposed to do? Send Gnup out to fight them for me? Barricade ourselves in and wait for them to set the roof on fire?' At that they both shook their heads slightly, involuntarily. They had both seen houses burn, without even thinking about Heithabyr. He bowed his head abruptly, as though ashamed, then turned back to Foldar.

'Do you think Frogunn does have something to do with it?' he asked. 'Do you think she really does care for Varin? I'd have thought she would have more sense.'

'So would I. But no one knows who will care for whom, I suppose. And she did seem interested in him, when we were talking with her yesterday. Helga was quite cross with her.'

Ketil smiled, though whether at the thought of Helga disapproving of someone liking a man or just at the thought of Helga, Sigrid was not sure. She felt suddenly irritable, and turned her back on the paddock to stare at the hall. To one side, she saw

Rannveig and Hrefna appear from Rannveig's longhouse, and vanish into the hall.

'I'm going back inside,' she said. 'Maybe I can get Varin to talk to me. I tried Sigvat, but it didn't get me far.'

'Hm,' said Ketil, showing no sign of moving from his place against the wall. 'Good luck.'

It took her a moment to find Varin – he had left his old place near the top of the hall and was over where he and Sigvat had been sleeping, though there was no sign of Sigvat. She was about to take this chance to talk to him when she saw he was watching something intently. She followed his gaze. Rannveig and Hrefna were about halfway between Sigrid and Varin, talking with Frogunn. Frogunn had almost to bend down to listen to mousy Hrefna, but she was nodding, agreeing to something. In a moment or two, all three women headed for the door at the back of the hall, but there Rannveig waved the other two through it and turned back to the hall, scanning the assorted mourners to see if they needed anything. Varin's gaze stayed fixed on the doorway, as if, with concentration, he could see and hear what Frogunn and Hrefna were doing.

Of course, he knew Hrefna from Kirkuvagr. Was he concerned at anything she might tell Frogunn? Whatever the matter was, he hesitated, like a bird on a wall, for so long that Sigrid again thought she might catch him. But even as she started towards him, just like that bird, he suddenly headed for the door and vanished.

She reached Sigvat's bed space, considering. A grubby bit of bandage lay on the floor and she stooped to pick it up, recoiling a little as she found it was damp. Not bloody, though: in fact, it seemed to have food of some kind on it. She held it by a corner and went to throw it into the fire. It was time to follow Varin, at a reasonable distance. But before she could, Rannveig caught her.

'Sigrid, can you help me serve the meal?' she asked. 'Frogunn's busy with Hrefna, and Helga hasn't appeared yet this morning. I know not all the men are here yet but,' she went on, lowering her voice, 'some of Bjorn's crew have been drinking since they brought his body back, and they'll need something to sober them up. If I bring in the dough, can you start on the flatbreads?'

'Of course, Rannveig,' said Sigrid obediently. In a way she was relieved. She had no wish to prove any conspiracy between Frogunn and Varin. And anyway, Ketil was outside: he could keep an eye on anything that was happening, if he looked in the right direction.

But in the end it was not Ketil who brought the story of what was happening outside the hall.

There was a burst of laughter at the hall door, and a number of people turned and glared. Oddr dropped his grin at once and moved quietly into the shadows of the hall to hide his embarrassment, made a sign of apology to Bjorn's body then looked around quickly to see who was there to share his joke with. Hrolf and Afi had still not arrived, so he was reduced to squatting by the fire next to Sigrid and her stack of flatbreads.

'I thought having Foldar in charge here would be good,' he confided in her, 'but if that can't happen, I think I've just been blessed with the next best thing!'

'Oh, yes? What's that, then?'

Oddr's magnificent whiskers almost sparkled in his enthusiasm.

'I was just heading here from home – don't know where Foldar got to last night but he was late doing the milking with Frogunn, and my knees these days just don't let me ... Anyway, she'd gone on ahead, and when I was passing one of the sheds out at the back, you know, beside the dairy, I saw Varin heading in to it. Odd, I thought, because it's women's work in there. Then I heard Frogunn greeting him from inside. Well! I thought. Maybe he's interested in our Frogunn! So I thought I'd hang around just to check – after all, a father has responsibilities, you know!' He nodded solemnly, glancing about the hall as if to make sure that everyone knew he knew what he had to do.

'So what happened?' Sigrid encouraged him.

'Ha! Well, he was asking her something about someone called ... I don't know, some woman. But it was all very, um, you know, teasing?' His fingers twitched in embarrassment on his bony knees and his whiskers bristled. 'And then – well, I could see them then through the door, they weren't paying any attention to me. And there was a bit of, well, fooling around.' He was definitely red now, his face glowing in the firelight. Sigrid wondered how long it had been since Oddr had participated in any fooling around. His wife had been dead for years. 'Then Frogunn sort of backed off, looking at him, and Varin looked a bit cross. And I was going to step in, but then Varin did something with the collar of his shirt, then he took her hand and smiled at her, and said, "Let's go for a walk," he says. "I want to go and find Sigvat – I think he went back up to the Brough." And I backed off just in time – with my knees! – and they came out and off they went. Ha!' Oddr slapped his knee and tried hard to contain his delight in the quiet hall. 'A wedding! Varin'll get charge of the hall now and my Frogunn will be his wife!'

'I thought you didn't want Varin to get it,' Sigrid countered.

'Aye, but with a local wife, a wife that belongs to Buckquoy – that's nearly as good as a local man, isn't it?'

Is it? thought Sigrid. When the man is Varin?

And what was Varin playing at, anyway? He had not seemed that interested in Frogunn before, whatever her interest in him. Yet just now he had followed her outside – her and Hrefna ... Had Hrefna told Frogunn something Varin didn't want her to know? Was Varin the murderer? No – he could not have killed Bjorn, could he?

Oddr was a silly man, though, and his eyesight was not good. Who knew what he might actually have seen? Sigrid glanced at him. Frogunn took after Oddr in build – Foldar was more graceful, though he did have Oddr's eyes.

Foldar had said that Frogunn would do anything for Varin and Sigvat.

Frogunn had been the only one tending to Sigvat's injuries.

What if those injuries were nowhere near as bad as they had thought?

Sigrid suddenly jumped to her feet.

'Keep an eye on those flatbread, Oddr, would you?' she snapped. 'I have to go.'

XXVIII

Ketil had allowed the fog to blow around him as he stood by the paddock wall. The misty air was nearly the equivalent of the darkness on the night of Thordis' murder, and he was trying to picture exactly what had happened.

Who had gone to all the trouble of making sure Afi and Bjorn were outside? Afi seemed to have gone first, but had wandered off over to the south to stare down at his beloved harbour and the boats there, so far as he could see them in the dark. By his own account, that seemed to have been where he was throughout the whole incident, only returning to the hall when Ketil himself was looking at Thordis' body. No one in their right mind would believe that Afi could in cold blood murder a woman, anyway. And he claimed to have seen nothing, either. No, Ketil thought, Afi was a distraction, though perhaps he had even been a mistake on the killer's part that might in the end tell them something.

Then Thordis herself had come out of the hall – presumably to go to the privies – and then Bjorn. Perhaps her murderer had also come out after her, or around the same time, or had waited for her outside? The darkness outside a hall in the late evening was the perfect place, Ketil thought, for a bold person to commit a murder. No one ever knew exactly who was where – unless someone happened to find you at the moment of killing, it would be hard to prove anything.

She had been found well away from the privies – the path there would have been too busy for safety for the killer, probably. Had she arranged to meet someone over here by the paddock? Or had someone met her and drawn her over here? If they had, the most likely candidates were Bjorn and Varin. No other men would have had much chance. But a woman ... He wondered about that for a moment. Could a woman have met her outside, and asked for help with something or told her to come and see something? That sounded not unlikely: even at that time of the night the women were often still busy. A woman ... a jealous woman, perhaps? The thought of Sigrid blinked in his mind, but he put it to one side. Jealousy over a man: a strong woman could have killed Thordis easily, helped by the element of surprise. And as for Bjorn ... as he had said from the start, surprise was the most important factor there, too, that and the fact that Bjorn had been kneeling. And even Foldar had had trouble, Sigrid had said, defending his sister. Frogunn could have done it all. Yet one thing kept niggling at Ketil's mind, one doubt – Frogunn was not a stupid woman, clearly, but still: was Frogunn really cunning enough for all that detailed organisation?

They needed to talk again to Frogunn and Varin. In fact, perhaps Sigrid was doing that just now, though Ketil did not hold out hope that she would draw much from Varin. He should probably go into the hall and see if she needed a hand. But there was something curiously comforting about standing there in the wet mist and the wind, like a young lad on guard duty: no complicated instructions, no mysteries, just a simple job to do.

Standing facing the direction of the Brough, though it was lost in the fog, he noticed a figure – or was it two, close together? – making their way past the paddock and off in the direction of the landbridge. The wind caught them as they left the shelter of the wall but he could see no detail, just the faded flapping of skirts and perhaps a cloak. They would need to be careful if they were heading across to the Brough in weather like this, he thought: nowhere but in these islands had he ever seen fog so persistent that no wind could blow it away. Not even the wind that was certainly making a good effort just now, as it had been all the last day and night.

He went over again in his mind his search on the Brough earlier. Was there anything else he should have looked for? Who else should they be asking? Had anyone seen someone leaving Thorfinn's hall in the middle of the night, or creeping back in? Groa? Probably not. Bolla? Perhaps. Bolla was a bright woman. But he had been there himself, as had Sigrid, and they had noticed nothing. What was wrong with them? Or were they looking for a shadow? A ghost? The fog was the perfect place for uncanny tales. He shivered, shaking them off. No ghost had strangled Thordis. No ghost had slit Bjorn's throat, even if it seemed that he had thrown away his luck when he tossed his amulet into the night.

'Ketil!'

He turned quickly. Sigrid was at the hall door and hurrying towards him.

'News?'

'Yes. Sort of. I think so. Have you seen Frogunn and Varin?'

'I don't think so.' He gestured to the fog. 'They'd have had to be quite close.'

'They were heading to the Brough, if Oddr's to be believed. If Varin's to be believed.' She was squinting into the fog, agitated.

'Together?'

'According to Oddr, yes.'

'I may have seen them, but the fog was too thick for me to recognise them. Not long ago?'

'Not very, no.' She gestured that they should go that direction, too, as she recounted quickly what Oddr had told her, or a shorter version, anyway. 'Oddr's delighted. But then I remembered Foldar saying Frogunn would do anything for Varin and Sigvat. The two of them – I mean Frogunn and Varin – could be plotting something more. The thing is, it's only been Frogunn who has tended to Sigvat's injuries.'

Ketil realised at once what she meant.

'So his jaw might not be broken?'

'Exactly. And if that's the case, either Frogunn is plotting with them, or she's in danger.'

Ketil frowned. One way or another, it made sense – and even if Frogunn happened to be a willing accomplice, he was sure that neither of the brothers was so attached to her that they would not dispose of her when she ceased to be useful.

'Oddr thinks Varin will ask for Frogunn's hand,' Sigrid tossed the words over her shoulder, and Ketil took two long strides to walk by her side.

'Would he agree?'

'Certainly – he was delighted by the idea. Next best thing to having Foldar rule the hall: have his daughter married to the ruler.' She coughed in the fog, but recovered, keeping up her speed. Ketil put out a hand to slow her down.

'Be careful,' he said. 'It's hard to see the edges in this weather.'

'Huh,' said Sigrid, annoyed. 'Remember when it was twice

this width? It wasn't that long ago.'

'You still can't see from one edge of it to the other in this,' he pointed out. The fog was growing more dense by the moment, it seemed, blowing round them like thick cloth, darkening the sky. To their right, not far below, he could hear how the wind was driving waves on to the jagged shore, angrily lashing the island. He took a firmer grip on Sigrid's arm, but she stopped abruptly.

'You don't think Varin would have just pushed her over, do you?'

'No,' he said firmly, not even sure why. He tried to think. 'Too dangerous, for Varin: too much chance he'd be seen. Too decisive. You said Oddr heard he wanted to go and find his brother?'

'That's what Oddr said, anyway.'

'Then he'd wait, and see if Sigvat agreed. I think,' he added, more quietly. But Sigrid appeared happy to be reassured, at least for the moment.

'Come on, then,' she said. 'If Oddr's right, we need to find Sigvat.'

The gate guards were huddled in the shelter of the gate, looking miserable but unusually alert.

'Anything could come from anywhere on a day like this!' one of them said, ominously.

'Have you seen Frogunn Oddr's daughter?' Sigrid asked.

'Aye, she was one of them!' said the other guard, as if it proved their point. 'With yon nephew of Einar's, the prinksie one. Not the polite one.'

'Both of them, good,' Ketil heard Sigrid mutter. They were swamped by the sudden shelter of the gateway, then slapped again by the wind as they emerged on the other side. 'The hall?' she asked.

'Best place to start,' Ketil agreed.

She went ahead of him, knowing the way to the hall's great door even in the poor light, the flags already worn and familiar.

The midday meal, barely started when they had left Buckquoy, was already over at Thorfinn's hall. Ketil scanned the remaining guests, spotting Geirod with his yellow dog talking quietly with some of Thorfinn's older followers. Sigrid, however, had seen Bolla, the maid.

'Is Sigvat around?' she asked as Bolla came past with a wet cloth.

'Sigvat? Where did I see ...' Bolla's eyes quartered the hall efficiently, then she remembered. 'That's what it is. He was over there, but his brother – is it his brother? The one that looks as if he's been gone over with a smoothing stone. His brother came in – with is it Frogunn? Oddr's daughter? And they went over to Sigvat and the brother said something to him, and Sigvat looked as if his meal had disagreed with him. Then he got up, and they all went outside.'

'Was that long ago?' Ketil asked. Bolla glanced at him, but gave the reply to Sigrid.

'You've not long missed them.'

'Any idea where they went?' asked Sigrid, but Bolla shook her head.

'I wouldn't cross the hall to find out what the brother was doing. I certainly didn't go to the door.'

'You'd have been busy, anyway,' said Sigrid sympathetically.

'Well, if Groa would pull her weight instead of arguing with Sigvat, some of us wouldn't have to work quite so hard,' Bolla growled, and stamped away before they could respond. Ketil and Sigrid met each other's eyes. Why was Groa arguing with Sigvat, now? Ketil groaned inwardly. He was beginning to think he would never be given leave to go to Heithabyr.

'Where should we try?' Sigrid was asking. 'If they went outside ... I don't think either of them has friends here, that they would be visiting one of the longhouses.'

'Let's try the chapel,' said Ketil. 'Anyone can go in there.'

They followed the wall of the hall back towards the chapel, no more visible than anything else on the foggy Brough. When they fumbled their way to the door, they found there was one small lamp burning inside, and Tosti was sweeping the flag floor. He glanced up in surprise when he heard them.

'Varin and Sigvat? No, I haven't seen them. Nor Frogunn, either.'

'Where now, then?' asked Sigrid. They stepped back outside, and Ketil raised his hand, listening. There were voices coming from somewhere nearby – hard to place in the fog and the wind.

'That's Frogunn!' Sigrid said in a low voice.

'Where, though?' Ketil leaned close to her, hoping that even if they could listen, they could not be heard. Sigrid frowned, concentrating. She raised a tentative hand to point silently, her eyebrows asking if he agreed. He did: they edged closer to the voices, painfully aware that one callous swipe of the wind and the fog would leave them completely exposed. He held Sigrid's arm again, wanting to keep her close in case they needed to speak.

'I don't know why you brought her here,' came Sigvat's voice, snipped and snatched by the wind. 'You could have just dealt with her at Buckquoy.'

'Well, you see,' said Varin, 'I wasn't sure how to do it, not there. I mean, I thought I'd better ask you. In case I made a mistake. Like the last time,' he added sulkily.

The last time. When he killed Thordis. Ketil felt Sigrid nudge him: she had realised, too.

'You made a mistake bringing her here. What if someone saw you with her?'

'In this fog?' Varin made a reasonable point.

'I am here, you know,' snapped Frogunn, and Ketil could picture her, arms folded, glaring at both brothers through the mist. 'And I'd just like to remind you –'

'Shut up!' said Varin crossly. 'Do what you're told! You usually do.'

'That was before I saw what you were wearing!' she retorted. Ketil looked at Sigrid. She scowled, then a light seemed to come on in her eyes. She gestured to her throat, indicating something hanging there. Ketil was puzzled, but thought hard. Could she mean Bjorn's missing amulet? Could Varin have the bear's tooth?

'Yes, she saw it,' Varin was telling Sigvat.

'You told me you'd hidden it,' said Sigvat, in a kind of resigned anger. He was well used to his brother's stupidity.

'It brought Bjorn luck! I thought it would do the same for me.'

'Well, it didn't, did it?' said Frogunn. 'Is that what you killed him for? You did kill Bjorn, didn't you?'

'We killed him,' said Sigvat with exaggerated patience, 'to get the hall.'

'And Thordis?' asked Frogunn, her tone now icy. Ketil felt Sigrid shiver.

'No good just killing Bjorn. That would annoy King Harald,'

Sigvat explained.

'I don't understand this bit,' Varin admitted, and Frogunn laughed. She seemed to be recovering from her passion for Varin.

'You wouldn't have to if you hadn't lost your patience with her,' Sigvat snapped. 'Couldn't stand seeing her with Bjorn. If you'd just waited ...'

'She was my betrothed, and she was sitting with him!'

'You didn't even care until she took an interest in Bjorn. But at least we were able to make use of it.' Sigvat sounded pleased with himself, but Frogunn was not stupid.

'You had to discredit him, didn't you?' she asked Sigvat. Ketil sensed Sigrid nodding suddenly. She stood on tiptoe to reach Ketil's ear.

'Make Bjorn look bad, then dispose of him. Harald won't take revenge for the death of his favourite.'

'And they wanted to trade with Harald,' Ketil added, turning to reply, brushing Sigrid's headcloth with his cheek. She nodded, excited now that they finally had answers.

Ketil said nothing more, wary of being heard. They could not be far away from the brothers and Frogunn, but whereabouts were they? It was so hard to tell. Sigvat was still talking, so at least he did not seem to suspect that there was anyone nearby.

'I suppose it is a little better up here,' he said grumpily. 'We could tip her over a cliff, and no one would question that. She might not even be found.'

'You can try,' said Frogunn. 'You might be clever enough with a knife, Sigvat, but I've watched Varin: all he does is strike a fine pose at the edge of the fight. I can't imagine why I thought that was a good thing! But just now it seems to me to be your disadvantage – Varin's a useless fighter, and it'll take more than just you, Sigvat, to push me over a cliff! You probably can't even tell where the cliff is!'

'That's true –' said Varin, and broke off with a grunt. 'Ow!'

'Now you shut up,' snapped Frogunn.

'My nose! You've broken it!'

There was a scuffle, and a thump, as of someone hitting something hard. Ketil stepped forward, uncertain, and at that moment someone blundered into Sigrid, knocking her from his grasp. Varin? It was impossible to tell.

And then it wasn't.

Doorways cleared in the fog, and they blinked as their eyes adjusted to the wavering light. They were next to a low wall. Sigvat had Frogunn pinned against it, with the additional emphasis of his drawn knife prodding her ribcage – it explained why she had not yet run, though looking at her face Ketil thought she was probably too angry to be fearful. In fact she must have elbowed Varin in the nose just now. Blood streamed bright from both his nostrils, and stained the sleeve of her blouse. For a moment, only the blood showed any sign of moving. Then Sigvat saw Ketil and Sigrid watching them.

He took a deep breath, and pressed his face into shocked concern.

'This woman's insane! Look what she's just done to my brother! We need to take her to Thorfinn: she seems to know all about the murders.'

'Frogunn! Are you all right?' Sigrid demanded, half-stepping forward. 'She's no more insane than you are, Sigvat! I thought you were the nicer brother.'

The look on Varin's face for the blink of an eye almost made Ketil laugh. But Sigvat was not slow. His handsome face took on a nasty expression, and Sigrid hastily stepped back again.

'I suppose you've been listening? Hiding in the fog?'

'We heard, Sigvat. It's you that needs to be taken to Thorfinn.' How long had they got? Already the fog seemed to be thickening again. Ketil edged forward, hoping this could be done without drawing his sword: it was hard to control two prisoners at swordpoint. Frogunn, the knife close to her chest, was breathing hard. Varin wiped his bloody face on his sleeve. Sigvat calculated.

It happened in a flash. Sigvat signalled to Varin. Varin, still clutching his nose, tumbled himself over the wall. Sigvat grabbed Frogunn around the neck, and, knife still pressed hard against her, dived in the opposite direction. And the fog descended.

'Sigvat,' said Ketil, and made for where he had last been visible. Better to catch him, and save Frogunn, than to go after Varin. But a flurry of noises came from the mist. Two grunts, one the echo of the first. A cry of pain. Running feet, heedless of the fog. A man's voice, swearing, and then, unexpectedly, the squeals of a very unhappy pig.

The first footsteps had died away even before they could

make out whose they were or where they were going. But more began now, over to their right, where Sigvat had headed.

'Follow me,' snapped Ketil. 'Take my cloak tail, but drop it if I say.'

Something in his tone must have deterred argument: Sigrid did as she was told, for once. He could feel a light tugging on the cloak as he moved forward, as quickly as he could, listening all the time for footsteps or breathing or – but the squeals of the pig were persistent, and cross. They were also heading in the same direction. He hoped that they were not just following the Westray sow on another of her escapes, but he was sure that the sow would be moving much more quickly on her own.

A wall surged up out of the fog, a high one this time, over Ketil's head height. He put a hand to it, and followed it. The pig and the footsteps were still ahead, but now a new sound surged up to compete: the crashing of the waves, somewhere nearby. He slowed at once. Were they at the cliff edge? But the building, whatever it was, reassured him. It must be the bathhouse, close enough to the cliff edge but still with a good broad path behind it – the path where they had found the Westray man with the sow. Ketil prayed that this was not just another pig rescue.

'Varin, what are you doing? Shut that pig up!' Sigvat's voice came from behind Ketil.

'I can't. It keeps squealing.' A mighty wave crashed below, and there was a nervous gasp from Varin. Somewhere in front of them? Around the side of the bathhouse? The fog made sound deceptive.

'Slit its throat, you fool!'

'I've dropped my knife! Oh, where's it gone? Damned pig ...'

'Drop it, then!' Sigvat's patiencewas silk-thin.

'No, it's my knife I've dropped,' Varin explained, misunderstanding. 'I had it out to use on Frogunn. The pig – oh, now what?'

'What?' Sigvat demanded.

'Oh, this cursed fog ...' There was a scuffle, and the pig expressed dissatisfaction. 'Oh, no – now I've lost my amulet. Bjorn's amulet! All my luck!'

An exasperated sigh from Sigvat cut through Varin's wail.

Ketil flattened his back to the wall, still not sure where the two men were. And where was Frogunn? At least he knew roughly where Sigrid was.

'Keep moving, then. We can't stay here,' snapped Sigvat.

'I don't think ...' came Varin's voice, tight with fear. What was happening? Ketil edged forward to the corner, then felt a sudden tug on his cloak tail. He pulled it towards him. No Sigrid.

'Ketil!'

Sigrid was breathless, but he could not see her, even this close. Where was she?

'Sigvat!' called Varin. 'I think Ketil's still following us!'

'Shut up, Varin, and get moving! It's all right – I have some protection for us.'

'Sigrid?' Ketil called out, suddenly afraid. For a moment he could hear nothing but another wave crashing against the cliff below.

'Don't follow, Ketil!' she called back. 'I'm sure I'll be all right!' She did not sound remotely sure.

'I have her, Ketil!' Sigvat called. 'So she's right – don't follow!'

'Sigvat!'

Varin cried out, and in response came a dreadful roar, a thundering, crunching rumble.

'Varin?' Sigvat called, then louder. 'Varin? Where are you? Oh ...'

'Sigvat! No!' It was Sigrid's voice. 'Ketil, the cliff has – has gone! Varin's gone! And Sigvat – help! Help!'

XXIX

The moment the words were out of her mouth she regretted them. Ketil would rush around the building to see what was going on, and then what? The cliff was crumbling beneath her.

'Stop!' she cried. 'Don't come any closer!'

But already Ketil had appeared round the corner, a dim, misty figure.

'Slowly!' she gasped. Then, as she saw he had taken in what was happening, she made herself draw in a breath, and try to calm down. Ketil had stopped, wary.

'Are you all right?' he asked, and she bit back a sarcastic reply. She was lying face down with both arms over a crumbling cliff, clutching the empty glove of the man she had just seen tumble to his death. Sigvat had followed his brother over the edge. How he had not dragged Sigrid with him, she could not say.

'The cliff is unstable,' she managed to say. As if it were not obvious. She began to wriggle backwards, stopping as she felt earth break away under her hands.

'I'll pull you,' said Ketil. She felt him take hold of her ankles. This was not going to be dignified. She bit her lip, and braced herself. And below her, as if trying to reach her, another wave slapped at the cliff, teasing away more tumbling rock only an arm's length below her nose.

He was certainly strong. He drew her backwards gently over the wet grass, just to the point where the ground was stable enough for her to sit cautiously upright. He was kneeling beside her, and drew her a little further back until both of them were leaning against the comparative stability of the bathhouse wall.

'Not sure I'd care for a bath just now,' she said breathlessly. 'You?'

'Even a dip in the sea is not that appealing,' Ketil agreed, nodding at the waves beyond the cliff edge. They worked ceaselessly through the fog, assaulting the cliff. There was no saying how long they, or the bathhouse, might be safe. But the path back around the building was even less secure, and for a moment she knew she would never be steady enough to walk along it. She felt Ketil's arm around her shoulders, holding her close. That was enough for now.

'They both went over?' he asked quietly.

'Varin first. I don't think he even knew what had happened. Then the fog shifted, and Sigvat could see Varin had gone. He rushed forward, and ...'

She glanced down at her hands. Her fingers were still entangled in Sigvat's glove. She straightened them, and laid it down on her lap, smoothing it flat.

'What about Frogunn? Where is she?'

'I didn't see her. Oh, Ketil, what if – what if he pushed her over first?'

'We thought he was the better brother,' said Ketil.

'We were wrong. He would have done anything to push Varin's success, wouldn't he?'

'I think so. Using Thordis to discredit Bjorn ...'

'Her death, anyway. Varin killed her and Sigvat used it.'

'He was the clever one.'

'I didn't like her, but that – that was awful. Like an unwanted piece in King's Table – cast aside for the sake of the bigger game.' Sigrid felt tears welling in her eyes, and tried to blink them away. The wind was working straight at them here: if it were not for Ketil beside her she would be frozen by now. How were they going to get back safely? At the moment all she wanted to do was to curl into Ketil's warm side, rest her head on his chest, and close her eyes. What on earth would he say to that? But his arm around her was holding her tight: he was not going anywhere, either. She turned a little towards him.

'What on earth?' he said sharply, and she jerked backwards – just as a small black snout poked its way under her arm.

'A pig!' Sigrid's mind whirled.

'The Westray sow,' sighed Ketil. 'Of course.'

'The pig that Varin had?'

'Our little fugitive,' said Ketil.

'She seems to like you,' said Sigrid, sitting up straighter.

'It's Skorri she's particularly fond of,' said Ketil. 'And her owner's neighbour. That's probably who she was trying to find.'

'Nevertheless, she's prepared to make do with you,' said Sigrid, watching the pig nestling against Ketil's side – just where Sigrid had been a moment before - as if she had found some particularly comfortable straw. Sigrid cleared her throat. At least the pig was happy.

'And then using Frogunn, too,' she said. 'Oh, where is she?'

'How complicit do you think she was?'

'I think she knew what had happened. Did she know before it happened, though? Varin and Sigvat must have asked her to pretend that Sigvat's jaw was broken, certainly: and she helped to make it look that way. But I don't think she knew Thordis was going to die. Bjorn, though ...'

'Why do you think she knew about Bjorn?'

'Because she asked Father Tosti to go and talk to Varin. If she knew Sigvat was going to do something bad, she wanted a witness who could say that Varin had nothing to do with it.'

'But Sigvat had his own ideas about that, and sent Groa in to seduce Varin.' Ketil nodded. 'Another woman pressed into service for Sigvat.'

'I don't understand what happened on the night of Thordis' death, though,' Sigrid admitted. 'People sending Afi and Bjorn outside, and all that. What was going on?'

'Maybe we'll never know,' said Ketil. 'Maybe it was all just coincidence.'

'That's an awful lot of coincidence,' she said. 'I think I want answers!'

'As far as I'm concerned,' said Ketil, 'it's what Thorfinn wants that counts in this. If he feels the matter is closed, and allows me to leave for Heithabyr, then I'm not going to chase any other hares.'

'Of course.' She had forgotten Heithabyr, and the fire, and Ketil's brother. And he was right: Thorfinn would be happy with the bigger answer, and not need to be bothered with details. Not enough to hold back his trusted officer, when the officer wanted to go. And then, indeed, Ketil would go.

And would he ever come back?

For a moment she was taken aback at the emptiness that

opened up inside her at the thought that he might not. Dusk was falling slowly through the fog, and the wall behind her was cold and damp. She stared out across the mysterious sea, vague thoughts of Heithabyr floating across her mind.

Then another huge, greedy wave surged up, rolled relentlessly towards them, and gouged another foot-length of cliff from just in front of them. They both snatched their feet away fast, and the little pig squealed.

'We need to try to crawl back,' said Ketil, 'or we'll just go too.'

'It's too narrow!'

'You can fall there or fall here,' said Ketil firmly. 'I think that's our choice. I'll take the pig.'

'Oh, Lord!' Sigrid breathed. The path beside the bathhouse, which had seemed narrow before, now looked barely more than a fringe of grass along the foot of the wall. Fall there or fall here ... and how could Ketil, so much broader than she, get along that safely with a pig under one arm? Heithabyr suddenly seemed a very long way away.

Then she heard a cry, and saw a light.

At the corner of the bathhouse, holding torches, were several figures. She could only make out fragments of their faces as the torchlight flickered, but Ketil was already yelling,

'Don't come any closer! The cliff is crumbling!'

'Yeah,' came a grunt. Geirod. Almost a friendly face: Sigrid, anyway, was very happy to see it. He seemed to be bending over, fumbling with something. 'Ach, Thor's teeth!' he muttered. 'Alf, do this, will you? My fingers aren't working.'

'Is Sigrid there? Are you all right?'

A woman's voice – Frogunn!

'I'm here, Frogunn!' Sigrid shouted back. Frogunn was alive!

'I'm so sorry, Sigrid! I was such a fool!'

'Maybe we'll talk about that later!' Sigrid called. Frogunn's guilt or stupidity was not foremost in her thoughts just now. The pig was growing anxious, wriggling against Ketil's leg.

'What are you doing, Geirod?' Ketil called. 'Don't come any nearer!'

'I've a rope,' said Geirod.

'Three,' came Alf's voice, precise as ever. 'Frogunn's got the other end of one of them. There are more people coming, Ketil.'

'I hope there's no one in the bathhouse,' said Sigrid. Her teeth began to chatter. 'They might find they're in for a colder dip than they expected.'

'I hope they don't think Frogunn can take our weight,' said Ketil. 'I hope she's not going to do something stupid.'

'Someone's going to have to do something stupid or we'll never get off here,' said Sigrid.

'It's probably going to have to be one of us.'

Her hand was braced beside her, against the bathhouse wall. For a moment she thought she felt the touch of his fingers – he was probably making sure the pig was all right - then came a shout from Alf, and a grunt from Geirod.

'Go on, now!' muttered Geirod, just audible past the sound of wind and waves.

'Ropes!' cried Alf, with a sweep of his torch.

And all at once Geirod's yellow dog was scrambling over them, tugging behind him enough rope to reef a sail.

Ketil wasted no time. One rope was clearly for the dog, and one for each of them. He undid one and passed it round her waist, and she took the end and knotted it securely, like the end of a braid. At once she felt more secure: she tried not to think about what the other end might be attached to. Frogunn could probably support her, but the combined weight of Ketil and a pig?

That pig ... Ketil was looping his cloak around the animal.

'Get past me. Go,' he said. 'I'll be just behind you.'

Already the dog was heading back, surefooted – almost – along the fringe of path, urged by Geirod's murmured encouragement.

'I can't get past you. You go first,' she said, nervous.

'Go between me and the wall,' said Ketil. 'I can reach over you, you know.' He showed her, pressing one hand into the flagwork above her head. 'Been able to for years!' he added, and she glanced up to see him smile at her. 'Go on. Now, before it's too late.'

She took a deep breath, trying to still her own shaking. It would not do to let him know how scared she was, she thought. Making herself as small as she could, she squeezed in between him and the wall, praying that his booted feet would keep a steady hold on the cliff edge. Had he tied his own rope? But had he done it properly? She should have checked. She could not stop now, or she might push him off the cliff. She was past him.

And now for the narrow bit.

Ahead, she could see Alf with his hands firm in her rope – Frogunn must be holding the torch. Geirod and the dog watched her intently, as if they could hold her safe just with their fixed gaze. She clung to the wall, feeling all her bones and sinews working, her fingers and toes, arms and legs, minutely aware of every detail of path and stone, ears on stalks listening for sounds from Ketil, instructions from Alf, a fresh crashing wave behind her.

She was almost there ... she was an arm's length away ... a couple of steps ... a step – and Alf, one hand still wrapped in the rope, reached out and seized her arm and pulled her to safety. Jiggling torchlight dazzled her and Frogunn's solid arm came round her shoulders, steadying her shivers. But at once she turned back to look: was Ketil following? Was he safe?

The jagged border of the path had taken her weight, but would it take his?

'What's going on?' came a voice behind her. It was Thorfinn: Skorri was with him.

'Ketil ... on the cliff,' she said, though she was not sure she was even speaking out loud. She should tell him about Varin and Sigvat, about what had happened to Bjorn, but not now. Now she could not string that story together for anyone.

Alf was speaking to Thorfinn, though, even as he arranged his long, thin hands around the last rope.

'Apparently Varin and Sigvat went over, my lord,' he was saying. 'Sigvat was dragging Sigrid, and Varin had a pig.'

'A pig,' said Thorfinn, as though it were inevitable. 'Not that Westray sow?'

'It looks like her, my lord.' Skorri looked round the corner anxiously. 'I recognise her wee snout.'

Alf's fingers paused briefly on the rope, as if he would have liked to laugh, anywhere else. Sigrid willed him on. The torchlight behind her sent flickers along the bathhouse wall, into the dusk, but she could just see Ketil's pale face, the line of his shirt. How Skorri could see the sow was beyond her.

'You'll need more men on the rope,' said Thorfinn, and took

a loop of it, passing it round his own stocky waist. Skorri followed him.

'I'm so sorry, Sigrid. So sorry,' said Frogunn, still holding Sigrid close. 'I was so stupid.'

'Come on,' Sigrid muttered. 'Come on, Ketil.'

'You all right there, Ketil?' Thorfinn shouted over everyone.

'I think so, my lord,' came Ketil's voice, calm as ever. How on earth would he use the footholds and fingerholds that Sigrid had found, with her small fingers? Frogunn was holding Sigrid's hand now, looking at it, but Sigrid paid her no heed.

'Come on, Ketil.'

A short, anxious squeal came from the pig. Everyone paused: Ketil's foot had slipped. But somehow he was making progress, long hands like spiders reaching stones and gaps Sigrid could never have used. And he was so much taller, of course: where she had needed three or four paces, he could sweep along in two. Slowly.

'Slippery bit by your right foot,' Alf said conversationally. Ketil adjusted his perch. They could all see him clearly now, and then, in a moment, he had taken a last, long step, and he was safe.

They all moved promptly back, away from the cliff edge, and Sigrid sank to her knees, hands to her face. It was only then that she realised what Frogunn had been looking at: her fingers were bleeding, torn and ragged. The pain shocked through her suddenly, and she found she was crying. She prayed no one would notice.

Ketil had been caught up by Alf and Skorri and Thorfinn, slapping his back, while Skorri took the pig into his own custody. Geirod was kneeling by his dog, making much of him, just next to Sigrid. Folding her fingertips into her palms, gritting her teeth, she turned and looked.

'Clever dog!' she said. 'How did you know he would do that? Go out towards us with the ropes, all on his own?'

'Because I asked him to,' said Geirod. His face was as grumpy as ever, but even in the torchlight she could see a touch of pride in his eyes.

'What's his name? I don't think I ever asked.'

Geirod glanced up at Alf and Skorri, their backs to him.

'He's called "Friend",' he said quietly. Then as if he could pretend the conversation had never happened, he stood and led

Friend away, leaning now and again to touch the dog's back with his good hand.

'Need to bandage your fingers, Sigrid,' said Frogunn.

'Fingers?' Thorfinn heard almost everything on his Brough. 'Are you hurt, Sigrid?'

Reluctantly she held out her hands, and Alf and Skorri whistled in dismay.

'That'll hurt,' said Skorri in sympathy.

'Back to the hall,' said Thorfinn. 'I need to hear the full story. And we could all do with some warm wine, too.'

On the way, Frogunn stayed close to Sigrid, not speaking, but the echoes of her apologies seemed to follow them along. Was it true? Was she really sorry, or had she been more complicit than they had thought? Sigrid went over as best she could all the conversation they had overheard between Frogunn and Varin and Sigvat. Sigvat had been ready enough to dispose of Frogunn, and Varin did not seem bothered at the idea, but did that mean that Frogunn was innocent?

At the hall, it was left to Thorfinn to decide.

'You knew what those two fellows were doing, didn't you?'

'Not all of it, my lord,' said Frogunn, 'but I confess I knew they were working against Bjorn. It was only when Bjorn died that I was really sure that they were bad. But I should have realised sooner – and I should not have been such a fool over Varin.' She could have hung her head then, maybe played for sympathy, but she held herself upright, concerned but ready to face her punishment. Sigrid glanced across the hall. Ketil was there, a cup of hot wine steady in his hands, looking as if he had spent his day relaxing by the fire instead of perched on a crumbling cliff edge. She held her own cup clumsily, aware of her torn and tousled clothing and blotchy face. It would be hard even to mend her dress, never mind finish those braids she had been working on. She wanted to go home.

'You know that Sigvat killed Bjorn?'

'Yes, my lord.'

'And you were hiding the fact that his jaw was not broken?'

'I thought it was at first, my lord. But yes, he asked me – Varin asked me – to keep quiet. So that Bjorn would look bad, they said. And when I thought Sigvat had killed Thordis, my lord, I was glad, because I knew she was betrothed to Varin.' She was sincere, Sigrid thought. She had not even known that Varin had killed Thordis.

'But did you know about it before it happened?'

'No, my lord.'

'You should have told someone when you did find out,' Thorfinn grumbled. 'It would have sorted all this out much faster.

'And saved Bjorn's life,' added Ketil.

'Not just his life,' Frogunn put in, looking wretched. 'His luck.'

'His luck?'

'Varin and Sigvat had amulets,' Frogunn began, looking about her as if to check who else had seen them. 'But after Bjorn survived Sigvat's knife blow, Varin was convinced that Bjorn's – his bear spirit,' she gave a breathless little laugh, 'was stronger. They were jealous of his luck. And then, at Buckquoy, I saw Varin had Bjorn's bear-tooth amulet.'

Sigrid could not help giving a little 'Ah!' of satisfaction. Frogunn barely paused.

'I knew then, definitely, what they had done, and how I felt about Varin just changed in that instant. But Varin realised I'd worked it out – I wasn't quick enough to pretend. But I tried – he said he wanted to go and find Sigvat and I should come too, and I went along with it – I thought ... I don't know, that I could stop them ... or trap them ... I don't know. I couldn't seem to think. Then in the hall here, when we came in, everything went so fast. I've always been able to cope with everything – I thought – I thought I'd find a way to make up for all they'd done ...'

Frogunn, always so competent, young and confident – and out of her depth. She would need a bit of looking after. And that could be done, Sigrid thought.

Ketil was focussed elsewhere.

'Ask her about the scratches on Bjorn's hands, my lord.'

Thorfinn raised his eyebrows, and turned back to Frogunn. But Frogunn looked bewildered.

'I saw scratches on his hands – Sigrid pointed them out to me. She wondered if he had got them from Thordis, but I thought they looked too fresh.'

Thorfinn looked at Sigrid. She cleared her throat awkwardly.

'That's right, my lord. And she was right: they were too fresh. Someone scratched him after he was dead, to make it look as if he had attacked Thordis and she had defended herself.'

'Someone trying to discredit Bjorn,' said Thorfinn thoughtfully. 'Well, if it wasn't you, Frogunn, it must have been Varin or Sigvat.'

'No, I don't think either of them went near Bjorn's body,' said Sigrid. 'Not after I had arrived, anyway. Frogunn? Were they near him?'

Frogunn frowned.

'Neither of them helped to carry the bier back to Buckquoy,' she said, clearly running through her memory. 'And I don't believe either of them was long in paying their respects – nor did either of them go very close to the body. But if one of them did it, then surely Sigvat did it when he killed Bjorn?'

'No,' said Ketil with certainty, 'Bjorn's hands were not marked when we found him.'

'Then who ...?' Thorfinn looked from one to another of them, but no one gave an answer.

Sigrid glanced again at Ketil, and found he was looking at her. He raised his eyebrows, but she shook her head. She thought she knew who had scraped Bjorn's hands with those long, regular scratches, but she was not quite sure enough to say.

XXX

With all they had heard, here and out in the mist, Ketil was content that Frogunn had known no more than she had admitted. She seemed to feel quite bad enough about what she had known and done: that did not, however, include the strange manoeuverings on the night of Thordis' murder. Who had sent Afi outside? Who had persuaded Bjorn to follow Thordis? He shook his head slightly. There was no need to be distracted by such questions. They knew who had killed Thordis and Bjorn and why, and that was all that was required. And they had told Thorfinn – now Thorfinn would allow him to leave for Heithabyr.

Heithabyr ... He looked about him in Thorfinn's hall. Grettir, the young man with the burned face was not immediately in evidence. Ketil had intended to talk with him again, when he was in a better position to take in what he had to say. Surely he had not left already?

But no: there he was, coming into the hall from some expedition outside. Ketil allowed him to find a place on one of the benches, then went to join him.

'I'm sorry I have not come to speak with you before,' he said.

'That's all right,' said Grettir. 'It's a good place to stay, here. I was in no rush to push on. To be honest, I lost most of what I had, so it's nice to get some decent food for a change.'

'Where are you going? Back to Heithabyr?'

The man shrugged, one-sided.

'Nothing for me there now. I'm going on to points south, see if I can ply my trade somewhere new. My idea was to get away from King Harald, anyway.'

'It must have been a shock to you to find that Bjorn Einarson was here before you.'

The man's steady gaze flickered slightly.

'Aye, yes,' he said. 'The Bear ...'

'And you met Sigvat, didn't you?' Ketil went on, conversationally.

Again, Grettir's eyes wavered.

'I'm not sure ...'

'Blond, good looking. Bandage around his jaw – probably.'

'Oh, that Sigvat! Well ...'

'What did he do? Persuade you that Bjorn was not a fit person to lead men here? Tell you he'd killed a woman? Ply you with hacksilver?'

'No!' Grettir yelped. 'No ... he said he might be able to set me up in business if I was able to help him.'

'What is your business?' Ketil asked pleasantly.

'I'm a boatmaker,' said the man. 'Sigvat said he had friends in – is it Kirkuvagr? They'd get me customers, find me somewhere to work.'

'He might have, at that.' Ketil sighed. 'You know he's dead?'

'What?' Grettir was shocked, but there was a kind of relief on his face.

'Went over the cliff. So no help with your business, I'm afraid.'

'Then it's south for me!' said Grettir.

'How much did Bjorn Einarson have to do with what happened in Heithabyr?' Ketil asked, and the good side of Grettir's face went pale. After a moment he said,

'Are you sure Sigvat's dead?'

'Pretty sure.'

'What about his brother? Not that he was so ...'

'No. I mean, yes, we think he's dead, too. They both went over the cliff. With quite a bit of the cliff.'

Grettir pressed his lips together.

'All right, then: no, I never saw the Bear at Heithabyr. And

I was at the water's edge. I saw fireships, and I saw a few ships off the shore, that must have sent them into the harbour. None of them was the Bear's.'

Anger at Grettir's deception fought with relief in Ketil's head. He had been right about Bjorn after all. Did it change anything? Would he have tried harder to talk with Bjorn that night if he had not thought him guilty of burning Heithabyr?

'You're sure?'

'I saw the Bear's ship down in the harbour here when I arrived. Someone pointed it out to me: I'd never seen it before. I'm a boatmaker, so I'd know,' he added, suddenly glum.

A boatmaker wanting to set up business, with nothing to bring to it. How much would Sigvat have done for him? After all, it was another useful oar in Sigvat's boat, another of Sigvat's clever little tactics, rumours spread to discredit Bjorn.

Ketil sat back, considering. A part of him had hoped that Grettir's whole story had been untrue, that the firing of Heithabyr had been a tale with no substance. He would still have to go and see his brother, still see for himself the destruction of his childhood home. His heart ached at the thought.

A movement caught his eye further down the hall. Sigrid and Frogunn had their shawls about them, and were heading for the door. Abandoning Grettir with a disgusted look, he hurried to catch up.

'Are you going back to Buckquoy?' he asked. 'It's dark, and the weather's no better.'

Sigrid's head was low.

'I just want to go home,' she said, and Frogunn beside her looked just as tired and dejected.

'Let me walk with you.'

'We'll be all right together,' said Sigrid. In the light of the hall's doorway torches he could see the pale bandages on her hands. No weaving for a while, then. What would she do?

'I'll come with you,' he said. 'I want to talk to Rannveig.' It was the first name he could think of, and it was easy to see that Sigrid was not convinced.

In fact the weather was better: the wind had dropped, the mist had cleared, and the waves were less greedy as they sucked at the cliffs. Someone had told him the bathhouse was still standing, perilously, but already Thorfinn had plans for a new one, nearer to the gate. It was too dark to see now, anyway. Ketil lit a torch at the door, and followed the two women to the gate.

Once they were past the guards, Sigrid glanced back.

'Is the pig all right?'

'Skorri has taken her back to the pigman,' said Ketil. 'But it's only a matter of time before she escapes again.' He would have to get someone to take the pig and Thorthr back to Westray. Maybe if Thorfinn made a judgement on the case, the two neighbours would listen.

He wanted to say more, but could not think of anything. He walked behind the women, trying to light their way with his torch without getting too close. Frogunn seemed inclined to take care of Sigrid, which was good. No doubt she would be looked after while her hands healed. He did not want to think it would be otherwise. He was cross with himself for not realising how hard that climb across the wall would be for her, yet he was not sure he could have made it any easier for her. Was she angry with him?

They were nearly to the paddock wall when at last, walking beside him now, Sigrid said,

'Why do you want to talk to Rannveig?'

He decided to be vague.

'Just to clear up the last questions.'

He could feel the look she gave him.

'Well,' she said, 'I think I know what happened the night of Thordis' death.'

'You mean the way Afi was sent out and then Bjorn?'

'That's right. I think I know.'

She nodded solemnly.

'Was it to do with Rannveig?'

'Oh, yes. Who else?' She called ahead. 'Frogunn, I need to talk to Ketil. You go on in: I won't be long.'

'All right.' Frogunn knew her way from here with no need for a torch, now the sky was clearer. Ketil wondered what she was going to say of her day to Oddr or Foldar.

'You know Bjorn believed he was protected by that bear spirit he claimed to have seen in the north?' Sigrid began unexpectedly. He leaned against the paddock wall beside her.

'Yes, of course. Hence the amulet.'

'That's right. It all sounds a bit – well, desperate, but I think we have had all the pieces for a while – Afi saying he was asked to go and do a favour for someone, Bjorn's missing cloak that reappeared, Rannveig busy with sacking, and Bjorn being sent out of the hall, somehow.'

'I'm beginning to see where this is going,' said Ketil, half-smiling.

'I think Rannveig was going to get Thordis to take the bearskin cloak, which she had in the sacking, out to Afi, who was just required to stand wearing it somewhere nearby so that Bjorn could see a great bearlike figure. Maybe they would ask Afi to point north, or something. Then Thordis and Rannveig could persuade Bjorn that it was a sign he should leave, go back to Norway.' She shifted uncomfortably, wrapping her hands in the tails of her shawl. 'Afi wouldn't question anything as long as it seemed harmless, and in a way it really was harmless. Rannveig just wanted Bjorn to go.'

'Was this something she arranged with Sigvat, then?'

'No, no: this was Rannveig acting alone. But then Varin killed Thordis, angry that she – his property – was apparently making up to Bjorn. He had no idea that she was doing something that he could have used to his advantage. Though who knows: Sigvat and Varin were so impressed by amulets and charms and so on, and Frogunn says they believed in the bear spirit, too.' She shivered. 'And then, finally, I think Rannveig scratched Bjorn's hands. A final attempt to take some kind of power – maybe to make Varin obliged to her. I don't know exactly, but I think she's the only one who could have done it.' This time her teeth were chattering.

'Come on,' said Ketil, 'let's go into the hall and see if we can eat there. Are you going to say anything to Rannveig?'

'Depends how brave I feel!' she said, trying to sound cheerful. He nodded. It did make a kind of sense, using Bjorn's belief against him. It was the kind of economical tactic Rannveig would use. No wonder she had been looking for Thordis that evening: she must have wondered why nothing seemed to be happening.

Sigrid seemed about to move off, and Ketil stopped her with a hand on her arm. She seemed to freeze: he hoped he had not inadvertently hit some bruise or cut from earlier.

'What do you think about Frogunn? Can she be trusted?'

Sigrid glanced over her shoulder, but Frogunn had already

disappeared towards the hall.

'I think so,' she said. 'I do. And she went for help for us, and came back with them. I think she's to be trusted.' She paused, and glanced back again at the hall. 'I hope so. I like her.'

That would have to do, for now. He tilted the torch.

'Come on, then,' he said again. 'Let's get something hot to drink, and then I'll see you home.'

'I can manage,' she said, but it was not completely convincing.

The hall had an unsettled feel. He saw that Bjorn's crew were half-packed, ready to go as soon after the funeral as they could. The corner that Varin and Sigvat had occupied already had an abandoned feel. He assumed that Frogunn had brought the news of the brothers' deaths, if it had not already reached Buckquoy by other means. Bjorn's great body still lay on its bier to one side: he felt surprised that it should still be there, but it was only a short time ago that they had found him lying on the Brough, his bear spirit fled.

The tables were laid out at the upper end of the hall so that the men could be fed, and Ketil found Sigrid a seat at the end of one of the benches. Her injured hands would be reason enough for her to sit and be fed, rather than serving, but she looked uneasy there, all the same. Perhaps it was simply the general air in the hall. He sat down beside her and accepted a bowl of broth from one of Rannveig's women. Frogunn was also serving broth, though she had stopped to talk to her father, he saw. Back here in her home, away from the need to defend herself to Thorfinn, she looked smaller. But he thought Sigrid was right: after Frogunn recovered from her embarrassment, she would be well, eventually.

'Go on, then – talk to Rannveig,' said Sigrid quietly, and he caught the light of humorous challenge in her eyes. Clumsily she pulled out her spoon, and managed a mouthful of broth without spilling it, though it was slow. She saw him watching, and said again, 'Go on!'

'I shall, when I'm ready.'

'Fortifying yourself first?' She waved a bandaged hand at his wine cup.

'Wouldn't you?' But he did not touch the wine: if he were really going to talk to Rannveig, he would need all his wits about him. 'I didn't tell you about Bjorn and Heithabyr,' he said, and pretended to himself that it was not a delaying tactic. He told her what the wretched Grettir had confessed.

'It doesn't make it much better, though, does it?' she said. 'Heithabyr is still fired.'

'But Bjorn wasn't involved. Like you with Frogunn, I liked Bjorn.'

She nodded.

'I know: he was likeable. He would probably have done well here.' She looked around the hall. 'Who will Thorfinn choose now?'

He shrugged. It would all be sorted out by the time he came back from Heithabyr, no doubt. If he came back: sometimes people didn't.

'Sigrid!' came a voice, and they both looked round. To Ketil's surprise, it was Hrefna, Ljotr's downtrodden wife. 'Oh, and Ketil.' She looked more nervous even than usual, a little breathless.

'Sit down, Hrefna,' said Sigrid. 'How are you? I haven't had much chance to talk with you since you came.'

'I've been talking to Rannveig,' she said, and there was something almost defiant in her tone.

'Well, that's nice,' said Sigrid.

'Yes,' said Hrefna, almost to herself. 'Talking to Rannveig. She's a strong woman, isn't she?'

'That is certainly true,' said Sigrid with feeling.

'I think I like her,' said Hrefna.

There was no time to respond to this surprising statement. The door at the back of the hall slammed open, and Rannveig herself strode in. Ljotr followed, his habitual grin fixed in fury.

'You can't escape me by running in here, woman!' he shouted.

Rannveig whirled to face him.

'Show some respect. Bjorn's body still lies here.'

'Aye, that's why you ran in here, so I wouldn't shout at you! But I care nothing for respecting someone I didn't even know. Why should I?'

He also seemed to care nothing for making a spectacle of himself, Ketil thought. Everyone in the hall had stopped to stare at Rannveig and her brother-in-law. Rannveig stopped, and visibly rearranged her angry face into something more placatory.

'No, no, you're quite right,' she said, holding out her hands towards him. 'Respect should be for those we know, shouldn't it? And for the living, too. For those who are earning it, like you.'

Ketil glanced at Hrefna. The little woman was gazing at Rannveig in stunned admiration. He could not quite see why: surely even Ljotr would see through the insincerity of Rannveig's words.

'That's right,' said Ljotr. 'I work hard, I'm doing well. That needs to be recognised.'

'I know it does, Ljotr.' Rannveig's voice had dropped, growing gentler. 'And that's how I can help you. I helped Einar for years, you know.'

'Well, that's true,' Ketil heard Sigrid murmur.

'I can be very useful to your business. I don't come without my own contribution, either: I have some wealth put aside to support me in my old age. It can be invested in your business, can't it? With your guidance, of course.'

'How does she do it?' Ketil was astonished. Ljotr's scowl was softening already.

'She says she'll teach me,' Hrefna breathed. 'Help me with him. *You* know,' she added to Sigrid. 'And I don't even have a brother to help me.' Sigrid looked blank for a moment, then turned to Ketil and mouthed,

'She means you!'

He nodded: he had remembered Sigrid's ruse.

'Some wealth, eh?' asked Ljotr.

'A little, yes,' said Rannveig, and you would almost think her incapable of counting it herself, let alone looking after her own interests. Ljotr licked his lips unattractively.

'And you could come right away? You can leave things here?'

'After Bjorn's burial,' said Rannveig. 'After that is done, I'll come back with you to Kirkuvagr.'

'She's going to come and live with us!' Hrefna turned to Sigrid. 'Isn't that wonderful?'

'That's perfect,' said Sigrid. 'The perfect solution for all of you, isn't it?'

'Leaving Einar's hall?' Ketil queried later. 'What advantage is that to Rannveig?' He was walking with her up to her longhouse: the hot food and wine had indeed cheered her.

'Well, Ljotr's a prosperous man.'

'And a wife beater,' Ketil reminded her.

'Not for much longer, I imagine.'

'You mean she'll prevent him from hitting Hrefna? I'd be surprised,' said Ketil.

'Oh, I think she'll manage,' said Sigrid, 'one way or another.'

'Ah,' said Ketil. 'You mean a permanent cure?'

Sigrid gave a little laugh.

'I'd be surprised if Ljotr enjoys a long and healthy life, wouldn't you?'

Rannveig and her potions – yes, Sigrid was right. The perfect solution for all of them. Well, for Rannveig and Hrefna, anyway.

Rannveig was as good as her word: she left Einar's hall with Ljotr and Hrefna the day after Bjorn's burial. The Bear had been laid to rest next to his father at the chapel on the Brough, not far from Thordis, three fresh graves in the tawny earth the markers of all the tragedy of the past days. Bjorn's crew departed on the same day as Rannveig. Some were sorry to leave, others eager to be on their way, and most of the Buckquoy folk went down to the harbour to wave them off with equally mixed emotions.

Only a few days later, Sigrid was on the shore again. The wind was whipping about the harbour as Skorri and Alf readied Ketil's boat. Geirod and the yellow dog stood nearby – Geirod's hand was still bandaged, but he would be able to help with the baggage. There was no sign of the pig.

'I thought you were going to take them back to Westray on the way,' said Sigrid. 'Thorthr and the pig.'

'We were,' said Ketil. 'Instead, Thorfinn has given us compensation to take to the pig's owner. He might not have wanted Thorthr to buy the pig, but he can hardly argue with Earl Thorfinn.'

'And Thorthr?'

'Has assumed temporary duties as Thorfinn's assistant pigman.'

Sigrid smiled. She thought she might go and visit the pig. She felt they had been through a lot together.

'And then it's straight on to Heithabyr?'

'Or what's left of it, yes. Grettir says the people who

survived the fire were setting up a temporary camp nearby. He thinks Njal should be there. I'll help him get the business established again, if I can. If that's what he wants.'

'Not that you're much good at business,' she heard herself say, and regretted it. But he smiled.

'I can take orders from Njal,' he said.

'That's good. You need someone to keep you straight.' She smiled back.

'Then come with me,' he said.

The shock she felt she saw reflected in his face. He had not planned to say that. And at once she tried to find excuses.

'I need to look after the farm,' she said. 'It's not fair on Gnup to expect him to manage. And there are the braids – I can't do them just now, but I need to talk to people, take orders, make dyes. You know.'

'I know,' he said, and she thought he looked relieved. He really had not meant to ask her to go.

She had watched the little boat leave the harbour, then hurried back here, home, where she could see it again after it had rounded the Brough and set off north. The sail had filled and the boat was making good speed. Ketil would be happy, anyway, back on the water. And she was happy, too.

She had worked hard for the rest of the day, sorting out all the things she had abandoned over the last days, reassuring Gnup that she was home. When she had finally gone to her bed, she thought she would sleep well, tired as she was. But she lay awake into the night, her mind wandering.

It was her home, just as she liked it.

She had been quite right to say it needed looking after, though. Gnup didn't know enough about the farm yet, and then there was her business – if you left people alone for a while, they began to buy their braids from other people, and that was not a habit she wanted to encourage. No, she needed to stay here. She was right.

She lay on her back, staring up into the darkness, enjoying the smell of the fire and its gentle night time cracks, the faint odour of the small dye pots she kept in the farthest corner, the feel of her old blankets around her, patched and worn and shaped exactly right.

Ketil could manage without her for once. He would be fine.

He would find out what had happened to Heithabyr, to his brother and Njal's family. It was all about his family. She had been right to let him go.

It wasn't as if he would be away for long.

It wasn't as if she would miss him.

She sat straight up in bed.

She was wrong. She should have gone with him.

Odd words in *The Bear at Midnight*

Claik	Gossip
Clart	Muck
Clegg	Horsefly
Climmer	Clamber
Kvarr	Merchant ship
Newsan	News
Oxter	Armpit (as in so many dialects)
Peedie	Small
Prinksie	Puffed up, full of yourself
Redd	Clean
Roo	Heap of stones
Speeder-legs	Crane fly, daddy-long-legs
Thole	Put up with

About the Author

Lexie Conyngham is a historian living in the shadow of the Highlands. Her historical crime novels are born of a life amidst Scotland's old cities, ancient universities and hidden-away aristocratic estates, but she has written since the day she found out that people were allowed to do such a thing. Beyond teaching and research, her days are spent with wool, wild allotments and a wee bit of whisky.

We hope you've enjoyed this instalment. Reviews are important to authors, so it would be lovely if you could post a review where you bought it! Here are a few handy links …

Visit our website at www.lexieconyngham.co.uk. There are several free Murray of Letho short stories, Murray's World Tour of Edinburgh, and the chance to follow Lexie Conyngham's meandering thoughts on writing, gardening and knitting, at www.murrayofletho.blogspot.co.uk. You can also follow Lexie, should such a thing appeal, on Facebook, Pinterest or Instagram.

Finally! If you'd like to be kept up to date with Lexie and her writing, please join our mailing list at: contact@kellascatpress.co.uk. There's a quarterly newsletter, often with a short story attached, and fair warning of any new books coming out.

Murray of Letho

We first meet Charles Murray when he's a student at St. Andrews University in Fife in 1802, resisting his father's attempts to force him home to the family estate to learn how it's run. Pushed into involvement in the investigation of a professor's death, he solves his first murder before taking up a post as tutor to Lord Scoggie. This series takes us around Georgian Scotland as well as India, Italy and Norway (so far!), in the company of Murray, his manservant Robbins, his father's old friend Blair, the enigmatic Mary, and other members of his occasionally shambolic household.

Death in a Scarlet Gown

The Status of Murder (a novella)

Knowledge of Sins Past

Service of the Heir: An Edinburgh Murder

An Abandoned Woman

Fellowship with Demons

The Tender Herb: A Murder in Mughal India

Death of an Officer's Lady

Out of a Dark Reflection

A Dark Night at Midsummer (a novella)

Slow Death by Quicksilver

Thicker than Water

A Deficit of Bones

The Dead Chase

Hippolyta Napier

Hippolyta Napier is only nineteen when she arrives in Ballater, on Deeside, in 1829, the new wife of the local doctor. Blessed with a love of animals, a talent for painting, a helpless instinct for hospitality, and insatiable curiosity, Hippolyta finds her feet in her new home and role in society, making friends and enemies as she goes. Ballater may be small but it attracts great numbers of visitors, so the issues of the time, politics, slavery, medical advances, all affect the locals. Hippolyta, despite her loving husband and their friend Durris, the sheriff's officer, manages to involve herself in all kinds of dangerous adventures in her efforts to solve every mystery that presents itself.

A Knife in Darkness

Death of a False Physician

A Murderous Game

The Thankless Child

A Lochgorm Lament

The Corrupted Blood

Orkneyinga Murders

Orkney, c.1050 A.D.: Thorfinn Sigurdarson, Earl of Orkney, rules from the Brough of Birsay on the western edges of these islands. Ketal Gunnarson is his man, representing his interests in any part of his extended realm. When Sigri, a childhood friend of Ketil's, finds a dead man on her land, Ketil, despite his distrust of islands, is commissioned to investigate. Sigrid, though she has quite enough to do, decides he cannot manage on his own, and insists on helping – which Ketil might or might not appreciate.

Tomb for an Eagle

A Wolf at the Gate

Dragon in the Snow

The Bear at Midnight

Other books by Lexie Conyngham:

Windhorse Burning

'I'm not mad, for a start, and I'm about as far from violent as you can get.'
When Toby's mother, Tibet activist Susan Hepplewhite, dies, he is determined to honour her memory. He finds her diaries and decides to have them translated into English. But his mother had a secret, and she was not the only one: Toby's decision will lead to obsession and murder.

The War, The Bones, and Dr. Cowie

Far from the London Blitz, Marian Cowie is reluctantly resting in rural Aberdeenshire when a German 'plane crashes nearby. An airman goes missing, and old bones are revealed. Marian is sure she could solve the mystery if only the villagers would stop telling her useless stories – but then the crisis comes, and Marian finds the stories may have a use after all.

Jail Fever

It's the year 2000, and millennium paranoia is everywhere.
Eliot is a bad-tempered merchant with a shady past, feeling under the weather.
Catriona is an archaeologist at a student dig, when she finds something unexpected.
Tom is a microbiologist, investigating a new and terrible disease with a stigma.
Together, their knowledge could save thousands of lives – but someone does not want them to …

The Slaughter of Leith Hall

'See, Charlie, it might be near twenty years since Culloden, but there's plenty hard feelings still amongst the Jacobites, and no so far under the skin, ken?'
Charlie Rob has never thought of politics, nor strayed far from his

Aberdeenshire birthplace. But when John Leith of Leith Hall takes him under his wing, his life changes completely. Soon he is far from home, dealing with conspiracy and murder, and lost in a desperate hunt for justice.

Thrawn Thoughts and Blithe Bits and *Quite Useful in Minor Emergencies*

Two collections of short stories, some featuring characters from the series, some not; some seen before, some not; some long, some very short. Find a whole new dimension to car theft, the life history of an unfortunate Victorian rebel, a problem with dragons and a problem with draugens, and what happens when you advertise that you've found somebody's leg.

Printed in Great Britain
by Amazon

24461225R00179